FURY

Rebecca Lim is a writer and illustrator based in Melbourne, Australia. She worked as a commercial lawyer for several years before leaving to write full time. Rebecca is the author of fourteen books for children and young adult readers, and her novels have been translated into German, French, Turkish and Portuguese.

Also by Rebecca Lim

Mercy
Exile
Muse

REBECCA LIM

FURY

The MERCY series

HarperCollins*Publishers*

First published in hardback in Australia by HarperCollins Publishers Australia in 2012
First published in paperback in Great Britain by HarperCollins *Children's Books* in 2012
HarperCollins *Children's Books* is a division of HarperCollins*Publishers* Ltd,
77–85 Fulham Palace Road, Hammersmith, London, W6 8JB.

The HarperCollins website address is: www.harpercollins.co.uk

1

Text copyright © Rebecca Lim 2012

ISBN 978-0-00-744308-6

Rebecca Lim asserts the moral right to be identified as the author of the work.

Printed and bound in England by Clays Ltd, St Ives plc

MIX
Paper from
responsible sources
FSC **FSC™ C007454**
www.fsc.org

FSC™ is a non-profit international organisation established to promote
the responsible management of the world's forests. Products carrying the
FSC label are independently certified to assure consumers that they come
from forests that are managed to meet the social, economic and
ecological needs of present and future generations,
and other controlled sources.

Find out more about HarperCollins and the environment at
www.harpercollins.co.uk/green

To Michael, with love always

Be sober, be vigilant; because your adversary the devil, as a roaring lion, walketh about, seeking whom he may devour.

1 PETER 5:8

CHAPTER 1

Picture, if you can, the ancient city of Milan in the dead of night, lashed by an unimaginable storm. Picture the rooftop of a vast, white cathedral that towers hundreds of feet above snaking, crowded streets of stone, wreathed in lightning so fierce it transfigures the oxygen in the very air.

Do you see it? Because it's what *I* see.

I stand within a mighty forest of spires and tracery, gargoyles and statuary, utterly dwarfed by what the hand of mankind has wrought.

And yet ...

I am the world, and the world is in me.

How can I make you understand this feeling?

I am myself, as I once was, when I was first created.

As potent, as piercing, as light.

Dizzy with power, drunk with it.

Capable of things you couldn't begin to imagine.

In this moment of rebirth and reclamation, I am a maelstrom of possibility — more powerful than the snow driving across this gothic rooftop I'm stranded upon, more powerful than the wind that squalls around me, more powerful than the lightning that splits the darkness overhead, more powerful even than the two winged demons shrieking curses at me from the skies above.

For I was never exiled from heaven like they were, all those years ago. I was sacrificed.

Sacrificed by the hand of the one who was supposed to love me more than life itself.

And though I might carry the mark of the exile upon my burning flesh, I am not guilty as Lucifer was guilty.

Pride I had, and vanity.

But I am no demon. Though I did not enter this world willingly.

I have been trapped here on earth, but it doesn't change what I am: an archangel.

No mere *malakh*, or messenger, but one of the *elohim*, most holy, most high. Who is more human now than one of my people has any right to be.

And the reason I'm feeling all the frailties, all the helpless fears and simple longings that bedevil humankind, is right here in my arms, rigid with cold, the sleet sluicing off his beaten-up leather jacket, soaking his dark hair, his heartbeat faltering beneath my fingertips.

'Ryan?' I say shakily. 'Stay with me.'

His eyes are closed, and his lips are blue with cold. The only thing keeping all six foot five of him upright is me.

Stupid, I tell myself fiercely as I lurch forward, the wind like broken glass against my face, Ryan a precious dead weight in my embrace. *What kind of damned angel can't even fly right?*

As I tried to land on the cathedral roof, I saw human figures, the size of giants, standing in stern rows upon the carved and fretted spires, their faces turned upon the city below. The lightning that had sundered the sky around us, transforming night momentarily into bright day, had made them seem alive, and I'd faltered and lost altitude.

No sanctuary for demons, they'd seemed to say.

Even to saints and martyrs made of stone, maybe that's what I'd looked like to them. Like a demon.

I was so disoriented, so crippled by my absolute fear of flying after all these years of being earthbound, that I came in at a bad angle. I fell too far, too fast, and collided with a spire, felt it pass right through me, clipping Ryan, hard, across the torso. In the shock of the impact, I dropped him from a great height upon the unforgiving flagstones of the cathedral roof.

Candoglia marble versus human flesh and bone. He has to be a mess inside from the way he's breathing. He's just barely holding on. There's blood on his mouth.

'Ryan?' I mumble against his hair, my eyes searching for the way down. 'I'm going to fix this, okay?'

But I don't know if I can fix him, because I can't seem to fix *me*.

The world around me seems too fast, too loud, as if I'm seeing everything through some kind of crazy lens, or filtering things through a blinding strobe light that's going off in my head alone.

On the surface, I seem the same as I used to be. I recognise these limbs, the glowing, sleeveless, white raiment I always used to wear. The surrounding storm can't touch me — before any sleet can hit the energy my skin gives off, it vanishes completely. But there's a flaw in me, I can feel it. Something's changed. Something small, yet fundamental; something I can't put my finger on.

In this moment, I may be power incarnate, but I don't feel as if I can channel it, or even hold myself together for much longer. It's the greatest irony: I always thought that the moment I got the old *me* back, I'd never again feel the sick sensation of being in a stranger's body, fighting desperately for control. Instead, one false step and I might shatter; blow apart completely.

I want so much to give in to this feeling of *building* inside me, but I know that if I do, if I allow myself to atomise, to be pure energy, pure light, the way my body yearns to — Ryan will die. And it will be my fault.

I need to control it. I can't control it.

The snow drives down as if it would bury the world. And the two demons that hunt us circle the forest of marble spires at a distance. Unable to come any closer, compelled to stay back, rending the air with their violence, their screaming. Even from so far away, I see how beautiful they are — the lethally muscular male with short, auburn curls and dead-looking, midnight eyes, whom I once knew as Hakael; his companion, Gudrun, Luc's beloved these days now that I am his beloved no longer. His minions, here to finish what he started.

In a moment of weakness, I lean the side of my face against Ryan's bowed head. His skin is so cold. In place of the exaltation I should be feeling, I'm filled with a crippling dread.

There's no time. There's never been any time for Ryan and me. As if it was the fate that was written for us once, a long time ago to find each other, then lose each other twice, three times over and we are merely playing it out.

I falter to a stop, my eyes raking the darkness, the steep

incline of the cathedral's peaked roof, holding Ryan so close that the unsteady beat of his heart could be mistaken for the one I don't possess. I remind myself fiercely that I don't believe in fate. Remind myself, too, that I have the power to kill and the power to heal in equal measure; that these things were in me when I was first created. I just need to get Ryan inside, away from the bone-piercing cold, from the demons screaming, *Haud misericordia! No mercy!* Then do what needs to be done. The other stuff, the tricky stuff — about *us*, and what that could even mean — I'll have to work out later.

The grip I have on Ryan is awkward, as if I'm locked in the arms of a drowning man who's dragging me beneath the water. I brace him against my right side, pulling his left arm over my left shoulder so that he's more upright against me and that's when I see it.

The fingers of my left hand are entwined with his, and they burn with flames of pure energy. The pain of this living scar, this proof of Luc's betrayal, is no more than a dull ache now, present but subsumed, though the flames still retain their hypnotic, corrosive beauty.

And I suddenly remember that when Luc had torn me free of Irina Zhivanevskaya's body, he hadn't bothered to unravel that last, tiny portion of my soul in which the Archangel Raphael had hidden my name. In these flames, in this flaw, is written my true name; the name that still eludes me. Raphael's gift. And his curse.

I will never be whole and perfect until I reclaim the name I was given. Until then, 'Mercy' will have to do, as it has done for the longest time. It was the last word I ever uttered as myself — until today. And it is apt. I think that, maybe, I have even begun to earn the name.

5

A flash of silver-grey, as luminous as it is subtly tainted, passes overhead, then another. The demons come as low as they dare, and the air is filled with a shirring sound, as of an approaching plague. Then living fire rains out of the sky — sphere after sphere, each perfect and distinct, no bigger than a demon's cupped hand. There's no time to run, nowhere to hide. All I can do is curve myself protectively around Ryan and pray that the end is swift, and that we might meet again.

But this place carries its own peculiar magic. The flaming spheres hit some barrier that even I cannot see, and shatter into waves of brilliant light before dissolving utterly. The sky is lit weirdly red as each missile implodes and dies away to embers — as if I stand beneath some kind of demon-born aurora borealis.

And then I remember to *move*.

But thunder loud enough to raise the dead peals out, followed by a flash of lightning that cracks the rim of night. In its light, I see a tall, broad-shouldered figure, outlined in silver, dressed in robes of black, with long silver hair flying loose about his shoulders in the storm. He stands upon the very apex of the crown of stone carvings about a hundred feet away. His face is youthful and beautiful and deadly, his stance relaxed; arms held loosely at his sides, fingers slightly curled. His eyes are untroubled, but watchful, as blue as the daytime sky.

Shock blazes through me as our gazes lock. The Archangel of Death craves the souls of the blameless; he cannot help but be drawn to them. It is his province, his peculiar calling. He has no use for the other kind.

Azraeil! I scream, for his ears alone. *You stay away from him! You stay away.*

Do I imagine his half-smile before the darkness returns? When I peer at the raised cross at the centre of the stone crown, it stands empty of life.

No one takes precedence over Death. It's part of our lore; a given. But I'll be damned if I'm going to let Ryan go before we've had a chance to work out what we are to each other. I am owed.

At the very least, I am owed some answers, and to give some in return.

I resume my stumbling descent down the treacherous roofline, cradling Ryan's head against the line of my neck. His left forearm is taut across my shoulder, his left hand still grasped tightly in my burning one. The argent flames seem to leap off my skin, begin to envelop his, yet he remains beyond reach, is turning slowly to stone.

For a moment, I imagine that his heart actually stops before resuming its faltering, thready beat. My fear causes me to break into a sliding run.

I realise with shock that Azraeil was standing almost directly above the flight of steep, stone stairs I've been searching for. With Ryan clamped tightly against me, I skitter towards them, along a rain-slicked, narrow canyon of stone. As I pass beneath a towering row of flying buttresses, Ryan's head slumped against the line of my jaw and collarbone, I hear the demons challenging me with their bestial voices from on high: *Haud misericordia!*

They can wait forever. I don't have forever.

At the end of the walkway, I reach a doorway cut into the stone: the entry to a great tower. Inside, is a staircase that leads down to the street, straight into the Piazza del

Duomo, the Duomo Square. I have not walked those stairs in centuries, but I remember. I know I'll have shelter enough inside that tower to try to fix the things inside Ryan that are broken.

As I step forward into the gaping darkness, Ryan's heart stops all together, and its shuddering beat does not resume.

I have no memory of how I got us inside the tower, but suddenly I'm crouched over Ryan's motionless form. He lies where he fell from my nerveless grasp upon the cold stone, his long frame curled awkwardly on one side. His skin is unnaturally pale and he's no longer breathing.

My terror causes me to wail aloud, causes my burning left hand to flame even brighter so that it's as if a small star is trapped in this narrow, breathless space. There's no time. There's never been enough time for us.

Outside, the demons screech their fury to the skies, seeking a way in, a way to get to *me*. But for now, we're in one of the few places on this earth where they may not follow, and it gives me the courage to plead to the dead air crowding us.

Azraeil! I feel your presence here and I ask you to stay your hand. Not yet, Brother, please.

It's too soon. Too soon.

We are deep within the tower, many twisted flights down, our bodies close together upon a narrow stone landing. Above and below, stairs stretch away into the gloom, each one worn down in the centre from centuries of human passage.

No doctor on this earth, no hospital, can save Ryan now. It falls to me alone to call my love back. I steel myself against what I am about to do, because it always, always invites in the unwanted.

Then I place my burning left hand upon his lifeless body, at the base of his cold throat in which a pulse no longer beats. And I atomise in the instant, becoming a rain of mercury, a rain of fire, letting the tide take me where it will.

I am light now, pure energy. I am overwhelmed by the memories of Ryan's life, his blameless, small-town existence into which a monster strode and took his sister, changing everything in the instant. I feel his horror and rage and helplessness as if I, too, lived every second of those years that Lauren was kept caged away from the sun. I relive all the fights, the dead ends, the building darkness within. In this moment, I know Ryan better than he will ever know himself. I see that he would give his life to save his sister; to save anyone he truly loved. He is by no means perfect, but he's the real deal; in the end, he would fall on the side of the line that really matters. His is the kind of soul that Azraeil searches for the world over.

And now I see myself, the way Ryan has seen me — as Carmen, as Lela, as Irina — and I feel him falling for me, life by life, encounter by encounter, harder each time. I see the effect I had on him when I was Carmen. When we met, he was frozen inside, and it made him unpredictable, savage, incredibly careless of himself. But something about *me* cut through the noise in his head. I gave him hope when it seemed the time for hope had long passed.

I feel his shock the moment Carmen woke in the hospital and denied ever meeting him before in her life; his piercing grief when Lela was gunned down before him. And I feel his love for me the instant our eyes met across that catwalk under the blue-lit dome in the Galleria Vittorio Emanuele here in Milan. A love so absolute and fierce and sure that, even now, it makes my soul shiver.

The heart will always want what it wants, his voice seems to whisper.

I can feel his love. Can almost touch it, as if his memories have reached out and enfolded me in an embrace such as I've never known. But it's fading, that love. And him with it.

The despair I feel makes me move with greater purpose, greater urgency. I rage through Ryan's dying frame, making of myself a healing fire, channelling everything that I am at the wounds inside him. Making the temple of his body whole again so that the flame might be relit, that it might return.

I am clumsy and unpractised, but my touch is electric. My power cannot be denied; it should be bringing him back to life. But, all around me, his body continues to slacken. Ryan's soul seems to flee before mine like a separate wave. The two of us moving in aching parallel across a lonely sea.

I sense his organs starting to fail at the peripheries, and the memories of his blameless life cease to stream into me. They waver and grow dim, as if someone ahead of me is turning out all the lights as they leave.

I almost imagine I see Ryan hurrying away from me down a long corridor, bounded by light on all sides. I can't bring back the dead. It's not my gift, not my province. Only Azraeil — and one other — can claim that as their right.

Ryan! I cry out. *Don't leave me!*

But his body continues to fail, and he seems to pull even further away. Hides his face from me, won't turn around.

It's growing too still, too quiet.

I'm going to lose him.

All I am, at this moment, is wild and undirected energy, shrill panic, unspeakable grief.

I force myself to still, to cease pursuing his ghost. To think.

The soul is ephemeral. The soul weighs less than the air a body needs in order to stay alive.

They say that the mind is the last thing to die. But the way … the way is in the heart. A holy man told me that, a long time ago, in another life, another time altogether.

Another wise man once said that the greatest evil is physical pain. But I've never shied away from dishing out pain, or taking it. And I know Ryan will forgive me, because I know of no other way.

I turn and gather myself. Like floodwater, like a rattlesnake striking. And hit him with the full force of *me*.

As if I have brought the lightning, the storm, inside, I beat down the doors of Ryan's heart, and the whole world immediately turns red with pain and heat and noise.

There's an abrupt sensation of coalescence, and I'm flung out of contact with Ryan's body. The instant I come to, shaking and swearing to myself that I will never again do this thing to another living creature, Ryan takes a great, heaving breath.

His dark eyes fly open and he chokes and claws at the rigid muscles of his neck, at the place where I laid my hand upon him.

I don't even think, I just pull him to me with trembling hands and bury my face in his dark hair. I'm holding him to me so tightly that the sound of his heartbeat, the murmur of his quickening blood, could be my own.

Thank you, I say silently and with reverence. *Thank you.*

He smells of rain and smoke and leather, and it's the uncanniest thing, but being this close to him, having somehow personally wrested him from Azraeil's grasp, I can *feel* his life force. I'm almost intoxicated by it.

It's something I never felt when I was cast *into* Carmen and Lela, all the others. I never got a real sense of the peculiar human energies of all the people around me. But now, in Ryan, I can somehow ... read it, or hear it, like music. It's singing out of him — who he is; what he is.

He's alive. He's so alive.

Two walls meeting to my right form a sheltering angle and I lean into it, taking Ryan with me, still held fast in my arms. He's retching and shuddering, and I remember how it was when I was trapped inside Lela's dying body and the Archangel Gabriel gave me a personal reminder of the evils of possession. It felt like live current moving through me, as if I was touching eternity. How must it have seemed to Ryan?

It's a long time before he can do anything except breathe with a raw sound, like someone who has survived a raging fire. All I can do is hold him and measure the passing seconds by the beating of his heart.

Finally, Ryan pushes away slightly, though he does not try to break my hold. I help him sit up, before reluctantly letting him go. This touching thing could get to be habit-forming, and the last thing I need now is a new addiction.

My left hand no longer burns with the mark of Luc's betrayal. For an instant, I'm mesmerised by the sight of my own skin, my own fingers — how long it's been since I've really seen them and felt as if they were a part of me. They are as unmarked and smooth as fired porcelain. I'm reminded with a jolt of Carmen's eczema-scarred wrists, Lela's small hands, Irina's slender, tapered claws. I've left them all behind me now, truly.

Ryan breaks my reverie by raising his head to face me at last. His eyes are pain-filled. He looks at me for the longest time; studying my features, my glowing, strong-limbed form. He told me, once, that he kept a picture of me in his wallet — something a sketch artist put together on the strength of Lauren's description. But he's never really seen me, the real me. He's only ever known me as a sharp-tongued presence, a wise-cracking ghoul, inhabiting a stranger's body. Is he … disappointed?

But there's awe in his expression, and a dawning gladness. There's something else, too, in his eyes. Some kind of new-found awareness that was never there before.

I wonder what he saw when he journeyed through the valley of the shadow of death. Whether he witnessed things that cannot be reasoned away. The path, for every person, is different, they say.

We sit staring at each other, side by side, our backs to the rough stone. I focus solely on Ryan, on his face. It's weird, but so long as I look at him, the feeling that I'm about to splinter apart, seems to lessen.

'What …' His voice is like something carried back on the wind from the afterlife. 'What just … happened? It felt like I was …'

'On fire?' I say quietly.

He nods, wiping the blood from his mouth with the heel of one hand. 'From the inside.' He struggles to swallow, grimacing when it causes him pain. 'I died, didn't I? I was d—'

I put a hand to his lips to stop him saying more, in case Azraeil should be reminded of how he was cheated and think to return.

Ryan turns his face into my palm. I want so badly to trace the line of his mouth with my thumb, but I quickly let my hand fall before I can give in to weakness.

'It takes a lot to heal someone,' I reply cautiously. 'And I don't have a great track record at healing things, so cut me some slack.'

'You *saved* me?' His voice is raw. 'You mean you were responsible for that ... that ...' He inhales sharply at the memory of the pain and his fingers curl involuntarily where they rest upon his knees. When he turns his gaze back on me his eyes are almost accusing. 'That was ... *you?*'

I say gently, 'Like I told you before, I'm not a "regular" girl, Ryan. And seeing as how I almost killed you, I figure we're about even now.'

He coughs as he pulls himself more upright against the wall, and that familiar fringe of straight, dark hair falls into his eyes.

'All I can remember is a bunch of steeples and ...' he frowns, 'people? Am I right? Were there *people* up there? All rushing up to meet us, then *blam*, I hit something. Lights out. Then I wake to find you watching over me. Like some kind of angel ...'

He looks at me sideways, deliberately casual, to gauge my reaction.

As I look down, discomfited by the intensity of his gaze, a strand of my own straight, dark hair falls across my face. Ryan bridges the gap between us, loops it gently behind my ear, briefly tracing down the line of my jaw as if he can't help himself. His touch is so shattering, so damned *human*, that some cold, hard part of me feels as if it is giving way.

'You feel so real,' he rasps.

Self-preservation is instinctual in me now and I move out of reach, warning him raggedly, '*Don't.*'

'Or what?' He sighs, leaning his head back against the

wall. It's so cold in here that his breath streams out white, like a cloud, or a soul departing.

'You know, I've had my own freaky theories about you for some time now,' he murmurs. 'I went away and did my research like you said to, between dealing with a mountain of self-pity and anger and ... grief.' He shoots me another glance. 'I don't know how it's possible ... how you're even possible. You've made me question everything I've ever believed in. I deserve a little more ... clarity.' His voice is strained. 'I think I've, uh, earned it.'

Warily, from the safety of my corner, I meet his eyes.

'For what it's worth,' he says, 'I feel like everything's new again between us. Like we've been given permission to ... start over.'

'Permission?' I laugh despairingly. 'In what universe could someone like you and someone like me make any kind of sense? Who "permits" this?' I look away from the tenderness in his gaze, the hurricane inside me begging to be set free.

'You need to explain things to me,' he insists. 'I need to understand who it is that I'm —'

'Dealing with?' I cut in.

Something flares in his eyes, and I'm instantly ashamed of my own cowardice because I know what he was about to say, the words he was going to use.

'You could put it that way,' he says, stung.

I look down at my hands, wanting to touch him, to tell him I don't deserve his love. Maybe I've never really known what love is; after all, I chose as my first love someone who soon after became ... the Devil.

I shudder. Ryan catches the movement and frowns.

'Trade?' he says so softly, I almost miss the word.

For a long while I don't answer, seeing landmines in every direction, seeing ancient history that could only cause Ryan pain, the last thing I would ever want for him. All the while, I struggle to keep my nausea at bay, to contain that sensation inside me of building, of escalation.

'You promised.' Ryan takes a shuddering breath. 'It's because of *you* I got broken in the first place.'

'And I fixed you!' I reply, turning on him like a wounded animal. 'So quit complaining.'

'I was broken the moment you left me the first time.' His voice is very quiet. 'Damn straight, it's up to you to fix me. And you haven't even begun to mend the hurt you caused. You can't hide from what's between us forever! You deserve ... love as much as anyone does.'

It's as if the word is ripped out of him. He's unaware that I've already read his heart like a map, like the constellations.

'*Let me in,*' he begs, murmuring again, 'you promised.'

'What?' I say, struggling to hold myself together, to hold myself apart from him. 'What did I "promise"? How was I even in any condition to promise you anything?'

I see his face soften as his eyes glide over my features, over my glowing form, the curls of energy that drift off my skin, then blur and fade.

'You promised that you'd never hurt me,' he whispers. 'Remember? When you were Lela. Then you went and *died* on me. It felt as if I was the one who'd been shot. I even looked down to see if *I* was bleeding ...'

I close my eyes, feeling again the ghostly impact of the bullet that ended Lela's life. 'I so badly wanted to go with you then,' I murmur, 'but it wasn't permitted.' I place the heels of my hands against my eyes, trying to stem the ache I still feel for that lost girl. 'I'm trying to protect you,' I mutter over the white noise in my head, 'for what it's worth. You don't know what you're asking.'

'That talk we were always supposed to have?' Ryan pleads. 'We're having it now, Mercy. So start talking. You're afraid, I'm afraid. But we're here now, you're *free*.'

'I may not be caged inside another any longer,' I say from behind my hands, 'but you have no idea how wrong you are, what you're up against. I will *never* be free.'

Of you, of him. Not while I live.

I see it again: the hills around Lake Como, the Galleria Vittorio Emanuele, all exploding in a kind of liquid flame, consumed by the wrath of demons and archangels colliding. In those memories, I see Ryan's death foretold, and I almost cannot bear it.

'Why are we even arguing?' Ryan whispers, his breath stirring upon my skin. 'Where have you gone?'

'Beyond the stars,' I whisper, hearing the static and the silence, the inexorable distance, in my head. How very far I fell, how far.

He places a tentative hand upon my bare and glowing arm; against all wisdom, I allow it to remain. Ryan always was brave, and foolhardy around me. We've always fed that impulse in each other, and isn't that what love is supposed to do? Lend you wings; grant you the strength and courage of Titans.

'So real,' he murmurs again in wonderment.

Through his skin I can read the chaos in his thoughts: love piled upon fear, layered upon hope and desire, anger and frustration. The weight of them, their metaphysical noise, is almost intolerable.

It feels *wrong* to have access to his innermost thoughts. Knowledge like that is so dangerous in the wrong hands. It's little wonder that Luc's ambitions have gained a certain purchase in this world: they are here for the picking, these mortals. Everything you need to know — their dreams, their vices — all flowing beneath the skin constantly, like a river. To be drawn from, or poisoned.

Without consciously recalling how it's done, little by little I turn Ryan down, tune him out. So that his inner energy, the random glimmers of thought and emotion I get from him now are almost bearable. It's not perfect, but at least I can think again. I drop my hands from my face, turn to look at him.

Finally, I tell him of home. And as I describe it, the way it was when it was fresh made and new, and every small thing seemed a miracle in and of itself, tears of fire spill down my cheeks, melting away even as they hit the chilly air.

'My kind,' I weep, 'were not created to feel sorrow. Everything about me, about *us*, is impossible, Ryan, so frightening, I can't see my way clear ...'

'You told me to go look up that word, *elohim*,' he says. 'The word for what you are. And I did, but I'm still missing something important. It can mean so many things. I'm no good at languages. Or history. All the stuff I read just confused me even more. I just want to hear what it means, from you.'

He puts his arm around me and hauls me close, and it's so electrifying, so longed for, that I can't think again, can't move. We're pressed shoulder to shoulder, hip to hip, and I'm so distracted by the achingly familiar scent of him, his human warmth, the life force surging inside him, that I close my eyes and give myself over to sensation, resting my head against the hard line of his shoulder. It feels so right. And so real. It's just a moment or two out of time. Even the Archangel Michael would grant me that much.

But then a bright, numinous light sweeps past the windows of our tower, followed swiftly by another, causing me to flinch, for I alone recognise its source. I can almost hear Gudrun breathing in the night, all her hatred, and that of her dead-eyed hunting partner, Hakael, bent towards me. They smell my fear. They seek to know where we hide inside this vast stone edifice. If Ryan and I had not reached sanctuary, I'm sure we'd already be dead.

CHAPTER 2

'Once,' I say, struggling to keep my voice calm as the sweeping, searching light recurs, and recurs again, 'there were upwards of a thousand *elohim*. Some created male, some female. Eight were made most powerful, most prescient, of all things that dwell in the universe: His regents. His princes. Tasked to discern His will.'

Their names rise like smoke in the icy air. 'Barachiel,' I murmur, 'Selaphiel, Jeremiel, Jegudiel, Uriel, Gabriel, Raphael, Michael ...'

A look of shock appears on Ryan's face. 'Mercy, those are the names of *archangels*. Beings that people actually ... worship.'

'And they were my friends,' I whisper, 'like my brothers. The name of God is woven into the very fabric of their beings, their names, as it is in mine, if only I could remember it, but something was done to me to make me forget, do you understand what I'm trying to tell you?'

There's baffled wonderment on Ryan's face. For a moment, I get a torrent of feeling from him, denial the strongest thread.

'And these eight, uh, archangels ...?' he says hesitantly.

'Were the ones who kept me "safe", who placed me inside a woman called Ezra, into another called Lucy, a girl called Susannah, then Carmen, Lela, Irina; and, before them all, an unbroken chain of human lives I can no longer recall ...'

Ryan frowns. 'Kept you safe from what?'

I pretend not to hear. 'Our people are further divided into *malakhim* — the messengers, who are sometimes seen to intercede with the living here on earth; and *seraphim*, *ophanim*, dominions, powers, others. There are many ... "castes", for want of a better word, but the *elohim* are highest of all.'

Ryan rolls his eyes. 'Castes? You've just described Paradise High. And, I guess, I used to be one of the *elohim*, too. Before I fell. So *snap!* Some pair we make.'

I return his grin with a startled smile of my own, but then my voice grows sombre again. 'There are three classes of being under God: bestial, human, angelic. And one thing is known and understood by us all: never shall they intermix, or evil is the result. I know it as if it is written on my soul in letters of fire.'

'Evil?' Ryan leaps on the word. I feel his sudden tension in the arm lying across my shoulders.

'When the Daughters of Man began to multiply upon the earth,' I explain, unsure of how I gained such knowledge, where the words arise from, 'some of our people lay with them, begetting a race called the *nephilim*. Some say they are murderous giants, some say devouring spirits.'

'Fairy tales,' Ryan scoffs.

My eyes sharpen upon his. 'The way the Devil and his demons are?'

'What we are isn't *evil*,' he insists.

'I don't know *what* we are,' I reply. 'And I'm not saying I agree. I'm just giving you an idea of the ... baggage that I come with.'

Two supernatural factions wrestling for control of my soul across the centuries, reduced to this one word: *baggage*.

Ryan's answering look is wry.

I recall Irina's roomful of bespoke luggage and give a short laugh. 'I'm just telling you that this is how we're ... wired. So if you don't think I come with the biggest damn warning sign you've ever seen, you aren't really looking at me properly. Why aren't you afraid of what I represent? Why aren't you already running?'

Ryan looks down. 'You know the answer to that. Don't make it any harder for me than it already is. And I'm not saying that the, uh, *nephilim* were a good thing. But the fact that they, uh, might exist,' his face is sceptical, 'shows that some of your people broke "the law" in the past, right? By mixing with us lower life forms. You might say you're programmed one way, but I see you questioning things all the time. Everything you've done since I've known you has been a process of trying to break free; to override what was done to you by eight of the most powerful beings in existence.'

I stiffen at his words, recognising both truth and heresy in them. It's true that I no longer comprehend the ways of my own kind; that, in some way, for better or worse, I've ... evolved. After all this time, I may be more human than not. Don't I feel pain, fear, grief, sorrow, when I was created to feel none of these things?

'Were they all there? The Eight?' Ryan asks, catching me by surprise. 'At the Galleria?'

I shake my head. In my mind's eye, I relive the instant Luc cut K'el down and pain explodes through me again. I rock forward, crossing my arms tightly to hold in the hurt.

'K'el's last act in life was to protect *me*,' I gasp. 'Even though I never loved him enough to deserve such sacrifice.'

'K'el?' Ryan seizes on the unfamiliar name, his grip tightening. I know what he remembers: a gleaming giant, tawny-haired, unyielding, honourable, bitter, with eyes like a young lion, who stood between me and Luc.

'Raphael was supposed to be there, too,' I whisper. 'But he never made it. Nor did Jegudiel. And Selaphiel's been … missing for a while now.'

'Missing?' Ryan queries sharply.

I hear his frustration as he struggles to piece together the little I've seen fit to offer.

'Taken,' I clarify bleakly. 'All three of them, by Luc's forces. K'el was just a stand-in; he was out of his depth, and his reward was an unjust death. He was singular and perfect, Ryan. And he will never be made again. I think that's all I want to "trade". You don't need to know the rest.'

Ryan grips me by the upper arms, turning me to face him with a hard shake. 'Why can't you trust me?' he growls. 'Don't underestimate me. Don't treat me like I'm something less than you are — I don't deserve that. *Who is he, Mercy? The one who was threatening you? He's* the reason K'el's dead, the real reason Raphael and the others are missing, right? The reason the Eight have had to hide you for so long, inside so many people? I'm not as stupid as I must seem to you.'

I begin to tremble as if I'm in the grip of a killing fever. *Don't make me tell you, Ryan. Please.*

'Who is he?' Ryan insists. 'That … archangel,' he stumbles over the word, 'who looks just like me? If he isn't one of the Eight, then who is he?'

Trust Ryan to cut to the heart of it, of me.

He gives me another shake. 'He was hurting you and I tried to kill him. Kill him!'

I hear his disbelief. He is wide-eyed now at the memory. I know that he's seeing what I'm seeing: Luc suspended sixty feet in the air, arms outspread, flames enveloping his living form, laughing wildly.

'He was *on fire*,' Ryan shudders, 'but he wouldn't die. And I *wanted* him to die because he was trying to hurt you. Tell me who he is!'

I look at Ryan again, really study him. For an instant, I see eyes as pale as broken water, as living ice, in place of his brown ones; golden hair where his is dark; golden skin where his is so pale. He could be Luc in disguise. Save mortal and vulnerable in a way Luc has never been and never will be. Could Ryan represent some kind of warning? I was never good at reading signs and portents, having fallen to earth before I could work out, for myself, who I was and what my purpose could even be.

'Who *is* he?' Ryan's voice is raw.

'He's no archangel,' I murmur. 'Not any more. I've always called him Luc,' I add reluctantly, 'but you would know him as Lucifer, Ryan.'

I see Ryan blanch as understanding finally dawns: that he is a dead ringer for the Devil Incarnate.

As if to underscore my words, a soul-rending scream pierces the storm-tossed night. It reverberates in the silence that has fallen over Ryan, over me, deep inside our stone citadel.

Both of us flinch as another scream sounds, closer this time, and louder. For a moment, a bright, constant light pierces the narrow window set deep into the walls above our landing, and we stare up at it, frozen with fear, before it suddenly extinguishes.

Ryan lets go of me abruptly, leans back against the wall.

I pull my knees up under my chin, tightening my arms around myself defensively. 'So you see how this is hopeless, you and me?'

In answer, Ryan just closes his eyes and tilts his head back, as if he can't bear the sight of me.

I never babble, I'm no good at small talk, but I rush to fill the silence with the oldest story there is. About a girl seeing a guy through a crowd for the first time, and falling in love.

'It was like a sickness,' I mutter. 'We were young, capable of things your people would deem impossible. We were ... *obsessed* with each other, with what we could do. We thought we were outside the order of things. That rules were only there to be broken. We sneered at the others — believing they didn't possess our depth of understanding about the way things *could* be. The whole universe was our playground, and Luc loved to walk in your world. He'd return with stories of some strange, rare place he knew as "Eden". The greatest irony is that he should be trapped here for an age, growing in vengefulness and spite and pure evil because of me ...'

Can Ryan hear my unspoken plea?

I did nothing but fall for the wrong person, Ryan. I picked Luc, when I should have picked Raphael, even K'el. But then I never would have met you ...

Even then, Luc had been trouble. He'd been wild. We'd been created to govern. We were responsibility and duty and

25

faith and principle made flesh, made *real*. But Luc had taken all the power bound inside him, all the unspoken covenants laid down between us and our creator — the covenants hard coded into the very matter of which we were made, *thou shalt, thou shalt not* — and he'd used them for his own ... sport.

It had been exhilarating, and frightening, being with him. Almost from the first, Luc had behaved like a god himself: creating, destroying, twisting the animate and inanimate world around him into anything he desired simply because he could. He was different from us all and somehow ... free. And more beautiful than the sun.

And I fell for that. Who wouldn't have?

Maybe I hadn't transgressed the way Luc did, but I never tried to rein him in. I was implicated, a witness; at the very least, I turned a blind eye, when I must have known he'd never be satisfied with things the way they stood.

I tell Ryan all of this and he doesn't say anything, or open his eyes.

'I had it wrong for the longest time,' I finish softly. 'It was never the Eight who cast me out of home, cut me off from everything I'd ever loved, everyone I'd ever known. It was Luc all along. The Eight did the best they could to keep me alive down here, but they couldn't stop Luc filling my sleeping mind with longing and lies. Some fatal bargain was struck between Luc and Michael, all those years ago. But Luc gave it a special twist, all of his own making, like he's always done. *He* was the one who exiled me and it almost killed me. But he didn't count on me surviving. And he didn't count on being cast down himself, by Michael. And because of a rash vow that Luc once made me, he's been trapped here on earth.'

I close my eyes in horror, whispering, 'Luc craves a monstrous empire. And I am the key, the touchstone. What he wants won't be possible until he has me back under his control. He will never stop pursuing me.'

Ryan still hasn't moved.

'And *are* you still … obsessed with him?' he says finally, without opening his eyes.

His voice is emotionless, steeled against more hurt.

'Yes,' I whisper over the hurricane inside. 'More than ever.'

Ryan swallows and opens his eyes and I see them shimmer with an unspoken devastation before he abruptly looks down at his clenched hands.

I watch the skin of his face tighten in rejection as I say, 'I am *consumed* — with thoughts of destroying Luc the way he destroyed K'el, the way he's been responsible for destroying and defiling more of your kind than you could begin to number, the way he tried to destroy me. He robbed me of time, Ryan, of choice, the two things I consider as precious as life itself. He raised his hand against me when all I ever did was love him beyond reason.'

Ryan raises his head as my words sink in. I hold up my aching left hand, which I've been concealing from his gaze, and the living flames rise off my skin as if they reach for him. He gasps, recoiling.

'I'm sick of being objectified by those who are supposed to "love" me,' I say fiercely. 'I've been a game piece for far too long. I want *vengeance*, Ryan. I want to rain down upon my enemies like a ruinous plague. But most of all? I'm ready to be loved, just for myself, no other reason. And I don't think you're strong enough to be with someone like me. No one is, not now.'

Ryan's continuing silence tells me everything I need to know. I feel such a sudden weight of sadness that, for a moment, the screaming, spinning world beneath my skin grows still. Abruptly, my burning scar extinguishes all together, ceases to ache.

Who could love me the way I am? Nameless, stateless, flawed.

'I have no name,' I say, my voice bleak. 'And there is a legion after me who would reduce you to blood. For what it's worth,' I whisper, 'I feel it, too. Felt it, almost from the moment I met you. When we're together, I feel so much less ... alone. And I would like nothing better than to lose myself in the human world with you, but that's a dream, Ryan. And I'm done dreaming. I'm awake now. Now and forever. And where I'm going, you cannot follow.'

A demonic shriek shatters the night, so close beside us that I surge upright in fear, only to have the entire world tilt through its axis as I struggle to retain my balance.

Ryan is on his feet immediately, steadying me.

He's so tall, taller than me, built like a line-backing angel.

I'm still Irina's height, still mortal-sized. I can't seem to find the energy, or the will, to dominate the space I occupy, to reclaim my true nature. There doesn't seem any point. I'm no "better" than he is. Not any more.

I struggle in Ryan's arms, but he won't let me push him away. Maybe I imagine it but, for a second, it seems as if my outline ripples, like Ryan's clasping a creature made of fog, I can see the ground below my bare feet, through them.

'Don't you *dare*!' Ryan cries, his grip momentarily tightening on emptiness as I struggle to draw myself together. 'Don't you dare disappear on me again. I know what we have is impossible to rationalise, but once I met you, my old life was over anyway. I was dead inside. All that stuff, that Ryan, they were already gone, already past. Only *this* matters. *Don't leave me.*'

I want to lean into him and draw upon his solidity, his indescribable, peculiar energy that I could pick out in a crowd, anywhere, but I'm falling again, falling.

I'm caving in, I'm vertigo.

'All that exists,' I gasp, as if saying the words will somehow protect me, 'is this present.'

It's something I told myself when I was Irina and believed that Luc was dead, and I'd never see Ryan again. Maybe it's the only thing capable of being true in a world like this one; that the moment we inhabit, is all we can ever really be sure of.

'That's it, that's it exactly!' he pleads. 'All I want from you is more *time*.'

The laugh that escapes me has the quality of hysteria.

'We need to carve something out for *us*,' Ryan exclaims. 'The big guy with the big sword said so himself. He ordered me to take care of you in the human world, which tells me that your time on earth is nowhere near over. And he thinks I can help. Somehow.'

The screwed up look on Ryan's face is almost comical and it hits me that he's the sweetest thing I've ever known. Then the world begins to spin in earnest and I feel his hold on me slip again.

'We take this moment, this *now*, and we draw it out, we turn it into a chain of time that will keep us together,' Ryan insists.

When I reply, my voice is almost inaudible. 'The "big guy with the big sword" is the Archangel Michael, and he overestimates his jurisdiction where I'm concerned. I've been taking care of myself in the human world for a very long time without recourse to anyone. Every time They put me into someone new? It all came down to *me*: me doing the starting over, me making things up as I went along. Being with me will only get you killed. I can't be responsible for losing you, the way I almost lost you tonight.'

The sense of vertigo is so bad now that Ryan seems fuzzy, as if I'm seeing him through a veil of light.

'You're already responsible,' Ryan implores. 'I'm a marked man. I could see it in his eyes when he looked at me. With you, or without you, I'm marked for death. And I'll take my chances *with* you. In any life, given the same choice, *I would choose you*. Are you hearing me?'

Ryan could be a being of fire, light is scattering off his skin. I reach out and touch his face with my fingers, feeling the energy spike beneath the surface of him, his iron self-control wavering. So much passion in him, so much life, all for me.

'I know what you're trying to do,' I whisper through the pain sweeping through me. 'And it won't work. This isn't a game, Ryan. *Run*, or *die*. Those are the choices. Am I worth that much to you?'

'I've got your back,' Ryan vows fervently, 'if you've got mine. You know it.'

He wraps his arms around me as if he would bind my energy to him. And the bright glow that my skin gives off seems to bleed into him, or draw tight around him, so he glows brighter to my dazzled eyes. It's as if we are bound together by light. Light is refracting off us onto the walls, the worn handrails, the uneven stone stairs, like some kind of chemical reaction is happening.

Ryan's breath is warm upon my face. 'Now, are you done throwing out challenges?' he asks. 'Maybe I lied a little when I said that all I wanted was your time, because I'm greedy for whatever you can give me. I'll steal what I can. Because there's something I've had to wait more than one lifetime to do, and I'm not waiting any more ...'

Before I can divine his intention, shore up my defences, Ryan tips my face up to his, curving me into the hard line of his body, lowering his lips swiftly to mine.

My eyes fly wide then shiver closed.

I am love, and desire, and fear.

I'm suffused with a roaring heat.

Those things are inside Ryan, too, surging beneath his skin.

We are two disparate energies colliding and the light around us, in us, through us, seems to build and build.

So potent a mix are we that the mere act of being, of holding myself together, becomes untenable and I shatter into a billion pieces, into ragged motes of light, like an exploding star, instantly dispersing.

Ryan is buffeted by a blast wave of heat and energy, it ruffles his dark hair, his clothing, and he's left to grasp the empty air, howling just one word, '*Mercy!*'

Thinking me already fled, gone, departed, as I have done so many times before.

I am the hurricane that was promised.

I am boundless.

There's nothing to stop me penetrating these stone walls and go slipstreaming into the night.

I am insubstantial, yet indivisible.

I feel inviolate, all-powerful.

It is as it should be. It is as it was.

But something holds me here. It's like an itch, a small and nagging cut dragging at my attention.

I know it. I can almost taste it: some messy human emotion I should put behind me forever, but cannot now ignore.

It's grief, Ryan's grief radiating into the icy air.

To every action, a reaction; it's something my people dismiss. We look down on all those below us and think that our actions, our inactions, have no consequence.

But mortals live in a storm of consequence, and Ryan has been hurt enough for one lifetime.

Somehow, that thought draws me back.

I am clumsy and unpractised, and my whole being yearns to be and remain weightless light, but still I pull my fractured energy together like a swarm of angry bees. I force myself to become a perfect simulacrum of a human being once more: fleshy, dense, solid.

Then I'm facing him again, and Ryan's eyes are still wide with horror and sorrow. He's close enough to touch, but neither of us makes a move towards the other. Now he knows what I have known all along: that touching is dangerous. It invites the unwanted.

I see suddenly, blindingly, how love and loss are two sides of the same coin. To know one is to know the other, even before it has come to pass.

Ryan pushes his hair out of his eyes. 'I thought you were … gone.' His voice cracks on the word. 'This time for good. It's never going to be easy for us, is it?'

I shake my head.

'You scare me, Ryan Daley. Even more than those demons outside that scream for my death. How is it that I want what you want? I've spent an eternity feeling powerless. *Love* did that to me — robbed me of all control. I never expected to feel this way again. I don't want to *feel*.'

'Neither did I,' Ryan rasps, 'because feeling anything at all was dangerous. If I let myself feel, then maybe I'd have to believe what everyone was saying — that Lauren was dead. But from the moment I laid eyes on "Carmen", *you* kept getting under my skin. At first, all you did was irritate the hell out of me, bailing me up that way outside my house, inviting yourself along for the ride when all I wanted was to be left alone. But that irritation turned into curiosity, which turned into something else, becoming this chain of, of … feeling that brought me here. I dropped everything for you. I veered left. And I'd do it again in a second. That's what "feeling" does. It tells you you're *alive*, it gives things … I don't know, proper *meaning*. You're still trying to maintain some veneer of independence? Toughness? Do words like that even apply to you? But I see through it, Mercy. I see through *you*. You're not that different from me after all, under your armour. Crumbs, Mercy, that's all I'm after. Just crumbs. It's not a lot to ask for.'

Ryan steps forward and tries to catch hold of me again and it's reflex what I do next.

I slam up a force-field between us, a seamless web of energy the way K'el reminded me was possible. And Ryan hits it with just his outstretched fingers. A crackle of intense, blue-white light is thrown up at the point of contact and he rocks back on his heels, cradling his stinging fingertips in his other hand.

He stares at me, wounded, before laughing ruefully. 'No sudden moves from now on, I promise, if you promise me something back.'

'What?' I say warily. 'I suck at keeping promises, remember?'

'Just promise,' he says, 'that you'll take me with you this time. You won't just fade out and leave me behind again. Just let me be with you, just stay for a while, that's all I'm asking.'

It hits me once more, that he's the sweetest thing. But I don't move any closer, though I want him more than anything.

What I want is impossible. And Ryan's given me the answer to this mess, the only answer that makes any sense.

The thought of what I'm about to say fills me with an ache so powerful that a terrible sense of dissolution returns.

'You might not need me,' he insists hotly. 'You might not want me, but you've got me.'

That force-field, that protective shell I've cast about myself, I let it drop. I hold my right hand out to Ryan, and both of us can see that it's shaking.

Hesitantly, he takes my fingers, then grips them tight, as if he will never let me go. I have to tune out everything I can feel beneath his skin, everything about him that unsettles every particle of my being, in order to speak.

'It's the one thing I can't do, Ryan: *stay*.'

He shakes his head violently and I whisper, 'Hear me out, *please*.

'I never took Luc's side in his rebellion against God. I was exiled before I could be forced to choose. So now — call it luck, call it chance, call it accident, because I will *never* call it fate — I remain *elohim*. Not demon. I still have a choice. And there's a way to keep Luc in Hell forever; a way that will mean placing

34

duty before desire the way the Eight always have, and always will. I have to leave, don't you see? It's something that part of me yearns for. I've been stumbling towards the light for the longest time, and now? *I might actually return.* I might actually be able to go home. If Luc can't find me, he'll always be contained here.'

Ryan releases me, shocked. 'You'd just abandon us to him? Aren't we worth saving?'

Such a tiny word, *us*, conveying so many things.

'But Luc would be trapped forever,' I say pleadingly. 'He'd never be able to leave, never be able to turn everything beyond your world —'

'Into a wasteland,' Ryan says fiercely, 'the way he'd do here if he ever discovered you were gone.'

'This place is already a wasteland,' I murmur. '*One law for the lion and the ox is oppression.* That's just the way it is. How things were laid down.'

The words slip out before I realise I've uttered them.

Ryan reels back from me as if I've punched him in the throat.

'So just *go*,' he chokes. 'Throw us to the lions, or whatever. Save yourself, your home. Just forget I laid myself on the line. Forget I spoke, that I pleaded with you on behalf of my entire *species*.'

'You don't understand,' I say quietly.

'Oh, I understand very well,' he replies. '*The greatest good for the greatest number*, right? They hammered that one home in sociology one year. We humans are ... what, just one rung above the animals? But when Luc takes out his vengeance on all of us because you slipped through his fingers, just remember what *you* sacrificed, Mercy, because it will all be your doing. Having more than a little personal experience of sacrifice, I'm guessing you won't want that on your conscience. It's a coward's way out. And you're no *coward*,' he spits. 'Or do I have that wrong?'

Every word hits me like a blow, and I'm hardly surprised when we are rocked by another blast wave of heat and energy that knocks us both off our feet.

Sprawled where I am on the ground, I only have enough time to raise my head before the Archangel Nuriel steps out of a vortex that seems to have opened upon the stairs just above us.

She's so beautiful.

Her long, dark, wavy hair snakes out around her shoulders as if she's a living Medusa. Her dark eyes are wide and unseeing, and she seems made of lightning; so bright in outline I can barely discern her form, the sleeveless garment she wears. She's weaponless, and there's an expression on her face that looks almost ... vulnerable. All of the joy I've always associated with her, is missing.

Ryan's face is tilted up towards her, enraptured, and I know the same look is upon my face.

'*Soror*,' Nuriel pleads. '*Salva me*.'

Sister, she's saying. *Save me*.

Though I kneel up and reach out to her, she does not meet my eyes as she drifts, weightless, above the stone. And I realise that this is a vision of some kind. She's a projection, she's not really here. Luc showed me that such a thing could be possible.

I rise and approach the vision cautiously, passing my fingers through the edges of Nuriel's constantly shifting, fraying outline. I feel nothing. She could be a hologram.

'*Festina*,' the vision whispers, '*ne delear ut K'el deletus est.*' *Come quickly. Or I will be destroyed, as K'el was destroyed.*

I close my eyes briefly in renewed horror at the mention of K'el's name.

'What is she saying?' Ryan says, getting up cautiously.

But I'm torn by the memory of Nuriel siding with Michael, with all the others, against me. And I do not reply.

'*Salva me, soror.*' Nuriel's voice is eerie and emotionless. '*Salva me.*'

Then there's a jump-cut moment — like a break in transmission — where I imagine for a moment that Nuriel's outline wavers, rippling outwards. Then she winks out of being, leaving Ryan and me circling the space between us warily.

'You could hear her,' I say bluntly. 'See her.'

Ryan nods, still puzzled. 'But she could have been speaking backwards. What did she say?'

'She was speaking in Latin. She wants me to save her.'

Ryan's face is, instantly, transparent with hope. 'So you'll stay long enough to free her?'

'It's a trap, Ryan,' I say flatly, and his face falls. 'The last time I "saw" Nuriel, Luc was chasing her down, above the waters of Lake Como. Luc's got her, I heard him say it. This vision is an elaborate kind of bait. Some measure of coercion was used. Torture.'

'But she's a friend of yours, right?' Ryan's voice is almost pleading. 'And she's in trouble?'

'Yes,' I say tightly, realising where this is heading.

Ryan challenges me with his eyes. 'So do it — if not for me, then for her. Stick it to Luc one last time. Defy him. I know you want to. If you're not going to hang around to defend us, at least leave us someone who can.'

I'm stung by his words. 'It doesn't change the fact that it's a set-up! You don't "get" what we are, what we're about. *We're not in it for you.* Anyway, Luc's not going to just let me walk in and take her. Even if I did decide to help her, I forbid you from going anywhere with me, so don't even think about it, it's non-negotiable.'

'So you'll do it?' Ryan says eagerly.

'I didn't say that,' I growl. 'I'm still thinking about it. You could die.'

In that string of non sequiturs is all my unspoken fear for him.

'It wouldn't matter what you said,' Ryan argues. 'I'd just follow you anyway. You can't stop me. I've had years of practice. You picked the wrong guy to mess with.'

'You have no idea what I'm capable of!' Worry sharpens my voice to a keen edge. 'And don't be ridiculous, you wouldn't know where to go. You couldn't do what I do, you'd never find me.'

'I'd just follow the trail of destruction,' Ryan says triumphantly. 'You've made a mess of things so far, all of you. It'd be a piece of cake. I'd just follow the trail of burning buildings.'

Or burning humans. I recall, with horror, those images of a fiery, melting world that Gia Basso and I had watched, side by side.

'Luc would squash you like a bug,' I growl to hide my fear. 'You'd be completely unprotected, trailing around after me with demons on the loose.'

'So let me go with you then,' Ryan says guilelessly. 'I could stand behind you when things get nasty.' He grins. 'Got no problem with that.'

'The sensible option would be to leave and never come back. Right now. You know it.'

'But where would the fun be in that?' he murmurs. 'And we're both due a little fun.'

'*Fun?*' My reply is incredulous. 'Walking into an obvious trap set by a bunch of first-order demons isn't defiance, it's not even fun. It's just stupid.'

'But we're a stupid and obstinate species.' Ryan grins wider at my expression. 'Argumentative. Tenacious. Just *go for it*. You've got to love that about us.'

'It's not "love" I'm feeling right now! You could die,' I say again.

'But I'd be less likely to die if I was with you,' Ryan wheedles. 'Because you'd do everything in your power to keep me alive. I know you would.'

'You'd just get in my way,' I bluster.

'The way you got in mine?' he shoots back. 'And see what happened? You found Lauren. You saved her life. Good things happen when we're together.'

He moves forward, taking my hands in his. 'So you'll let me turn the tables on you? Let *me* tag along this time? One last joint mission before you leave me forever?'

I stare up into his face, troubled, seeing demon fire that resists water; that turns flesh to an ash so fine it can be borne away on the wind.

'With one condition,' I murmur. 'If we do this, if we try to go after Nuriel together — you're free to leave at any time. You don't have to stay to see how it pans out. You have my permission to run when you feel like running. I won't hold you to anything.'

'Free to bail,' Ryan agrees solemnly. 'No strings.'

Though there are. We can feel the ties that bind us together, even if we can't see them. Our words are at once empty of meaning, and brimming with it.

He folds his arms around me and places his lips against my forehead, tentatively, half-expecting me to scatter into a formless cloud of light, before looking down into my eyes with a crooked grin.

'You know I'll just keep chipping away at those defences,' he murmurs, 'working up your tolerance levels, taking you outside your comfort zone. Consider yourself forewarned.'

He feels me shiver in answer, and gives a low and sexy laugh. Is about to say more, maybe even kiss me again, when the night is shattered by a chorus of nightmare: a score of voices shrieking wordlessly, converging from many directions at once, speaking no language ever devised by the *elohim*.

Ryan and I clutch each other in mounting horror as light begins to punch through the windows of the tower in a staccato, scattergun motion. Searing light, with a sickly grey tinge at its heart, like a cancer. Demonlight. Time seems to speed up and slow down all at once as the metal window frames ripple and flex, then fly inwards, propelled by some unimaginable force, their glass exploding a second later, shredded into a powder so fine it fills the atmosphere.

CHAPTER 3

Ryan turns his head away sharply, coughing, as the glittering, granular powder disperses through the air and the warped window frames hit the stone with a sound like gunshot.

The light streaming in through the windows, the high-pitched shrieking, grow and grow until they are almost unbearable and I know that he's out there, Luc's out there.

Ryan stumbles away from me suddenly, up the stairs, tripping and cursing as he rounds the corner, out of sight. And I fall to my knees, my arms wrapped around my head in agony, wondering if the noise has driven him out of his mind the way it's invading mine.

Through the monstrous screaming, I seem to hear Luc whisper in my ear, almost as if he's standing over me. *I'm coming for you. If not now, then soon. I am wolf to your hart, hound to your hare, and I will bring you down. Believe it.*

An incredible surface pressure suddenly builds, as if the atmosphere is somehow twisting and condensing, pushing down upon me. It's as if the air around me is becoming molten. I feel an indescribable rage, a terrible malice. Luc cannot physically touch me, but he's manipulating the air itself into a kind of weapon, the embodiment of his anger. It pushes at me from all directions, reaching in through the paneless windows as if it would kill me where I lie.

'Ryan!' I cry out, fearful it will crush his mortal frame.

The light outside, the heat, the screaming, all build and build. There's a *crack*, a sonic boom so vast I wonder that it does not level the city, this cathedral.

An instant of light, so searing it's like being at the heart of an atomic cloud, and then darkness returns. The pressure begins to recede rapidly, like the tide turning. The air grows cool and thin, the way air should be. And I know with absolute clarity that Luc is gone, for now, taking his demons with him.

I spring upright, screaming, 'Ryan!'

I am the only visible thing left in this place. The darkness inside the tower is absolute. The cold air streaming in from the open windows is like needles against my skin, though the night is still and silent now. There's no snow, no sleet, no wind. The storm that has been raging all night, the storm to end all storms, it's over. Gone with Luc.

I feel Ryan before I see him: his familiar energy, the hum of him growing stronger to my senses. His boots strike the stone stairs with a clumsy sound, then a crunch and slide upon powdered glass as he turns the corner. He collapses beside me on the landing, breathing heavily.

'I headed higher up,' he gasps, 'thinking the view would be better, but all the windows are so high and narrow. I couldn't grab on to any of the window ledges — they're cut so that they slope down.' He grasps my arm, his gaze and words feverish. 'I had to jump to see out properly. And I'd just left the freakin' ground when something gripped me hard, like a fist, holding me there. I couldn't breathe, couldn't move. I saw all these streams of light twisting together like a rope that got sucked back into the hole in the roof of that Galleria place.'

I feel his thoughts running hot beneath his skin; let myself see how it was through his eyes.

'They were ... demons, right?' He swallows, still unable to grasp the physical existence of such creatures. 'How could something so beautiful be so ... evil?'

Again I get that disorienting flash of Luc — superimposed over the features of the young man before me. I shiver, whispering, 'Take it from me, it's possible.'

Still shaking, I head up several steps to the window above our landing, needing to see for myself. The narrow aperture lies just beyond reach, uncovered now against the night air, the glitter of pulverised glass beneath it. Ryan described it accurately: the window is set in deeply, and impossible to keep a grip on. But I tell myself fiercely: *You can do it, you can do anything.* Then I leap lightly into thin air ... *and I'm floating.* My feet aren't touching the ground.

Will it and it is done. That's how it's supposed to work.

Yet, I am vertigo. I am panic. I am nausea. It feels too much like flight for comfort. I wonder if it will ever feel natural again: leaving the earth behind me.

As I drift there, unsupported, I glimpse black smoke still pouring from the ruined roofline of the Galleria Vittorio Emanuele; the steady pulsing of the lights of the emergency vehicles parked haphazardly behind hastily erected crash barriers on the Piazza; tiny figures getting slowly back onto their feet, gesticulating at the sky in fear and wonder.

My view is truncated by the decorative angles of the Duomo, but at the horizon I see the faintest lightening. Daybreak is coming at last.

I land as lightly as I left the ground, though I stumble as my feet reconnect with the stone. Ryan stares at me in silence, his eyes reproachful at the reminder of the chasm that lies between us.

I voice the thought I've been carrying around inside me. 'We can't stay here. I make everything around me a target; enough has been done to this city, to its people. The demons are gone for now. Michael, Gabriel and the others must have drawn them away somehow, long enough for us to leave here. So if you really want to do this, if you want to try and carve out some time for us, pull off one last "joint mission"? We've got to get ready to go. It's almost light.'

'How?' he asks. 'We can't just walk out of here. They'll see us. There's nowhere safe in the world when they can destroy something without even touching it.'

He shudders. I take his face in my hands, letting the warmth bleed from my skin into his, hoping he will mistake it for confidence.

'We can,' I whisper. 'We have an advantage they do not possess. We have the ability to think like mortals and act like mortals in this mortal world. It's something none of them — angel or demon — has ever really "stooped" to do; at least not in the way I've been forced to. They persist in treating you like unthinking cattle when you've demonstrated, over and over, that you are capable of rationalising the mind of God. You are miraculous.'

I lean my forehead against his and he closes his eyes at the warming touch.

'When it grows light and the tourists begin to spill out into the streets,' I murmur, 'we'll move. Everyone loves a catastrophe. The Piazza is already crawling with people. And more will come. A tide of humanity is going to flow up this staircase today. The Galleria has become a tomb for the dead still inside, and this roof provides the best view of it. The reporters and thrill-seekers and ghouls will flock here. When the first sightseers begin to leave, we'll leave, too, hidden among them.'

Ryan pulls away from me, his laughter disbelieving. 'And I'm asking you again, *how*?' He backs away up several more stairs so that he's staring down on me from above. 'Have you looked at yourself lately? You're the most beautiful thing I've ever seen. You're electric. And you've got as much chance of slipping out of here unnoticed as, as …'

I see his eyes grow round, see him fall backwards in genuine fear, as I do what K'el, what Nuriel, what even Gudrun reminded me was possible.

I shape-shift.

Permutations, combinations — they should flow seamlessly, one from another. But I'm rusty, still fighting the feeling I could fly apart at any second. So it seems to take a lifetime to finetune and discard, add and subtract, borrow and enhance, drawing on shattered memories, old abilities, forgotten powers, until I'm satisfied with the eyes, the nose, face shape, hair colour, height, the works.

And while I do all of it, Ryan's face reflects his own fascination, and nausea.

When I'm finally done, I'm an equation, I suppose. A strange amalgam.

45

I look sixteen, maybe seventeen at most, because it's the way I'm feeling inside: so strangely confused and vulnerable and unformed.

What I remember distinctly? Is being young, and so in love with Luc that I couldn't see beyond that. Then whole human years, whole human lives, must have intervened between the creature I was then — the creature who fell — and the thing I am now. But all I can clearly remember out of all that lost time — years that could have happened to someone else — are recent memories. Like waking as a battered wife called Ezra, with blood caking my face, a hairline fracture in one eye socket.

So in honour of Ezra, I've given myself her sun-kissed skin. And I have gifted myself Lucy's green eyes because I'd look every morning into the cracked mirror in her stinking apartment and wish I was somewhere else. I have Susannah's dusting of freckles across the bridge of her long, narrow nose. And I have her dimples, one beneath the apple of each cheek so that when I smile, I appear open-faced, uncomplicated and friendly, the exact opposite of Susannah's nightmare of a mother, who made her life a kind of hell. I have Carmen's wild, black, curly hair and I'm wearing it bound back in the kind of low ponytail that her nemesis, Tiffany, used to favour. I have Lela's fine bones, elegant wrists and ankles. But I have Irina's heart-shaped face and long, tapered fingers, her long limbs and her height, because I would miss seeing the world from her vantage point, miss being able to place my head on Ryan's shoulder without having to strain to do it.

But there's something of my own strong build and features in this new persona I've created: an in-joke for an audience of one. Irina looked breakable, which is something I will never, ever be, or permit myself to seem.

I could pass as a citizen of almost anywhere; I'm both anonymous and unique, interesting to gaze on, but just shy of true beauty. I'm a deliberate collection of quirks.

'Who the hell are you supposed to be?' Ryan says, staring into my face.

'Close your mouth,' I tell him, laughing softly. 'What do you think?'

I do a little twirl on the spot, resting my hand high upon the curve of my left hip, the way Irina would.

I'm wearing ordinary-looking clothes: a black, hooded goose-down jacket over a heavy, black, rollneck sweater, skinny, dark grey jeans and soft, sand-coloured, flat-soled boots that end just below the knee. They're all fake, of course, all props, shifted out of the very energy of which I'm made. Here because I need them.

Ryan blinks several times as he studies me. 'This isn't funny — I don't know you like this,' he says finally.

I frown as I drift slowly up the stairs towards him. 'Look closer. You recognised me inside Carmen, inside Lela, in Irina, when you shouldn't have been able to. I'm the same person I always was. It's just a shell. I'm still here,' I insist. 'You know me.'

I sit down beside him, but he shifts away, as if horrified by what I've done.

'What else are you people capable of?' he breathes. 'Every time I think I've come to terms with what you are, what you can do, you freak me out all over again. I just got you back, damn it! I just got you back and you go and do this.'

'They won't be looking for someone wearing this face or form,' I say sharply. 'It'll keep us alive.'

Ryan's eyes flash. 'That may be. But you're still glowing. They're gonna see that, right? If you could, uh, dial down the whole shining thing, well then, maybe it would work.' He flicks the fingers of one hand at the gleaming surface of my skin.

I freeze, astonished that I could have forgotten such a fundamental detail.

'What would I do without you?' I murmur, staring down at my luminous hands.

When I was Carmen, I'd only ever glowed very faintly in the dark, when there were no other sources of light around. In the daylight, I'd looked like everyone else. But I can't afford to do even that now — glow in the dark — not when the stakes are so high and any tiny slip up could get us killed. Ryan's right: I need to 'dial down the whole shining thing' altogether. But can I do it?

I bend my will inwards, the way I've relearnt to do, imagine locking the light away inside me, the way my soul was anchored deep inside the human vessels the Eight procured for me over centuries. Ryan gasps as the glow that surrounds me begins to dull and fade until I'm indistinguishable from the darkness inside the tower. I hold the light cupped inside, buried so far down that only I could know it's there.

'What do you think?' I ask again softly, my voice seeming to come from everywhere and nowhere at once. 'Dialled down enough for you?'

Ryan is silent for a long time. His eyes appear blind as they struggle to pinpoint me. I realise suddenly that he can't see me at all.

I can feel his apprehension. He thinks I'll leave him behind, because he's useless. But he's so wrong. He's my reality check, my secret weapon, the only real reason I'm still holding myself together. Everything I value in life is right here beside me, close enough to touch.

'I'm lucky to have you,' I say fervently, and I mean it.

Ryan replies flatly out of the darkness, 'I don't see how. I can't do what you do. I lost everything at the Galleria — I left my duffle bag with the coat-check girl, dropped my pack, which had a tonne of things in it, useful things. All I have is my phone, my wallet, passport, a folded-up picture of you that looks nothing like you, not any more. I'm bringing exactly *zip* to this little "mission" of ours. I can't do any … magic,' he ends falteringly, 'not your kind, anyway. I'll just hold you up. Get you killed.'

'It doesn't matter, Ryan,' I whisper, reaching out and taking his hand unerringly in the darkness. 'Right now, I couldn't do this "magic" without you, and that's the truth.'

He gives my hand an answering squeeze, and I feel his relief.

'So you've still got my back?' I remind him sternly of his words.

'Always,' he replies without hesitation. 'Even when I can't see a damned thing.'

I laugh and pull him to his feet, and he's suddenly *take charge*, like the Ryan I remember from Paradise.

'We need to get our bearings,' he says, gripping me tightly, not letting me withdraw. 'Work out how we're supposed to get out of here without attracting any attention. But this place won't open for hours. So, first, I want to see how far we've come, where we crash-landed.'

'*You* crash-landed,' I say sheepishly, turning him in the direction of the roof.

Ryan's usually possessed of a natural, athlete's grace; strength in every sense of the word. But the darkness has robbed him of any certainty and he stumbles as we begin to climb up the winding, uneven staircase in the dark. Even our linked fingers, my own unfaltering eyesight, can't make him see where the handholds, steps and landings begin and end. In the light, the staircase defies logic. In the dark, to human eyes, it's an impossibility.

'We need to get back to the lakeside town I saw in my dream,' I say over the laboured sound of Ryan's breathing, the scuff of his boot heels on the stone. 'I think I know where she is; there was a villa there, a large estate, with a smaller outbuilding of some kind, and a pier, on the water. I can still see it all in my head. We'll work our way from there, okay?'

The plan sounds better than it is. Ryan can't know that, at this point, there are way more holes than plan. What town? What villa? Where do I even begin to locate them when all I have are visual cues I picked up in a dream in the dead of night?

I'm pounded by another sudden wave of dizziness, and am so shaken, overwhelmed and nauseated that I think I will pass out. I don't think I've ever been more afraid of the task ahead, and it makes me miss a step.

Even sightless as he is, Ryan catches me before I fall, his strong hands grasping me around the waist unerringly.

He turns me to him clumsily. 'Forget what I said before,' he breathes, feeling for the contours of my face. 'Glow or no glow, whatever you look like, you're still beautiful, and I'd know you anywhere.'

In the dark, Ryan can't see me searching his face. He can't see in my eyes all the fear I feel for him. Before I can change my mind, I reach up and pull his head down to me, kiss him lightly, lingeringly, upon the lips, before drawing back.

I ignore the lick of fire that thrills through me like live current that seems to whisper: *Forbidden*.

It's just a kiss, I tell myself fiercely. I must have done so much worse, in my time.

Beneath my hands, Ryan is shocked into stillness.

What I feel for him is so different from what I felt for Luc. Loss, sorrow, regret: these things are already built into every word we utter, every glance we share, accompanying us moment by moment, like spectres at a feast. They only serve to heighten the complex, hard-won love that has somehow flowered between us. People say that you don't know what you've got until it's gone. But I *do* know. What we have is precious and rare, and so utterly terrifying.

I can tell that Ryan hadn't really expected me to kiss him again. Not after what happened the last time. He'd actually meant what he'd said about crumbs being enough. He'd been teasing me when he talked of *tolerance levels* and *comfort zones*.

His love is so humbling that I'm suddenly glad he can't see me.

'Maybe that's the secret to working "us" out,' I laugh awkwardly to cover my terror, 'taking it one tiny step at a time.'

'Here's to more steps like that one,' Ryan answers shakily.

'You deserve so much more than this,' I murmur. 'Than me.'

I can't bring myself to tell him I love him, for fear it'll all go to hell the way Luc and I did. I'm cursed, and maybe I always will be.

51

'I couldn't even dream up someone like you,' Ryan mutters, his hands tightening on me, drawing me closer, wanting more, in the human way of things.

But then I hear the sound of something mechanical, far, far below us. A noise so faint it could be the sound a pebble makes hitting the bottom of a dry well.

'What is it?' Ryan says, confused, as something primal flares in me, some instinct for danger.

Fear propels me instantly into motion. I start moving upwards again, hauling him along by the front of his leather jacket.

'*C'è qualcuno?*' a man says below, faintly but clearly in Italian. *Is anyone there?*

'*Cosa c'è?*' another voice replies sharply, also in Italian, also male. *What is it?*

'Noises — listen,' the first man replies.

Ryan's footfalls, his laboured breathing, sound so terribly loud.

'I hear nothing; you're jumping at shadows,' the second voice says dismissively after a pause.

'I tell you, I heard something,' the first man insists.

'Pietro's voice is loud enough to wake the dead,' comes the reply. 'He's probably on his way to meet us with the others.'

There's the faint sound of tapping. The noises move steadily closer, and I'm starting to pick up the interior buzz the two men give out, as if each carries a hive inside him: of thought, feeling, imagery, energy.

'Ryan,' I say, my voice low and desperate. 'You have to *hurry*. We can't be seen here. We can't be questioned.'

'By who?' Ryan says, exasperated, unable to hear the echo of footsteps from below. 'What are you talking about?'

'I tell you, there's someone up there!' The first voice is insistent. '*Pietro?*' he calls.

'We can't be found here, Ryan!' I hiss, exploding back into motion. 'I won't allow myself to be trapped again.'

We stumble towards the doorway that leads out onto the lower level of the roof. As we exit beneath the stone lintel onto the north-facing walkway, I'm immediately hit with a sensation of vertigo so powerful, I have to lean against the inner wall, let Ryan take in the jaw-dropping view on his own until the world ceases to buckle around me.

When my sight grows clearer, I see a faint pink line streaking the far horizon, growing steadily all the time, eating away the edges of night, the roofline of the Galleria smouldering to our left. Though there are miles of open sky all around me, I feel like a rat in a cage.

'We have to hide!' I tell Ryan pleadingly.

Ryan doesn't turn, still awed by the whole of Milan spread out before him. 'Not before we get our bearings, Merce, there's still time. There's no one up here and a million places to hide.'

He tries to draw me towards a double row of intricate stone lacework, the stones set one behind the other like shark's teeth, that forms a kind of natural barrier to the dizzying drop below.

'Come see,' he says, leaning out, looking down. 'It's so beautiful. You're never going to fall. Not when you're with me.'

I shake my head, look back fearfully at the doorway we just came through. But Ryan takes me by the hands and draws me in front of him, crossing his arms around my waist, pulling me against him so firmly that I cannot move, cannot fall.

His cheek is against mine as he says, 'Look. Just look. It won't erase what he did to you — nothing could ever do that — but every time you face down your fear is an act of *defiance*.'

Just for a moment, against my better judgment, I let myself lean into Ryan. And though I must close my eyes briefly to overcome a chill horror at the distance we are from the ground, little by little I find myself gazing further outward, taking in the march of rainwashed streets and buildings that appear to crowd right up to the horizon in every direction. Milan seems to radiate outwards from the Duomo as if the cathedral is the city's literal heart.

I turn in his arms and point shakily to the north, at the line of hills I see there, purple in the wintry light, the jagged line of mountains rising behind them. 'That's where we need to be.'

I peer down at the northern edge of the Piazza del Duomo so far below. Immediately to the Galleria's right, opposite us, stands an undamaged stone building roughly the same height, with a series of imposing arches marking the ground-level entryway. Solid and austere, it has a modern rooftop terrace with a curve-fronted glass and steel structure rising behind it. Both are deserted at this hour. A barrier of live greenery about chest height runs along all three sides of the terrace, and there's a head-high barrier of glass and steel that stands between the hedge and a collection of outdoor umbrellas and groups of matching tables and chairs, set out in neat rows.

'Seems close enough to touch, doesn't it?' Ryan says, echoing my own thoughts. 'It's like we could just step down and take a seat. If you ignore the, uh, massive drop.'

Then time seems to slow, and speed up, at the same time.

For I see three men appear on the stairs at the far end of the walkway, all dressed in plain, black, heavy robes and shapeless black overcoats, a small stain of white at the base of each man's throat. They are framed in a succession of flying buttresses with identical rectangular doorways set beneath them, each doorway cut to the exact same dimensions as the next; the whole vista so detailed, so dreamlike, it could have been lifted from a work by Escher. The old men stop dead at the sight of us, just standing there. The one in the lead gives a shout.

I feel Ryan's arms go rigid around me as he sees them for the first time.

'*State lì*! Stop! We would talk with you!' the priest says, flinging one hand out towards us.

My head fills with the sound of their distinct energies, their peculiar human signatures, drawing closer and getting noisier as they move towards us along the walkway. I take in the terrifying drop before me — almost one hundred and fifty feet down — and feel the chill wind of vertigo sweep through me, that sensation of falling as if I will never, ever stop.

The elderly priest, arm still outstretched, shouts from the other end of the narrow corridor of stone, '*Che vuole con noi?*' *What do you want with us?*

'Pietro? Is that you?' I hear from inside the stairwell.

I feel that sense of convergence strengthening, the cacophony of five separate living beings moving towards me, all set at different frequencies, concerned with vastly different issues, their thoughts a mixture of the alarmed and the mundane.

'Mercy!' Ryan gasps, turning his face in the direction of the new voice, then back towards me. 'What do we do?'

I turn to face him, grip him fiercely by the arms.

'Are you sure this is what you want?' I say feverishly. 'You and me?'

'You know it is,' he gasps, 'but why do you ask?'

His last word turns into a yelp as I grasp him tightly beneath the arms and vault onto a carved stone finial that forms part of the first of the stone barriers. We teeter for an instant as I take in the way the tiled roof drops away from me into the second barrier and then into empty … space.

'Mercy!' Ryan yells, unable to process what he's seeing: the ground so far below. I'm doing the impossible, balancing here, taking the whole of his weight easily when there's no solid ground beneath his feet, or mine.

But Ryan's with me, and if he's with me, I won't ever fall. That's what he told me and it's what I tell myself now.

I turn my head for an instant, the chill breeze lifting the curling ends of my dark hair, my eyes narrowing first on the astonished trio of men clustered at one end of the roof, then on the young man with dark eyes and close-cropped dark hair just emerging from the stairwell to my right.

Then I snap my eyes forward. Look at the place I need to get to, where I need to be. It's funny how desperation feels a little like love. Makes you do things your conscious mind would never countenance.

But I am what I am, and that means I will always have a choice.

And then I throw myself into thin air, Ryan held fast in my arms.

'Mercy!' he yells again, feeling the magnetic pull of the world beneath us.

Though I am beset by fears that none of my kind has ever faced before, I soar — against gravity, against all reason.

Freedom is all that matters. Freedom, and Ryan.

As I cross the abyss that lies between one solid surface and another, I know that I am power, and that I'm *back*.

CHAPTER 4

I land badly as usual, on the rooftop terrace beyond the double barrier of greenery, glass and steel I'd glimpsed from the roof of the Duomo, almost taking out a row of chairs and tables. One seat teeters for a moment, then makes an iron clanging sound as it falls over. It sounds like an explosion.

We were there, and now we're here, and it's only taken seconds. I'm exultant, half-disbelieving, yet also strangely clear-headed. Ryan was right. Every time I face down my fear is an act of defiance that can only make me stronger.

I release my death grip on Ryan, who sways a little on the spot, wordless at feeling a new surface beneath his feet. I look back at the Duomo and see five figures in black gathered beyond the barriers of stone that resemble shark's teeth. They're waving their hands, discussing us heatedly. I see the younger one, the one from the stairs, run back up the walkway and disappear. The old priest stares down at us across the chasm, awe and astonishment on his lined face.

'Where ... *are* we?' Ryan slurs, feeling around for a chair and sitting heavily. 'When my brain is ... working again, you'll have to tell me what the hell just happened. You have this way of making me … lose my grip on reality. Being with you is like being in a dream —'

'You can't wake from?' I finish softly. 'Welcome to my world.'

Ryan looks up at me for a moment, as if he's imprinting my new face, my travelling face, upon his memory, or making his peace with it.

'Ready?' I say quietly. 'We've got to keep moving.'

Ryan blinks, taking in the silent terrace around us, the overturned chair, his eyes widening as he spies the watching men gathered on the roofline opposite. 'What are we still doing here!' he exclaims. 'Let's go.'

There's the sudden wail of an alarm being triggered, then the *snick* of a lock or bolt, a door opening.

I turn my head sharply to see a man in uniform emerging out of the curved structure of steel and glass behind Ryan. The young man is of average height, with a slight frame and receding jawline that makes him seem even younger. Beneath his peaked cap, he's breathing heavily and nervously training a handgun on me.

Between us, there's a sea of rain-speckled tables and chairs. He takes in our clothes, our builds, weighing us up. I get snatches of the panicky argument he's running against himself in his head: *thieves?* he's thinking. *Or … terrorists?*

Ryan stiffens as I murmur aloud, 'They're saying maybe the Galleria was a "terrorist attack", he thinks we're armed.'

This is some kind of high-end department store, I realise suddenly, getting a flash of the building's interior as the man relives the heart-stopping moment he spotted us from the inside, through the floor-to-ceiling windows.

'Police!' he calls out shakily in Italian-accented English over the blare of the alarm. 'Raise the hands.'

I feel his intense fear. He's only a few months into this job, and he was supposed to go off duty in twenty-two minutes precisely until his commanding officer ordered him to respond to some nonsense from a bunch of priests about people on the roof. I skim all that out of the white noise in his head, and his name, too, because he's yelling at himself in the third person. Humans are like radio transmitters; it's hard to think with the air jammed so full of their noise. I know I should be afraid, but for the first time in a very long while, I feel an absolute calm.

'Vincenzo,' I say loudly, and the young man gives a start, goes pale, at the mention of his name. 'You need to let us leave.'

His eyes widen and he shouts, 'Impossible, *signorina*. Raise the hands.'

Without taking my eyes from Vincenzo's face, I draw Ryan to his feet. The chair legs scrape a little as he straightens up and turns around slowly. Vincenzo's expression flickers fearfully as he looks from me to Ryan, now standing side by side. We both have our backs to the barriers now.

Vincenzo moves closer. 'There is nowhere to run,' he says anxiously. 'Raise the hands, or I will be forced to shoot you. Not to kill, you understand,' he adds almost pleadingly, 'only to wound.'

Still holding his gaze unwaveringly, I take another step backwards towards the head-high glass wall, the screen of trees behind it, one hand on the sleeve of Ryan's leather jacket.

'What are you going to do?' Ryan mutters, sounding

panicky. 'He's got a gun. You know what happened last time.'

'What happened last time happened to Lela,' I say fiercely. 'It's not going to happen to us. I need you to go with whatever I ask you to do. I need you to trust me.'

Before Ryan can reply, a burst of static issues out of a black device clipped to Vincenzo's belt and I catch the word 'localizzato'; located.

Vincenzo fumbles for the receiver, his gun hand wavering a little. While he's distracted, Ryan and I keep inching backwards.

'Not far now,' I say. 'When you feel the glass screen behind you, move right. Whatever you do, even if we're separated, just aim for that corner.' I see Ryan nod out of the corner of my eye. 'Wait for me?'

Ryan's eyes fly to mine, and I remember: *wait for me* were the last words I ever said to him when I was Lela.

A second man in uniform suddenly charges through the door Vincenzo left open. He's stocky and tall, with a dark, even tan, massive shoulders and arms like sides of beef. One of his big, broad, black-gloved hands is wrapped around a semi-automatic identical to Vincenzo's. He thrusts Vincenzo aside and snarls: 'Get down! Get down! Or I shoot the boy first, and then I shoot you.'

I let the flow of his thoughts wash through me and I know he'll do it. In his world, everything can be solved with guns, with beatings, with violence. He'll take Ryan down first, because he's bigger, more of a threat. Then me.

I feel Ryan's fingers tighten around mine, his palm slick with apprehension. Something dangerous rises in me and I push Ryan back behind me, the fingers of my right hand still linked through his.

61

'We're leaving,' I say loudly and slowly. 'We don't want any trouble. We're just going to walk away and disappear. You won't ever see us again.'

I feel Ryan pause for a moment before beginning to move slowly to the right between the glass screen and the outermost row of chairs and tables.

The second officer narrows his eyes, not bothering to reply. Then he points his gun up into the air and pulls the trigger. One shot, skyward. A flock of pigeons explodes upwards, scattering and wheeling in all directions. Even over the shrilling alarm, the gunshot is very loud and seems to reverberate in the air for the longest time. This place will soon be swarming in uniformed men.

'Ryan!' I say sharply, looking back at him. 'Go!'

I see his unwillingness to leave me: it's in his eyes, in the tense line of his body. Then he releases my fingers, bends low and sprints full tilt towards the eastern corner of the terrace without looking back. In that single, telling gesture is all of his faith in me.

I keep drifting slowly in the same direction, my eyes never leaving the faces of the two policemen, the gap between Ryan and me widening all the time, making myself the target.

'Get down!' the bigger one screams, his neck muscles cording, the ropy surface veins along his temples swelling with angry blood. He points his gun at Ryan's fleeing figure, then at me, uncertain who to take aim at now. 'Get down!'

From the peripheries of my sight, I catch the outline of my left hand ... a flicker. As I raise it to my face, it begins to ache. An argent bloom moves over the skin, envelops the fingers, and that voice inside me, my inner demon, whispers: *Cave. Beware.*

The instant I raise my eyes to the second officer's face, I register the tiny muscles around his eyes tighten, see the sudden flare of his nostrils, his lips go white. As my eyes widen in realisation of what he is about to do, he pulls the trigger — not to wound, but to *kill* — and the air in front of me seems to displace with the heat of a thousand suns.

Both men cry out, fall back. There's a long, flaming broadsword in my left hand, its blade rippling with a pale blue luminescence. Giant, gleaming wings unfurl across my back, catching the light, intensifying it. As if the shot itself were a call to arms. I look down at my burning left hand upon the sword's grip, study the elaborate pommel and cross-guards of its double-edged blade, uncertain if I can remember how to wield it. The sword weighs nothing at all, yet it is absolute power, a physical manifestation of my anger, indisputably mine.

As I gaze at its blazing hilt, I see the bullet enter my abdomen almost in slow motion, slicing neatly between two press-studs on the front of my black, goose-down jacket. The surface of my jacket seems to swallow the small, superheated projectile before growing smooth once more. The bullet leaves no trace, makes no impact upon me. But if I were the ordinary human girl he believes me to be, I'd be dead now, dead like Lela. I suffer a genuine moment of *déjà vu*, so terrible, so chilling, that I have to remind myself that this is a different time, a different place, altogether.

I level the tip of my flaming sword blade at the man who shot me as if it were an extension of my arm. 'On your knees!' I roar, and my words ring with a sonic after-bite that causes the men to fall to the ground, dropping their weapons, clutching at their ears in agony.

'Use violence against me again,' I snarl, *'and you will suffer violence.'*

The sword vanishes into my palm, the shining wings dissipating with a shredding, swirling afterglow of energy. I turn towards Ryan and see the black-robed men on the Duomo roof lined up like gaping crows, their hands clasped before them as if in prayer.

I cover the distance to Ryan in seconds, and before he has time to speak, I slide an arm around him and take us up and over the barriers, over the edge of the terrace, across the entire breadth of the Via Santa Radegonda.

This time Ryan just yells in the kind of visceral terror that goes beyond words as I throw us almost blindly through space. We land badly on the rooftop adjacent to the department store, Ryan crying out as I skid over the edge of the stone railing, losing my footing, almost pitching us both headfirst onto the narrow, open walkway running along the front of the building.

As I haul him upright by the hem of his leather jacket, Ryan chokes, 'Being with you is going to *kill* me!'

I don't trust myself to answer; it's the very thing I fear. I just touch his face reassuringly and keep moving, knowing he'll follow.

There are loud sirens on the Piazza below, as if we have stirred up a nest of wasps that are now questing in our direction. The facade of the building we're crossing is longer than the one we just left, and irregular. Looking back over one shoulder, I can no longer see the watchers on the Duomo roof. We've left the cathedral behind, as we've left behind the Duomo Square and its sea of milling officials, flashing lights and cordons.

I'm debating whether or not to just keep going across the rooftops of the city when Ryan passes me unsteadily, heading left around the corner of the building. Surprised, I swerve left, too, almost running into his back.

He turns to me, eyes wide and bloodshot, face pale from exertion. 'There's no way down from here,' he mutters, a clear note of panic in his voice. 'No way down. I can't, Mercy, I'm not like you. I don't think I can keep doing this.'

His eyes dart fearfully across to the next building, his sides heaving. I can see he's reached some kind of physical limit. He's only holding himself together, only submitting to the crazy things I'm putting him through, for *me*.

There were always more holes than plan, anyway.

I make my decision almost the instant I say gently, 'There's always a way down.'

Though I wish there were an easier way for me to return us quickly to solid ground, I pull Ryan to me tightly with my left arm, cover his mouth with my right hand, and take us up and over the edge of the roof. Down, down, into Via Agnello. I can feel him bellowing through my fingers as we plummet to earth, making no sound as we fall from the sky.

I count six floors on the way down. The windows we pass show rooms full of merchandise, mannequins, furniture, but are otherwise empty of life. It still isn't opening time in central Milan, luckily for us. But in one hour, two at most, people will be clamouring to be let into the Duomo, the Piazza, into all of the surrounding shops and buildings that remain undamaged by fire, untrammelled by tragedy or death, because life goes on. It can do nothing else. We have to hurry.

The only person on the street below is a woman with a dark, wavy, shoulder-length bob, wearing a fashionable tweed overcoat, skinny jeans and slouchy tan boots, a striped tote bag on one shoulder. She's heading away from us to the northwest, past a couple of parked cars pointed in the same direction. But as I land, I stumble against a stationary bicycle that's been leant haphazardly against a parking sign located right by the wall. The commotion as it falls over causes the woman to turn and look at us. We're clasping onto each other like drunks, Ryan and I, and she stares at us for a while, before turning and moving away again, slowly, jerkily. There's something awkward about the way she walks, as if she's in the grip of some kind of degenerative disorder, though she can't be more than thirty, thirty-five.

I take my hand away from Ryan's mouth and he starts yelling. 'Don't you *ever* —' Then his shoulders sag and he mumbles, '"Don't" isn't really a word that applies to you, is it?'

'It's all new to me, too,' I say softly into his exhausted face, 'just having you here. Till now, it's always been me fighting some impossible corner on my own. I've been battling my own set of major ...'

'Adjustment issues?' Ryan mutters.

'Something like that,' I say ruefully. 'You've noticed?'

'And I thought it was the effect I was having on you.' His laughter turns into a fit of coughing.

I shake him gently. 'We'll try and do things your way for a while, okay? We're going to find you somewhere safe to rest.'

It starts off as an empty platitude, but then a tiny idea takes root in my head. It seems so outlandish at first that it couldn't possibly work. But if it did? It could mean help for him and help for me. And I'm more than willing to take advice these days, provided it's solid. I've been on my own for long enough.

Ryan shivers, weaving a little on the spot. 'So cold,' he says absently.

There's a deserted underpass across the street, bisected by a zebra crossing; an empty bar beside it with a torn, maroon awning flapping a little in the breeze. Melted run-off thunders through subterranean pipes somewhere far below our feet. I look into the distance. Via Agnello, with its pizzerias and public car parks, cheap souvenir shops and menswear stores, didn't look like this when I was last here. But I know with unerring certainty where we are and where we have to go. I point up the narrow, one-way street in the direction the woman is walking.

'Think you can go just a little bit further?' I say brightly.

I'm lying through my teeth, of course. We're going to have to go the long way around to avoid the mess around the Galleria, but Ryan doesn't need to know that. And we have to hustle. The streets around here are an illogical warren laid down over centuries, but people will still come looking for evidence of the crazy *turisti* who leapt off the terrace of one of the most prestigious department stores in town. They'll be looking for body parts. It's only a matter of time.

Ryan closes his eyes, and I feel him shivering uncontrollably inside his clothes. 'You're like some kind of learner archangel,' he mutters. 'Like that guy who was mad, bad and dangerous to know. That's you. They could've been describing you.'

'Free to bail,' I remind him quietly.

He coughs a little as he opens his eyes and I see that they've grown unfocused. 'Can't,' he slurs. 'Can't escape fate.'

I give him a shake, appalled at his words. 'I'm not your *fate*, Ryan. I'm your *choice*. Remember that when everything is going to hell around us.'

I'm not sure if he can hear me any longer. I pull his arm across my shoulders again and we stagger forward, trailing that lone woman who shoulders her stripy tote as if it contains all of the sorrows of the world. I don't get any sense of what she's thinking, and I'm glad of it, because all I can see, hear, smell, touch, taste is Ryan's bone-deep exhaustion. His eyes are fixed on the ground below his stumbling feet and he can't stop shaking. If it weren't for me, he would already have fallen. He needs things I can't give him. We have to hurry, though doing things Ryan's way — the human way — is always going to take longer.

I march him on ruthlessly while I warm his icy hands in mine. I describe all the buildings we're passing in a low, cheerful voice while I scan the rooftops continuously for any hint of demonsign. Ryan eventually ceases to respond, and my sense of quiet desperation grows.

As we turn right into Via Ulrico Hoepli, I catch glimpses of faces and forms moving about at upper-storey windows. This late-rising city is beginning to stir. I get the sudden buzz of a middle-aged man in an elegant overcoat, scarf and suit exiting a coffee shop just across the street, something about the end of the world in his thoughts. Then I pick up the ambient thoughts of a couple of men wrangling a new armchair into a delivery van outside a furniture store we're passing. They hate each other, hate the armchair, and can't understand why, after everything that's happened in this city, they still have to deliver it. *Today*.

I turn left up Via San Paolo, with Ryan braced tightly against me, his every footstep dragging. As we move along the upper edge of the Piazza della Scala, I begin to pick up a tangle of human energy: thoughts expressed in a multitude of languages, emotions that grow louder and more insistent the closer we get, amplifying in timbre, volume and complexity, all the time.

Then I *see* the crowd of shouting people gathered around a police roadblock at the southern end of the square, a larger crowd milling around another roadblock on the western side.

Something else across the square makes me freeze in my tracks. Ryan sways against me, exhausted, his fringe of straight, dark hair falling forward over his eyes, body on autopilot. I'm staring directly at the northern face of the Galleria Vittorio Emanuele, the building we've been trying so hard to go around. Two banners hang one on either side of the giant archway that serves as an alternative entry point to the vast shopping arcade. The left banner is badly damaged; you can barely make out the playful model with the striking eyes and sky-high beehive wearing an evening gown from the 1960s in Giovanni Re's signature red, *rosso Re*. But the right banner is largely intact, and I stare at the mesmerisingly powerful image of a warrior-sorceress with her burnt caramel-coloured hair wild and loose, wearing a long, flowing gown of molten gold, her hands wrapped around the pommel of a bejewelled sword. I gaze into Irina Zhivanevskaya's huge, smoky, smouldering eyes and feel for a disorienting moment as if I'm staring into a giant mirror, so recently have I fled her body.

I'll take it as a sign that I'm doing the right thing.

The air smells of burning. If I concentrate hard enough, I can actually taste ash on the air. As Ryan and I stagger on past the roadblock facing onto Via Santa Margherita, the handsome, copper-skinned, hard-faced policemen behind it wave their arms dismissively, shouting, 'Go back! Go back!' in Italian, in English, as people try to argue their way into the restricted zone.

The street we're moving down now is packed with banks and insurance houses that occupy elegant, towering mansions standing shoulder to shoulder. A few people begin filtering past us, afflicting me with their thoughts, their random energies. The dark-haired woman is only a little ahead of us now, and her gait has grown so slow and torturous that we finally overtake her.

'Not much further,' I tell Ryan distractedly as I glance at the woman's shuttered face in profile, note her youthful features and strangely clouded blue eyes.

It hits me a few feet later. The wrongness about her. The way her old-woman shuffle doesn't sync with her smooth skin and shining hair, her robust frame and fashion-forward clothes. I stop and look back at her over my shoulder, wondering why I get no sense of *her* at all: of what she's thinking, or feeling, or even any sense of her peculiar life force, her human energy. What I *do* feel is something incredibly faint, but insistent. Almost ... familiar, that's setting up a distant, almost painful hum in my bones.

Then, without warning, the woman crumples forward onto the footpath. The palest, gleaming blur, like a mobile patch of sunlight, seems to shriek away from her still figure — as if ejected, or rejected — darting and rebounding off all the faces of the buildings, the street signs and manhole covers, before fleeing back in the direction we've just come from. It's rapidly lost to sight.

What I want to do is run, but I don't. Not yet, because I need to be sure.

I tell Ryan to wait, and force myself to walk calmly towards the woman lying facedown on the pavement. I kneel beside her and turn her over, relieved to see she's still breathing. I place my hands against her chalk-white face and she gives a great choking breath, her eyes opening. I'm sure that the fear and panic in her eyes are mirrored in my own.

She looks up at me as I cradle her head off the ground. Her blue eyes are clear again, though huge, in her pale face. 'Where am I?' she asks in Italian, and when I answer her gently in her own language, she says, bewildered, 'But what am I doing here?'

People have seen us; they hurry towards us from both sides of the street. I leave the woman in the care of a small, gesticulating crowd and return to Ryan, who is standing exactly where I left him, with his head bowed, hands in the pockets of his jacket, feet planted shoulder width apart to stop himself from toppling over. All I can do is hug him to me tightly, in horror.

The *malakhim* are blunt-force instruments with none of the subtlety of the *elohim* about them; so-called lesser angels, they were created to do our bidding, and they will always leave signs that my kind can read. That woman's flesh contained a signature, and I am certain it was left by the same tormented creature I came across when I was Lela, and again when I was Irina — something that was once angelic, but is now no more than a shattered remnant. Weak as it is, can it somehow still sense me? It came to Milan with a warning for me from Michael, about Luc. What warning does it bring me now?

As Ryan and I enter Via Victor Hugo, a sense of *déjà vu* returns so strongly that my eyes fly at once to a three-storey, grey stone building across the road. I study its graceful Palladian roofline intently, half-hoping to see K'el still outlined there by storm clouds of such brilliance they could be a portal to another world. But of course he's not. The pale blue sky is cloudless from end to end and I have to take the sudden anguish I'm feeling and drown it deep within me, like the light I have hidden away, that is the essence of being *elohim*.

I see her before she sees me. She's standing beside the bonnet of a familiar-looking black limousine that has more doors than a normal car and rides a little too low to the ground because it's armoured. She's arguing fiercely with someone, as usual, because she's tough and resourceful and it's her job to stand up to tyrants and crazies on a daily basis. The bruising along one side of her face is still a livid purple-red, and there's a nasty red weal on her neck, like a burn, but she looks surprisingly well for someone who somehow survived a celestial firefight inside the Galleria.

A passing car draws her gaze, and her eyes widen when she takes in Ryan and me standing still and silent across the road. She recognises him first, of course, because I'm a stranger to her. She's never seen me before, not like this.

She steps without hesitation around the front of the limo in her artfully studded, black patent-leather biker jacket, her precision-cut, glossy China-girl hair blowing across her eyes in the stiff breeze. She shoves it back impatiently and shouts, 'Ryan? Ryan Daley?'

When he doesn't answer, doesn't even lift his eyes to acknowledge her, she looks at me, really looks at me, and says, tentatively, 'Mercy?'

We cross the road towards her, and she tells the scowling, balding, suit-wearing gorilla she was arguing with that he just has to wait, she's got no orders. 'It's just too bloody bad.' Then she moves towards me briskly and slings Ryan's other arm around her shoulders without me having to tell her to.

Wordlessly, we haul him together up a grand circular driveway lined with luxury sedans and limos, and through a revolving front door of high-shine glass and bronze. It spits us out into a palatial hotel foyer crowded with antiques and chandeliers, and I'm immediately assailed by muzak and human noise, the smells of disinfectant, air freshener and the kinds of expensive, towering floral arrangements that I've come to detest.

The male concierge in maroon and gold livery standing behind the immense, marble-topped reception desk almost steps back from us in disgust. Ryan's hair is a little matted now and he could use a shave. He looks wasted beyond redemption. But the concierge recognises Gia Basso immediately and says, icily, '*Signorina*,' his pale grey gaze flicking from Ryan to me, before he favours her with a small smile, an almost imperceptible nod.

When the lift doors open, Gia fumbles a security card out of the back pocket of her skin-tight, black, waxed jeans, shoves it into a slot on the control panel and punches a floor number.

The brass and mirrored lift reflects us back to ourselves from all angles; we three appear infinite. Ryan's head keeps lolling into the crook of my shoulder and there's a rip in his jacket, running up under the right arm, that I think I might have caused. It's clear from the way Gia's wrinkling her nose that Ryan could use a shower.

'Jesus,' she mumbles, looking over his bowed head at me, unable to tear her unusual eyes — one blue, one brown —

away from my face. 'You're both still alive. When the shining giants with the swords and, uh, wings appeared,' she shoots me a sharp glance that seems to come back at me from everywhere at once, 'some clumsy idiot smacked me in the face and then the whole place just exploded in flames. I'm ashamed to say that I lost sight of everything except getting to the nearest exit. I'm glad you made it. You look ...' she hesitates, '... good. Uh, different. But good.'

From the strange expression on her face, I can tell that she somehow recognises me, though my features, my voice, my body, aren't even remotely familiar. There's no doubt in her mind about who I am.

'So do you,' I reply, almost suffocated by sudden gratitude, a fierce affection for this prickly, practical woman. 'Nice,' I say, indicating her body-hugging, shiny jacket bristling with shoulder spikes, buckles and intricate quilting because that kind of stuff seems to matter so much to her. 'It's so very ... *you*.'

She bares her teeth in a sudden, shark-like grin and lifts up a cone-heeled, patent-leather, black ankle boot for my inspection, which also bristles with matching short, sharp metal spikes all over the toecaps and heels. 'The jacket I had on yesterday was trashed beyond salvation. It smells like a barbeque. I felt like I needed armour today — I've been kicking heads since the phone rang this morning at three seventeen. I figured, if people didn't pay attention, I could just impale them with my footwear.'

We grin at each other for a moment, and Ryan shifts restlessly against me, his head against my cheek. And it hits me how little time we have left together, and how it's things like this I'll miss most: friendship, the warmth of human contact, love. Just the small things.

'Too sophisticated,' Ryan mumbles suddenly, struggling to focus on Gia beside him, and she looks obscurely pleased by the comment.

'He looks the way I feel,' she notes almost kindly. 'Seedy.'

'Considering I almost killed him twice today already,' I say quietly, 'he's doing all right.'

Gia's face is suddenly serious. 'You didn't decide to drop by just to approve my wardrobe choices, did you?' she says in her cut-glass British accent.

I shake my head, and indicate Ryan between us. 'He needs food, sleep, the usual things.'

'Human things,' Gia says sharply. 'And what do *you* need?'

'Help,' I say immediately, and her strong, dark eyebrows fly up into her glossy, slanting fringe in open disbelief.

The lift doors slide open, and we're walking under the same Murano glass chandeliers, across the same elaborately patterned royal blue and gold carpet I strode down yesterday on my way to the catwalk parade, as Irina. And it's completely disorienting to be returning like this when everything *I* am has changed beyond measure.

I get an echo of my own thinking from Gia, but her thoughts are indistinct and hard to read, as if she's somehow trained herself to hold her cards close, even from creatures like me. She's like a steel trap, this one. Good at keeping secrets.

She clears her throat delicately. 'Irina still hasn't come around since you ... left. She's like Sleeping bloody Beauty. There isn't a mark on her, not a scratch. All the vital signs are good, she's breathing unassisted. But she might as well be dead. It's like she's just a shell; zero response to external stimuli. We're debating whether to move her or wait it out. But the medicos say that if her vegetative state persists the body's going to ...'

'Die,' I finish.

'It sounds as if you know what's wrong with her,' Gia replies. 'I was hoping you might.'

'I have a few theories,' I say grimly.

'I want to leave,' Gia says suddenly. 'Leave this city, leave Irina, leave this bloody business for good. But I'm not going to do it while she's frozen inside her own body like Snow White after eating the apple. She's a "beeeetch", the queen of bitches, actually, but she's got no one right now. Burnt too many bridges. And don't look at me like that.'

'What?' I say, straight-faced. 'Like I was about to accuse you of having a heart? *Never.*'

Gia hoists Ryan's heavy arm up awkwardly while she punches her security key through a brass slot by the door to Irina's suite. 'I'll do what I can to help you,' she says in a low voice. 'You know I'd do it anyway. You were a good boss, better than what I'm used to.' She favours me with a crooked smile. 'In return, all I ask is that you do what you can for me?'

I nod without hesitation and Gia throws wide the door.

'Welcome to the madhouse,' she mutters, then calls out loudly, 'Carlo! Your assistance, please, dead man walking,' as we wrestle Ryan into the formal sitting room.

CHAPTER 5

The sitting room is full of people. There are a couple of youngish suits I don't recognise, both speaking in English, both on their mobile phones and perched uncomfortably at different ends of a long, low, French Empire-era settee that doesn't seem sturdy enough to hold them. A thin young woman with shoulder-length, curly auburn hair in a navy pantsuit and sensible shoes moves past with some fluids and medical instruments on a tray. Juliana Agnelli-Re is there, and her impeccably dressed family physician, the man who treated me after I leapt off the roof of a moving limousine, cutting up Irina's feet badly.

Carlo and Jürgen, from Irina's personal goon squad, surge to their feet at the sight of us and move forward to brace Ryan while Gia opens the door to her own set of rooms, then pulls down the covers on her own king-sized bed.

'Boots off, lay him down,' she orders. 'Gently does it. He's been through the wars.'

Carlo and Jürgen meekly do as they're told, and Gia pulls the covers back up to the level of Ryan's waist. 'Dottore Pellini?' she calls out through the doorway of her bedroom. 'If you'd be so kind?'

The doctor moves towards her.

I'm still standing by the front entrance, taking everything in. The suits haven't given me the time of day, and Juliana ... I survey her forlorn figure sharply. She's staring into space, still dressed in the burnt-orange pantsuit, filmy chartreuse blouse and vintage-looking lime and dark green Mary-Janes she was wearing at the haute couture show. Her crazy two-tone hair — dark roots, bright yellow ends — is looking pretty rough. Like Gia, she's carrying a few bruises, cuts and weals around her head and neck, but she's surprisingly whole for someone who made it out of the Archangel Michael's presence alive.

'She's taken over global design duties at Atelier Re,' Gia murmurs beside me. 'Private Label, Black Label, resort, diffusion, menswear, accessories. Everything rests on her shoulders now. Effective today. Board rushed it through, unsurprisingly. She was the Chosen One, in any case. Only now it's official.'

I'm so surprised at the news I can't stop myself blurting out loudly, 'But what about Giovanni?'

At the mention of her uncle's name, Juliana looks across the room at me with tear-reddened eyes. Gia places a restraining hand on my arm; the gesture tells me all I need to know.

Juliana calls out in her heavily accented English, 'Were you a friend? He had so many friends.' She looks down suddenly to disguise the sheen in her eyes. 'It was instant, they say. He was already very sick.' She gives a loud sob that she instantly tries to swallow.

I can't help walking over to her and placing a hand over hers where it lies on the dining table. Just touching her gives me a brief window of access to her memories: the technicolour past seems to flash up at me in stereo, from out of her head. I see, feel, hear, exactly how it was to her the moment her uncle died. She was standing just a few feet away when he was crushed by a portion of steel beam the size of a car. He hadn't stood a chance.

I *am* Juliana as she tries in vain to move the steel pinning down Giovanni's bloodied figure. Flames tower over us and we're gasping for air, constantly buffeted by a fleeing, hysterical mob that's been reduced to impulse and reflex alone. For a moment, at the periphery of our sight, there's a tall figure dressed all in black, a lock of his long silver hair falling forward as he bends his youthful face low over Giovanni Re's prone form, touching him only briefly. The stranger vanishes before we can beg him for help and is lost again in the sea of constantly shifting faces, lost in Juliana's memories. Just one among many. Azraeil meant nothing to her; she doesn't even consciously remember him. But the Archangel of Death was there, in the chaos. It has always been his way to come and go unheralded. He would have been busy last night, beneath the Galleria's palely blue-lit dome.

I release Juliana's hand and the memory vanishes instantly. 'Giovanni didn't suffer,' I say quietly, with absolute certainty.

She doesn't answer, crying in earnest now. She covers her face with both hands, her shoulders shaking with raw grief. The men on mobile phones grimace at the sound she's making and get up from their settee, move towards the door.

Gia raises an eyebrow. 'While the going's good?' she reminds me.

I nod and approach Irina's bedroom, place my hand on the gilt-edged wooden door panelling.

One of the suits looks up sharply from his conversation and says, 'Miss, you can't go in there. Did you hear me, *Miss*?'

'This is an old friend of Irina's,' Gia retorts. She crosses the index and middle fingers of her right hand and holds them up. 'Until yesterday, these two were like this, okay? Inseparable.'

I see her mouth twitch; she may be trying to suppress laughter.

'Irina will not even know I am here,' I pipe up in Russian-accented English, making my voice sound young and naive.

Gia looks at me, startled at my pitch-perfect inflection, which is a little bit Irina herself, a little bit Dmitri Dymovsky.

'Well, make it quick,' the man huffs. He waves a hand dismissively before returning to his call.

We enter Irina's bedroom and I recognise every single thing in this insanely over-decorated space, other than the saline drip and feeding tube, the pushcart filled with meds and dressings, and the unused respirator machine standing in one corner.

Irina's lying in silent state on the king-sized bed beneath a crisply mitred blanket and top sheet pulled up to just above her waist. Her roses and cream complexion is unmarked, and her narrow chest rises and falls steadily below her unflattering hospital-style gown. It's the strangest feeling to be standing here looking down on the body I was last incarcerated in.

Irina's so beautiful, even in sleep, with her caramel-coloured hair loose and shining all over her pillow. But this is no ordinary sleep. I have to concentrate hard to even feel she's alive, her soul's buried so far down. When Luc wrenched me free of her body, he didn't bother to release the strange slipknot that keeps her soul captive inside her.

The nurse bustles in behind us, deposits the now empty tray on top of the fussy, bow-fronted armoire near the en suite, before leaving again. Through the open door behind us, I can hear the two men winding up their phone conversations.

'We don't have long,' I tell Gia, and she crosses quickly to the door and shuts it, before moving ahead of me to the bed.

'What's *really* wrong with her?' she says.

When I don't answer, she looks back at me impatiently, then gasps. For a fine bloom of light has swept across my skin, my entire form, and I'm already changing, my outline is already shredding into vapour.

Within seconds, I draw myself up and up, looking down into Gia's awestruck face. Then I collapse into a towering cloud of fine, silver mist, swirling and dense, taking all the heat in the room with me. Immediately I'm pulled into that terrifying, alien raceway that the human body represents to those of us who have no need of a chemical, mechanical presence. This time, I'm not looking for a way out, not yet. I'm searching for that knot, that kernel, that Irina's soul has been reduced to.

Where is it?

Luc tore me free. There must be some disjuncture, a loose seam, a clue.

And then I chance upon something ... like notes written in living blood, in cellular walls and electrolytes. The signature of my brethren is here: elegant, luminous, their intentions joining together like plain song to create a safe harbour for me within another living being. I read their haste; and then I read the work of another — one whose touch had once made me feel like I was the most beautiful thing in creation — rendered here in hatred and fury and spite.

And then I find it … a seam, a thread, a clue. So tiny I almost missed it.

I follow it back to its source, and the pattern and energy of her is there. So compressed and distorted it's a wonder I could find her at all.

Mercy! I seem to hear a desperate voice echoing all around me, though I have no ears to hear, am nothing but pure, directed energy. *Hurry.*

I take that tiny fray and tug at it, unravelling it further and further, letting it stream out behind me like an unfurling ribbon as I follow the linkages, the switchbacks, the false trails, the complex broken pattern that Irina's soul was cast into. Smoothing, untwisting, laying bare, so that the flame might be relit, so that the soul might return.

Pressure begins to build, a vast electrical storm, and I feel everything that Irina *is* convulse as if her body were a building being shaken to its foundations. I feel her soul struggling in mine. I hear the sounds that are torn out of her, as if she is being tortured. *Possession.* In this moment, I could truly be classed as demon. She does not want me here, she feels me like a burning presence that must be cast out. I can't begin to tell you how wrong this feels.

Mercy! I hear it again, the voice disembodied, desperate. *Please. Quickly.*

I can't wait to go, can't wait to get out. There's a sensation of abrupt coalescence, and I'm flung out of Irina's body. For the very last time.

I come to on the floor beside Irina's bed and turn to see Gia across the room, her back braced against the closed bedroom door. It's clear from her strained expression that someone's trying to open it from the outside. The warning voice I'd heard was hers.

She looks at me, white-faced, with wide, desperate eyes. 'Do something,' she hisses, indicating the telltale gleam coming off my skin. 'Can't hold it much longer.'

'Open this door!' a man roars. 'Open it at once!'

And this time, the door jumps open an inch or two before Gia slams it shut again, pushing back with every ounce of strength in her slender frame.

The pounding and rattling intensify. '*Mercy*,' she pleads.

It feels as if it takes forever to extinguish the glow, but it can't be more than a few seconds because I'm suddenly standing at the foot of Irina's bed and the surface of my hands, the ends of my curling hair, my clothing, of *me*, is matte and dull once more. I give Gia a nod. She takes a deep breath and pushes away from the door, which bursts open immediately. One of the suits — tall, dark-haired, overweight, red-faced — thrusts through the knot of concerned people at the entrance.

'What are you doing to her?' he demands, trying to see around me to the bed. 'We heard the most terrible sounds. As if you were trying to kill her.'

'Like the *animale*,' the nurse says with a shudder, entering the room behind him.

'Old Russian remedy,' Gia improvises smoothly. 'Quite the eye-opener.'

'Like the prayer,' I say in my girlish Russian accent, fluttering my eyelashes a little. 'Only with the growling.'

'Don't forget the screaming,' Gia drawls, and only I can tell how truly shaken she still is. 'The screaming's integral to the whole cure. The louder, the better. We all joined in actually, it was quite cathartic. That's what you heard.'

'*Dio!* Miss Irina,' the nurse cries out suddenly, 'you are awake!'

'She's awake?' the man exclaims.

I turn to see the nurse with her hands clasped together against her lips, and Irina drenched in sweat, her eyes wide with shock. Her arms and legs are stretched out and rigid, hands curled into claws upon the rumpled mattress, her blanket and top sheet a crumpled heap of fabric on the far side of the room. The red marks of her own nails are on her neck. She reminds me a little bit of me, that time I woke in Carmen's body. There's a wild look in her eyes that I recognise.

'Give her a leetle time,' I say casually in my heavy Russian accent. 'Then she will be — how you say — as good as new.'

I look down at the fingernails of one hand, like a ditz, as if I'm bored. But I'm almost as shaken as Gia is. I think I just pulled off bringing a captive soul back to the surface, the same way Gabriel himself might have done with me. And Irina might be suffering her own set of adjustment issues right now, but she's struggling to sit up, she's trying to speak. And, in my book, that's got to be better than one rung above *dead*.

'No, really, what did you do to her?' the man demands.

He scrabbles in his jacket pocket for his mobile and starts dialling, as the nurse scoops up the bedding and smooths it back over Irina's body.

'All she did,' Gia says crisply, grabbing me by the arm and walking me away, 'is remind Irina of how good it feels to be alive.'

I can't help looking back over my shoulder at Irina, and she suddenly rolls her head and eyes in my direction, raises one long, thin, pointing finger at me accusingly.

'*You* ...' she gargles.

Gia pulls me out the door. 'Irina was *convulsing*, foaming at the mouth,' she mutters, 'clawing at her skin. And her eyes ...' She swallows hard. 'And the sounds! *God*. It was like something out of a horror film except it was all *real*. I almost passed out.' She stares into my face, crossing her arms tightly. 'One day, you're going to have to sit me down, buy me a beer and explain to me what I just saw.'

'It's because she was fighting me,' I reply into her haunted eyes. 'Two sentient souls suddenly sharing one body. It's never going to be pretty unless something ... gives.'

Gia shudders and says fervently, 'Let nothing like you *ever* come after me that way. *Please.*'

It's no comfort, but I say, 'The sooner we get out of here, the less likely you'll ever hear from any of us again. What happened at the Galleria was an ... aberration.'

'Let's hope it stays that way.' Gia's eyes are troubled as she adds, 'Now a deal's a deal, and, by God, you delivered and then some. Tell me what you need and I'll make it happen.'

We're at her open bedroom door now, and I see Ryan's sleeping form on the bed, his head thrown back carelessly, his dark hair spilling across the pillow, blankets rumpled down to his waist. As if he feels my eyes on him, he shifts in his sleep, mumbling some word I can't catch.

Dottore Pellini joins us, telling Gia discreetly in Italian that there's nothing essentially wrong with Ryan that a little less partying wouldn't cure.

'What he really needs is rest,' I tell Gia regretfully when the doctor has moved away again, 'but there's something I need to do and he's insisting on coming with me. So, could you get him some food and drink? I don't know when his last square meal was. His clothing's torn, and he needs a new pack. He also needs … props.'

'Props?' Gia says, confused.

I frown, unable to think of the right word. It's my own shorthand for shape-shifting, and Ryan's no shape-shifter.

'You know, *things*. He looks too much like himself,' I say, 'and too much like *him*.'

In my mind's eye, I see Luc glaring across the catwalk at Ryan, Ryan at Luc, one so dark, one so light, like the negative and positive sides of a single image. With me caught in the middle.

'Oh, the sexy ex,' Gia replies in sudden understanding. 'The blond god sitting beside Gudrun who made my mouth go dry with lust the moment I set eyes on him?'

'It's his speciality,' I reply, horror dawning in my face as the thought suddenly crystallises. 'Gia, Ryan's in so much danger. When they can't find me, they'll go looking for him.'

'So it's best if you stay together then,' Gia replies, trying her best to sound reassuring. 'Watch each other's backs.'

'Which is just as well,' I say miserably, 'seeing as I can't seem to give him up.'

Gia grins, looking Ryan over again with an expression of amused regret on her face. 'Like sugar, or cigarettes. I completely get it. Look, I'll get Tommy onto it. He can put together a man bag for him. But what about *you*?'

'All I need is information,' I reply instantly. 'An update.'

Gia's expression sharpens immediately. 'Shoot.'

I search her face. 'Remember how you told me about the fires that destroyed Domaso, Gravedona, Rezzonico, Menaggio, Tremezzo, Argegno, Laglio, Urio?'

She nods, hugging herself even more tightly, as if she's cold, the wicked spikes on her shoulders catching the brilliant lights in the room.

'What happened after Urio?' I ask. Gia frowns. 'Was there anything ... more?' I add.

'I couldn't honestly tell you,' she replies. 'But Juliana would know. She has a villa by the lake, as did Giovanni. Her staff will be keeping her informed.'

I trail Gia back across the room to where Juliana is still seated at the dining table beneath vast windows. She seems shrunken in her grief, all her usual vitality, her habitual curiosity, leached out of her. Gia repeats my question to her in rapid-fire Italian, and she looks up, startled.

'I'm told that Moltrasio was partially destroyed before it all ... stopped. After Moltrasio there was no more ... burning.'

'As if the cause of the fires was interrupted?' I ask in perfect Italian.

Gia's eyes widen for a moment in surprise, before her expression goes bland.

Juliana nods, looking perturbed. 'Yes! It is exactly how it was described to me — as if the arsonist was interrupted. Though the arsonist must have been in league with the Devil, for it should be impossible for fire to behave that way, as if it were alive ...'

She shivers and crosses herself, then says to Gia, 'Bianca St Alban's family estate is in Moltrasio and I haven't even called to ask after her, or to let her know that I've decided to give to her as a gift the haute couture pieces she ordered. Nothing in Giovanni's final collection will ever be reproduced again, for anyone. But he would have wanted Bianca to have the gowns she selected before he ... before he ...' Juliana looks down, but not before I see her eyes filling rapidly. 'The police are only letting locals into the area,' she whispers. 'I could deliver them myself, of course, but I don't have the heart to see it. It is too much ...' Her voice trails away.

I have to look away quickly so that she will not see the sudden flare of excitement in my eyes. My voice is casual, unhurried, as I study my booted feet. 'I could do it for you. I have business in the area. And Bianca knows me. We spoke only a few days ago in fact, face to face.'

I glance up just as Juliana looks at Gia dully. 'You would vouch for this young woman? Can she be trusted to take the two pieces directly to Villa Nicolin? Deliver them personally into Bianca's hands? A price cannot be put on those dresses now, but I would sooner harm my own children than touch them again.'

Gia's expression doesn't waver for an instant as she stares into Juliana's grief-ravaged face. 'Absolutely. She is —'

'A creature of my word,' I interject. 'If I say I will do something, then it will be done. Without question.'

Juliana turns her reddened eyes upon me. 'Then please do so, with my thanks.'

She looks away from us towards the vast sash windows that dominate the room. 'See to it,' she tells Gia. 'Give her every assistance and Atelier Re will make good any trouble it has caused you, twice over.'

Gia nods and calls out across the room, 'Carlo.'

'Miss?' he replies, rising from the low-slung and impossibly fragile-looking Louis XV-style armchair near the front door that he'd somehow folded himself into.

'Mercy must be given the exclusive use of one of the cars today,' Gia barks. 'Clear it with Gianfranco. Atelier Re will meet the expense. She needs to leave as soon as some gowns arrive and her friend has had a meal and bathed.'

'One way or return?' Carlo says, surprised, raking one large hand through his head of short, tight, black curls.

Gia raises an eyebrow at me and I say, 'One way. The driver's to drop us and go. No waiting.'

Carlo is already dialling from the in-house phone when he looks up again, at me. 'Destination, Miss? Where shall I say the driver is going?'

'Moltrasio,' I reply, and Carlo's olive skin goes pale. 'To the Villa Nicolin.'

His eyes fly to Gia's for confirmation, and she gives him a terse nod before tapping away on the seamless screen of her slender, black phone. She is making things happen the way I'd hoped, prayed, she would.

I bend over Ryan's unconscious form and his eyelids flicker. Someone's taken off his leather jacket and jeans and thrown them across an armoire beside the bed. He's just wearing the long-sleeved tees he was wearing when I last saw him in Australia, one blue, one grey, both looking a little grey now around the neckline. I want so badly to trace the exposed line of his collarbone that I have to turn away and busy myself in the marble en suite bathroom.

I perch on the side of the massive stone spa that dominates the room and start drawing him a bath, dumping in an array of bath salts and potions from all the little brand-name bottles lined up neatly beneath a vast urn of white flowers on a ledge beside me. I play my fingers beneath the running water and allow the flesh of my hand to turn opaque and vaporous. The water runs right through it, and I find that it's still easier to make myself a creature of mist than it is to hold this human form that I've chosen. But the dizziness, the disorienting sense of dislocation, of vertigo — they're lessening all the time. I pull my hand back together, rebuilding it until the water ricochets once more off its sleek, solid surface.

'Mercy?' Ryan calls out uncertainly.

I turn away from the running water and rise quickly, unable to suppress the smile that spreads across my face. It's echoed by Ryan's grin.

'You don't have to do that,' he says softly as I approach him. 'Run me a bath, I mean.'

I lower myself down on the edge of the bed beside him and reply cheerfully, 'The weird thing is that I *want* to, and I can't understand why. I'm the most selfish creature alive. Anyone will tell you that.'

He sighs, shifting across the bed, making room for me beside him. I shake out my head of wild, dark curls and lie down on top of the covers. Both of us turn inwards to face each other so that we are eye to eye. There are still dark circles under his eyes, but that sense of him that I get is no longer clouded by sheer exhaustion. He reaches out, tracing the line of my nose; and when I smile, he touches the dimples beside my mouth, my laughter lines, and traces them, too.

'I could get used to this,' he murmurs, playing his fingers through the ends of my curling hair, then says hesitantly, 'You know what I was most afraid of? It sounds so dumb even saying it. I was afraid ...'

He swallows, tries again. 'I was afraid that I'd never be able to *compete*. That maybe what I thought you felt for me all this time was just a pale reflection of what you really felt for *him* ...'

'Compete?' I say dazedly.

'Yep, compete.' Ryan laughs self-mockingly. 'As if anyone would ever win in a play-off against the Devil.' He laughs again, softly.

'Brenda wasn't my first serious girlfriend,' he says in a weird rush. 'Before we moved to Paradise, I was crazy-in-love with a girl called Edie Nolan who dumped me after she caught me drunkenly helping her best friend out of her shirt at a party. Edie would never let me touch her, and I was *dying*. You'll have no idea what that feels like, what I'm even talking about. After that, I couldn't have moved towns fast enough. First kiss at seven, in the dark, in the gym, on a pile of smelly old gym mats with a girl called Nikki whose dad ran a bar. Our teeth kept clashing. She'd just eaten a cheese sandwich. I remember thinking it wasn't all it was cracked up to be, kissing.' Ryan's words are almost tripping over themselves.

I see them, those girls. I let myself see them through his skin, and then I tell myself to shut it down, to stop torturing myself, though the damage is already done. Edie walks through my mind — a gentle-looking, strawberry blonde; the best friend, an up-for-anything brunette; Nikki — a tough-looking kid with straight, sandy bangs.

'And maybe Brenda and I were bad for each other,' Ryan almost gabbles. 'But after Edie, being with Bren was like being with a, a … *blowtorch*. If what happened to Lauren hadn't happened, we'd probably still be together.'

'I don't understand why you're telling me all this,' I whisper.

'I need you to know,' Ryan insists softly, 'about me; I need you to know *me*. But it's coming out all wrong.'

I feel the rising heat beneath his skin, read his intention the same instant he leans forward gently and takes my mouth with his, reaching out and cupping the side of my face with one hand, his fingertips tangling in my hair, the kiss deepening until my entire world, my entire horizon, is Ryan, and every sense is flooded with him.

Some dim recollection steps forward: of Bernie drunkenly kissing Ezra under moonlight, of me in a score of past lives being kissed or kissing someone in return. But did I ever feel this sense of flowering? Did I ever feel as if it meant something more than mere mechanics? Did it ever touch *me*, the real me, the way Ryan is doing now?

'You overwhelm me,' I murmur against his lips, staring into his hooded eyes, the pupils so dark and dilated. And it's true. I can feel his peculiar energy singing against me, breaking against my skin. He's like a kind of wild music running through my head, the living energy of him. He's transfixing.

He pulls me closer, kissing me harder, and there's nothing grating or unpractised about his mouth now. He is heat and velvet, and the salt-sweet roiling sea.

He rolls me over onto my back, bracing himself so that he's lying half across me and the two of us are hopelessly entangled in the bedclothes. It's a new kind of imprisoning, but one that does not engender loathing or anger. Just wonder.

Love plays out so differently among the *elohim*. We guard ourselves, our essential natures, from each other. We were created with self-knowledge, and, as a consequence, are so wary, so loath to cede control, that it's rare to know what courses through the mind of another of our kind.

There's that lick of fire along my nerves. I can't recall even the Devil's kisses burning me this way.

Ryan's eyes flash open suddenly and he scrambles back from me with a gasp. 'You're so *hot*,' he says.

'And that's ... good, right?' I reply, puzzled.

He shakes his head, looking at me wide-eyed. 'No, *hot* as in *scalding*. Like trying to kiss a candle flame. Not that I'm complaining,' he adds hastily. 'It just makes things a little ... trickier.'

We stare into each other's eyes. Only a few inches separate us, but they could be light years.

'Food's on its way,' Gia calls through the door we'd forgotten was wide open. She leans against the doorframe, grinning. 'You two look cozy.'

Ryan says, 'Aaaaarrrrr,' and flips over onto his back, covering his face with his hands. I see the faint blush on his skin beneath his outspread fingers, a hint of sexy stubble roughening his jaw.

'Gia!' I growl. 'Push off. We're working something out here.'

'Ah, young love,' Gia smirks, 'so relentlessly hopeful, so nauseating.'

The doorbell to the suite peals loudly and Ryan takes his hands away from his face, looking up at the ceiling. 'What *now*?' he sighs.

Gia's expression grows serious. 'The dresses are on their way, and Tommy's arriving separately with a ton of looks for Ryan to try out. So stop trying to put the moves on her, Romeo, and haul ass into that bath. You're a mess. No one in their right mind could possibly want you the condition you're in. When I come back, you'd better be up to your neck in suds.'

Ryan makes a roaring sound of frustration, throws off the rumpled bedclothes violently, then snares his jeans off the chest of drawers and heads for the bathroom. He shuts the door with unnecessary force, moving so quickly that all we get is a glimpse of long, leanly muscled legs in motion beneath the fraying hemline of his tee-shirts.

'To *die* for,' Gia pronounces lightly, already on her way out. 'Tight in all the right places. You don't deserve him.'

For a moment, I get something from her that has the feel of loneliness to it, or envy, before her iron control is back in place.

I sit up, hugging my knees tightly. 'He doesn't deserve *me*, you mean.'

She turns instantly, prepared to defend him, her eyes softening when she sees the anguish on my face and catches my real meaning.

'I'm *weak*, Gia,' I say in a low voice. 'To allow this to continue, to let it get so far out of hand ...'

'Snatching a little happiness for yourself isn't weak,' she replies gently. 'It's just human.'

At the look on my face, she says quietly, because there's nothing else *to* say, 'Uh, right. Point taken. I'll get the food.'

CHAPTER 6

Tommy doesn't bother to knock, he just barges right in in his OTT brown leather aviator jacket with the oversized shearling collar and cuffs and de rigueur hardware and pocket detailing, skin-tight black leather trousers, black lace-up boots and black knitted beanie, toting an enormous canvas carryall.

'Where's the patient?' he calls out in his light, silvery voice.

His eyes skim over me briefly and without interest before he heads straight for the closed en suite door and throws it open.

Ryan shouts, 'What the …?' and I hear a great *slosh* as he ducks beneath the water so the soap bubbles cover just about everything there is to cover.

'You want me to disguise *that*?' Tommy exclaims to Gia. '*Why* in God's name?'

He sets his bag down on the marble tiled floor and slides his beanie off his cropped, dark blond hair, stuffs it into a pocket of his leather bomber. He starts unbuckling that, too, saying wickedly, 'It's hot in here. Are you hot?' before slinging the heavy jacket onto a gilt footstool near the marble-topped sink. Underneath it, he's still the last word in street fashion, wearing his customary slogan tees under a fitted leather waistcoat covered in hundreds of glittering safety pins.

Ryan glares at me through the doorway. 'Get these people out of here!' he yells.

'They haven't even begun to do a number on you yet,' I say, drifting in and standing behind Gia and Tommy. 'This is *nothing*. Consider yourself lucky no waxing or exfoliation will be involved.'

Tommy looks at me again, quizzically. 'Do I *know* you?' he asks. 'I don't think I've ever worked with you before, but there's something about you that seems familiar.'

He purses his lips and scans me from head to toe, as if the answer might lie in the shape of my calves or the way I'm standing.

'I've got that kind of face,' I tell him. 'What's in your bag of tricks?'

He kneels and rummages through it, pulling out bottle after bottle of hair dye. 'Take your pick!' he says. 'We can put some highlights or lowlights through it, or take him back to a dirty blond, or maybe a dark auburn — so distinguished. Silver is so last season and will completely wash him out, as will a deep black. Too gothic against his pale skin. We could even go two-tone, like Juliana out there. Radical, but different.'

'No!' Ryan exclaims, horrified, from within his nest of bubbles. 'What's this all about? You're not touching my hair.'

Tommy ignores him. 'I've got wigs, weaves, facial hair, lashes, fake goatees, the works — a truckload of man make-up, caps, hats, frames.' He gives Gia an accusing stare. 'You *were* rather cryptic on the phone. I had enough trouble getting the finance department to release the gowns to me and arrange for a letter to be typed up *stat* saying they were a gift from Atelier Re — Domenica almost burst an artery on the spot when I dictated that part.'

'Will someone tell me what in hell is going on?' Ryan splutters. '*I'm right here*. And the answer is *no*, to all of it.'

I scan the items littering the bathroom floor and settle on an instrument with a wicked, saw-toothed blade on the end, an electrical cord trailing from it.

'The dye idea will take too long,' I say. 'Can you clip it? Right back?'

'Sure I can,' Tommy replies, frowning. 'But are you sure? It would be a damned shame.'

'Mercy?' Ryan says uncertainly, seeing something in all our expressions that tells him this is no joke.

'Luc likes to wear his hair *long* as a general rule,' I say quietly, not quite meeting Ryan's eyes, 'when he's not showing up in the front row of fashion parades in a bespoke three-piece suit and designer stubble. So a buzz cut would be perfect, Tommy, thank you.'

I bend and study the hats and caps on the floor, selecting a dark grey woollen beanie and an anonymous-looking navy baseball cap with a discreet, embroidered logo on it that looks like a quartered wheel. I look up to see Ryan blanching in sudden understanding of what this is all about.

'It's got to be lo-fi, Tommy,' I murmur, shifting my gaze back to the slight young man standing beside Gia. 'We'll be on the move anyway, and he's less of a target if he isn't staying in the one place. But I can't change the way he walks, or speaks, his foot size, his hand span or how tall he is. So in case someone *does* spot him, I need something that will completely change the way they register his face.'

Tommy and Gia exchange glances before Tommy says, 'Well, it's obvious really.' He bends down and picks up a pair of plastic, rectangular-framed, dark tortoiseshell spectacles with clear lenses, and a pair of wraparound sunglasses with impenetrably black lenses, like bug's eyes. 'If it worked for Clark Kent,' he murmurs, straightening up, 'it'll work for *him*. Both frames are so heavy they'll completely swamp his face. They'll be all anyone takes in at first glance. Pair them with a hat and he'll be just another schmo with bad dress sense.'

'It'll have to do,' I murmur, scooping up the electric clippers and handing them to Tommy, who passes me the two pairs of spectacle frames in return.

'We'll wait for you outside,' I tell Ryan gently as Gia and Tommy precede me out of the room and I close the door behind us.

Tommy moves one of the antique dining chairs across the room, and unplugs a beautiful but useless lamp, plugging in the clippers in its place. With the air of someone about to be executed, Ryan finally emerges, clean-shaven, with still-damp hair, from Gia's rooms in a tee and jeans and bare feet. He sits reluctantly in the dining chair.

As Tommy fires up the clippers, the doorbell to the suite peals again and a concierge wheels in a clothing rack on which hang two gowns, each zipped into a hand-sewn, protective cover made from some diaphanous, shimmering fabric I can't name. I recognise both gowns immediately as Designs 13 and 28 of Giovanni Re's final collection: the first one, slim, one-shouldered, sleeveless, in Giovanni's signature *rosso Re*, with a complicated neckline and plunging back; and the second, silver, strapless, 1930s in feel and heavily sequined. The night I met Bianca St Alban at Atelier Re, they'd been laid out for me to model for her, but I never got around to trying them on.

It's strange seeing them again. From life to life, I've never been able to carry anything concrete with me. My existence to date has had a terrifying aura of impermanence, of hallucination, as has the entire objective world. Until Ryan. When he and I collided, everything began to change. And now the room is filled with people I've met before under vastly different circumstances, and the rooms themselves, the dresses, are known and familiar things. It's a seismic shift for me, the effects of which I think I'm only beginning to feel.

Juliana barely glances at the two dresses before telling Gia in a low voice to take them away. As the gowns are wheeled back out of the suite, Gia catches the look on my face and murmurs, 'Don't worry, they'll be there in the car. What's so important in Moltrasio anyway? Nothing could make me go there. You saw the footage. There's nothing there now except death.'

'Death has been and gone and taken what he wanted,' I reply absently, thinking about how those two frivolous gowns give Ryan and me a reason to be in the heavily compromised lakes region. Once they're delivered into Bianca St Alban's hands, I can start looking around Moltrasio for traces of Nuriel: in the sky, in the water, the soil, the trees. You can't just make one of the *elohim* vanish into thin air, especially one that doesn't want to go. Knowing Nuriel, she would have left some clue.

Juliana signs the letter of introduction on Atelier Re letterhead before she and Dottore Pellini take their leave together. All the while, Tommy administers Ryan's buzz cut in the background, with Carlo and Jürgen looking on in sardonic amusement, pointing out places he's missed.

The doorbell sounds again, and Gia and I supervise the laying out of a mountain of dishes and beverages that emerge from the trolleys wheeled in by two female hotel staff in maroon and gold uniforms. Irina suddenly lets out a bloodcurdling shriek, followed by the loud *clang* of something metallic hitting her closed bedroom door. The young women exchange covert glances before excusing themselves from the room.

Gia grins at me. 'Bet Magdalena the nurse wishes Irina was still under.'

'I'm done here,' Tommy calls out.

Gia and I turn away from the dining table and I'm shocked by how changed Ryan appears. He looks thinner and older, the dark shadows under his eyes, the pallor of his skin, the remarkable lines of his facial bones, his skull, all accentuated.

'Oh, Ryan,' I say softly, appalled at what I've allowed to happen.

'I like it,' Gia says in a no-nonsense voice. 'I think he looks edgy, hot. Kudos, Tommy, you didn't even draw blood this time. *You*,' she indicates Ryan curtly, and again I get that faint wash of unhappiness from her, 'get over here and get stuck into this feast.'

Tommy sets down the clippers and rolls up the newspapers he laid out around Ryan's chair, bundling up lengths of shorn-off hair in the process.

'Is it that bad?' Ryan replies, getting up and walking over to me.

I don't reply, still troubled by the transformation in him.

He doesn't ask for a mirror, or even look for one, and that's him all over. He just doesn't give a shit about the way he looks or the impact he has.

He holds my gaze challengingly and says, 'It's still me.'

And you're still heart-stopping, I think. *Even to those not in possession of an actual heart.* All I say aloud, gruffly, is, 'Eat.'

As Ryan wolfs down what looks like his body weight in food and drink, Gia hands me a black and grey backpack with splashes of fluoro green across it. We go through the contents together: that all-important letter of introduction, the beanie, the cap, the spectacles, the sunglasses, a lighter, a cylindrical silver flashlight, a handful of chocolate bars, a bottle of water, a pocketknife, a disposable razor, a small canister of deodorant, a travel-sized bottle of whisky, a small chamois cloth, a bar of soap, an Atelier Re-branded five-pack of black boxer shorts in size M, two pairs of hiking socks, and thirteen hundred and seventy euros in notes.

'Because that's all I have on me,' Gia says crisply when I try to return it.

'It's too much,' I say, looking at the pile of bills in my hand — tens, twenties, fifties, hundreds — in candy colours.

'Take it,' she insists in a fierce whisper. '*You* might be able to walk through walls, but Ryan needs to survive like the rest of us do, the regular way, and that takes dough. Buy me a meal if you ever swing by North London and we'll call it quits, though, by the look of things, food's optional for you lot, isn't it?'

She runs a purple fingernail idly through the contents of the bag. 'The rest of this stuff is a jaded old fashionista's take on what a Boy Scout bag ought to look like. It may come in handy, it may be completely useless. I wouldn't know. I don't do *le camping*.'

After Ryan pushes away from the table, looking slightly sick, Tommy leads him back into Gia's bedroom and bullies him into changing out of his grimy tee and jeans while Gia and I look on, amused.

'These are fair-trade organic cotton,' Tommy mutters as he yanks a couple of long-sleeved tee-shirts over Ryan's head and leanly muscled bare chest, one cream, one black, before thrusting a black zip-up hoodie with a subtle cable running up either side of the zipper into Ryan's hands. 'Cashmere angora blend,' he says. 'Feel it. Lightweight, unbelievably warm. From this season's collection.'

I can tell from Ryan's face that he just doesn't get it. He gazes at the hoodie bemusedly and zips himself into it. 'Uh, thanks,' he says, shooting me an imploring look. 'Fits great.'

Tommy hands him a slim-fitting pair of dark indigo jeans. 'Also organic, hand-whiskered. No two pairs are ever the same.'

'They're, um, nice,' Ryan replies, shrugging into them hastily and half-turning away from us to do up the fly and top button. I see that they're a perfect fit.

'The way this *isn't*,' Tommy says with a sniff, holding up Ryan's beaten-up dark brown leather jacket. 'It's torn. You can have mine. It was too big for me anyway. I'm already over it. They give me a new one every year.'

'If it's okay with you,' Ryan says firmly, 'I'd like to keep wearing mine.'

'It's revolting,' Tommy insists. 'And it's only got two pockets,' he adds, like it's a crime.

The two men — one so tall, one so slight — stare each other down for a moment.

'It's important to me,' Ryan says finally. 'And, actually, it's got three.'

He takes the jacket out of Tommy's hands and turns back the right side to reveal an interior pocket. He unzips it, reaches inside and takes out a flat, black mobile phone like Gia's, a small booklet with a blue cover so dark it's almost black, a small black leather wallet and a folded-up piece of paper that's starting to tear along the creases. He throws everything onto Gia's bed except the paper. Wordlessly, he unfolds it, and I look up at him, startled, realising what it is a second before Tommy and Gia crowd around to look at the image in his hand.

It's a colour pencil drawing of an unsmiling young woman with an oval face, a long straight nose, lips that are neither too thin nor too wide, large, wide-set brown eyes, brown hair that hangs down to just past the shoulders. A strong face that is all angles and planes. *My* face. The one I must try to keep hidden while Ryan and I search out a vanquished archangel.

'It's a reasonable likeness,' I mutter. And it is. Quite remarkably like the face that used to stare out at me from inside the reflections of strangers. It's weird seeing myself captured this way.

'She's beautiful,' Gia muses. 'Such a strong and unusual face.'

'Who is she?' Tommy calls out, heading for the bathroom waste bin with Ryan's old tee-shirt balled up in his hands, before coming back and studying the hand-drawn image again.

'I was wearing this jacket when I first met this girl,' Ryan says obliquely, his eyes holding mine, 'and I've been chasing her for a while now. So the jacket stays. It's non-negotiable.'

Gia looks from Ryan to me, sudden comprehension in her expression, and says softly, 'Well, good for you. You'd look utterly ridiculous in Tommy's jacket anyway.'

'It's a three-thousand-dollar jacket,' Tommy exclaims, wounded.

'It's a traffic stopper, Tommy,' Gia agrees, straight-faced, 'and you know it. But I don't think that's quite the effect these two are after. The words *low* and *key* are not in your vocab, darling.'

Ryan pulls his old leather jacket on over the black hoodie and zips it right up under his neck, before sitting down on the edge of Gia's bed and shoving his bare feet into a clean pair of thick, khaki-coloured hiking socks and his worn-out boots. Then he gathers up the valuables he scattered across Gia's bed and returns them to his inside jacket pocket, together with the hand-drawn image, and zips that, too.

He looks up at me and says, 'Ready?'

He smiles, and there's so much youth and love and eagerness in his eyes that I feel a terrible foreboding.

If You're listening, I think feverishly, *keep him safe. Let him survive me.*

'It's been fun, kids,' Gia murmurs, looking into our faces intently before handing me the backpack to sling over my shoulder. 'But *con te partiro*, as they say in the classics: time to say goodbye.'

I can't help the chill I feel at her words as she and Tommy walk Ryan and me to the door.

Gia tells Carlo to take us down to the car and her expression is very severe.

'It's been real,' she drawls in her posh voice, her eyes

suspiciously bright. 'You ever at a loose end, you look me up, you hear?'

Ryan enfolds Gia and her spiky jacket in a careful bear hug before shaking Tommy's hand awkwardly.

'I don't know what you're thanking me for,' Tommy snipes lightly, 'seeing as how I practically *vandalised* you.'

He gives me a nod, frowning slightly as he struggles again to place where he could possibly know me from.

Gia just glares at me, sounding choked up. 'Don't touch me, don't even say anything, or I will *cry*. Now get out of here. And use your powers for good, not evil, got that?'

Carlo opens the door and ushers us out into the hallway like unwelcome guests. And just like that, the door is shut behind us, and Irina and I are done. I don't think I will ever lay eyes on her again, except maybe on a magazine cover, and I almost feel something like regret.

Ryan puts a hand in the small of my back as we walk towards the lift and I imagine I can feel it burning there.

'Thank you,' he says softly, 'for finding Gia, for doing that for me.'

I'm suddenly so indignant, so furious, on his behalf that my reply comes out more harshly than I intended. 'For putting you first for a change? The way no one ever did while Lauren was gone?'

In reply, he lifts my curtain of dark, curling hair and kisses the back of my neck once, lightly. I actually shiver. As he lets my hair fall back down, he trails his fingers through its ends before returning his hand to the small of my back.

'There are ways to play with fire,' he says lightly, 'without getting burnt.'

And I shiver again, inside.

We follow Carlo into the sound-deadening lift and Ryan's eyes widen in surprise as he catches his own reflection from seemingly infinite angles. I dig through the backpack before the lift doors open onto the ground floor and hand Ryan the cap and the tortoiseshell frames with the clear lenses, both of which he puts on reluctantly.

'I might not know the first thing about fashion,' he complains, taking the ugly backpack from me and shouldering it, 'but even *I* know that right now I look like the world's biggest *dork*.'

'It's what's on the inside that counts, darling,' I remind him acidly as we renegotiate the glittering lobby, the slow sweep of the continuously turning front door, Carlo leading the way.

The black limousine with the gleaming silver hood ornament of a winged woman in flight is waiting for us right by the hotel entrance, ostentatiously blocking the upper curve of the circular driveway. A few guests stare curiously as Carlo, Ryan and I approach the car, because we don't look rich and we sure as hell don't look famous.

Carlo opens the rear door, saying solemnly, '*Signor*,' and Ryan ducks awkwardly to get his head and lanky frame into the vehicle before lowering himself into the seat on the far side. Already lying across the seats opposite him are the two couture gowns in their protective sheaths. There's an opaque screen up between us and the driver.

'Get that lowered,' I tell Carlo sharply. 'And tell him to keep it down. I need to be able to see the road ahead.'

Carlo taps on the driver's side window immediately. The opaque screen vanishes smoothly and I see that our driver is the man Gia had been arguing with, his face even unhappier, even more tight-lipped, than when I last saw it. Carlo gives him last-minute instructions in rapid, low-voiced Italian, then says coolly, without the slightest hint of recognition, '*Signorina*,' and hands me in after Ryan and slams the door.

He thumps on the roof of the limo and the car sails smoothly away from the kerb. We're down the hotel drive and on our way before Ryan's even finished his awestruck inspection of the limo's interior.

'I always wanted to ride in one of these!' he exclaims, wriggling deeper into his seat with appreciation, before raising the wide leather-clad armrest that separates us and putting his arm around me as if it's the most natural thing in the world. He looks out the tinted window beside him for a moment, then back at me, his warm, deep voice teasing. 'Buses and trains not good enough for you people?'

But that's just it. It's so loony it's almost implausible: an archangel, a human, two evening dresses and a stretch limousine. It sounds like the start of a joke, but it just might work.

I turn my head and stare out the window, seeing not the man-made canyons of stone rising all around us, the watercolour sky, but Nuriel's vulnerable face and pleading eyes. And I feel a sudden flash of anger so intense that it curls the fingers of my left hand where they rest upon my leg, as if I am grasping the hilt of a mighty sword. As we sweep up Via Bochetto, that small voice inside me whispers: *For the time of their punishment is coming.* In a chauffeured, armoured car with a built-in minibar and surround sound.

'This is the last thing they'll expect,' I murmur, so quietly that Ryan has to bend his head to hear me. 'They're never going to see us coming. It's perfect.'

It's mid-afternoon, the sky a pale blue with just the faintest ripple of cloud, like the way the wind can carve patterns in a sand dune. Even with the detours and roadblocks we encounter at almost every turn, Moltrasio is only a short distance away to the north. We should be there well before nightfall.

Ryan has fallen asleep again, his mouth slightly open, his head tilted at an awkward angle against the side of the car. I scan the rooflines of all the buildings we pass; the people getting into and out of vehicles, moving along the sidewalks in their sleek furs and overcoats, holding briefcases, satchels and shopping bags; the motorcyclists in full leathers, the scooter riders in their retro-looking helmets, some with passengers riding pillion. In and amongst this sea of seething life, of human defiance, I'm searching for errant gleams of light that refuse to obey the laws of physics; beings of fire masquerading as ordinary men and women. But all I see is that Christmas is coming. It's in the neon signs everywhere, the sparkling electric lights and happy, tacky decorations taped to windows and doors.

As we navigate the narrow streets filled with aggressive drivers and raucous groups of handsome, olive-skinned young men and women, I realise something. It's a change so stealthy, yet so fundamental, that it takes me some time to understand it. But when I do, I'm electrified, and my gaze transfers wildly from my window back to Ryan's, then to the front windscreen, in disbelief. Something has happened to my eyesight. Or, at least, to the way I perceive *language*. The street signs and shopfronts we drive past haven't changed overnight, but I have. I can read *everything*. Any language, any script, I register it for what it is: Italian or Chinese, German, Arabic, Korean, Turkish, Hebrew or Hindi. Wherever words or characters occur — scrawled across the windows of tobacconists and takeaway shops, spelt out in electric lights outside bars and restaurants, furriers, mini-marts and low-rent fashion emporia — I discern their meaning immediately.

For block after block, my eyes move across words and phrases in languages I don't even recall knowing. That ancient ability I must once have possessed — to speak all the tongues of men, and of angels — has somehow been restored with my own restoration. Half of me wants to wake Ryan to tell him — because these days he's always in my thoughts, almost my first consideration, like a running snatch of music that won't leave me alone. But the other half, the sensible half, tells me to let him sleep, that I'm already freaky enough in his eyes without making myself seem even freakier.

I relax a little in my seat the further we get from the city. The streets are still crowded with vehicles and people, lights and blaring noise and signs in every language under the sun, but I can't see that we're being followed, or even monitored. And I wonder what it's cost Michael and the others to keep Luc at bay in order that I might escape.

I know that I shouldn't still be here, should already have left the face of this world far behind me. But as I glance across at Ryan sleeping, I know why I can't leave.

As we hit the autostrada, passing under signage for Lake Como, I take Ryan's hand in mine, overcome by the simple need to touch him. He awakens immediately.

'What did I miss?' he says quickly, looking around. 'Why didn't you wake me sooner?'

We approach a turn-off marked *Malpensa* and traffic suddenly slows to a crawl. It continues this way for over an hour, and the source of the hold-up becomes clear the closer we get to a massive police roadblock that's been set up across the breadth of the motorway near signage that reads *Como Monte Olimpino*. Every car ahead of us is being rerouted to the west. Beyond the roadblock is a mess of police vans, cars and motorbikes, and beyond them, the motorway to the east stretches out emptily, like the kind of roadway you might glimpse in a dream.

I see our driver's neck, his head, go rigid with tension. Though he's speaking softly beneath his breath, I understand every word of the guttural, colourful Italian invective he uses. *Of all the days*, he's thinking. *Of all the places. Why me?*

When it's our turn, a single policeman steps forward from the large uniformed group that's edgily talking and joking there, some great and secret fear on all their faces. Our driver slides down his window, explains in Italian that we are rich foreigners, friends of the St Alban family with urgent business in Moltrasio.

The young, clean-shaven, blue-eyed policeman in his dark peaked cap and handsome uniform — a fitted navy jacket with gold seals, knee-high black boots and tight-fitting breeches with a contrast band running up the side — replies coldly in the same tongue, 'Residents only, no exceptions.'

'They are expected,' the driver wheedles, and I hear the deep unease in his voice. 'They have a letter.'

'I don't care if it's a letter from God,' the policeman barks, 'residents only. Move left.'

I release Ryan's hand and lean across him to hook up the backpack before depressing the button set into the contoured armrest in my door.

'I'll take it from here,' I tell the driver in fluent Italian as my window slides down.

The dark-tinted driver's side window is smoothly re-engaged and our driver points his blunt and craggy face forward once more, but I can tell from his stillness that he's listening.

The policeman takes a step back in surprise, placing one hand on the weapon on his hip, before recovering. He looks me over coolly, Ryan, too, and I don't look away. To Ryan's credit, neither does he. I open the backpack and take out the letter of introduction.

'Your Italian is remarkably good for a "rich foreigner",' the policeman says sardonically. 'So you will understand very well when I tell you again that only residents are permitted past this point.'

'Read the letter,' I plead, handing it to him. He takes it reluctantly. 'It is signed by Signora Agnelli-Re herself on behalf of Atelier Re. We are expected at Villa Nicolin, by Bianca St Alban.' I see the police officer's eyes flicker as I name-drop shamelessly. I point out the two gowns lying across from me. 'We are already late.'

The young man's countenance wavers for a moment before his expression hardens again. 'I'm sorry, *signorina*, but we have our orders. Some roads are impassable. The dead — they are still being recovered.'

'Please,' I say quietly. 'Read the letter. Call the number you see there. It was Giovanni Re's dying wish that Signorina St Alban have these gowns. I know that you know who he was, that he was a great man. A true Milanese, and a good person. I don't have much time. It's imperative that I deliver these gowns today.'

The police officer takes his time reading the letter before returning his gaze to me. Then he turns on his heel and walks back to the contingent of armed men and women strung out loosely along the barricade and I see him confer with several of them, each person scanning the letter, surprised.

Somewhere behind us, an unwise driver lets loose a few impatient blasts on his car horn, which sets off a bunch of other drivers. Through my open window, I see several of the officers peel away from the roadblock, wending through the gridlocked traffic on foot in search of the jokers responsible.

'We're holding everyone up,' Ryan murmurs, frowning. 'What's happening out there?'

The young policeman is nowhere to be seen.

'Maybe he's calling that number,' I reply, more confidently than I'm feeling. 'Gia had it all worked out, they've got to let us through.'

We wait, silently and on edge, the smell of smoke and ashes drifting in through my open window, slowly poisoning the air inside the car.

A flurry of activity at one end of the roadblock draws my gaze. I see cars and vans being shifted around to allow a helmeted police officer on a motorbike to roar through the gap that's been created. He executes a tight loop around our limo, before pulling up to my open window, engine growling, the front wheel of the bike facing the gap in the barricade. He pushes up the visor of his helmet with one black-gloved hand and I recognise the young officer's cool, blue-eyed gaze immediately.

'I'll escort you to the Villa Nicolin personally,' he says curtly. 'Look neither right nor left or you will have cause to regret your curiosity.'

He snaps his visor down and accelerates away from us, and a few seconds later our driver is sliding the car past the hard-eyed policemen and women, past the jumble of blue and white police vehicles.

My hand finds its way into Ryan's automatically, gripping it tight.

The road rises, winding gently, and Ryan and I take in the tiers of low-rise buildings with terracotta-coloured roofs nestled into the foothills all around us, the late-afternoon sun giving them an almost rosy cast. It's so incredibly beautiful when we see the lake for the first time, ringed by tall pines and graceful dwellings, the snow-capped peaks of distant mountains rising behind.

'What do you think he could have meant about not looking around?' Ryan says wonderingly as we follow the shore of the lake, the road strangely deserted. 'I've never seen a place as beautiful as this, ever.'

But that pervasive smell — of smoke, of ashes — is growing stronger. And I begin to discern patches of darkness in the distant canopy; a strange, dark blot upon the handsome facade of a dusky rose-coloured villa built right up against a curve in the shoreline, far across the lake. As we enter the main street of Moltrasio — a narrow canyon of shopfronts built shoulder to shoulder in cheerful colours — the first thing that hits me is the utter desolation, followed by the realisation that it's filled with people.

There's a fire crew still hosing down the smoking ruins

of what must once have been a wine shop, because a river of melted glass seems to flow out of it, into a car park filled with the remains of vehicles, similarly rendered down into a kind of metallic tallow. We drive without stopping past the shattered front windows of a burnt-out delicatessen; a photographer's studio hollowed out by fire that's missing most of its front facade; a shoe store that retains a front door but is now open to the sky. Our driver has to slow several times to navigate over or past jumbles of semi-liquefied stone and concrete, brick, steel grillework and tile; around dangerous cracks and potholes that have opened in the road.

Through the ruins move ash-covered figures, drifting as if dazed, bending to scrabble through the rubble on the ground as if they've misplaced something, or raising their hands to the sky, faces twisted in agony. None of them seem to engage with the uniformed emergency personnel who are struggling to shore up structures on the brink of collapse, their desperate shouts piercing the hazy air.

Moltrasio was only partially destroyed, Juliana said. This scene must be amplified in town after town all along the lake from here to Domaso. I clench my left fist, feeling that old agony rising in me.

'What *is* that?' Ryan's voice cuts across my thoughts.

He draws my attention to a shadowy stencil on a honey-coloured shopfront wall just ahead. It's a weird kind of graffiti — like the rough outline of a man drawn freehand in a faint, powdery, black substance, like charcoal.

Beside the strange image stands a tall man, bald-headed, slack-faced, his suit, skin, eyes and hair covered in a thick grey dust, no hint of colour about him, not even a rim of pink around the eyes. He might be made from ash — even the whites of his eyes seem ashy. He raises both arms towards me, palms upward, as we pass him in our car, as if pleading for help. And that's when I see it. The shape of him. The shape of the shadowy stencil rendered on that shopfront wall.

'Did you see him?' I whisper to Ryan. 'The streets are filled with people just like him.'

I turn and kneel up on my seat to look out the rear window at the man standing by the wall, as if anchored there by his pain. His eyes follow our car in numb supplication. I point him out to Ryan, who is kneeling on his seat, too, scanning the war zone we're leaving behind us.

'What people?' he asks. 'All I can see are search crews. But it doesn't look like there's anyone left alive to find out there.'

And then horror seizes me fully and I understand what that man is. What all those drifting, dazed and voiceless people are, so divorced from all the frantic activity around them. They are those that Azraeil had no use for, those who were not blameless. And that mark on the wall? It was the agony of one man's passing, caught there in his own life's blood.

It's a ghost town, I think, sickened. *As it was in Hiroshima, as it was in Nagasaki.*

And it is Luc's doing, all of it.

I will bring you down, I hear him say again in that dark and smoky voice that used to play havoc with every sense I possess. *Believe it.*

CHAPTER 7

The back wheels of our limo grind and scream uselessly, unable to get traction as the driver crunches the gears, trying to accelerate out of a giant pothole within sight of the towering gates that guard Villa Nicolin.

Our police escort salutes us from his motorbike and roars away.

I pop the lock on my door and tug on Ryan's hand. 'Come on,' I say, jumping out of the shuddering limo, the elegant dresses upon their padded hangers hooked over the fingers of one hand.

The pothole looks recent. When I stare at its clean edges, I imagine that I see the faintest trace of phosphorescence, of melted, cauterised earth. Nuriel must have fought Luc so badly.

Ryan shoulders the daypack and we walk up to black wrought-iron gates. They are at least twenty feet high and set into the centre of a towering stone facade built to resemble the entry to a medieval keep. Dusk is falling, and as we draw closer, automatic sensors flood the area immediately around us with a dazzling light. Four sleek, fine-boned shapes materialise out of nowhere and throw themselves at the gates, thrusting their muzzles at us through the bars, teeth snapping, foaming and yowling.

Ryan yells, 'Holy crap!' and leaps backwards, but I remain where I am, watching the light strike the glistening, bared fangs only inches from my fingers.

'Italian greyhounds,' I say absently as I turn and press the buzzer on the intercom panel set into the gate. There is no nameplate on it, no address.

A faint metallic chiming sound comes back at us from the built-in speaker. The camera lens that's set into the centre of the panel swivels minutely in my direction. From the corner of my eye, I see Ryan slip on the fake spectacles, adjust the cap on his head so that it sits low over his eyes.

The intercom speaker suddenly crackles into life. 'Business?' a woman's voice says pleasantly. I place the accent a second later as Irish.

'Juliana Agnelli-Re sent us with the gowns for Miss St Alban,' I say smoothly, holding the dresses up in front of the lens.

Ryan and I turn as, with a squeal of tyres, the limo shoots out of the pothole and does a rapid U-turn before burning back the way we came. Ryan runs the fingers of his right hand through the ends of my loose hair, and I give him a stern look, twisting it back into a knot behind my neck with my free hand. It stays there.

He grins. 'Neat trick.'

'Focus,' I reply repressively.

The intercom remains silent, and I look over the heads of the baying, scrabbling dogs at the estate. The wide driveway — paved in smoothly rounded, dark and light stones that mark out an intricate pattern — seems to go for a mile past gently playing fountains and manicured lawns before curving around the side of an imposing three-storey Palladian-style villa with cream-coloured walls and dozens of windows framed by forest green shutters. It's a house with scores of rooms and chimneys, entered by way of a grand central portico supported by stone pillars. The huge carriage lamps on either side of the front door suddenly come on, as do all of the floodlights lining the driveway. Immediately, the sky seems darker, heightening the impression of Villa Nicolin being a kind of fortress against the outside world.

'Tomaso will be right with you,' the woman's voice says through the speaker.

Minutes later, an olive-skinned man built along the lines of a silverback gorilla, taller even than Ryan, in a sleekly fitted three-piece suit, with short, greying hair and an earpiece, approaches the gate. He looks us up and down expressionlessly, before looking at the dogs going mad at his heels, drenched in sweat.

He drags the dogs away by their collars around the side of the house, then returns and points some kind of remote unlocking device at the gates. They swing away from us almost soundlessly, and as we enter, the man indicates wordlessly that we should submit to a search. He sets the gates closing again with the remote, before pocketing it and patting Ryan and me down individually for weapons, the touch of his hands feather light and impersonal. Beckoning for the dresses, he wrings each one lightly, then rummages through the daypack. Finally, with a jerk of his head, he indicates that we should follow him up the drive.

As we walk along the pebbled roadway towards the villa, we can still hear the faint howling of the dogs. I know they will continue until they are hoarse from screaming, or can no longer sense me. Ryan's dogs had reacted to me in exactly the same way. It must be my essential inhumanity that they discern, my utter alien-ness.

'I bet they're jumpy from the fires,' Ryan says hastily, but Tomaso doesn't even turn his head to look at us. Just keeps walking swiftly, almost silently.

It's almost second nature to me now to try to tune out any trace of mortal energy around me, and little by little I'm getting better at it — I can choose to accept what I wish to accept and discount the rest. But I let myself see, for a moment, how this man must see us. I get no sense of alarm, no curiosity as to why the dogs are behaving so out of character for their breed. He believes we are what we appear to be — troublesome young foreigners on some frivolous errand — and I relax a little as I take in my surroundings.

The villa is set on a steep hill above a vast garden that runs down in immaculately maintained tiers to the lake's shore far below. The level below the forecourt features a formal parterre garden built around a series of small circular ponds. Below that, there's a grove of miniature citrus trees scattered with curved stone benches. Below that again, a classical statuary garden filled with the frozen forms of nymphs and satyrs. Running water features cascade down either side of the wide central staircase that leads to the portico of the main house and bisect the top three tiers of the formal garden. There's also a cleverly concealed winding driveway that connects the main house to a much smaller, sleekly modern one-storey guesthouse of glass and steel at the foot of the hill. A high stone wall with another pair of tall, black, wrought-iron gates set into it separates the property from a narrow street that runs along its lowest boundary.

'Holy crap!' Ryan mouths again, looking around. He points out a long, narrow jetty jutting into the lake opposite the lower gates of the property. A large cruiser and a couple of smaller motorised runabouts are moored to it. The jetty had caught my interest, too, almost immediately.

'Worth checking out,' I mouth at him behind Tomaso's broad back.

He nods to show he's understood, reflected light glinting off the lenses of his fake glasses.

As we step onto the large, complicated, Renaissance-style symbol picked out in polished black and white stones just below the front portico, a slight woman in a long-sleeved white dress and white bib-fronted apron, with curly, jaw-length blonde hair and ruddy cheeks, opens the tall, heavily carved front door to the house. When she sees us, a smile lightens the anxious expression on her thin face. She walks towards us, hands outspread in welcome.

'Thank goodness you've reached us safely,' she says in her lilting voice. 'When Signora Agnelli-Re's office called to let us know you were already on your way, well, I ...' A shadow crosses her face before she adds brightly, 'Now let me take those from you, you must be exhausted.'

Ryan and I exchange glances. I hoist the hangers in my left hand a little higher.

'I'm sorry ...' I begin, and pause.

'Clara,' the woman says. 'How rude of me. Clara O'Manley.'

'Clara,' I continue smoothly, 'but I have strict instructions to deliver these personally to Bianca St Alban. Mrs Agnelli-Re was quite adamant. As you will be aware, a value cannot be placed on them now. They are museum pieces, you understand.'

Clara's expressive face cycles through surprise, sorrow, comprehension, then a studied neutrality. 'Tomaso,' she says to the silent hulk standing to one side of us, 'have Gregory call down to the *dépendance* to see if Signorina Bianca is available to receive …' Now it's her turn to pause.

'Ryan Daley,' Ryan says immediately, his manners impeccable, holding out his right hand. 'And Mercy.'

'I have one of those impossible names,' I add quickly, shaking her hand, too, which feels calloused, cool and dry. 'Just Mercy will do.'

Tomaso moves around us silently, entering the villa through its open front door. Neither name will ring any bells with Bianca St Alban. She's never met Ryan, and when she met *me* I was the notorious Irina Zhivanevskaya. But she's staying in the guesthouse at the foot of the estate, near the lake, and that's where I want to be. All I have to go on is that terrible dream in which I somehow saw inside Luc's mind, *was* him as he pursued Nuriel across the dark waters of Lake Como. I need to look at the shoreline from the perspective of the lake itself and maybe then it will become clear what happened to her.

My voice is deliberately casual as I say, 'We'd be happy to walk the dresses down to Bianca ourselves. We spoke only a few days ago, in fact, at Atelier Re, just before the couture show. That's the guesthouse, the *dépendance*, down there, I take it?'

Clara nods. 'You're friends of hers? She's been something of a recluse lately ...'

I nod. 'When Juliana told me she needed to get the gowns to Bianca, and we were already headed this way, well, it made sense to stop by. All that business with Félix de Haviland ...' I frown. 'So shocking, and so, so *sad*.'

Ryan blinks for a moment, struggling to recall where he's heard the name before.

'You know, darling,' I purr, turning to him and putting a hand lightly on his arm. 'You and Justine were talking about it only the other day, remember?'

Ryan's face clears. 'Félix always was an idiot,' he says disapprovingly.

'Félix broke her heart,' Clara murmurs, gazing down at the guesthouse. Light spills from its floor-to-ceiling windows onto the lawns, casting shadows in pretty patterns. 'She'll be so happy to see some familiar, friendly faces. Her parents are travelling between board meetings, like they always do this time of year. She was already feeling under siege, so alone, you know? And then all this happened ...'

She touches the back of my hand and, for a moment, I get a clear sensation of her terror when she'd woken that night to see strange lights in the sky. The estate had become a kind of island, marooned by a fire that had seemed somehow to be *alive*. She'd watched from her upper-storey bedroom, scarcely able to breathe, as trees and buildings had burst into flame all around the shoreline. Lines of fire had appeared across the surface of the lake, like holy writing, though she hadn't been able to make out any source. She'd seen the main street of the town burning in the distance and had recited the words of every prayer she'd ever been taught as a child, because she hadn't known what else to do.

I shake off her touch lightly, knowing it's imperative I get down to the lake.

'We're visiting other friends in the area,' I say, 'just to see how they're getting on. We'll duck in and have a quick chat with Bianca, drop the dresses, and be on our way.'

'We'll be gone before you know it,' Ryan adds warmly, and he's so solid and reassuring and boy-next-door handsome in his kooky get-up that Clara can't help twinkling up at him.

'Oh, go on,' she says with a shooing motion. 'I expect she'll be glad of the distraction. Head past the little folly to my left there, and you'll find the start of the driveway that will take you down.'

She waves at us before re-entering the house. As she shuts the door behind her, I hear her call out, 'Tomaso? Tell Gregory —'

'For an honest guy, you make a convincing liar,' I tease Ryan in a low voice as we walk towards the marble and wrought-iron folly — like a miniature rotunda — set on the far edge of the property.

Ryan takes the heavy spectacles off his face, slipping them into his pocket with relief as he rubs at the bridge of his nose.

For a moment, we linger beneath the delicate ironwork canopy of the folly, looking up at the first stars of evening appearing in the sky. Then, by some unspoken consent, we lay our separate burdens down upon a curved marble bench seat within the folly, and Ryan hooks his arms around me from behind, pulling me close into his body. We gaze together across the darkening lake as the wind rises around us, ghosting through the folly, through the pines that tower overhead. The view is astounding. Twinkling lights ring the foothills, mirroring the lights in the sky, as if strings of stars have somehow fallen out of the firmament and come to rest beside the water, just for us. And I'm suddenly filled with an intense gladness, for each light represents at least one living soul, someone who survived Luc's malevolence, the way I did.

'I'm glad it's you,' Ryan murmurs, 'that I'm seeing this with.'

'Don't ever forget this,' I reply softly. 'Don't ever forget me.'

When he starts to protest, I say fiercely, 'It happens. Memories die, they can be twisted, shattered, stolen forever. I'm proof of that. Remember this, Ryan. That we managed to find each other. That we were together, here, just for a little while.'

That I love you. I'm too much of a coward to say the words.

I turn in his arms and look up into his eyes, place one hand against his warm human skin, letting the energy of him wash over me for a moment, the song of him play through me, before I turn back to face the lake, leaning back into the hard line of his shoulder. It's dark beneath the folly's fretwork canopy. The moon is almost overwhelmed, only a thin sliver. Dominated by its paramour, the sun, the same way Luc once had me in thrall.

'Do you know what I'm thinking right now?' Ryan's voice is very quiet as he tightens his arms around me.

'Yes,' I whisper without hesitation, because lying to him would be like lying to myself. I turn my head so that his heartbeat is just beneath my cheek. 'I do. And I'm humbled by you.'

'It's the first and last prayer I think I'll ever make,' his laughter is ragged, 'that God might let me "keep" you; that we can be together for always. You've paid and paid. Why must you keep risking everything when there are others who can take the fight up to Luc?

'We were both like dead people,' he murmurs. 'Why show us what's possible only to take it away? Why doesn't *He* ever help us, anyway? Why does He allow all this bad stuff to happen?'

He flings an arm out at the lake, at the world, and in that gesture I understand the frustrations of an entire, uncomprehending species. I think of Lauren and what was done to her, how any sense could be made of a thing so unspeakable. I've asked myself the same kinds of questions, and yet I am one of His weapons, His anointed. It's an irony to me, that I should keep finding mysteries within mysteries; that life is a puzzle box without end; that if you peel back every layer, there are more beneath.

'He knows,' I reply, more hope in my words than certainty. 'He knows and sees, I really believe that, but I think He's gone beyond the point of intercession. I think we were all set in motion a long time ago; we exist now inside this bell jar, as do the parameters, the rules, the cycles, and it's up to us — all of us, even the *elohim* — to weather the conditions. We are pieces of Him, all of us, from lowest to highest. Whatever we do, we do to Him also; whatever happens to us happens to Him. We are His great experiment, and if we suffer, He suffers with us. We have to believe that, for the alternative would be unbearable.'

'Have you ever *seen* Him?' Ryan asks, turning me to face him, and I feel his terrible need: for reassurance, for answers.

I shake my head. 'I have felt His presence, like a breath of holy fire, of life. Maybe only the Eight ever have. They hold us together at the centre, when many may have drifted.'

'The way Luc did?' Ryan says.

My voice is troubled. 'And the others. K'el said a hundred *elohim* fell with Luc, and who knows how many from the ranks of the *malakhim*, the *seraphim*, more ...'

Ryan's voice is very quiet, very controlled. 'You know what really scares me? That maybe this is *it*. We get this one shot at things and then I never see you again. I don't think I could stand it if this is all we're ever going to have. It's not enough. It isn't fair.' His laughter is self-mocking. 'Listen to me.'

Around us, the wind whistles, and scudding clouds cover the moon until what little light there was has turned to shade.

'Just don't ever leave me without saying goodbye,' Ryan says suddenly, violently. 'Don't leave me at all.'

Then he lowers his head to capture my mouth, and I turn and wrap my arms around his neck, letting all the words I can't bring myself to say to him, all the unspoken fears and longings inside me, speak of themselves in this one kiss.

There's that lick of fire along my nerves. But Ryan and I remain locked together, saying everything that can be said through touch alone; though what we are is pain, an impossibility.

He finally tears himself free against his will — unable to bear being with me, or away from me — and I place my fingers against his wounded mouth and take away the hurt, instantly.

'You're like fire and water,' he gasps against my hand. 'You've spoilt me for anyone else in this life, any life, you know that, don't you?'

'You'll get over me,' I reply sombrely. 'The way others have.'

I suddenly recall Gudrun's red-painted nails resting on Luc's arm; the way Luc's sapphire cufflinks struck fire from the lights beneath the dome of the Galleria, complementing the shade of her brilliant eyes exactly. *He tried to kill me*, I think wildly. *I can't still love him.* But, despite everything that's happened, I can't help the sudden stabbing pain I feel, wave after wave. I bury my face in Ryan's shoulder, rigid with grief for what Luc and I once were to each other. It might have been Luc here, in my arms now, if everything were different.

It's still so fresh for me. Luc has had all the time in the world, but for me, it *was* only yesterday that I went from being everything to him to being his quarry and his prey.

'He may be the Devil,' Ryan growls disbelievingly, placing his lips against my hair and binding me to him so fiercely it almost hurts, 'but he's still a moron. There's no getting over someone like you.'

I almost say them aloud then, the words Ryan longs to hear.

And I do love him, with every particle of my being, but it's a love complicated by so many things. And the words can't change the fact that we're already out of time; that it was too late for us before we even got started. So I choke them back and they remain unsaid.

'You deserve so much more than I can give you,' I whisper raggedly.

'Shut up,' he says fiercely, and the short, hard kiss he uses to silence me is almost brutal.

'What's the plan?' he sighs finally against my skin, the tone of his voice more normal, more gentle.

'I need to get my bearings,' I murmur thickly through the lingering vestiges of my grief and shame. 'Nuriel's close,

I can almost feel her. Luc couldn't have had time to move her; he was in such a hurry to get to me. I want you to take the dresses to Bianca, tell her I stopped to look at a bunch of statues on the way. And while you're distracting her with your wit, charm and superficial good looks,' I feel his lips curve against me, involuntarily, 'I'll take a look around.'

Ryan pulls back from me and looks down into my eyes. 'I can't tell you what you can or can't do,' he says gravely, 'because you'll do it anyway. You always do exactly as you please. But don't just vanish again because it's easier than trying to work things out. *Stay safe.* Come back to me as quickly as you can. My, uh, charms are a little rusty these days.'

He retrieves his fake spectacles and shoves them onto his face, blinking, and it startles a laugh out of me. I flick the bill of his cap so that it falls backwards off his head and he has to bend to retrieve it with a grunt, jamming it back onto his buzz-cut scalp.

'When you reach her, lose the cap, lose the glasses,' I say with a grin, 'and you'll soon have one of the world's most eligible rich girls eating out of your hand. She's beautiful, too. Stunning. It could be love at first sight.' I bite my lip. 'Which could be a good thing, in the circumstances ... a merciful thing.'

Ryan gives me a crooked smile. 'Good try, but I'm not biting. Lightning never strikes twice, not with me.' He pulls me close again. 'Come back?' he breathes against me, so tentatively that I wrap my arms around him tightly to contain his fear.

'You know I will,' I say fiercely. 'I'm not Carmen any more, I'm not Lela. It's not going to play out the same way.'

I turn and pick up the pretty dresses, then hand Ryan the backpack, which he puts on without even registering he's doing it. Then I take him by the hand and lead him out of the folly. Low lights set into the edges of the driveway point the way down to the guesthouse, and I feel time recommencing, reeling out of my hands the way it always does, like an angler's line.

Ryan's worn-down boot heels slip a little on the steep, slick surface. Below us, I see the front door of the guesthouse open, and there's a slender silhouette of a girl in the doorway, surrounded by a halo of electric light, looking up at us, just waiting.

As the driveway switches back and the guesthouse is momentarily lost to sight, I thrust the dress hangers into Ryan's hands and whisper, 'Be seeing you.'

Before he can frame a reply, I let my outline shred into a pale white mist, let myself break down, dissolve. Then I am ether, scattering into a billion pieces, soundlessly.

I see him step back in shock, looking around him wildly. 'God, Merce, I *hate* how you do that!' he exclaims.

It makes me laugh, and he flinches at the low sound that seems to come at him from everywhere and nowhere at once.

Trailing faint motes of light, I circle him once, twice — lighter than an embrace, than a kiss — before slipstreaming away into the night, down through the gardens of Villa Nicolin and through the bars of the tall iron gates that mark the lower boundary of the estate.

Down, down, to the waters of the lake.

I flow along the length of the narrow, private jetty, unseen and soundless. The boats moored there bump and creak as I head out over the water, skimming low, slicing through the rising wind that howls like a live thing and buffets the tall trees lining the shore. It's so very dark, but I'm still able to

discern the clouds that are once more building in the sky —
massive, unnatural, like the sails of ghostly galleons.

Something wicked this way comes. The elements herald
its very progress. I can feel in every particle of my being that
dark forces are on the move.

*I need to find Nuriel before Luc discovers I've already
left Milan.*

When I'm out over the water, I turn, a disembodied
zephyr, and scan my surroundings. And that's when it becomes
obvious that I've seen this place before; I once dreamt of it so
vividly I'd imagined that Luc and I inhabited one body, and
that all the evil he committed that night was wrought by my
own hand.

Luc was on the point of cutting Nuriel down with his
sword when she made one last, desperate, spiralling attempt
to pull away from him. In my mind's eye I see them again —
how her feint caught Luc by surprise. How he lost precious
seconds before turning and pursuing her. They had exploded
through the physical world — hunter and hunted — leaving
destruction and incandescence in their wake. It makes sense
to me now, how the main street of Moltrasio was destroyed;
all those people turned to ash. When angels and demons
collide, collateral damage is the only certainty.

In my dream, there was a vast estate by the water's
edge. A great house atop a hill, with a smaller outbuilding, a
private pier, at the base of the property. From the water, it's
clear that Villa Nicolin is the house I glimpsed at the moment
Nuriel dove down out of the sky. If Luc was acting in haste
that night, if he'd wanted to secure her, but also lay a trap
for anyone bent on saving her, the only place he could have
hidden her would be *in* the lake itself.

I rise high into the air and gaze down at the black body of water below without fear, without sickness, and see immediately where Nuriel is being held. There's a glow deep below the lake's surface, so faint it would be undetectable to human eyes. Though I'm as insubstantial as air, no more than a faint pocket of turbulence in the night, it still makes my soul shudder to see the quality of the light. It's numinous, incandescent, but subtly tainted. Not the pale blue luminescence of holy fire at its heart, but the creeping grey of corruption.

Demonlight.

It flares and subsides, pulsing within the dark waters of the lake like some monstrous, beating heart. Strange eddies play upon the lake's surface, as if the tide beneath runs counter to nature; is being moved by inexplicable forces.

I don't hesitate. I begin to narrow, to spin, funnelling all of my energy, my anger and fear, into a weapon that may be wielded. I make of myself an arrow, a spear, and fall towards the black surface of the water, piercing its dark membrane without sound, without raising so much as a ripple.

As I cleave through the water towards the depths below, all I can hear, with every fibre of my being, is screaming. It is the voice of a living soul in agony, in its death throes.

CHAPTER 8

I follow the sound of unspeakable anguish to its source, driving swiftly down through the water until the darkness begins to give way, begins to roll back at this crushing depth, as if the world has been drowned and the sun has been shackled to the filth upon the lake bed.

But what I find shackled there instead — to a tall, obelisk-shaped rock over a thousand feet down — is a bright, winged figure, her cloud of long, dark, wavy hair shifting loosely with the strange currents in the water. She's bound in chains of bright fire that crisscross her torn and bleeding figure. Her sleeveless robes are rent and despoiled, and the surface of her skin is marked by deep wounds that continually bleed light into the water.

I settle silently upon the lake bed at Nuriel's feet, stretched tauter than a membrane, just a collection of particles indistinguishable from the lake-bed ooze. An archangel usually comes wreathed in light and anger, like a thunderclap, a clarion call. But not me. The human world has taught me wariness and subtlety. I must take my sudden, murderous fury — that urge to transform into something vengeful, something monstrous, blazing with fire — and bury it deep within the mud and silt and sand that I've become.

Nuriel's entire figure is rigid, as if electrified. Her head is thrown back at an unnatural angle, eyes blank with anguish, her mouth stretched wide in that terrible, endless, wordless scream.

Though every part of me aches to release her immediately from her bonds, I know there's more to this than I'm seeing. It seems too easy that she's alone here. And I know what I saw through the water — demonsign. *To know your enemy is to have some measure of control over that enemy*: Luc himself taught me that. It's an irony that I'm using his own wisdom against him now.

Above me, Nuriel suddenly convulses. Light begins to stream out of her, off the surface of her skin, building around her in a dense cloud, and I almost rise, thinking in horror that it's her death I'm witnessing, that the energy of which she's made is dispersing, never to return. That I'm already too late.

But my inner voice, which is always one beat ahead of my waking self, whispers: *Wait, watch. It is demonlight.*

I freeze, waiting to see what form that light will take.

Nuriel's head falls forward suddenly, her body slackening within its fiery bonds, her screams choked into a fearful silence. The light coalesces rapidly, taking the shape of a winged man of such pale and mesmerising beauty that I can see who and what he once was: Remiel, one of the *elohim*.

He had worshipped Luc, been part of that pack of beautiful creatures that had hung off Luc's every word, lauding every crazy stunt he pulled. I know, because I was one of them myself, and I remember Remiel well; remember, too, his strange ability to sow discord wherever he went.

I see that Remiel worships Luc still, and that it has transformed him irrevocably. If anything, he's more beautiful, more otherworldly, than I remember him, with his pale skin and silver eyes, his long pale hair, also like spun silver. His heavily sculpted torso is bare to the waist, and he rolls his powerful shoulders as if they ache, his gleaming wings trailing curls of tainted energy into the water. He turns and scans his surroundings as if he can sense something, and I see that he is ... *shaking*. It's faint, but noticeable, the tremor in his formidable hands, and I wonder at it, for the cold should not trouble him as it does not trouble me.

There's a flaming mark at the base of his throat, like a scar. I realise what it is, because I carry something similar upon my left hand. It is the mark of the exile, the place where judgment was administered. Someone — perhaps even the Archangel Michael himself — once placed a hand at the base of Remiel's throat, a long time ago, and cast him down. Down to earth to be a demon.

Seeing nothing but rocks and mud, weed and silt, for miles in every direction, Remiel encircles Nuriel, his voice taunting. 'She's not coming for you; no one is. It's likely Luc already has her. Ananel returns now to finish you. And if you survive the punishments that await you at his hands, then I will return, and return, and return, until all that remains of you is a *scream*.'

He slurs the words, as if he's drunk. Then he launches himself slowly away through the water, almost clumsily for someone so lethal and beautiful. Immediately, everything seems darker.

When Remiel is finally lost to sight, I surge out of the filth at Nuriel's feet in my true form, mud cascading off my blazing figure, my blazing broadsword in my hand. And I cut her free, her bonds shrivelling, blackening and dissolving the instant my weapon meets them. She falls forward into my arms as my sword vanishes into the palm of my hand. Her wings, like mine, instantly shred into nothingness. She lacks even the energy to remain upright in the water. Her open wounds seep a constant light, like blood.

The instant I touch her, I know what has been done to her. *Possession*; a sustained possession of the worst kind that has infiltrated every particle of her soul, assaulted even her consciousness. First Remiel, then Ananel, the cycle repeated over and over until all Nuriel craved was death, or the death of time itself.

It is the pattern that Luc himself must have set so long ago when he first came across this Eden; the pattern that repeats itself in the world he walks today: human and demon continually feeding each other's worst impulses. When we *elohim* were created, there was no rape, no torture, no enslavement, no war. But Luc saw the thing in our design that was both gift and curse: that some of us were created male, some female — the pattern repeated in angel, in man, in beast. And he exploited that flaw for his gain, pitting man against woman, against beast, against world, from the very first.

Nuriel has been missing for days. Days in which Ananel and Remiel have tortured her to the point of death with every means at their disposal. For angels and demons do not abide by treaties of war; we follow no accords regarding the welfare of our hostages. We are black and white, all or nothing. And this is the result: broken angels, like broken people. In everything, a dark symmetry.

I gather her tenderly to me, preparing to bear her swiftly back towards the surface. But she's like a wraith in my arms, impossible to keep hold of.

Mercy. I feel the ghostly whisper of her voice in my mind. *They cannot abide the cold, having turned away from first light. Avenge me.*

I tilt her face towards mine, but her eyes are closed and her outline is wavering. She seems like a creature of mist, more insubstantial than the water we're suspended in. I know that she's succumbing to her wounds, unravelling. It would have been kinder if her captors had killed her outright.

Desperation makes me roar, 'Nuriel, if this is some kind of ploy to get me to do your dirty work, I'm done taking orders. *Avenge yourself.* You stood by and watched as Luc and Michael used me as some kind of live bargaining chip. You stood by and watched as Luc cast me out. *You owe me.* You want to take Remiel and Ananel down? *You do it yourself.'*

At my words, a small frown appears between her straight, dark brows. Her wide-set eyes flicker open, her outline solidifying in my arms. 'I don't owe you anything,' she replies, struggling out of my grasp, focusing with difficulty on my face. 'Not a damned thing!'

She drifts before me, skin palely gleaming, her long, wavy hair a dark cloud about her face, like a drowned girl. Her voice is very faint as she says accusingly, 'I *warned* you about Luc. I warned you, and you ignored me.'

'He was a shit,' I agree mildly. 'He's an even greater shit now. I really should have listened.'

My words cause her to blaze suddenly incandescent with rage and pain, the way I mean her to.

'*Should have listened?*' she shrieks. 'You're responsible for what was done to me. *You.* All your doing. No degree of friendship is worth *violation.*'

I shrug. 'It can't have been worse than what I've had to endure over the past few centuries. You're alive, aren't you? It was nasty and brutish, but at least it was *short.*'

I hate hurting her like this, but the Archangel Michael himself taught me that anger can be channelled; it can be used when there's nothing left in your soul to draw upon.

Nuriel launches herself at me through the water, screaming like a banshee of myth, her fingers curled into talons, blazing bright.

I catch her by her narrow wrists before she can take out my eyes, and murmur into her face, 'Now that you're feeling more like yourself again, what do you mean they cannot abide the cold, having turned away from first light?'

Nuriel seems to sag beneath my hands, and the light of her grows more tolerable to my eyes.

'I meant what I said,' I challenge softly. 'I'm done with riddles, with being pushed around. You want vengeance? Then tell me what I need to know. The rules have changed since I've been gone. Give me something I can use against them.'

Nuriel hugs herself tightly, her eyes wide and unseeing. 'I think it was the only thing that kept me alive,' she says, her voice thready and strange. 'Luc set two of them to watch over me, but it was always only one of them ... at a time ...' Her fingers fly up to her face in horror and she whispers through them, 'They cannot withstand the cold for long, not like we can, because they chose to turn away from first light ...'

I feel my eyes widen in comprehension. 'In a way that *I* did not; for the cold troubles me not at all.'

Nuriel nods, hanging her head, her hair drifting ghostly about her in the water. 'It felt like a lifetime before I worked it out. While one of them took me apart, piece by piece, from the inside,' her voice flies up the scale in anguish, 'the other always went away for a time, weakened by the cold of the lake water, but always returning ...'

'Strong again,' I finish. 'Renewed.'

It makes sense now, how Remiel seemed so clumsy, almost punch drunk, as he veered away through the water.

Nuriel glimpses something behind me. 'Ananel,' she gasps, and I see death and madness in her gaze. 'He returns. *He returns.*'

I spin in the water and see a pinpoint of brightness in the distance, growing larger second by second. He's moving swiftly. We don't have long, if he hasn't seen me already.

'*Hide,*' I tell Nuriel, pushing her down towards the murk of the lake bed. 'For once in your life, don't stand there clothed in glory, the way all of you do, dazzling each other with your rank, your pomp, your powers. Be like the water, be like mud — *invisible.* I'll take care of the rest.'

Her expression is wild as she scatters into motes of light, fading away almost instantly. One second I'm there, too, and the next I'm gone, indistinguishable from my surroundings.

Ananel surges towards me, bare-chested and heavily muscled, sleek and predatory, a gleaming dagger with a short, lethal blade clenched between his teeth. Silver bubbles slipstream through his long, midnight hair, the ends of his luminous wings, past the burning scar that lies along the top of his hip, as he sweeps overhead. I see him freeze in disbelief when he spies the rock to which Nuriel was bound, now empty of all life.

But he's stronger than Remiel was, no longer punch drunk from the cold, and he can sense something, something close, because he grasps his weapon in his right hand, turning and calling out sharply, 'Nuriel?'

He spins in the water, his shrewd grey eyes scanning the drowned landscape before he hisses, 'Don't make me hunt you down, or you'll wish yourself already dead. We have been greedy, Remiel and I, in keeping your sweetness to ourselves. But, *sister*' — at the word of endearment, I have to smother a gasp of revulsion — 'if you do not show yourself now, I will throw you to the legions at my command so that your agony may be made *infinite.*'

I flicker into sight just out of striking distance, and Ananel smiles, though it does not reach the darkness in his grey eyes.

I drift before him like a drowned girl, my hair a dark cloud around my shoulders, my luminous robes torn and trailing, bleeding light from the wounds that crisscross my body: all fake, all props. But I see from Ananel's expression that he believes without question he's looking at Nuriel, for I've made myself a simulacrum of her, a perfect copy, down to the tiny, gleaming defence wounds along the inside of her fingers, the madness in her eyes.

'Be merciful,' I plead in her sweet, high voice as I drift there with my hands outstretched in supplication. 'For I always loved you. Even after all you've done to me — I love you still.'

Ananel's eyes widen for a moment, though he's quick to disguise his shock. He lowers his blade uncertainly, the deadly weapon vanishing into the palm of his hand. Love is a thing he has not felt for aeons. A demon like he is, denied the kind of love that once surrounded him as freely as the air, must crave it like a drug.

He knows as well as I do that Nuriel doesn't lie. She can't. It's not the way she's wired. She's quick-witted and resourceful, but also gentle, true and faithful. Her one flaw, if you can call it that, is that she possesses no capacity for deceit. I see him thinking all of this, hardly daring to believe.

'You ... *love* ... me?' he whispers. 'Even after ...?'

'I will give myself to you freely, and in love,' I murmur, my dark eyes huge and haunted in my heart-shaped face, 'if you promise not to bind me to that rock again. I shall be yours, yours forever, if you keep me safe from that animal Remiel, if you keep me close.'

'What are you asking?' Ananel says as I drift closer to him, tantalisingly close. Close enough to touch my lips to his.

He is between me and the rock now. He is one of Luc's fiercest *daemonium*, one of the original hundred who fell, more than my match in every way — but I think I actually see uncertainty in his grey eyes.

'Take me,' I murmur, mere centimetres from his mouth. My voice is low with a desire I do not feel, and my eyes never leave his for an instant, the way one must keep watch upon a venomous snake that is poised to strike. 'Keep me,' I whisper. 'Kiss me.'

He reaches out, almost despite himself, and cups the side of my face with one hand before tangling his fingers into the roots of my hair and pulling me close. Our lips meet and his mouth opens over mine, and his kiss is like a numbing, drugging venom that is turning me to lead. He is heat and corruption and a voracious need, every dark impulse clothed in a staggering beauty.

I can't keep my eyes open. There's a heaviness in my limbs, a growing paralysis, and as he deepens his devastating kiss,

I feel myself changing, the false face and form I've assumed sloughing away like dead skin. I can't hold it, can't hold any thought or feel anything except his mouth on mine and the terrible heat and power of him. My stupid plan — I can feel it all rapidly going to hell, as defiance, my will, seep away beneath the relentlessness of his mouth, his touch. Somehow I can see everything that he's ever done, felt, thought, caused, over aeons. I know him for what he is, and he is truly a monster.

Ananel thrusts me away from him suddenly, though he keeps one hand buried in the roots of my own straight, dark hair. I open my eyes with difficulty. His own eyes are wide with shock and a growing recognition as he holds me away from him.

'Who —' he gasps.

Before he can say anything more, or begin to utter my name — my true name, which can be used as a means of control, as a weapon against me — there's a blazing short sword in my left hand, a twisted, lethal blade with pale blue fire playing across its length. Without hesitation, with the speed of reflex born of a terrible fear, a soul-deep disgust, I drive it straight through his throat and into the rock behind him, pinning him there.

'H—' he starts to say, his grey eyes wide and staring as the dark matter of him, his dark energy, flows rapidly out of him into the water, like blood. I am covered in it and imagine I feel it burning me, like acid.

The light of accusation in Ananel's gaze is dimming as Nuriel reappears at my side. I only realise now how badly I'm shaking. I've just taken a life; a terrible perversion to be sure, but still a *life*. The first I have ever reaped.

As we watch Ananel begin to unravel before our eyes, both our faces are filled with horror at the thing that I've become. At once *elohim*, but also liar; seductress; killer.

When Nuriel and I break the choppy surface of the lake, there's a small boat maybe thirty feet away, buffeted by the waves, motor running. It makes straight for us as I pull Nuriel free of the strange currents that seek to hold us below. I recognise Bianca St Alban at the tiller, in a dark rain slicker, her sleek, dark hair bundled into a heavy plait that lies over one shoulder. Ryan is balanced in the bow.

We wait, drifting just above the waterline, our feet not quite meeting the surface. I see awe mingled with fear on Bianca's face as the runabout draws closer. There's recognition, too. She *did* see me that night at Atelier Re, the way she'd claimed to. I had somehow pulled free of Irina Zhivanevskaya's body, just for a moment, and she caught a glimmer of me, a glimpse.

I tighten my grip on Nuriel, murmuring in her ear so that she understands, through the haze of her pain, what I'm asking her to do. As the boat moves alongside us, we make ourselves wingless and human-sized, so as not to overwhelm Bianca and Ryan. We wear the simple, sleeveless raiment that we always effect when we are ourselves.

Ryan leans out to help Nuriel aboard, and looks as if he's going to be sick when he takes in the number and severity of her injuries. No mortal could survive what she has survived.

Bianca spreads a blanket hastily along one bench seat and Nuriel lies down upon it silently, curling herself into a tight ball before closing her eyes. The light of her dims, fading until her skin is almost matte, almost human, and only I can see the luminosity that seeps slowly out through her pores.

So quickly that none except me caught the shift, she has changed her outward appearance so that she's wearing the same pale blue puffy down jacket, blue jeans and snow boots I first saw her in, outside Atelier Re. The same Fair Isle knitted cap is jammed low over her long, wavy, dark hair. She looks almost peaceful lying there, as if she's asleep. But I know that it's a sham, that she's holding all her hurt inside. Her wounds are still there, disguised beneath her unremarkable veneer. Though her eyes are closed, her suffering is so tangible, it's leaching into the air.

Ryan holds out his hand to me, but I shake my head. His eyes go flat and he is instantly wary and still. 'Don't,' he says fiercely.

'I need to take care of one more thing,' I plead. 'I'll explain later. Get her back to shore? Keep her safe? *For me?*'

He nods tightly, muttering, 'Isn't it always? But yeah, sure. Whatever.'

Before he can say anything more, before I can lose my nerve, I dive back below the surface of the water, shedding shape and colour as I go.

I'm almost too late.

Remiel is already at the rock, witnessing the last vestiges of Ananel's energy melting away into the dark water. In seconds, all that remains is the blazing weapon I used to kill him, its twisted, lethal blade still embedded in the stone, almost up to the hilt.

Remiel pulls the weapon free, trying to determine its make and maker, cursing as it flares brightly in his hand before it, too, scatters into nothingness. And I'm reminded, suddenly, that only the one who created such a weapon can hold it.

He gives no sign that he can sense me. But he's wily, and his power has been fully renewed. As I drift closer, he turns suddenly, his great hands reaching through the water, twisting into me, the stuff of which I'm made, seeking to hold me fast though he can't see me. I twist and struggle, as invisible as the current, as he roars, '*Appare!*' *Show yourself!*

And despite everything that I am, everything I've regained, his voice is like a terrible invocation that cannot be disobeyed. I am suddenly there before him, in the water.

For a moment, we are eye to burning eye. I glare into pupils the colour of molten silver. The eyes of an animal, or a ghoul.

One of his great hands is around my neck and I can't pull free of his fingers; it's like they're knotted in me, as if he's merging into me the way he forced himself upon Nuriel, and all I can feel, hear, see, is *pain.*

With his other hand, he keeps my slender wrists imprisoned upright between our two bodies, so that it's impossible to manifest any kind of blade against him. If I do, he will use my own weapon against me.

I see the moment of recognition dawn in his eyes. His lips draw away from his teeth, beginning to form my name, as Ananel tried to. The pain in me seems to treble, to explode. If he utters my name, I will be powerless to do anything. The punishment that Ananel promised Nuriel will be mine.

Remiel still holds my wrists imprisoned. He's too close for me to use a blade, too close.

Time seems to speed up and slow down all at once as I watch his mouth form the first syllable: 'Han—'

Hell roars open in my head, as though every part of me is rejecting the name that is as much a part of me as the light.

My soul, my very soul, is tearing apart at the sound of my own name.

Suddenly, as though answering my need for a weapon, there's a gun in my hands: sleek and heavy, with the look of a semi-automatic about it. A perfect replica of the real thing, requiring no speed, no strength, no *finesse* to wield. Only proximity and dumb luck.

I am fear, I am disgust, as I force the muzzle up underneath Remiel's jaw, then pull the trigger. A single shot, the bullet as deadly as any cutting surface I ever devised. It blows him away, and a blast wave of heat and energy and dark matter knocks me to the lake floor.

When I open my eyes, there's nothing left of him. All that heat, all that venom, that negative energy, already returned to the universe, already dispersed.

I stare at the gun in my hand, catching a rivulet of blue flame playing quickly across its surface before it disappears. Just a single lick of fire, the only sign it is not a weapon of this world. Then I let the gun fall from my trembling fingers, revolted, and it, too, disperses, melting away into the water.

CHAPTER 9

My head breaks the surface of the seething water near the jetty, and I see Ryan waiting for me, sitting with his back against one of the pylons, his cap pulled down low against the wind, the hood of his sweater pulled tight over its crown, knees up under his chin, just staring out over the lake like a statue. He is the living embodiment of everything that's good about this world, and something catches in me when I see him.

I pull myself out of the water so silently that he gives a yell when he realises what he's seeing.

'Christ, Mercy,' he says as I lie down beside him in my true form, but human-sized. '*What happened to you?*' He bends low over me, but even then the wind rips the words out of his mouth. 'It's been hours. It's almost midnight. I've been out of my head ...'

I crawl into his arms and just lie there for a while, my bone-dry skin gleaming white-hot in the absolute absence of light. There's a dark, building belly of cloud overhead, roiling like smoke, like a live thing. I can't seem to put my horror into words; at what was almost done to me, what *I* did. Without hesitation.

I'm a killer. Only chance separates me from the creatures that Ananel and Remiel became.

'What happened?' Ryan insists, turning my face up to his.

When I still don't reply, unable to force the words past my lips for fear I will see revulsion on his face in place of that steady, anchoring love, Ryan stands suddenly, bends down and swings me into his arms.

'*Let me,*' he says fiercely, looking down at me as I struggle. 'You think it's been easy for me to let you just walk away? Help me salvage a little pride here. It scares me when you're like this, all frozen, with that look on your face. Don't shut me out. Talk to me, damn it. *Come back to me*, the way you said you would.'

I stare at my hands, imagining the blood of demons on them.

Ryan strides down the jetty and up a set of stone stairs, talking rapidly as he goes. 'You know the thing that gets me the most? Is that you don't actually *need* me. In this entire scenario, I — am — completely — unnecessary.'

He's almost roaring the words, and I know I deserve his anger. He waits for me faithfully, holding out for love and forever after, and what do I do? Act as if I can neither see him nor hear him, like he's invisible.

'You're necessary,' I croak, so quietly that he snaps, '*What?*'

'Necessary,' I repeat through the strange knot in my throat. 'You're necessary. To me. Without you, I'd go mad. Without you, I'd have no compass.'

His arms around me suddenly seem less rigid, but his voice is still angry. 'Welcome back.'

He crosses the deserted street running in front of the enormous cast-iron lower gates to the St Alban estate. Still holding me off the ground, he punches the buzzer set into an intercom panel identical to the one at the villa's main entrance. No one demands that we state our business this time; the huge gates just swing open, shutting smoothly behind us once we're through.

It's only a short walk to the guesthouse, which is no longer ablaze with light. Ryan sets me gently down on my feet at the front door. But before he can ring the bell, Bianca yanks the door open, her pale blue eyes tracking me fearfully as Ryan and I cross the threshold.

The house is overheated, the air heavy with the scent of burning incense as if this were the inside of a church.

Ryan pushes his hood back, stuffs his cap into a jacket pocket, as Bianca mutters, '*I remember you.* From Atelier Re. You were the ... the ... woman I saw. I wasn't imagining things. You're *real*.'

She circles in front of me, slender and slightly above average in height, with an oval face and dark, perfectly arched brows, light olive skin. In her simple, grey crew-neck sweater and black skinny jeans, her face free of make-up, feet bare, dark, glossy hair still bound in a heavy plait, she looks even younger today than the spoilt-looking couture client I remember.

She stretches a hand out tentatively, as if she would touch me, before catching herself and lowering it. 'Tomaso is literally *freaking out*,' she murmurs, unable to take her eyes off my shifting, blurring outline, the curls of energy that I give off into the surrounding dimness. 'After I told him I'd take care of the security at this end on my own, he's had me checking in every ten minutes. Now that you're both back inside, maybe he'll get off my case. She's ... through there,' she adds hesitantly, pointing down the long, narrow hall. 'Excuse me while I call him.'

She flips her plait over one shoulder and hurries into a room just to the left of the front door. I hear her lift the handset of a phone.

Ryan takes my hand firmly in his as we head down the corridor, which is lit only by lamplight. I see several more rooms facing onto the hallway from either side, each generously proportioned and elegantly furnished, with modern pieces interleaved with antiques and arresting artworks. The wind rattles the floor-to-ceiling windows that dominate the lake-facing rooms, shrieks at the skylights set at intervals into the unusually pitched roof.

We stop at the end of the hall and gaze into a vast informal dining area. It's separated by a wall of glass from an even larger outside pool and entertainment area that overlooks the lake below. Beyond the dining area is another short hallway that peters out into darkness. One level down from the dining area, accessed by a set of open ironwork stairs, is a sunken living room filled with broad, comfortable couches and groupings of lamps, games tables and armchairs. I see stereo equipment; shelving overflowing with reading material, records, compact discs and board games; a television the size of a small billboard; a vintage pinball machine.

More stairs lead down from the recessed living area into darkness, and it's clear that there's more to the house than meets the eye, that there must be yet more rooms, more levels, below ground. But the wondrous, mazelike steel-and-glass house is nothing in comparison to the tall, pale, dark-haired figure lying on a couch in the centre of the sunken living room, the faintest telltale gleam coming off the surface of her skin, the ends of her hair, her ridiculous knitted hat, her clothes, her booted feet.

I see that her eyes are wide open. She's staring up through the clear skylight above her head as if she's communicating with spirits. I follow the line of her gaze and watch the unnatural progress of the dark clouds that have swallowed the moon, the entire shining firmament in which it resides.

Ryan can read my incredible tension and he squeezes my hand, indicating wordlessly that I should go to Nuriel, that what he and I have to say to each other can wait. As I walk away from him towards the stairs, he draws out a seat at the dining table with a loud scrape of chair legs, and I hear him unzip his leather jacket. I turn my head for a moment, get a glimpse of the screen of his mobile phone flaring into life, before I begin to descend. The wind booms hollowly as I get closer and closer to the one I once considered my dearest friend in life.

Nuriel shifts her shattered gaze to mine as I settle lightly on the edge of the couch beside her. We look at each other for a long time, unsmiling, almost in disbelief at finding ourselves together like this, after all that's happened.

She breaks the silence first, whispering, 'You know what the hardest thing was? That you never recognised me. Not once, in all those years, all those times I watched over you. I could see *you*, but it was like you were a witless, soulless ... wraith. It was only when you were Irina, and I looked into your eyes on Via Borgonuovo, that I saw ... recognition. You can't know how that felt. To finally have confirmation that some part of *you* had survived your long ordeal.'

'Raphael did his work too well,' I reply quietly. 'If Luc had not begun seizing the Eight, one by one, I would still be trapped in the manner Raphael devised centuries ago.'

I take her hand and she grips mine fiercely for a second, before the pressure of her hold slackens.

'He loved you,' she murmurs, her eyes huge with pain in her pale face. 'He always has.'

'So I'm told,' I reply quietly, seeing Raphael the way he was: sable-eyed, dark-haired, olive-skinned, ready laughter curving the lines of his beautiful mouth.

I get a sudden flash of true memory: of Raphael's hands upon me, his voice warning me against Luc's towering vanity, his terrible pride; how, in the end, I would be hurt. I must not have listened. For another memory follows quickly on the heels of the first: of Raphael facing me across a great distance. He was standing just behind Michael's shoulder when Luc uttered those final, fatal words, my left hand clenched tightly in his right: *Then, as an act of faith — of goodwill, shall we call it — take that which is most precious to me. I permit it.*

And, as if I'm actually there, somehow reliving the moment, I suddenly see how Raphael's eyes flew wide, how he divined Luc's intent before any of us could have. See, too, that he was unable to act in time to prevent what took place. He and Michael had both started forward — like sprinters leaping away at the starter's gun — trying to catch hold of me. But I was already gone, already lost, the instant Luc cast me down with every ounce of his strength.

How blind I was then, how blind. So undeserving of the love, the web of protection, these *elohim* wove about me all the long years after.

Nuriel turns her head away, curling over in agony, and the past instantly dissolves. 'I imagined,' she gasps, 'that when we met again face to face, and you knew me for who I am, everything would be all right again in my world. It would all be the way it was, it would all be *fixed*.'

She gives a laugh that is one-part madness, and as she turns her face back to mine, I see with horror that she's *weeping*, the way I've learnt to do.

Tears of light course down her face as she cries, 'I'm not as strong as you are. I don't think I can survive this. For years, I watched you suffer in this human world as an animal suffers — with just your native arrogance, your indomitable will, to keep you alive. And yet, you remain; you are essentially yourself. Shining and whole, despite the cruelties you have suffered, all the unspeakable things that befell you. As strong and fast, as fierce, as you ever were.'

As she speaks, her form ripples, changes, and she lies before me hatless, bare-limbed in her rent and sleeveless shift. My hands fly to my mouth as I catalogue her wounds that are no longer hidden from sight. There are the marks of demonic weapons upon her flesh, terrible burns; it's as if she's been mauled by wild animals. She's bleeding light, scarcely alive, and I'm so shocked, I can't think or speak or move.

She rears up and grabs hold of my upper arms, her self-loathing so evident and so potent, I wish I could take it all upon myself.

'I want to die,' she pleads. '*Die*. Or at least be granted the kind of mercy you've had to endure — freedom from memory, from all comprehension. Teach me how it's possible to forget, for I can no longer heal myself. I have lost the art. I feel no forgiveness, no love. I'm *empty*.' Harsh sobs rack her gleaming, bleeding form in earnest as she falls back from me.

I place my hands on either side of her face and feel her wildness slowly begin to abate. 'I'm a strange hybrid these days,' I whisper. 'Corrupted, debased, weakened. Luc said so himself. You don't want to be like me.'

'And yet you slew Ananel,' she murmurs, almost accusingly. 'I saw you do it.'

'And Remiel, too,' I reply fiercely.

Her eyes fly to mine.

'He is finished,' I say. 'He will never trouble you again.'

Her gaze grows unfocused. 'Except in nightmare,' she whispers, 'for he will always be alive there.'

'Stalking the corridors of your dreams?' I murmur. 'Yes, I know. But that is all they are: dreams. Just distant echoes.'

I speak more confidently than I'm feeling, for my dreams have always troubled me, have always seeped beyond the boundaries of unreal into *real*.

I stroke her dark, curling hair away from her forehead. 'I can't heal those kinds of wounds,' I say softly. 'Only time can do that. To be in this world is to suffer cruelty and beauty every minute of every hour. But you just hold on to the beauty and try to let the rest of it ... I don't know ... wash away. That's what I've learnt. You need simply to *be*. You need beauty and stillness and time. That's all the wisdom that I, who was never wise, can offer you.'

She closes her eyes and, little by little, as I continue to comfort her, the physical marks of her suffering melt away, until, on the outside, she seems as glorious and perfect as she ever was. But underneath, something's shifted, something's given way, and she will never be quite the same again. It's a feeling I myself know only too well: how life itself is an affliction that can harden you like a diamond.

'How I've missed you,' she says raggedly. 'You should never have left us, left *me*. Not like that. It changed everything.'

She opens her eyes and they seem a little clearer now, a little calmer. 'As damaged as you claim to be, you've done what few *elohim* have achieved while sane, whole and in the fullness of their power: you've taken down two of Luc's inner circle. While the lower-order *daemonium* can always be ... replenished,' her mouth twists in revulsion, 'in a way that the *elohim* and *malakhim* may not, Remiel and Ananel were irreplaceable to Luc. Pray he does not know it yet, but you've hurt him, you've struck back.' She sits up slowly, the shadow of a smile upon her lips. 'You are a force for good these days, whether you like it or not.'

She grasps my hands tightly, her voice urgent. 'Free Selaphiel. He was the first to be taken. I *saw* the place in Remiel's mind, in Ananel's — they could not keep it from me when they, when they ...' She grips my fingers harder. 'It was the place you took yourself to ... to die. *That* is where they hold him. In an empire of death, ruled by bones. Underground. Do you remember it?' she finishes hesitantly.

I recoil from her, horror-struck, as I get a flash of that place, located far, far beneath an old human city. Above ground, the living had scratched out a mean, jammed existence, infecting each other with their uproars and grievances and foul pestilences. Below ground, there had been a blessed, blessed silence, but also chambers and passageways filled with water and putrescence, piled high with the jumbled bones of the human dead: skulls and femurs, finger bones and vertebrae, fat, hair, skin, gristle, all mixed and intermingled.

The worldly remains of *thousands*. The scent of death that lay so heavily upon me, it lay upon that place, too. The carrion stench of it had seemed to reach its fingers up through the city and beyond. It was what drew me there in the first instance, that smell of death. To the creature of nightmare that I was — a burnt and blasted thing, barely alive, a being composed solely of ash and anguish — it had seemed a fitting place to end it all.

But the Eight had run me to ground there, at long last. And They'd forced me to *live*.

'I see it even now,' I whisper. 'If Hell had a gateway, it would be that place. But I cannot recall the name of the human city it formed part of. It's as if the name has been burnt out of my memory ... by me? By others? Who can say?'

'Paris,' Nuriel replies harshly. 'The Eight found you in Paris. At Cimetière des Innocents. Ananel and Remiel were with Luc when he located the burial chamber where you'd lain only hours before. But nothing of you remained, and Luc's fury was terrible as he tore apart gravesite after gravesite, chamber after chamber, looking for traces of you, unleashing a powerful plague into the ground water, into the very soil, to sicken all of Paris itself. It is what he does best, after all — come at us from below, from the dark.'

I try to pull away from Nuriel, but her grip is surprisingly strong and she will not let me go.

'Selaphiel is held in a place bound by bones,' she tells me. 'If *I* am any measure, he will have suffered even more terribly. I would do it, I would save him, but I am a husk. I am spent. *Free our brother.* Call it your debt to me. And if, in so doing, you are able to hurt Luc further, then all to the good. Thinking you almost within his grasp, vengeance has driven

Luc to move against the Eight now, after all these years. Punish Luc in the same spirit. Avenge me. But also yourself.'

There's a loud sneeze above us, a muffled curse, and Nuriel makes a startled movement, eyes wild again, as if she would draw a weapon, or take flight. I turn to see Bianca's and Ryan's shadowy outlines huddled high above us, on the stairs, listening intently.

Nuriel turns back to me. '*Free him,*' she insists. 'And if you see Michael, tell him I broke when I could not bend; that I could do no more, and I am sorry. It may yet turn out to be true ...'

I and the mortal watchers on the stairs are buffeted by a blast wave of heat and energy as Nuriel grows brighter than the stars for an instant, before scattering into a billion pieces. And then she's gone, like a vision, or a dream.

Ryan drops down onto the couch first, then Bianca lowers herself, cautiously, on my other side, her arms crossed tightly against her chest.

'I'm sorry, but I couldn't help ... eavesdropping,' she says. 'Don't blame Ryan — he tried to stop me, but I couldn't stay away. You have no idea what you look like together, do you? You seem so powerful, so beautiful ...'

'And if I hadn't sneezed,' Ryan says, disgusted with himself, wrapping his arms around my frozen form and pulling me to him, 'maybe I wouldn't have scared her away like that. She probably had a lot more to tell you.'

'She had to go,' I murmur into his shoulder. 'She needs to heal. And you probably overheard what she wants me to do. Go to Paris, kill more demons.'

I start to shake then.

Ryan tips my face up to his, saying gently, 'I'm sorry I gave you a hard time when you came up out of the water. It's hard for me to understand that other side of you, the, uh, freaky side. Whatever you did tonight, down there in the lake, it was justified. Seeing Nuriel that way reminded me so much of Lauren when you found her, of how helpless I felt. You're not helpless.'

'I'm a killer,' I whisper, appalled.

'A demon killer,' Ryan clarifies, struggling to sound as if he's entirely unfazed by the idea.

'Which, by definition,' Bianca interjects hesitantly, 'is entirely acceptable.'

She draws her legs up onto the couch and sits cross-legged, facing us. She takes a deep breath before meeting my eyes. 'Ryan's already filled me in on a little of your … situation. You and he need to get to Paris, and I've got a way of getting you there quickly and discreetly. As stupid as it may sound to you, I want to help, if you'll accept it.'

'You're not coming to Paris,' I tell Ryan immediately, looking up into his face.

'Am too,' he retorts. 'I *want* to see Paris. Thanks to you, I finally left home, left that little box I'd carved out for myself, and I don't want to go back.' He grins at me. 'Plus, I've decided, after further thought, that I'm not completely unnecessary. My role is to provide cover for you.'

'*Cover?*' I can't hide my incredulity and draw back from him, but he tightens his arms to halt my progress.

'You're fairly crap at acting human on a good day,' he says, a gleam lighting his eyes. 'Consider me your veneer of normality.'

'I was supposed to get Nuriel out of here, then *leave*,' I remind him quietly. 'And you were supposed to run screaming from the freaky girl with the freaky powers at the first sign of trouble. That was the plan.'

'Plans change,' he murmurs. 'Until I met you, I was the guy most likely to get a football scholarship and marry Brenda Sorensen. In that exact order.'

'And Félix and I were supposed to be on our honeymoon in the Serengeti right about now, but here's where the story ends,' Bianca adds forlornly, looking down at her bare feet. 'Which leads me right back to my point. I can have one of our jets fuelled and ready for take-off at daybreak. We have a private hangar. You'll get into Le Bourget by mid-morning. It's that easy. You just have to say the word.' Her gaze flicks back to mine.

'No one's going to expect an archangel to travel by Gulfstream,' Ryan says almost gleefully. 'A Gulfstream with *two* coffee makers on board.'

'Honestly, Ryan,' Bianca says, half-appalled.

He grins. 'You can always trust me to zero in on the important stuff. And yes,' he continues, seeing the stony expression on my face, 'you *are* being railroaded. We worked it all out.'

'But I don't *want* to go to Paris,' I wail.

Bianca leans forward. 'But you *have* to,' she insists.

I turn my head and glare into her eyes so fiercely that she actually scrambles backwards across the couch, banging into the armrest at the end, her hands raised before her defensively.

Ryan pulls me more tightly into him, steadying me, his arms crossed about my waist. 'Hear her out, please,' he whispers into my hair.

Bianca sits straighter, tucking her legs back beneath her before shoving her heavy plait back over one shoulder. 'I see certain ... symmetries between us,' she says falteringly. 'We've both been utterly taken in, utterly betrayed, by the most toxic and despicable ...' She looks down, takes a shuddering, composing breath, before her startlingly blue eyes flick back up to mine, a bright sheen of tears in them. 'People I have known, places I love that hold only the happiest memories for me ... they've been swept away. They only exist now *in my head*.'

I realise from her unfocused gaze that she's speaking of her old life with Félix, but also of her life here. She's been twice bereaved, in such a short space of time.

'I know that you understand what I'm talking about. And I don't know what we did to deserve having our ... our ... worlds ripped apart,' she says, her voice rising in anguish, 'but you're what I wish I could be. You have the power to *hurt* the person who did this to you. Don't underestimate the healing qualities of simple vengeance, of retaliation, when you are absolutely in the right. God, what I wouldn't give ...'

She clenches her hands into fists upon her knees before something seems to recall her to our presence. Her voice is almost normal, almost calm, as she says, 'The St Alban Group is primarily known these days as a financial services powerhouse. But centuries ago, we built our fortune upon shipping, and we still have a global logistics arm that even *Satan himself* could not rival. We move bullion, livestock, even weaponry, all around the globe daily, point to point. Getting a guy and his ...' her expression is nonplussed, '... freaky girlfriend into Paris would be child's play.'

'A freaky girlfriend with no papers,' I remind them both with an edge to my voice, remembering the small, dark booklet amongst Ryan's things. 'The sovereignty I hail from doesn't issue those.'

'One passenger on the manifest,' Bianca says brightly, refusing to be cowed by what I represent. 'We get the cabin crew to turn a blind eye, or we minimise the number of crew, smuggle you on board somehow —'

'We wouldn't need to,' Ryan interrupts softly. 'Mercy can take care of getting herself on and off unseen.'

'One passenger it is then.'

Bianca digs around in a pocket of her jeans and fishes out an embossed business card, holds it out to me with shaking fingers. I don't take it, and her hand almost drops at the palpable hostility I'm giving off.

'You act as if it's already decided,' I say menacingly. 'Given my troubled history, I dislike feeling like I'm being *cornered*.'

'I warned you about that,' Ryan tells Bianca ruefully. 'She doesn't like being told what to do. The counsellor at Paradise High used to tell me I had issues with authority, but she ...' He gives me a little shake. 'She'd have to be off the charts.'

Bianca's voice is small as she continues holding the card out to me. 'The choice is yours. But if I wanted to twist the knife into someone who deserved it, and a person offered me the means of getting from A to B to Z just on the strength of a phone call, I'd already be there, twisting the damned knife.' Her voice drops further so that it's barely audible. 'When we're young, they teach us about "turning the other cheek", that vengeance isn't a valid response. But this is *Lucifer* we're talking about, Mercy. To save someone you love from him could never be wrong.'

I take the card, finally. It has the words *StA Global Logistics* embossed across the top and a logo featuring a galleon in full sail centred over a pair of crossed keys. There's a single telephone number printed below, commencing with a plus symbol. The card offers no useful information to a casual reader.

'That's the family hotline,' Bianca says. 'Anyone wants to move a lover, a vintage car, a carton full of contraband for our own personal use, we call the wizards that man this number. I'm not saying I approve or disapprove, I'm just saying that's how it goes. Borders are porous, and all borders can be worked — it's almost a family motto. I'll get you into Paris, and this is a free pass, if you need it, to get out of there again. You just say where and when, and it'll happen like magic.' She blinks rapidly and her eyes grow shiny again. 'Just quote *Crespigny19A* when asked — the name of Félix's favourite dog and our apartment number on the Upper East Side. Stupidly easy to crack, but I haven't got around to changing it yet. Something that will shortly be rectified.'

I hand the card back to Bianca and she looks down at it, crushed. 'So you won't do it?' she says in a small voice. 'You won't go?'

'Merce?' Ryan's hold tightens as he looks into my eyes.

'The dark place that Nuriel finds herself in now,' I whisper, 'Paris represents that place for me. The misery I felt then was *nothing* compared to the torment that Nuriel has endured, but I was at my ... lowest there. I don't think I will ever again be as alone, as lost, as *forsaken*, as I was in Paris.'

Bianca leans forward as if to touch me comfortingly, and I draw back into the solid warmth of Ryan's body.

'I don't need your card,' I say quietly, and her dark brows draw together unhappily. 'I don't need it,' I go on, 'because I've already memorised the number and the magic password. I won't forget them, not now. You can keep it.'

Bianca sits upright, letting the card fall from her fingers. 'So you'll do it?'

I can see her immediately working out what she has to do, what she has to say, to make the magic happen.

I nod wearily within the circle of Ryan's arms. 'No other course would honour Selaphiel's compassion for the monster that I was, nor Nuriel's selflessness. They never deserved torture, and their bravery deserves mine. Those that guard Selaphiel were drawn to the darkness below, and in the darkness they must remain, or die — there are no innocents among them. Luc's people have made a desert enough of this world. If I — who never had a task, never had a purpose — must be the one to slay the dragons that guard the gates of Hell in order to save Selaphiel, then so be it.'

I look up at Ryan. 'But it's not your fight, and you don't have to do this. You should take up Bianca's offer and go home.'

'Damned with you,' Ryan whispers, smoothing my hair back off my forehead, 'damned without you, remember? You've got cover, whether you like it or not.'

CHAPTER 10

The house is quiet now, with all the phone calls made, details exchanged.

Earlier, Bianca paced the dining room, working a telephone, laptop and scanner furiously, while Ryan trawled through the contents of her industrial-sized refrigerator, answering her questions between bites.

Excluded from talk of permits and clearances, flight-plan filing, catering requirements and ground handling procedures, I drifted through all the elegant, expensively furnished rooms of the house like a restless ghost, beset by a formless fear, struggling to remember the shape and contours of the ancient, sprawling city I'd once gravitated to to die. But though I dug and dug, my memories were chaotic and fragmentary — no more than snatches of sound and colour, a stench, vague impressions, a glimpse of a woman's face, mouth stretched wide in a scream, eyes fixed in terror on something. *Me?*

The only clear memory I possess of that time is waking with the Eight standing over me, deep within the putrid heart of Cimetière des Innocents. It would have been my eternal resting place, too, but for Their interference.

When the planning was done, Bianca retreated to her rooms near the front of the house, exhaustion shadowing her blue eyes. 'Tomaso will have the car brought around at six,' she'd said. 'He's arranged for a police escort to take you from the police blockade to Malpensa airport. There'll be a full VIP meet and greet at the hangar, Ryan, that will speed you onto the plane. And when you reach Paris,' she'd added quietly, 'I promised you point to point, exactly as if you were family, and I meant it. One of our drivers will be waiting on the tarmac at Le Bourget; he'll meet you straight off the plane. Customs and immigration will happen onboard, Mercy, so make yourself scarce at that point. If you're seen, and your presence can't be explained, I'll have no choice but to deny any knowledge of you.'

She'd refused to accept our thanks before turning and hurrying down the hall.

Now, I stand at the floor-to-ceiling windows in the lamplit master bedroom, waiting for daybreak. I am looking across the troubled, black waters of the lake when Ryan emerges from the en suite bathroom, the light streaming out behind him, his hair still wet from the shower, a half-eaten apple in his hand. There's a pale blue towel knotted tight and low around his narrow hips. Droplets of water gleam upon his broad shoulders, catching the light like faceted gemstones. I don't think I've seen anything more beautiful for a long time.

He smiles instantly when he sees me, dropping the apple onto a nightstand and holding his hand out to me. But before I can move towards him, I get a disorientating flash: of Luc, bare-chested, similarly wreathed by light, holding his hand out to me in the same way. I shake my head, stepping backwards, genuinely frightened and confused.

The dark versus the light, though the dark and the light are inverted and distorted.

I see confusion grip Ryan, too, at my weird reaction. Then a deep anger flares in his expressive face, which is rapidly overcome by a bemused tenderness.

'This is *so* messed up,' he sighs, bending down and grabbing one of the large, overstuffed pillows off the top of the bed, punching it a little before leaning it up against the wall. He sits with his back against it, on top of the coverlet, watching me steadily as he finishes his apple.

'*I'm* messed up,' I correct quietly as I move across the room towards him.

When I reach him, I look down into his face. And it's both familiar and unfamiliar, a signifier I have neither the wit nor the talent to read.

Ryan doesn't hesitate; he does what he always does when I get close — pulls me into him like we're two halves of the same whole, though we can't be, it's impossible. I'm falling again, but this time I feel no fear. I end up half-sprawled across his lap, the towel between us damp from being drawn across his skin, laughing as I try to keep some semblance of balance, of distance. The skin of his chest is warm and yielding beneath my fingers. I feel the play of his muscles as he draws his arms around me tightly and just breathes me in, for a time.

'Why is it,' he murmurs wonderingly, 'that you smell of snowfall?'

He is a jumble of contradictions, every part of him like velvet-wrapped steel.

He tips me over, suddenly, onto my back, catching me unawares the way he has done from the very beginning, somehow getting in under defences that were wrested in place by the hands of archangels. He lays a line of fiery kisses from the hollow at the base of my neck up to my jawline, and I arc up to meet him. He only pulls away when he reaches my mouth, and I feel his reluctance to do it.

'Now you know how it feels to be *me* around *you*,' he murmurs, his mouth breaking into amused and sensual lines as he braces himself over me. 'Jittery, psyched, out of control, out of my mind. We're right back where we started, you and me. All that separates us is a damned *towel*.'

My eyes widen, grow dark with my desire, and he sees how devastated I am by his actions, his words, exactly the way he intended me to be.

He opens his mouth over mine, kissing me, moulding me to him, flesh to flesh, energy to energy, until I feel the heat bloom under his skin of steel and velvet, an answering rush of heat rising in me. He tastes of apples and mint and the salt-sweet, roiling sea. There's that thrill of fire, of warning, along my nerves, but I dig my fingers into the muscles of his shoulders, his back, unable to pull away, because we are magnetic. We are two disparate energies colliding. And I grow so hot beneath him that he gasps out loud and has to push away from me, shield his eyes because I'm wreathed in light.

He shudders and drops back onto the bed, covering his face with his hands. He gives an involuntary groan.

'Why do you persist,' I say, accusing and anguished, 'when loving me is a kind of *hell*? K'el, Raphael, even Luc — they're proof that I bring the darkest end upon all who claim to have loved me. I am the siren's empty call, Ryan, I am a *plague*. I'm cursed, and I will drag you down the way I did those others. Why, *why* do you persist?'

He uncovers his face and looks at me, his expression unreadable.

'Give me up,' I whisper brokenly, as the light within and around me fades until it is tolerable once more. 'Renounce me utterly, so that I might come to my senses and set you aside, too. I don't have a *heart*, Ryan. I can pretend that I do, even fashion one for myself as the circumstances require, but I don't *need* one. I don't need food or water or air, sunlight or rest, to keep me alive.'

I see his shock as I add, 'I want you more than anything, but I can't give you what you want. In all my "lives" upon this material earth, you're the one thing I've reached out to, again and again, against all reason, every obstacle. But *this* could never be enough for you. How could it?'

Ryan suddenly launches himself off the bed without looking at me, and I'm too afraid to reach out and read the turmoil in his mind for fear of what I will see there. He hooks a tee-shirt and a pair of sleek, black boxer briefs off the back of a chair before striding into the bathroom, and emerges a few seconds later, dressed and without the towel.

'This is not Hell,' he says, and his voice is shaky with emotion. '*Hell* is keeping vigil in a hospital room at the bedside of a weird, prickly girl you think you've fallen for, only for her to wake and deny ever meeting you before in her life. *Hell* is thinking I'd found you again and then watching you "die" right before my eyes. If you think the only thing that's keeping me here is the prospect of some hot sex,' a faint flush appears high on his cheekbones, 'then you don't know me at all.'

He throws himself down on the bed beside me and turns his back to me.

'I need to sleep,' he growls softly. 'You can keep insulting and cheapening this thing we've got going on, so long as you do it quietly. I'm beat.'

I don't move, don't speak, until I see the hard lines of his body slacken into sleep. Then, and only then, do I move up beside him and mould my form into the sweet shape of his, placing my cheek against the back of his neck, hooking one arm around his waist to keep him close, to keep him safe.

And then I close my eyes, too.

I'm not really sleeping; I'm thinking. But it's a state of consciousness that starts as an acute awareness of my surroundings, of Ryan breathing deeply and evenly beside me, and gradually evolves into a state almost of grace, or meditation.

I find myself deep within the waters of the lake once more. I see Anael surge towards me, and it all happens again, as if for the first time: his deadly, envenoming kiss, the flare of recognition in his eyes. And, again, I find myself with a blazing blade in my left hand, which I drive through his throat without hesitation. What else could I have done?

But this time Anael does not die.

He is pinned to the rock by my killing energy, but the light of his grey eyes does not fade. Instead, they begin to change, in shape, in colour. The lashes grow longer, more luxuriant, dark gold in place of black, and the irises bleed from grey to a blue so pale and lustrous, they are like living ice, like broken water.

And his face ... my God, it is not Anael impaled upon my blade, but *Luc*. The Luc of Milan, of *this* world, the one I've never really known, his golden hair worn shorter than

I remember it ever being, that sexy hint of stubble along his jawline.

The instant I see his face, pain floods through me. I feel myself physically convulsing within this false dream, this twisted memory, and I know that he's causing it; he's reaching across time and distance to hurt me in the here and now. It's as though I've somehow called him to me, though I no longer want him in my mind or in my life.

As I thrash in agony in the water, Luc's mouth widens into a grin as predatory as it is devastating. He grasps the hilt of the weapon that is buried deep within his throat *and pulls it free.*

The weapon does not obey the laws as they were laid down in the beginning; it does not vanish in his hand with a flare of light. Instead, he holds the twisted, burning blade aloft, and I watch the light of the flame change instantly, so that the pale blue holy fire is eaten away by a light that holds the taint of demon-grey at its heart.

Time seems to speed up and slow down all at once as I watch him open his beautiful mouth to speak my name. But I can't hear it, because Hell is opening in my head and I am deaf, dumb and blind with pain.

Luc roars my name as if it were the darkest incantation of the blackest, most evil magic, and I feel one of his long-fingered hands encircling my throat, pressing deep, beginning to merge into my flesh.

Then, with a rush of violence, he bears me down into the filth of the lake bed, the water churning with our velocity. There, he lies atop me, writhing against me, in some terrible parody of the way we might have lain together in our secret garden. I feel him place the tip of the short, flaming blade beneath my jaw as if he would drive it through.

As I struggle to scream, I hear Luc say softly into the space between my eyes: *Little fool, you've told me exactly where you are more clearly than if you'd used words.*

And I scream at myself: *Wake!*

My eyes flash open into Ryan's concerned gaze. I'm so disoriented, so wretched and distressed, to see that face, *that beautiful face*, leaning over me, that I scramble away from him and throw myself off the bed, dry-retching on hands and knees on the floor. I've never been good at reading the signs, but this time I know what my inner voice, my inner demon, is trying to warn me of. The threat is too real to be ignored.

'We need to go,' I gasp, finally comprehending where I am. 'Luc knows I've left Milan. If Michael and the others haven't still got him cornered, he's going to come for me. For *us*.'

After a second of stunned incomprehension, Ryan is by my side on the floor, pushing my heavy hair off my face. He pulls me upright against him.

I'm shaking so hard I can barely articulate the words. 'We can't let him find us here. He can't know of Bianca's involvement. It would be a death sentence for her.'

I surge to my feet and stagger across the room, and begin feverishly stuffing our scattered belongings into the daypack Gia gave us.

'But what did you *see*?' Ryan asks, looking up at me from where he's still kneeling on the floor.

'I was thinking,' I murmur, 'meditating. Maybe even dreaming, I don't know. But the first of the demons that I …' I falter to a stop, remembering the violence of the kiss and the violence that followed.

Ryan doesn't drop his gaze from me as he stands and dresses quickly, automatically checking the inner pocket of his leather jacket for his valuables, for that picture he keeps of me like a traveller's medal.

'Go on,' he urges, as he shrugs into his jacket, steps into his worn-out boots.

'It was Luc I saw. In place of the demon I ... I ... killed. And Luc overcame *me*. He saw how Ananel died, he knows it was me ...'

'But how could he know?' Ryan scoffs, still unable to put much credence in a dream. 'That can't be possible — you're making it sound like he has some kind of celestial GPS for you. No way.'

'Then how did he find me in Milan when I was Irina?' I wail. 'I still don't understand how, after all this time, he was able to work out *who* I was, *where* I was, when he'd never been able to do that before.'

Ryan shakes his head, unconvinced, and I grasp his arm, the leather of his sleeve cool beneath my burning hand.

'We've always had this strange connection, Luc and I. Maybe because he was the one that marked me, I don't know, I've never been able to work it out. It used to be that when I slept he had access to my thoughts, he could reach out to me across any distance and we could speak with each other as if we were face to face, like you and I are now. But even with that weird connection, he's never been able to find me, not until now. If he can still get into my head, if my thoughts aren't safe from him, then we need to move. We need to reach Selaphiel before Luc can figure out what we're doing. And we're putting Bianca at risk every second we stay here. Luckily for us, he didn't see me at Villa Nicolin, he saw me at the lake. Let him think me still there when we've already fled for ... Paris.' I shudder as I say the word. 'We've got to go. *Now.*'

Ryan picks up our backpack, finally catching the flame of my urgency. I can see from his face that he knows very well what the Devil is capable of. Ryan lives in his world. This is the earth that the Devil has made, as much as any other, and it would serve no purpose to remind a Son of Man what Lucifer is capable of. Every thought, every deed, every breath, the Devil would claim his stake in, if he could.

Ryan looks out the windows, but to his mortal eyes it's still dark as night out there. 'What time is it, anyway?'

'Five fourteen,' I say unerringly.

'Close enough,' he says. 'Let's wait for the car out front.'

Bianca opens the door to her bedroom before we reach it. She's wearing an elegant pair of man-style pyjamas in oyster-coloured silk, piped in navy, but her eyes are heavy with sleeplessness.

'You're too early,' she says without preamble, looking up into my eyes, into Ryan's. 'I'll come fetch you when I hear the car being brought round. Try and get a little more rest.'

'The way you have?' I query softly.

'I don't sleep very well these days,' she murmurs, shrugging. 'Bad dreams.'

'I get those, too,' I say, making my voice as even and calm as possible. 'And the last one I had convinced me that you have to throw together a bag of personal possessions and move up to the main house. Now. Better still, you, Clara, Tomaso and whoever else you've got working here, you all need to leave with us. It's just a feeling I get.'

Bianca turns her bemused gaze on Ryan and he says quietly, 'You should do it. I'd trust those "feelings" of hers with my life.'

'My God,' she murmurs, appalled. 'What have you *seen*?'

'The Devil,' I reply, watching her face tighten in horror. 'When he discovers Nuriel gone, there's no telling what you'll see out there on the water. Call your neighbours and organise an evacuation, get to higher ground. Or leave the country.'

Bianca hurries across the hall into the room with the telephone. I hear her speaking in fluent, harried Italian. 'Send the car around now,' she insists, 'to the *dépendance*. They need to leave now. Yes, I know it's too early, but they can wait at the hangar. Get all the men and their families into the great house. The lake looks like it may … rise. And call Villa Cavallino and Villa Pironi. Then make an anonymous call to the emergency services. Untraceable. Same information. The lake may rise, something looks like it's happening, get away from the water's edge … I don't know … Yes, I understand it sounds crazy. *Just do it.* Okay?'

She reappears in the hallway, saying distractedly, 'Excuse me, while I change, pack a few things.'

She doesn't bother to shut her bedroom door, and I hear wardrobe doors being opened and closed hurriedly, the sound of a zipper being pulled. She emerges about five minutes later with a small holdall, dressed in the same grey sweater and black jeans we first saw her wearing, her hair bound back in a low ponytail, feet in heavy black boots, a bunch of keys dangling from the fingers of one hand.

'Why don't you come with us?' Ryan says with concern, as Bianca switches lights off all around us, then presses numbers into a glowing keypad by the front door before ushering us outside. As she closes the heavy, wooden door behind us, I hear the security system emitting a rhythmic *beep, beep*.

Bianca shakes her head at Ryan's question. 'There's nowhere safe from the Devil, is there? Some of my men are the great-grandsons of the people who originally worked here; this is all they know. They'll want to stay and defend their homes — if it comes to that — as do I. Leave that part to me, as I leave the liberation of ... of ... archangels to the two of you.' She gazes at my blurring, shifting outline with that expression of fearful wonder on her face.

I detect the faint purr of a car engine, the crunch and squeal of tyres sliding slowly across stone. I put a hand on Ryan's arm as headlights swing into view high above us, and he nods to indicate he's seen them. We watch the car slowly descend before the driveway switches back again and the vehicle is momentarily lost to sight.

'Ryan,' I say hurriedly, 'while you're in the car, you're not going to see me or hear me. But I'll be with you, I'll be near. You won't see me board the plane either, but I'll join you when I can. Okay?'

I see uncertainty leap in his eyes, and place the back of one hand against his face. '*I'll be with you*. It's no trick. You and me, me and you. That's the deal.'

Bianca places a hand tentatively on my arm at last, the way I know she's been dying to. 'You feel so ...'

'Real?' I reply with a crooked smile, which is echoed by Ryan's. 'That's what people keep telling me.'

'And warm,' she adds, a small frown pleating her forehead. 'I hadn't expected that. You look so, so ... flawless that I'd imagined you'd feel cold, like marble.' She drops her hand. 'I'm sounding crazy.'

174

I say quietly, 'Not to me.'

'I don't know how to wish you luck,' Bianca mutters, 'but I know that you'll need it.'

'As will you,' I tell her. She seems too slight, too frail, to withstand what is headed her way, but courage comes in many forms. It's something I've witnessed firsthand. *'Bona fortuna,'* I say formally. 'Godspeed.'

'And to you,' she whispers.

I bow my head in thanks, in admiration of her strength. Then I let it all go; hear Ryan gasp, see Bianca's face go pale. I let my outline shred into a pale mist before dispersing silently; just lean into the atmosphere and somehow become of it until I'm weightless again, I'm air.

By the time Tomaso steps out of the wide, black, low-slung luxury sedan with its heavily tinted windows, its high beams on to ward off the pre-dawn darkness, I'm nowhere to be seen. Only Ryan is standing there, the pack slung across one broad shoulder, wearing his faux glasses, his peaked cap jammed down low over his face, Bianca at his side.

'Where is the girl?' I hear Tomaso ask his employer sharply.

'She could not wait,' Bianca responds, meeting his gaze steadily. 'She went on ahead.'

Tomaso's reply is faintly derisive. 'Then she is either very mad or very brave.' He holds the door open for Ryan, indicating he should get in.

Ryan and Bianca exchange glances, then he extends a hand politely, awkwardly, and she takes it, gripping it briefly with both hands before letting go.

As Ryan ducks his head to enter the vehicle, I flow up and across the back of the car, a pocket of turbulence, indistinguishable from the metallic black of the paintwork. I crouch weightlessly upon the roof like a runner, giving myself perfectly uninterrupted 360-degree views in every direction. By the time the driver enters the deserted street that runs along the lake's shore, the gates are already closing against us and Bianca and Tomaso are quickly lost to sight.

As the car picks up speed, it becomes obvious that a thick and unnatural fog is building slowly but steadily over the lake, rolling outwards towards the banks on both sides as if it would swallow the world.

Bona fortuna, I whisper again, my thoughts flying up to that household of brave souls upon the hill. *Godspeed*.

CHAPTER 11

The fog brings the dead to the lake's shore.

I see them in the faint blush of light that signals daybreak as our car sweeps down the deserted, winding road that runs right beside the water, the wind soughing eerily through the pines that line it. There are scores of them. They drift along the road, down through the terraced gardens, anguished and confused, responding in some speechless, primal way to something in the water.

As we pass, every wraith lifts its head as if it can scent me, turns to follow my progress though I am nothing to the human eye, just a patch of turbulence, a cloud of energy, surfing by on top of a sleek and anonymous European car. But, still, they seek me out, and I feel a ripple, a chill, move across my soul at the sight of them all gathering.

Our driver does not see what I see; has no clue of what surrounds us. He ploughs the car straight through the grieving figure of an old man drifting in the centre of the road, dressed in the same shapeless cardigan, button-down shirt and suit pants he was last wearing in life. The car shreds him to pieces. When I look behind me, the apparition has already re-formed:

his ashen face and eyes trained on our disappearing taillights, arms outstretched as if pleading, before recommencing his mindless passage down to the water.

The fog builds and builds upon the lake beneath a heavy sky brimming with leaden, menacing clouds that the sun cannot break through. We travel through a weird, yellow-grey half-light, as if traversing some scenic boulevard of the underworld. After a time, there are no more dead lining the road, which tells me we have left Moltrasio and its new-minted spirits behind.

As we fly down a road that suddenly turns inland, away from the water, there's a vast, rending sound, a giant *crack* — like sustained thunder — and the ground ripples beneath the wheels of the pitching car like fabric, before steadying. The streetscape we move through — wealthy compounds hidden behind high, vine-covered fences and massive iron gates; the pastel walls of two- or three-storey dwellings built right up against the edges of the road; neat rows of compact cars parked nose to tail; the branches of spreading chestnut trees — seems to shimmer for a moment, to tremble.

In response, the driver floors the accelerator. I feel his fear in the way he's handling the powerful car beneath me, feel his panic in the way we almost fishtail around the bends though the road here is dry and in near perfect condition.

I hear car alarms go off, see lights flare into life in the windows of some of the buildings we flash past. But the booming sound does not recur, and, mile after mile, we leave its unseen source behind us.

We cross a bridge at a punishing, rattling pace, and the lake once more swings into view. We hug its mighty contours for a stretch before turning inland again and losing sight of it altogether. But that last, quick glimpse fills me with a greater apprehension — nothing can be seen of the water's surface, save that rolling white fog.

For a moment, I imagine I hear a high, whining sound in my inner ear. A questing sound, the kind that might herald the sort of intense pain Luc caused me only hours ago, when he was trying to get inside my head and I didn't want him there. My reaction is fierce and immediate. I imagine myself as a closed box, a walled compound, smooth on all sides, impervious to attack from any direction — and the sound is cut off, does not recur. Even though I know I'm kidding myself, concentrating hard on shutting Luc out gives me an excuse not to dwell on what lies ahead for me, in Paris.

We head further downhill, further inland, and I begin to see headlights winding up through the foothills in the far distance.

As our driver brakes on approach towards the same police roadblock we encountered yesterday, there's consternation amongst the gathered officers when they catch sight of our numberplate. A lone officer is sent striding our way, and I hear the hiss and glide of the driver's side window, then the window on Ryan's side of the car slides down. The grim-faced officer bends and glances swiftly around the interior of the vehicle, beckons for identity documentation, scans it, returns it, and raises a hand sharply. Moments later, two helmeted *Polizia di Stato* motorcyclists roar up on either side of our vehicle and we resume our journey southward, one motorbike ahead, the other falling in behind.

Four lanes of normal-looking traffic build up around us as we make a turn to the northwest, and the landscape grows more heavily industrialised. The presence of the two police outriders smooths our passage enormously: gaps in the traffic continually appear, as if by magic, and our driver makes the most of every one. I catch the curious glances directed towards our little convoy from the cabs of other vehicles that pass by, but the thing that draws my attention most is the sky. It's a normal winter sky out here: steel blue with just a scattering of cloud; a normal morning for this time of year: cold and clear, with only a light breeze riffling through and around me. The contrast to the lake country is startling.

There's one more major turn-off before the roar of jet turbines fills the sky above. The air grows heavy with the scent of burning aviation fuel and, in no time at all, we're on the tarmac of a busy airport, with cargo planes and private jets taking off and landing all around us. The noise is immense.

Before our car comes to a stop inside a canyon formed by shipping containers and private hangars, I've already vaulted off the roof. I hit the ground silently and upright, nothing more than a vaguely humanoid shimmer of energy, a heat haze. I make my way directly towards a large hangar where a sleek, silver, twin-engine jet with tip-tilted wings, six porthole windows and *StA Global Logistics* stencilled on it is parked. On the jet's tail, which is shaped a little like a swallow's tail, there's a logo of a galleon in full sail centred above a pair of crossed keys.

The police motorcyclists roar away in formation, back in the direction we came from, as I drift up the collapsible staircase towards the Gulfstream's open doorway. I enter a cabin that smells of leather, coffee and attar of roses, and see that there are two pilots and a single female crew member already on board.

And the fallen archangel enters the belly of the mechanical bird, I think bleakly, *bound for Paris to wreak vengeance on her enemies in the company of the man she loves.*

There are so many things wrong with that picture that I don't even know where to begin.

Ryan's 'VIP meet and greet' takes almost an hour. I spend the time roaming the plane, taking in the exits, the tiger-striped carpet in two shades of cinnamon, the flame-walnut inlay and gold fittings in the spacious washroom, the two coffee makers Ryan was so excited about, and the layout of the seating. There's enough room to fit twelve passengers comfortably. Up near the cockpit there's a built-in kitchenette area, then two groupings of two chairs with the aisle running between them. Each pair of facing seats has a small, blond-wood table between them, and a small plasma-screen TV set above each table. Midway back, there's a grouping of four chairs around a central table positioned across the aisle from a wooden storage unit with a larger plasma-screen TV fixed over it. And at the rear of the plane, two long couches face each other across the central aisle, before there's another smaller kitchenette area and the OTT washroom.

I watch the short, curvy female crew member in her smart, dark grey suit, filmy white blouse, bright red shoes and coordinating lipstick, her smooth, brown hair pinned in a low chignon, move around the cabin, plumping pillows and moving floral arrangements and in-flight reading material from one surface to another.

When Ryan finally gets onboard — his daypack slung over one shoulder — I see her eyes light up with interest. When he removes his cap and glasses, shoving them carelessly into a pocket of his leather jacket, then running a hand across the severe buzz cut Tommy gave him, I feel her interest intensify, even from where I'm drifting, weightless, at the back of the plane.

I forget, sometimes, how breathtaking he is with his warm, dark eyes and downy skin, the ready smile that lights up the incredible bones of his face, his tall and rangy athlete's frame. Gia reacted the same way the first time she saw his face on the screen of her tiny mobile phone. It's funny how true beauty can be immobilising when you come across it. Luc had been like that for me: he'd pulled my focus immediately in that crowd of beautiful creatures the first time I saw him. And he'd inhabited the absolute centre of my world from then on, until he'd casually torn it apart when he decided he was done with me.

I see the young woman struggle to put words of greeting together, the colour rising in her face as she gazes at Ryan with shining eyes, and feel something ugly move within me. They only talk about inconsequential things, like whether he wants his jacket stored, how the plasma touchscreens operate, how he takes his coffee, but it's all taking way too long for my liking, and she keeps finding excuses to touch him.

By the time Ryan extricates himself from her and takes a seat at that table for four, halfway down the plane, I'm seething with a possessive emotion that is completely unwarranted but that I can't help feeling. Love has treacherous faces, too, I've learnt. As do I.

And it hits me then, the resemblance. She reminds me of Luc's Gudrun, with her blood-red lips and nails, her impeccable grooming and curvy, flirtatious ways, her chatty, overly familiar demeanour.

When I slide, still just a heat haze, a faint shimmer in the atmosphere, into the seat opposite Ryan's, my words emerge from the thin air before his face quickly, acidly. 'Tell her to keep away from you for the duration of the flight — make up any old excuse. Unless you prefer her company to mine, that is. Then by all means flirt away, buddy. Knock yourself out.'

Ryan gives a startled yelp that brings the stewardess hurrying back down the aisle towards him. She places a hand on his shoulder and I can't seem to tear my gaze away from her blood-red nails where they curve down across the leather of his jacket.

'What is it, Ryan?' she says in her melodious Italian accent, because, of course, Ryan's insisted she use his first name. 'Is there anything I can help you with before take-off?'

Just try it, I think nastily, as Ryan shakes his head, staring with wild eyes at the space where he thinks I am.

'Could you just, um, keep back as much as possible, Rosa? I think I'm coming down with something … uh, something viral and really disgusting.'

He coughs loudly and stagily for emphasis, and I see Rosa step back a little, removing her hand from his shoulder with unflattering speed.

'I think I'll just lie down on one of the couches back there and sleep it off,' he adds. 'Just get the captain to, um, wake me when we're about to land. No need to check up on me, I won't be needing anything during the flight.'

She nods, backing away with a weird mix of relief and disappointment on her pretty face. 'Wait until after take-off, Ryan, then by all means sleep. I shall not disturb you.'

'Happy?' Ryan whispers as the plane begins to taxi towards the runway, Rosa safely buckled up in her crew seat near the cockpit. 'You just dudded me out of the freshly brewed coffee I was really looking forward to. But if you join me on the couch after take-off, I might let you make it up to me. Maybe.'

I do growl, then. Low and menacing, like a wolf.

Ryan just chuckles, putting his hands behind his head in an attitude of complete relaxation as I flow huffily away from him down the plane.

The group seating for four effectively hides the occupant of the couch behind it from sight if said occupant is lying down.

I hear Ryan stand up, hear him unzip his leather jacket before taking it off and dumping it across the table in front of him. Then he makes his way around to where I'm stretched out. He stands there looking down at me for a moment, and there's a weird expression on his face again. I know it's because I'm in the human form I first gave myself at the Duomo, with its black, curly hair, dark green eyes and skin of near perfect, unshiny humanness.

'We're not amongst friends now,' I murmur apologetically, 'people who understand what I am. This will have to do. In case I'm seen.'

He eases himself down beside me, places his head on the wide armrest beside mine and turns to face me. 'It still feels like I'm lying next to a stranger,' he complains quietly.

'I *am* a stranger,' I reply, inexplicably wounded by his words. 'In some way I'll *always* be a stranger because I can't get close to you. It was *written*, remember? We're just finding out about it now, that's all.'

Ryan's dark gaze softens and he reaches up and brushes a long, dark curl back from my face before grinning. 'You could get closer,' he murmurs, 'if you'd take off that stupid black puffer jacket you keep insisting on wearing. We might even gain a couple of inches of togetherness …'

He startles a laugh out of me that sounds almost tearful.

'Better?' I reply, shifting so quickly and imperceptibly that I'm wearing just the simple black turtleneck and jeans before he's even registered the jacket is gone.

He wrinkles his nose. 'What you've got on still has to be the opposite of sexy.'

It's done before I can call it back. In a fit of pique, I shift so that I'm wearing the filmy white blouse and slim-fitting dark grey skirt of Rosa's uniform. 'Sexy enough for you?' I say through gritted teeth.

Ryan recoils, almost falling off the couch in his haste to put some distance between us. His voice is reproachful. 'Now you're just being a bitch. We were only *talking*. You don't get the right to act like a jealous girlfriend when you won't even tell me what I mean to you.'

I shift back into my black turtleneck and dark grey jeans, but Ryan doesn't move any closer, and I say rawly, 'What else do you expect from a monster? I'm no good at any of it. At being *me*, at being like this. The Eight should have put me down the way I begged them to. I was born to trouble, to bring trouble upon others. I'm a freak …' I cover my face with my hands.

'You begged the Eight to *kill you*?' Ryan says in a hushed voice.

He pulls my hands away from my face fiercely, shaking me, his expression brittle with shock.

'I woke in that place — that place we're hurrying so hard to get to — so horribly burnt and wounded it was a wonder I ever woke at all,' I whisper. '*They* were all staring down at me, mocking me with Their incredible beauty, Their terrible power. But though I begged to die, They refused. Michael said it was against everything we stood for to end the life of one of our kind — even though I was vain and proud and the personal muse of the greatest force of destruction our universe has ever witnessed. They would not do it, though I threw my unspeakable pain, my deep rage and confusion, in all Their faces. And *this* is the result of all that care of me, all that love and protection that has never been warranted and can never be repaid. I'm a mess. In. Every. Single. Way.'

Ryan pulls me into his arms, holding me, rocking me, until little by little I stop shaking and my hurt begins to ease, at the edges.

'You should have seen the look on your face,' he murmurs, changing the subject valiantly. 'It was like you wanted to rip the poor girl's throat out.'

I give a shaky laugh. 'I always look that way. Get used to it.'

We don't talk for a long time after that; we just hold each other, the heat of our two bodies mingling. After a little while, when Ryan's hold slackens, I see that he's fallen asleep, and it makes me smile, how he can sleep anywhere.

I reach up to place a small kiss upon his wide, full mouth and that's when I notice a shadow falling down the aisle towards us. I look back up the plane, but Rosa's already fled, making a small, terrified noise as she runs towards the cockpit. She knocks frantically, then pulls open the door.

Ryan's still sleeping, one arm thrown across his chest, one leg bent slightly outward, when Rosa returns with one of the pilots. He's in his shirt-sleeves, hatless, his shaved head gleaming under the lights of the cabin. He flicks his light, hazel-coloured eyes from Ryan back to Rosa, his lashes and eyebrows such a pale ginger-red, they're almost colourless.

'I don't see the problem,' he says quietly in Dutch-inflected English. He strides towards the washroom door, opens it, looks quickly around inside. 'How could there be a girl? There's no one here.' He looks back up the plane and throws his hands out wide in confusion. 'There's nowhere to hide on this plane. *What girl?*'

When he shuts the washroom door with a firm *snap*, Ryan wakes with a start. He sits up, instantly alert when he sees Rosa and the pilot standing there looking at him.

'What? What is it?' he says, looking around warily, and I know that he's searching for me. 'Have we arrived?'

The pilot pins a genial smile on his face though I can tell he's annoyed. 'We're about to start our descent, Mr Daley, so perhaps you would care to return to your seat now?'

He indicates the table for four behind him with a sweep of his hand, before turning and striding back towards the cockpit with Rosa following at his heels, flustered and upset.

'But I saw her, I tell you. He was holding her. Why didn't you ask him? *Ask him.*'

I see the pilot shake his head and reply shortly, 'And what? Sound like a lunatic? *There's nowhere to hide.* You probably saw the ghost of one of Maxi St Alban's many mistresses; one he arranged to have thrown off the plane, I don't know. Like people say, Rosa — suck it up, okay? We're almost there.'

'Rumbled,' I whisper in Ryan's ear ruefully, and his eyes widen in understanding. 'See you on the ground.'

<hr />

After the plane comes to a stop outside the dedicated StA Global Logistics hangar at Le Bourget and the customs and immigration men enter the plane, I slip down the collapsible staircase and immediately see the anonymous, black, luxury sedan with the tinted windows waiting about thirty feet away. There's a slender, youthful-looking man of average height leaning against the front of the car. He has dark eyes, a triangular, clean-shaven face, and short, light brown hair that's been waxed so it sticks up in artful spikes all over his head. He's wearing a stylish camel overcoat over his navy suit, everything tailored to fit him perfectly, and his hands are buried deep in his coat pockets.

The wind is icy — the temperature can't be more than about five degrees, and the sky is slate grey — but all looks and feels normal for this time of year. December in Paris. The notion suddenly fills me with so much dread I almost can't bring myself to move towards the car.

But I make myself drift closer, circling the vehicle and its driver at a wary distance. He has an observant, watchful air about him, an expression that reminds me of Gia Basso. He gives out the same kind of muffled, complicated energy she does, too. It's hard to get a handle on what he's thinking.

After a roughly twenty-minute interval, the officials re-emerge onto the staircase of the aeroplane, one of them roaring with laughter at something the other has said. As they descend, I see Ryan appear at the door of the Gulfstream. I get a brief glimpse of Rosa behind him, her expression as frozen as her body language.

The driver pulls himself upright languidly when he sees Ryan and moves to open the rear passenger door on the driver's side. Though he seems relaxed, I see him size Ryan up with narrowed eyes.

As he comes off the stairs, Ryan checks to see that the officials have driven away before jamming his cap back onto his head, placing his fake spectacles onto his nose and hunching his shoulders a little to make himself seem shorter, like a different person.

I'm just a drift of energy on that chill, chill wind as I circle him and whisper, 'Tell the driver to stop the car just as you round the hangar marked *IRL Industries*. I'll be waiting.'

Ryan's a pro, because he doesn't even check his progress at my words, just sweeps on towards the car, shouldering his pack, keeping his head down. The guy nods at him and he nods at the guy, and the door's shut, the driver's back behind the wheel turning the engine over, and I almost don't make it to the corner before they do.

The black car slides to a stop beside me — the me of the Duomo, black puffer jacket and all — and the driver gets out and opens the rear passenger door again. He nods, says neutrally in his gravelly voice, '*Mad'moiselle*,' without a hint of surprise, before helping me into the car.

The word actually makes me wince as I slide in next to Ryan. He reaches over and buckles me in tenderly, like I'm a child, like I even *need* a seatbelt.

The driver shuts the door. There's no window between us and him; it's just a normal car, like the one that picked us up at Villa Nicolin — if you count a top-of-the-range black European sedan that's almost as wide and heavy as a tank as normal. So when the driver picks up the radio handset and says in his own language, 'Yeah, I got him. He's some big, dumbass rich kid who can't even tell me where the hell we're

supposed to be going. We stopped to pick up his girlfriend —
too tall for me, nothing to hold onto. Maybe she'll have more
idea. I will let you know directly,' my first reaction is to cover
my ears and put my head on my knees.

Ryan's shaking me suddenly and saying, 'Now you're
really scaring me,' while the guy mutters under his breath,
'*Que Dieu nous défendre contre les mioches riches et idiots!*'
God defend us from rich and stupid brats!

I curl into an even tighter ball, trying to block out the
sound of the mellifluous language. I can't bear its cadences,
its rhythm, even though it's one of the most glorious man has
ever devised. Hearing it again is like having hot irons placed
against exposed skin. This is something I *know* I've tried to
erase. To survive what I've survived, I must have put in place
some formidable defences, must have sabotaged vast areas of
my own cognition.

'*Monsieur?*' the driver says loudly. '*Mad'moiselle?* Where
are we going?' He adds beneath his breath, '*Une réponse
aujourd'hui serait préférable. Nom de Dieu!*' *An answer
today would be preferable. Christ almighty.*

The epithet cuts through me. I must have heard it spoken
at least a thousand times — by fishwives, barrow boys and
innkeepers, by casket makers and clergymen and those whose
job it was to dispose of the dead.

I raise my head suddenly and almost roar in fluent
but rusty-sounding French, 'Take us to the Cimetière des
Innocents. Take us there and wait until I say you can go. Do
you understand me?'

The guy's good at hiding his surprise. He raises his
eyebrows only slightly before facing forward again. He says
smoothly, without turning, in insultingly fluent English, 'You

are sure you want the Cimetière des Innocents? The place where it *was?*'

There's a strange emphasis on that word 'was', but I'm in so much agony — an agony of remembrance that has given rise to an almost physical pain — that I snarl, '*Oui.*'

And he floors it in response.

CHAPTER 12

'There's no point asking if you're okay,' Ryan says quietly with a quick glance at the driver's back, 'because clearly you're not. *Tell me what's wrong.* I can't help you if you don't talk to me.'

Our entwined hands rest upon his jeans-clad thigh, and I think I might be breaking his fingers, I'm gripping them so tightly. But, as always, he takes what I dish out without complaint.

I whisper, 'You're my compass, remember? You're here to light my way in the darkness of this world. This place is just a shadow from a distant past, but for me it has such a long and terrifying reach ...'

I try to ease my hold, but he won't let me move away. So I continue to grasp his hand in silence while we travel through a vast urban sprawl I don't recognise in the slightest, passing motorway signs that read *La Courneuve* and *Aubervilliers*. But it's hardly any time at all before we enter central Paris with a tide of other traffic, and I begin to see, here and there, a building, a church, a tower, a narrow street that brings with it a suffocation of feeling. Years ago, I crawled across a landscape that is buried now, submerged under a weight of modernity and progress. But the footprint of the old city I once knew is still here, underneath. I feel its pull.

As we pass a massive train station that was centuries from existence when I was last here, and motor down a broad boulevard that crosses over one unfamiliarly named street after another, I know where we are. I look up to see a sign that reads *Boulevard de Sebastopol.* The name of the street is no longer the same, but it's here, that place, under our feet. I tell the driver to stop, and he does, leaving the engine running.

'Where are we?' Ryan asks, looking out the window.

'Les Halles,' the driver replies in his gravelly voice, shooting us a quick glance before staring back through the windscreen. 'In the first arrondissement.'

All I see are large apartment buildings of great beauty and symmetry, well-tended stands of trees, their branches largely bare, everything regular and orderly and clean.

'Les Halles, yes,' I mutter, 'but where is the great market itself? It stood alongside a vast parish cemetery filled to overflowing with the dead. A horrifying place, stinking of lime and decomposing flesh, bounded by the bones of the exhumed on all sides, piled high, like kindling ...'

The young man at the wheel turns and gives me a strange look. 'That "great market" you speak of, it has not been here since, eh, the 1960s. Many years before I was born.'

'I don't care about the market,' I say sharply. 'Where is Cimetière des Innocents? The place bound by bones?'

That was how Nuriel spoke of it. Surely there could not be two such hideous places in all of Paris?

In reply, the driver starts the car and turns one corner, two, draws up in front of a small square with a large stone fountain at its heart. When I peer through the tinted glass at the fountain, I'm almost overwhelmed. I cover my mouth with my hands. I know it, I recognise the carvings on it. It was once located elsewhere on this street, the Rue St Denis, which has also altered almost beyond recognition.

Ryan doesn't ask if it's okay, he just leans forward and enfolds me tightly in his arms from behind.

The driver disengages the window on my side of the car. 'This is all that remains of Cimetière des Innocents,' he says. 'This square, this fountain. The bones, they were all moved a long time ago, over two hundred years. Nothing remains here of the cemetery you seek.'

'Where were they moved to, the bones?' I whisper, staring at the gently playing fountain, the pretty square beneath the bleak winter sky that is like smoky grey glass.

'Officially? To Place Denfert-Rochereau,' he says, 'in the fourteenth arrondissement. I will take you there.'

In minutes, we are on a bridge crossing over the mighty River Seine that bisects Paris into north and south, right bank and left bank. Ryan gazes in awe at the crowds of people on the tree-lined boulevard, the ancient and vast complexes of buildings lining both sides of the street, the gothic facade of Notre Dame Cathedral flying by. I recognise it, and recognise, too, the delicate spire of Sainte-Chapelle towering over the streetscape. There are centuries of 'modernity' all around me, one layer intruding upon another, but there's no time to reflect further on how much the Île de la Cité has changed because we've already left the island in the slipstream of a fleet of minibuses bearing southwest. Every few feet, I see something that triggers an image or stirs up some strong feeling that I thought I'd never see or experience again. I feel as if I'm under attack by random ghosts.

There's a sense of unreality about everything I'm looking at, as if I see two cities superimposed one on top of another and the only real things in this world are Ryan and I, the driver and this car. I lean against the solid wall of Ryan's chest to try to contain the sensation that I'm floating, that this is all a hallucination. All I let myself hear is his heartbeat; I do not admit the voices, the sounds, the chaos, of those days.

I'd assumed Selaphiel was being held in the Cimetière des Innocents, and my foolish assumption has cost us precious time. If we had any kind of lead at all on Luc and his forces, it's probably vanished.

'Stupid,' I snarl aloud before I realise I'm doing it.

'It is not a common mistake,' the driver says over his shoulder, 'but no matter. If you wish to see bones, you will see millions at the Catacombes de Paris, all arranged most strikingly. The tourists, they love it.'

When we finally reach Place Denfert-Rochereau, the car sliding in between a couple of maxi tour buses with side mirrors like the down-bent antennae of insects, Ryan says in surprise, 'Uh, it looks like a museum.'

There's a line of people dressed in layers of colourful, cold-weather clothing — hats, scarves, coats, gloves, boots — outside an unremarkable stone building. Some are sipping from thermoses or eating food from paper bags. Most carry backpacks and cameras, some have umbrellas. There are children among them. It has to be some terrible mistake.

Ryan reaches the same conclusion almost immediately. 'Would it make sense, do you think, for, uh, Selaphiel to be imprisoned in a place with a queue of people outside —'

'— wearing polar fleece and waiting to pay an entry fee?' I cut in, my voice rising. 'No, it would *not* make sense. This can't be the place. But if this isn't the place Nuriel saw, then where could he be? *They cannot abide the cold, having turned away from first light*, that's what she told me. He's in a place bound by bones, yet there can be no such place accessible by the general public. Nothing she told me lines up.'

Our driver's voice is studiously casual as he interjects. 'This is only the visitors' entry. There is a mile of tunnel underground that the visitors are permitted to see, and they are pushed through it like sheep and emerge, blinking, into the light on Rue Dareau. But l'Ossuaire Municipal stretches much farther than this. There is a giant network of tunnels, of old quarries — *carrières* — beneath our feet. The Left Bank is riddled with them. We took the stone from under the ground to build Paris, and now much of Paris is built on air.' He chuckles darkly, before continuing. 'Yes, the bones were first brought here. But they had men below, moving the remains, night after night, year after year. There are many more bones — from des Innocents, from all the ancient, condemned graveyards of Paris — scattered throughout *les carrières*. The bones of millions of Parisians could not fit into this pleasant display that has been constructed for the tourists. There are many, many more entrances to the underworld, and many, many more bones.'

His words are electrifying.

I sit straighter within the circle of Ryan's arms and say eagerly, 'Can you show me another way into this ... underworld?'

He gives me a quick glance. 'I could, *mad'moiselle*. But it is not worth my neck, you understand. The catacombs, they are dangerous. They say some do not return from playing there ...'

Ryan leans forward. 'We'll take care of ourselves. You just get us down there, then tell your bosses you left us on a street somewhere: we wanted to explore, we didn't come back.'

Our driver shakes his head. 'Still not worth it to me, *monsieur*. If rich young foreigners go missing, there are many unpleasant consequences for men like me.'

'Give me your cell-phone number,' Ryan says, turning on his own phone. 'I'll send you a message from my phone saying where and when we'll meet you, and if we fail to show, you're to assume your services are no longer required with no repercussions.'

'Nice,' I say with admiration.

Ryan gives me a dark look. 'It's called forward planning, and I learnt it from the best in the business. How else do you think Justine Hennessy now has a home to call her own?'

'Lela wasn't supposed to die,' I remind him quietly.

'Yeah, well, I have no intention of doing that today either,' Ryan retorts. 'So I'll take care of the cover-*his*-butt part of the adventure, then it's over to *you* to get Selaphiel and the two of us out of there, because I sure as hell can't see in the dark.'

'You have a torch,' I point out evenly, trying hard not to smile.

Both of us start laughing, maybe out of sheer terror.

The driver watches us narrowly as if we are mad. Finally, he reaches across the seat back with his right hand extended. Ryan grips it and shakes it.

'Henri Séverin,' he says, returning his hand to the steering wheel. 'And I must apologise — I misjudged you, I think. You are not —'

'Rich and dumb?' I interject acidly, remembering his conversation with his handler over the in-car radio.

Henri gives a self-deprecating shrug, unembarrassed. 'I have been with this company for seven years. There is a type, you know? You look very much of that type. How was I to know?'

He starts the car and pulls away from the official entrance to the catacombs, rapidly leaving the snaking line of brightly dressed tourists behind.

'Those tourists are the stupid ones,' he snorts. 'Underground it is always fifty-five, maybe fifty-seven degrees Fahrenheit. In summer, in winter, always the same. The living always overdress to meet with the dead. They fill themselves with food, with drink, only to discover that when they are deep underground, there are no toilets, no exits, no escape. It is not far to la Petite Ceinture,' he goes on, looking over his shoulder as he overtakes a small lorry. 'Nearby, there is a *grand entrance* the cataphiles use — one of Paris's worst-kept secrets.'

I lean forward, my fingers twitching as if reaching for the grip of a weapon. 'Hurry,' I say. 'We've lost enough time already.'

Ryan says sardonically, 'With her, Henri, you made a bad mistake. She fits no "type".'

Henri glances at him shrewdly in the driver's mirror. 'She may be more machine than human, I think, but you, *monsieur*, must be —'

'Badly in need of a coffee, some breakfast and a toilet,' Ryan interrupts ruefully, 'like the tourist I am.'

Henri parks on a quiet street on the outskirts of the fourteenth arrondissement and we walk to a bridge that overlooks a set of overgrown train tracks. It's just past noon, and traffic on the bridge is jarringly loud, incredibly fast. Hard to imagine such a place giving onto a gateway to Hell, but Luc was always imaginative.

Before we go over the bridge wall, Henri and Ryan bust out their mobiles. Ryan types up his butt-covering text message and hits *send*.

Henri types into his phone: *I understand, M. Daley. If you and your girlfriend do not return by 3.30 pm, I am to leave. I will inform my company. But please let me know if your situation changes. I am here to help. And please enjoy your explorations of this beautiful and historic region.*

He shows Ryan the message and Ryan nods. Henri presses *send*, and, like that, he has his alibi and Ryan and I are free to vanish underneath Paris.

Ryan, being Ryan, automatically offers to give me a boost over the wall. I can't keep the look of offence from my face, and he throws his head back and laughs before pulling himself up and over.

Henri moves forward to assist me, but I say to him quickly and quietly so that Ryan will not overhear, 'If we don't make it back, Henri, try and ring the number he gave you. Keep trying, even if you're far from here. He needs to get back to the plane that's waiting for him at Le Bourget. I'm not important — I truly can take care of myself. But he's the dearest thing to me in this world, and he has a whole other life without me that he can easily return to. Keep trying. Try until your shift is over, because he needs to get home. Would you do that for me?'

Mystified, Henri nods. 'Sure, I will call. There is nothing to lose. It will show that I am a good guy, that I am concerned.'

'Hel-*lo*?' Ryan yells impatiently from the other side of the wall.

I feel Henri's eyes on me as I pull myself up and over easily, landing silently on my feet in the tall grass on the other side. Ryan looks at me enquiringly, but before he can say a word, Henri's flushed face appears above the wall, and he drops down, landing badly.

'A moment,' he puffs, embarrassed, from where he's fallen amongst the weeds. He rises, brushes himself off, the corners of his mouth turned down in distaste, then gestures for us to follow him down the slope towards the railway line.

When we reach the tracks, Ryan looks both ways with a worried frown.

Henri laughs. 'It is abandoned. Only ghost trains use it now.'

We walk, and walk. And the further we go, the more my fear and tension climb, like vines grappling towards a distant sun.

Finally, a vast train tunnel appears up ahead and we slip from a wan kind of daylight into a darkness that must feel absolute to Ryan and to Henri. They slip and stumble gracelessly behind me, until one runs into the other with an *ouf*, and they stop.

'*Merde*,' Henri says gloomily, fumbling for his mobile phone.

He lights it up and holds it forward, but it's almost useless in here. The air ahead of us is inexplicably foggy. It has an acid-sweet smell, like exploded sugar.

'Smoke bombs,' Henri says. 'Cataphiles use them to conceal their way. It is illegal to be underground, you understand.'

'Great,' Ryan sighs.

I hear him rummaging around in the pack and, moments later, the bright white beam of his silver torch plays across the railway sleepers, the stones beneath and around them. The light barely makes headway into the surrounding darkness, the foggy air.

'To the right,' Henri directs gruffly, uncertainly.

We move forward slowly, Ryan playing his light ahead of us and across the right wall. There are still only weeds and stones all around us, that strange and foggy darkness. Then the edge of the flashlight picks up a flattened juice carton, a candy wrapper, a scattering of stomped-down beer cans, a broken plastic torch. I see it first — a gap in the rock, a breach between the tunnel wall and the earth beneath it. Two, maybe three feet across at most. For a moment, we three ring the opening, quietly appalled.

'You're kidding,' Ryan says incredulously. 'This is the "grand entrance"?'

Henri's voice seems muffled. 'There are many other ways in and out, they say. But this is the only one I know of. I came here once, for a party. We ate *crêpes*, danced, listened to music. It was like a dream. Hundreds of people underground. I've never forgotten it.'

I grasp his hand briefly and he returns the pressure to show that he understands.

Aloud, he says in his gravelly voice, 'And now I leave you two lovers to your gentle explorations of this beautiful and historic region.' He glares into our faces. 'I am a selfish man. Give them no reason to come after me with their questions, I beg of you.'

In his own way, he's telling us to be careful. He doesn't say goodbye, just drops out of our circle of light and stumbles back the way we came, his mobile phone held out before him, complaining under his breath all the way. I watch until the dim light of his phone merges with the distant, faint glow of the yawning tunnel mouth we first entered.

Ryan approaches the gap in the rock more closely, and we both crouch down, looking into it.

'Being with you,' Ryan says, turning to look at me with wide eyes, his pupils like pinpoints, the flashlight wavering a little in his hand, 'I am *always* scared. Scared of what you'll do next; scared of saying the wrong thing; scared you don't feel the same way I feel about you. But this? This is a whole other level of scared.'

'*Shit scared*, the Australians call it,' I reply, feeling fear take wing through me like a live, trapped thing. I swing one booted foot into the hole. 'It used to make me laugh whenever I heard someone say it. I didn't understand it at all, until Justine explained.'

'I get it,' Ryan mutters. 'I get it completely.' Then he puts a hand on my arm to stop me going in. 'I'll go first,' he insists gallantly, though he's literally sweating with fear. 'I've got the torch.'

I lay one hand against his clammy cheek. 'It's not a contest about who's bigger, who's badder,' I murmur. 'I appreciate the sentiment more than you could ever know, but I don't need the torch. Let me go first.'

He backs down reluctantly, loosening his grip. Before I can give in entirely to the fear, I'm scrambling through the crevice in the rock, and feel my feet hit the floor of a tunnel.

What I notice immediately? There's no light. And the air reeks of limestone, of bone dust.

CHAPTER 13

We walk for an hour through a maze of tunnels that fork
and branch and turn suddenly into chambers and openings
and junctions. Sometimes, there's ankle-deep water
underfoot. More often, the passages are dry, and thick
with dust. Occasionally, we are forced to duck our heads or
crawl on all fours, and weird things leap out at us from the
walls — graffiti tags rendered in brilliant colour, life-sized
portraits of men or women, monstrous sculptures chiselled
straight out of the stone itself as if caught mid-leap, mid-
snarl. And all I hear from Ryan is 'Shit!' repeated over and
over like a protective mantra, the laboured sound of his
breathing.

In a vast, cool, eerily silent chamber we find a finely
carved stone dining table rising straight out of the stone floor,
and Ryan breaks out a chocolate bar and some water. He
salutes me with Gia's travel-sized bottle of whisky, offers me
a sip. I shake my head, remembering the vodka laced liberally
with liquid meth that had caused Irina's heart almost to stop
while I was in her body.

'That stuff is poison,' I say quietly.

'I know,' Ryan replies, coughing a little as he replaces the cap on the bottle and tucks it back into the bag. 'But it feels as if I'll never be warm again. Plus, being with you would drive any guy to drink.'

We grin at each other before he indicates I should lead the way again.

We start moving steadily downwards and begin to see large deposits of bones, tossed into dead-end passages like refuse or driftwood. There are broken skulls among them, vertebrae, pelvic bones and mandibles, the teeth still lodged inside.

Ryan pulls his hood up over his head, hunching his shoulders against the cold, against the weight of the stone above us, the human remains that keep appearing like a warning from God. He starts to cough from all the dust in his throat. Whenever I turn and look into his face, he seems strung out with fear, as if he's fighting himself just to keep putting one foot in front of the other.

All the while, I desperately search for signs that Selaphiel has passed this way. But it's been over a year now since he was taken, and I see nothing; hear nothing but the distant rumble of a subway train passing somewhere overhead, the play of water through some subterranean aqueduct, the squeak and scuff of Ryan's boots on the dusty, rocky floor, the sound of his breathing, and of his coughing.

These passages must go for miles underground. When we come to a tunnel with an arrow painted on the wall, then a rough, life-sized cartoon of a man rendered in scarlet paint, I follow the markings with my eyes and discern a small opening, almost concealed by the uneven stone walls. There are rusty metal rungs set into the walls inside that dark space, a basic kind of ladder that extends upwards into darkness.

I grab Ryan's right wrist and duck inside, forcing him to follow, to crowd in with me. The sound of his breathing is very loud. I point his hand, the flashlight in it, upwards.

'I think that's a manhole cover way up there,' I say casually, letting go of him.

He lifts the torch higher, struggling to make out anything with his human eyes.

'I could get you out if you feel like bailing,' I offer.

He peers upward, still not seeing what I see. He shakes his head numbly and says, 'But then who would get *you* out?'

I'm so overwhelmed by his words — so brave, so foolish, so certain — that I move straight into his arms, and they lock around me, tightly.

'I'm holding you back, aren't I?' he murmurs against my hair. 'This has to be the most frightening place on earth. I've never felt so ... paralysed. It's like I'm moving through quicksand, like there's a giant block of stone on my chest and I can't breathe. But I can't leave you down here on your own. You'd never do that to me.'

I nod, because it's true. He's got me there.

He places his left hand against my face and runs his thumb down my cheek. 'None of this seems to touch you. Why do you seem less afraid now, when before you were a mess?'

I turn my face into the palm of his hand and my lips meet it briefly. 'Because I think I'm beginning to realise that this is just ... scenery. The place I went to die, it doesn't exist any more, so it no longer has the power to hurt me. When I was Carmen, and I woke to find myself in chains, with Lauren and Jennifer chained in the darkness nearby, that was real evil, living evil. So far, nothing in here even comes close to that.'

We re-enter the passageway, coming to a fork that seems a little different from the ones we've come across so far. I look back at Ryan for a cue, but he stumbles to a halt, saying wearily, 'I don't know, Merce, I don't have a feel for any of it. You choose.'

He doesn't say: *How much longer? How much farther?* And the sudden surge of love I feel for him is like a wave breaking through me. I may not need food or water, air or sunlight or rest to keep me alive, but Ryan? Ryan is necessary. I wasn't lying when I said it before.

One of the forking tunnels is organic looking, in the sense that it's hewn from the stone and stretches onwards into darkness. The other is sealed by concrete — and sealed recently — but there's a man-sized hole drilled through the base of the concrete plug. The entryway is littered all around with empty spray-paint cans.

I start moving towards the drill hole and Ryan groans.

'If it's too easy,' I say cajolingly, 'it ain't fun. It's something I used to tell myself when I was Lucy, to help me survive. It helped me keep her and her baby alive when I didn't know the first thing about her, or about me.'

I crouch down, preparing to go through, but as I stretch my hand towards the breach in the concrete, I feel a shift in the air and hear footfalls, drawing closer, fast.

I bump into Ryan as I back away and he tenses instantly, saying, 'What? *What?*'

'*Shhhh*, listen. Can't you hear it?'

He's still shaking his head when I grab him by the front of his jacket and push him hard against the wall behind him, just as a pack comes at us through the drill hole. Then a pair of hands comes shooting through the gap, then a head, and a kid covered in white bone dust slithers out and falls on the floor, like he's just been born.

He's fourteen, maybe fifteen at most, just starting to really grow, and he's already snatched up his pack, is already sprinting, before we can call out to him to stop. I feel the surge of his energy as he passes us, his body a psychic scream of fear, eyes wide. He turns his head briefly, taking us in, his mouth a round O of shock, before he disappears out of sight up the tunnel we just came down, his sneakered feet seeming not to touch the ground.

Another boy shoots out of the hole — also wearing a thick dusting of white — in the same urban uniform of hoodie, canvas sneakers, distressed jeans. He reaches back in for his pack, tugging at the strap, unable to yank it through, his fear carving a sizzling arc through the air around me. Then he spies us watching him, and gives a long, unearthly scream and runs, arms around his head, abandoning everything.

Five minutes we give ourselves, before we move. Nobody else comes through, physical or otherwise.

Ryan exhales in a rush when he sees me crouch down to look through the hole again. Cool, quiet darkness beyond. But there's something inhabiting that darkness that made a teenage boy abandon his precious swag and run, shrieking, like he'd lost the power of speech.

'It's the first sign of anything alive down here,' I say apologetically. 'You know we have to take a look.'

Ryan's still standing, frozen, up against the wall.

'It has to mean something,' I insist.

'What it means,' he says through gritted teeth, 'is that I've passed shit scared and gone into orbit on the fear-ometer. You're amazing, you know that? Most people would be falling apart right now.'

'Of course I'm afraid,' I say softly. 'But placed in the balance against hope — which is what those two kids represent — *hope is winning out*. You, of all people, understand what it feels like to have someone you love imprisoned in darkness. Selaphiel may be the closest thing to family someone like me will ever have. He is the gentlest, the most unworldly of the Eight; so kind, so absent-minded, so intent upon the workings of the universal, that he is blind to all else, including personal danger. And I owe him my life.'

I add quietly, 'Something is alive down here, I can feel it. And I understand if you want to turn back now. If you head up through that manhole back there, you should make it back to Henri in time. You've got his number. Call him — he'll have to pick you up. If I can, I'll catch up with you, I promise. But I have to do this. I have to keep going.'

Ryan hesitates, clearly torn, and I say fiercely, 'It's not about *fate*, Ryan. No one owns anyone else. I am the last creature on earth to want to trap you, to keep you here against your will. It's about gut instinct and reaction and choice. It's about what you can handle. If this feels bad to you, I release you. I won't hold it against you. You are already peerless in my eyes. I have … trouble saying the words you want to hear because I've been burnt so badly, so literally, I shouldn't even be here. But you know what I feel about you, and you have to know that it's *real*. One day, maybe, we'll have that time for ourselves, just to *be* and be with each other. But not now. You've seen things no human being should ever have to see. If you love me the way you say you do, you'll *go*.'

I rise to my feet and kiss him, tasting that all-permeating dust on his lips, the familiar salt-sweet tang of him. Everything I feel for him in my mouth, in my hands.

But I tear myself away before there can be that lick of warning fire that whispers: *forbidden*. Then I bend and wriggle through the drill hole without looking back.

When I get to my feet, I'm in a long, narrow tunnel with a blind corner ahead. What I notice immediately is the uneven line of spray paint running along each wall, black on one side, green on the other. The paint's fresh; I can smell it, sharp and heady. One boy, one can, each unimaginatively vandalising the seamed stone as he walked.

There's a *bump* behind me and I turn instantly, my outline beginning to shred protectively into mist, into vapour. But I recognise the pack that's come through the drill hole, and Ryan follows it, hands first, moments later. I coalesce immediately, the outline of my human form solid and unremarkable in the darkness, and watch him straighten with my green, green eyes. I know that he can't see me in the absolute absence of light.

'Tell anyone I almost lost my nerve, angel girl,' he whispers, 'and there *will* be repercussions.' He dusts himself off self-consciously before feeling around and picking up the pack.

I grin, and look down at the skin of my hands, expecting to see them gleam with the joy that I can't seem to contain: that he chose *me* over safety. But my hands are matte and unrevealing in the darkness, and Ryan fishes his torch out of his back pocket and flicks it on, his dark eyes settling first on me, then on the graffiti.

We walk again, me ahead, following the black line, the green. I reach the blind corner, Ryan at my shoulder, and we suddenly find ourselves standing ankle deep in bone shards. For a moment, I feel the chill flash of ancient memory rise up: of waking atop a stone dais in a chamber choked with bones, to find the Eight waiting and watching.

The chill intensifies as we walk forwards, and the ground drops away until the fragments of bone rise up to the level of our knees. Ryan scans the area around us with his flashlight, his hand shaking badly.

'I don't like this,' he mutters, as the torch picks out the eye sockets of broken skulls that stare at us lifelessly from the sea of bones surrounding us. 'I don't like this *at all*.'

The ground rises again beneath our feet and we're into another long passageway with the tags of green paint and black on either side. I read rising terror in the unsteadiness of the lines.

When we reach the next fork, we turn into the passageway that's marked by spray paint, but then it peters out, both lines running partially down the wall before stopping completely.

There are three gaps in the rock wall ahead of us. The left opening leads to more tunnel, blank and unrevealing. The middle one, more of the same. But in the third tunnel, I see a faint gleam of luminescence trailing low upon the wall to the right, as if something injured came this way, and recently. I imagine broken wing feathers bleeding light.

Even Ryan can make out the smeared and glowing uneven line near where the wall and the floor meet. The fear he's radiating spikes up, and stays up, and no matter what I do, I can't seem to block it out because it's in me, too.

We follow the glowing smear of light for at least a mile. I know the boys must have come this way because we pass a can of green paint dropped on the ground, then find the black one abandoned on a natural ledge of rock on one side of a narrow opening.

The opening is only just wide and tall enough to accommodate me, and I hear Ryan grunt as he ducks his head to pass beneath it. From our narrow corridor of stone we stare out into a cavern that's vast and high and filled with murky, grey water from end to end. On the other side of the cavern, another opening leads on into darkness, but it's what's positioned inside the huge chamber that catches my attention immediately, makes me place a shocked and stilling hand upon Ryan's sleeve.

No wonder those boys ran. I would run, too, if this were not the very place I am seeking.

Rising out of the great underground lake are two stone statues on pedestals, like funerary monuments, at least thirty feet of slowly swirling water separating them. Each figure is male and flawless, at least eight feet tall, winged and rendered from a pure white stone that captures every feather, every fold of the wearer's sleeveless robe, as if he'd been caught mid-movement. The figures are half-turned away from each other, giving the sensation of imminent motion, of imminent flight.

The one on the left has long, waving hair about his shoulders; a steely, forbidding expression. Inscribed upon the pedestal on which he stands are the words: *In flagella paratus sum. I am ready for the scourge.* The stone angel grasps a triple-thonged whip in one long-fingered hand, and I recognise it immediately. It was always his weapon of choice. None could wield it like he could.

'Jegudiel,' I whisper aloud, shocked.

My eyes flash across to the other winged being in dawning horror, and I see that he holds an open book in one hand; an orb shaped like a globe, or a planet, in the other. His eyes, his face, are lost in thought, beneath a head of shoulder-length curly hair. In life it would be sandy-coloured. A coronet of stylised stars rings his brow.

'Selaphiel,' I murmur, appalled.

The inscription on his pedestal reads, simply: *Bellator Deus. Warrior of God.*

The words are in bad taste. A taunt. For Selaphiel has no warrior side, it is not his *métier*. He is only contemplation and quietude, as mysterious as the universe he meditates upon.

The footage of Uriel drifting across the surface of an icy Scottish loch suddenly flashes into my mind. Jegudiel somehow located Selaphiel when Uriel could not, but something went terribly wrong. Jegudiel never made it to the Galleria Vittorio Emanuele in Milan that night because he was trapped here; taken while he was trying to free Selaphiel. They are caged within these stone effigies, I would wager my life on it. Beings of energy, of light, weightless and airy, cast into blocks of heavy, lumpen stone. What I am looking at is a deliberate and calculated provocation, an insult.

'How ...' Ryan begins, but I place my hands on his shoulders, pleading with him in a low voice to wait.

I move forward into the strange lake. Immediately, the water around me bursts into flames, which ignite the entire surface of the lake with a roar. I understand immediately what these flames are for — a special effect to keep out the mortal, the unwary, who might think to enter this chamber in which celestial beings are held captive in plain sight.

I turn and look back at Ryan, his skin lit by a weird red glow, his eyes showing his helplessness.

'Be careful,' he mouths. 'I love you.'

I nod to show that I've heard, give him a crooked smile.

I turn back and study the stone angels, their faces averted as if each can't bear the sight of the other. The smokeless flames lick at my boot-clad ankles, my denim-clad legs, but I do not burn. Oh, the flames are hot enough. But my own energy these days is equal to them, and they trouble me not at all.

I move forward through flaming water that is soon up to my waist, feeling the broken bones of a multitude of human dead shifting underfoot. Though there is demonsign aplenty, there are no demons in evidence. And I wonder at it, whether this is some elaborate trap. But nothing comes screaming at me from out of the darkness above or the waters below.

I cover the last few feet to the statue of Jegudiel at a stumbling run, and place my hand upon the stone that looks so cold. But it is warm beneath my fingers, and that warmth tells me all I need to know: that a being of fire is indeed bound within the rock.

I leap up onto the pedestal, and it's reflex what I do next. I plunge my hand through the surface of the stone, feel my own energy run in and through the hard, crystalline structure, seeking some thread, some flaw, some sign. Though Jegudiel himself eludes me, I can somehow read the signature, the pattern of him, within the rock. For his hand once wrote upon my soul the way I now seek his, and I will always recognise him now.

'Where are you?' I growl, half-merged with the stone, almost feeling something then losing it again.

Something seems to shift inside the rock. I feel him coiled there, like a serpent, and then the serpent begins to *move*. But something continues to hold him there, and I'm too afraid to give myself over to the stone completely in case I, too, am lost.

In frustration, in a voice with a ringing, steely edge to it, like a tolling bell, I cry out, '*Libera eum!*' Free him!

A vast, cracking sound echoes across the underground lake. The stone statue blows apart, into splinters, the mocking inscription instantly obliterated. I fall back into the water, shielding my face automatically, as a mist rapidly gathers in the place where the statue once stood, forming into the towering, glowing figure of a winged man that crumples forward silently.

He hits the flaming surface of the water and goes under, and I can't find him with my hands, though I search and stumble, crying out his name, throwing up a glittering spray all about me that reflects the firelight. Underfoot, the bones slide and tumble and tangle.

'Mercy!' Ryan screams, and I hear the awe in his voice. 'Over there.'

I turn and follow the line of his pointing finger and see Jegudiel staggering out of the water at the feet of the other stone angel, the one that wears the cosmos as his coronet. Flaming water sheets down off Jegudiel's powerful figure, cascading down through the folds of his bright and luminous robes, his wings. I see that some of their end feathers are bent and broken and trailing.

He plunges his hand into the stone angel before him and roars out, as I did, '*Libera eum!*'

The second statue flies apart, raining fragments of stone across the blazing lake surface.

It seems an age before Selaphiel's palely glowing figure coalesces and grows recognisable. Like Jegudiel, he falls forward and hits the flaming waters of the lake, going under. But he does not rise again.

Jegudiel spins, throwing up a desperate flurry of spray, his eyes seeking to penetrate the oily, burning water that swirls and shifts with some unseen current. As he looks up, he meets my eyes, and I see shock flare in his. The flames reflect on their dark surfaces so that it seems, for a moment, that he is on fire from within. A whip appears in his hand and he gathers himself like a lion, then surges towards me with a fearsome war cry loud enough to shake the cavern, intent on striking me down.

He believes me human, I think in wonder, in terror. *Or demon. My disguise must be absolute. He does not know who I am.*

Jegudiel has already half-covered the distance towards me, his whip raised high, before I relax the control I've fought so hard to maintain. I let my outline ripple, let it blur, so that he sees *me* before I reassume my human guise like a cloak.

He stops dead the instant he catches the shift, then the shift back, and his weapon is suddenly gone from his grasp.

'Find him!' he pleads. 'He's almost past help, Mercy. This could end him.'

CHAPTER 14

Immediately, both Jegudiel and I dive beneath the surface of the burning water and I feel his trailing wing feathers brush across my face as we spear through the airless, roaring depths, seeking our fallen brother. There's nothing but darkness and filth and noise below, bones a foot deep in every direction, everything washed red by fire.

I surface, surging upright to see Ryan lunging through the flames at the lake's edge as he drags the gleaming figure of a slack-limbed giant, wings bedraggled, up onto dry land.

Jegudiel appears on the far side of the chamber and prepares to re-enter the water, but I cry out, 'Look to the mortal!' — for Ryan's name would mean nothing to him. 'The mortal has found him.'

Jegudiel turns, astonished. He's crossed the length of the flaming lake and is looming over Ryan like a creature of nightmare, faster than I can move to stand between them. Ryan steps away from Selaphiel's prone body, his hands up and open in a gesture of parley, eyes wide, head tilted back, as he takes in Jegudiel's terrifying countenance so far above his.

'Who are you?' Jegudiel roars. '*Speak.*' And the whip in his right hand twitches.

I place my small, human-sized hand upon Jegudiel's side, but he does not turn to acknowledge me, just continues staring at Ryan as if he would turn him to stone with his eyes.

'Brother,' I say quietly, 'he's with me.'

Jegudiel's head whips around, his dark gold hair momentarily tangling in the feathers of his wings, and stares at me in disbelief.

I step out of the water and around Selaphiel's still form sprawled across the stone. I grasp one of Ryan's hands in mine. 'He's with me,' I say again, my voice stronger. 'His name is Ryan, and he's a good guy. Azraeil would claim him in a heartbeat — he's already tried to.'

Jegudiel looks at Ryan in consternation. 'But how could he "be" with you? He's *human*.'

Ryan lifts his chin. 'Nevertheless,' he says defiantly, 'I love her, we're together, and we came to get Selaphiel out.'

Jegudiel's eyes widen in astonishment. But then he turns and scans the cavern. 'This is no place to talk of *love*. Neqael and Turael — those who enslaved us inside the rock — will soon return. We are closer to Hell than you think: they move constantly between the fiery stronghold that gives them life and all the cemeteries and bone pits of Paris. And what they find there, they use to create ... monsters; *daemonium* enough to overwhelm all life.' His eyes snap to me. 'Since Selaphiel has been imprisoned here they have sent that foul legion against him for their own amusement, for sport. Time after time, his body has been broken almost beyond repair, but they "heal" him only to ready him for another contest, another indignity. They planned to pit us against each other when he was strong enough to face me. We must be gone before they return.'

Neqael: a name I haven't heard for millennia. She, too, had loved and followed Luc, and had seemed to me — in form, at least — as lovely and as fresh, as frail, as a wildflower. She had hair like russet leaves, cornflower blue eyes and the slyest sense of humour that could cut you to the quick.

Turael was just another hanger-on, dark eyes, dark hair, a beautiful boy in a pack of beautiful boys. Easily impressed, easily swayed. A sycophant; the type I've never been interested in.

'They are not as you remember them,' Jegudiel says harshly. 'These days, they are harder than the stone angels they create from the broken headstones of the ancient dead. They are angels of rage — and they will brutalise you without hesitation or remorse. We need to *go*.'

I bend and touch Selaphiel's flawless face. His eyes are closed. He could be a beautiful youth sleeping on the ground. There's not a mark on him, not a single wound, but the energy he gives off is terrifying and strange; and as we three stand over him, he seems to gutter, to flicker, and his wings shred and vanish before our eyes, as if he lacks the strength even to hold his own form.

Ryan gasps as Selaphiel begins to grow in brightness, increment by increment. I get a flash of the instant K'el died at Luc's hand. How his form grew hotter, brighter, even than the sun, before his energy exploded outward, dispersing back to the universe, never to return. The same thing is happening to Selaphiel.

Jegudiel's voice is raw with an uncharacteristic emotion.

'I have to get him *home*. His body may not appear broken, but his mind, his soul ... who can say?'

'*Mercy!*' Ryan yells suddenly, and his voice sounds so strange, so fevered, with so much terror in the word, that for a moment I think he's begging for clemency, not calling my name. 'The water!' he shouts. '*Look at the water.*'

Jegudiel and I turn to see yellowed skulls, scores of them, rising out of the burning water behind us, their eroded, fleshless faces topping a travesty of mismatched bones. Some of the skeletal figures have two legs, others four, others have whipping tentacles of bone in place of limbs, like the tails of scorpions. All of them move towards us, firelight gleaming on them, through them. The energy this army of bones gives out is utterly inhuman. It's low level, just enough to animate, but so utterly *wrong*.

At the opening in the rock on the other side of the cavern, I glimpse something shining. It moves so rapidly it's but a blur, and the energy it gives off is discordant and inhuman, too, but powerful.

'She comes,' Jegudiel snarls, brandishing his whip high. 'Get them out, Mercy. That boy should never have come here. God willing, I'll find you. *Go.*'

The deformed army of bones throws itself at the narrow spit of stone upon which we stand, and Jegudiel begins to scatter skulls and bony limbs in every direction with fist, with violent whip lash.

Still they come — a phantasmagoria of nightmare rising out of the lake. They are joined by more misshapen, skeletal forms that pour out of the opening on the other side of the cavern, single-mindedly entering the water and moving in our direction.

Ryan and I exchange wild-eyed looks as he grasps Selaphiel beneath the arms and I gather up the rest of him and we lurch forward, angling him awkwardly out through the narrow breach in the rock.

'He's a giant that weighs almost nothing,' Ryan cries disbelievingly. 'How's that even possible?'

Ryan's moving backwards and he stumbles over something and almost goes down, but somehow recovers, like a cat, like the athlete he used to be, and we follow the line of green, the line of black, the smear of luminescence, back the way we came. Selaphiel's form grows steadily brighter beneath our hands, throwing a stark light, like daylight, onto the tunnel walls around us.

We plunge into that pit of bones that so disgusted Ryan before, and this time the bones seem alive. They grasp at our legs, seeking to drag us down. Ryan goes wild at their touch, leaping and swearing and twisting until we are back on solid ground again. There's sweat streaming off his face and down his neck, every muscle in his tall frame poised for flight.

The passageways rise and rise, until ahead of us we see the concrete barrier with the drill hole at its base, just large enough to accommodate one man.

'What do we do?' Ryan almost howls. 'We'll never get him through there. It's impossible.'

I seem to catch a dense plume of roiling, smoky vapour passing overhead, then another flees by. Selaphiel's eyes suddenly flash open as the last of the smoke hits the concrete wall beside us, high above our heads, vanishing instantly. His gaze settles upon my human guise without recognition.

Joy turns instantly to fear; his eyes — once such a crystalline blue — seem sunken and cloudy and racked with pain.

'Selaphiel,' I gasp sorrowfully.

Ryan looks down at the being in his arms, doing a double-take when he sees that Selaphiel is conscious. Selaphiel's eyes move slowly across Ryan's face, the way clouds will pass across the face of the sun, touching nothing, altering nothing. He doesn't speak, doesn't struggle.

As we set him gently down against the wall, there's a distant rumbling sound that grows louder, moving up the corridor towards us with a low roar, like an approaching train. The stone beneath our feet begins to buck and ripple, the air filling with a choking dust, and Ryan and I are thrown to the ground.

'The stone!' I cry in horror, feeling it shift and protest beneath my fingers. 'It's coming down behind us!'

Selaphiel burns now with an almost blinding light. I push up off the tunnel floor and crouch before him, placing my hands upon his face to make him see me, for an instant, the way Jegudiel had. As he catches the shift, the shift back, his blue eyes widen, his mouth parting as if he would speak. But no words come.

'There's a way out!' I shout over the sound of rending stone, pointing at the concrete seal across the passageway. 'It's close, and this human, Ryan, will help you reach the surface, reach the light.' I indicate Ryan sprawled beside me on the floor, his eyes, wide, on both of us. 'But you need to do one last thing, brother, you need to *shift* as I've done. Do you understand what I'm asking of you?'

In reply, Selaphiel's eyes close and his form seems to slump and shimmer. For a moment, I think I see the surface of the rock through the outline of him.

'No. *You*. *Don't*,' I say fiercely. 'You don't give up. You don't get to. You're too important.'

I grab him and pull him close, cradling him against me, letting him feel the terror seeping out of me: for him, for Ryan, for all of us. The sound of falling stone buries my words, but I know that Selaphiel can hear them through my skin as I speak them.

'Don't let it be true, Selaphiel! Don't let it be said that I was responsible for the destruction of everyone who ever loved me. *Shift* if you want to live. It's the only way we can help you. If that boy dies, it will be my death sentence, too. *I love him*. Please, I beg of you. Shift that we may all live.'

'Mercy!' Ryan cries again, torn between wanting to run and wanting to stay with me, always with me.

Selaphiel suddenly struggles feebly in my arms, pushing me away. He raises a shaking hand, like a gesture of benediction, mouths a single word I cannot catch.

Instantly, the concrete barrier tumbles into pieces, falling outward, away from us. Ryan and I act like a single organism: we don't look at each other or even speak, we just each take one of Selaphiel's arms and haul him off the ground at a run, fleeing before the advancing rockfall. Lumps of stone — each big enough and deadly enough to end a man's life — erase the passageway behind us.

As we stumble forward through the choking dust, Selaphiel does what I begged him to do — he shifts so that he's scaled along more human lines, so we're able to hoist him higher across our shoulders and *run*. But the brilliant light he gives out keeps intensifying, until he's so bright, he's only discernible in a kind of numinous outline. It's like we're cradling a dying star between us. Ryan can barely stand to look at him.

'What's happening to him?' Ryan gasps, as we reach the narrow crevice in the wall we've been searching for.

I don't answer, catching a flare of light to my right. Digging my heels in, I turn my head to see what's causing it. It's Jegudiel in the distance down the passageway, grappling with a shining, winged female figure that can only be Neqael.

I can't see her face, but her trailing russet hair, her wing feathers, every inch of her, gleams with that foul, grey-tainted light. The folds of her diaphanous, long-sleeved gown billow around her as they struggle. I know that the other, Turael, can't be far behind. Demons seem to hunt in pairs, and if we leave now, Jegudiel will have to face them both alone.

'Mercy!' Ryan cries, indicating the rungs of the rusty ladder behind him that are mounted directly into the stone wall. 'Move it!'

I'm still standing in the entryway, my figure blocking both Selaphiel and Ryan from sight.

'Go. *Climb*,' I implore Ryan, entrusting Selaphiel to him completely, trying to push them both deeper into the cleft. 'Keep yourself alive, keep Selaphiel safe. Find Henri, do whatever it takes. Get to the plane. I'll find you. I'm not leaving without Jegudiel. No matter how much I've provoked him in the past, he would do the same for me. I get that now.'

Ryan gives me a hard, searching look, his heart in his eyes.

'It used to be all about how much *I* could take out of every situation,' I tell him in a rush of words. 'Individual liberty — it was always my paramount consideration, my guiding principle; Luc's. Hers.' I point at Neqael's gleaming figure in the distance. 'But I'm not alone. None of us is truly ever alone. We may feel as if we are, but our actions matter.

Every single act impacts on this web of souls we form part of, and it's a web that stretches backwards in time, forwards. I could never see that before, but now I do. It's not ever just about you, or the person you ... love above all others,' Ryan's eyes darken with emotion, 'it's about awareness and respect and gratitude. Everything in its place or it is chaos. That's our creed — the creed of the *elohim*. I used to think it meant "know your place", don't get ideas above your station, and it used to infuriate me beyond measure to have that continually thrown in my face — but I was wrong. What Gabriel was trying to tell me is that liberty is important, but it has to take place in a context: of others, of a community. Evil has no community, Ryan. It feeds itself, upon itself, it considers itself above all. I have to help him,' I finish desperately. 'Don't you see? It goes beyond what you and I want. It always has, and I was too blind to see that.'

Ryan bends and kisses me, swiftly, then he and Selaphiel are gone, out of sight, and I hear his boots striking the first rungs.

And even though I told him to go, I can't help feeling utterly bereft without him.

I turn back to see Jegudiel in the demon's embrace. They could be lovers, they could be dancing — though Jegudiel's profile is tight and hard, like granite — for she has her arms around his neck, and I see her lay her head against the side of his face, turning him giddily, laughing. She's wreathed in a robe that is gleaming with light, but also tattered, crepuscular, like a moth-eaten shroud. As she turns again, with Jegudiel held fast in her arms, I see the mark of the exile shining across her shoulderblades, between her wings.

She's facing me now, over his shoulder, and I'm shocked to see dark markings crawling across her face, her neck, her arms and hands, like tattoos rendered in acid, or poison. Her hair and form are alive with a dark electricity, a tainted light, that serves to make her cornflower blue eyes — the only part of her I truly recognise — seem unhinged and feral. She meets my eyes and grins, and I reel back in horror from her teeth — each one with the appearance of having been filed into a point, resembling the canines of wild animals.

I see recognition in her gaze as the ground below me ceases to shake and the sound of falling stone stops. The corridor is as silent as a grave now and she purrs into that silence, 'Did you truly think that your passage through the underworld would go unnoticed … *Mercy*?'

So quickly I barely have time to register the movement, there's a short, flaming blade in her hand and she pushes the tip of it into the smooth column of Jegudiel's throat from the side. He cries out in agony. She keeps the blade there, deliberately holding its point inside him, inside his throat, and I see light leaching steadily out of the wound as he struggles to hold his head high, his bright hair flowing down his back, down between his wings, like a torrent of gold.

'Let him go,' I say quietly. 'If you want me, if it's true, as Luc has said, that I have always been the prize, then let him go.'

'The way we let that eunuch Selaphiel go?' She laughs. 'We can always pick him and the boy up later, can't we, Turael?'

A chill moves through me at her words and I turn to see a gleaming male figure standing before the rockfall at the other end of the passageway. He's at least eight feet tall, the end feathers of his grey-tinted wings trailing in the dust on the floor, and there's a burning scar on his chest as large as an archangel's handprint. He has the dark eyes and dark hair that I dimly recall, but all else about him has changed, and changed utterly. He bears an intricate flowering of black markings around his left eye that only heightens his wild, male beauty.

Maybe he was standing there the whole time and saw the way Ryan and I looked at each other — the way everything we are to each other was in our eyes — because there's an ugly expression on his beautiful face, a promise of pain.

'Turael,' I say evenly, trying not to betray my fear, 'why on earth do you still affect to wear wings when all you and Neqael do these days is crawl in the earth like *worms*?'

He opens his mouth and hisses at me like a snake, and I see that his teeth are also sharp in appearance, like the canines of wild dogs.

'Shall I bring you his head?' he says, flexing his powerful hands. I go cold at his words. 'Or would you rather not know the manner in which the boy dies?'

Neqael swings Jegudiel around to face me. I see the dark talons of one long-fingered hand stretched down across the front of Jegudiel's torn robe like the claws of some predatory bird. She holds her short, flaming blade hard up against the front of his throat with her other hand.

'It's impressive,' she says, 'how ordinary and insignificant you've managed to make yourself. Even more ordinary and insignificant than you once were. It's a mystery to us all what our Lord Lucifer saw in you. None of us could ever understand it. You had no more to commend you than any of us did.'

'He saw her *fire*,' Jegudiel snarls. 'He saw her strength and her indomitable will. She is worth an *infinity* of you, and there will be a reckoning. It is coming.'

He inhales sharply as Neqael pushes the edge of her burning blade into his throat so that it bites deep.

'Reminiscences bore me,' she snaps. 'Take her, Turael. Let us be celebrated, let us be raised up at last, for I am sick of playing gaoler, of being a keeper of bones and dead artefacts and dust. She shall restore our fortunes, and the order of all things will be remade in *our* image. It has been too long in the execution, our homecoming. Let her see for herself what Hell is like.'

I feel Turael moving closer behind me, feel the dark shirring of his energy, am nauseated by it.

'I will hold them off for as long as I can,' Jegudiel says, regret in his dark eyes as he looks at me.

'That won't be necessary, my friend,' I murmur, as Turael's weapon springs into his hand at my back. I hear the sizzle of the blade as it pulses with that tainted light and heat peculiar to the fallen. 'Just remember to duck.'

A fleeting look of puzzlement crosses Jegudiel's face as I slowly pivot so that I'm side-on to Neqael, to Turael. I take a small step back so that I have a perfect line of sight in both directions.

'You know what?' I say conversationally. 'You're antiques, you two. You're stupid. And you know why you're stupid?'

Neqael's laugh is discordant and derisive. 'This coming from *you*, who could not resist showing off your "cleverness" to Jegudiel, to Selaphiel. Turael *saw* you. You're as dimwitted as the humans you consort with these days.'

I continue softly, as if she hasn't spoken. 'You're so consumed by malice, so focused on universal domination, that you've completely missed the point. You bring out the very worst in humankind, but you don't *see* them, you don't comprehend what they've done, what they're capable of.'

'Oh, I see well enough.' Neqael laughs, exposing the sinuous line of her throat that is wreathed with dark markings. 'They possess a fine capability for depravity of every nature, but beyond that, they are animals. And now you consort with animals — and therefore you are their whore, the way you were once Lucifer's whore, *H—*'

I see her tattooed mouth begin to form the first syllable of my name, I feel Turael grasp me by my long, curling hair, lifting me off the ground easily, and I have no choice. They leave me no choice, and I'm almost glad as pain begins to explode in me.

I let Turael swing me towards him, and I turn my face as if I would place one last kiss upon his cheek. Then, like a reflex, like the speed of thought, there's a gun in each of my hands: sleek and heavy, with the look of the semi-automatic, a single lick of blue flame passing across the surface. They require no strength, no *finesse* to wield, just proximity and dumb luck.

I feel the muzzle of the gun in my blazing left hand connect with Turael's jaw as the gun in my right rises towards Neqael as my eyes meet hers. My wrists are crossed before me, and it happens so fast that I've already pulled the trigger of each weapon simultaneously in the time it takes for Neqael's eyes to widen in recognition of the things I hold in my hands.

Her mouth falls open and I see her thinking: *But guns are stupid things; human things that humans use upon each other. They have no bearing upon angels, or upon demons.*

Until now, until *me.*

It's just a single shot from each weapon — small and insignificant against the majestic, blazing blades of my enemies — but the bullets are as deadly as any cutting surface, sped by thought, infallibly accurate, because I am the scope, I am the accelerant.

Just a small sting, like the bite of a mosquito.

But I imagine I see Jegudiel wrenching himself to the right as the blast wave of heat and dark energy that once was Turael knocks me to the tunnel floor. I'm deaf and blind to everything, my entire being resounding with pain as if my body were a tolling bell. So I don't see the second bullet connect, I don't see Neqael die. But I feel it. I feel the atmosphere compress then expand almost beyond bearing as the passageway is filled with the roar of her dark matter returning to God.

Then Jegudiel and I are all that remains in this silent, tomblike place.

I crawl across the cold and filthy floor towards him and say into the still place inside his head: *Brother, you're hurt.*

Jegudiel sits up slowly against the wall and his damaged wings shred into nothingness. He just looks at me with his dark eyes. I kneel before him, almost in an attitude of worship, dwarfed by his scale.

Raphael kept insisting you'd changed. His voice in my mind is very quiet. *And I confess, I did not believe it possible.*

Raphael is missing, I reply. *He was not in Milan. He has been taken, too. But not here. Taken somewhere else.*

Jegudiel seems to slump at the news. Then he gestures in the air, making the fingers of his hands into unfamiliar weapons, into guns. *How …?*

229

The smile I give him is sad. *When you have lived long enough in this world, you will understand how I am able to manifest something so utterly foreign to everything we are.*

I reach out to him, and as my small fingers connect with his, he takes both my hands gently.

'You do me good,' he murmurs aloud. 'To have you restored in this way — it gladdens me beyond measure.'

'My memory is still riddled with holes,' I mutter, 'like this place. I'm not complete, not the creature I was. I may never be whole again.'

'You don't need those memories,' he replies firmly. 'You no longer have them — whether by your own doing or Raph's — for good reason.'

His gaze grows distant. 'Selaphiel can't remain here — you know that, don't you? This world will only kill him. I need you to do something for me ...'

It's probably something impossible, but I say anyway, without hesitation, 'Yes, of course. Name it.'

Jegudiel refocuses his gaze upon my face, and his smile, now, seems sad. 'Do you know how he does it?'

I shake my head, knowing that he speaks of Luc.

'Fault lines and surface weaknesses: those are what he uses to move himself and his forces around the human world unseen. He's had years to work out where the pressure points are; he's also more than adept at creating new ones.'

Jegudiel shifts uncomfortably against the rough stone at his back and I know he's wounded inside, too. Perhaps badly.

'Go on,' I say softly.

'We Eight also have our meeting places, our secret haunts. Michael will not thank me for telling you this, but the

Majlis al-Djinn is one such place; also the crypts of ancient Carthage, the peak of Mount Pilatus, the limestone terraces of Pamukkale, and many others. After Milan ...' his gaze shifts inward again, '... we were to regroup at a place mortals know as Sōfu-iwa or Lot's Wife. Do you know it?'

I shake my head. 'Where is it?'

'It's part of a chain of isles, the Izu-shotō,' he murmurs, sitting straighter against the wall. 'Hundreds of miles south of the city known as Tokyo, Japan.' He gives me a wry, sideways glance. 'You've seen that city ... in another life. Sōfu-iwa is the southernmost of them all. An isle so sheer and uninhabitable, and located in such rough seas, that it is virtually impossible for any human to disembark there. Perfect for our purposes. Whoever survived Milan was to go there immediately and wait. And plan.'

He grasps my hands tighter in his, and his face is grave. 'I need you to tell whoever you find there what transpired here: that I am alive; that Selaphiel yet lives and has been taken out of Luc's reach. Can you do that for me?'

No small thing. But those who have risked their lives for me cannot be denied; and I know now where this compulsion, this need to repay, to make things right, springs from. It has gone beyond simple vengeance, beyond redemption. I'm beginning to see that maybe only love and fealty have the power to move me now. The demon killing that I must engage in sickens me. I do not delight in revenge the way that I thought I would. But I would do it again, and again, in a heartbeat, for the right reasons.

I nod, finally.

Jegudiel stands slowly, pulling me to my feet before releasing my hands. 'Go as quickly as you can, by whatever means will take you and your ...' He stops momentarily, perplexed. 'Your mortal companion to Sōfu-iwa.'

'He hates flying, you know,' I say. 'My way, not the human way. For so long I couldn't fly; and when I finally regained my freedom, I almost couldn't make myself do it again. But now, when I *can* fly, there's Ryan to consider ...'

Jegudiel looks down into the human face I wear and smiles. It makes him almost too beautiful to gaze on. 'He must be very strong, to love you,' he says quietly. 'He'll survive.'

His outline begins to shred as I follow him back down the tunnel towards the crack in the wall that conceals that ladder to the surface.

'Selaphiel is my concern now,' he murmurs, almost to himself. 'Mine alone.' He looks at me over his shoulder and I know I will always remember this moment — the instant he was before me and then gone, vanishing into motes of light, his laughter resounding, ghostly, his voice saying out of the ether, 'As to the mortal boy who loves you? I leave it to you to explain to him where you are going and why. You were always ... inventive.'

Then I know that he has vanished into the cleft in the rock and I — so weary in spirit, wanting nothing more than to be, and to be with Ryan — have no choice but to follow.

CHAPTER 15

I hear Ryan yell out as the gust of force that Jegudiel is hooks Selaphiel off the rungs of the ladder below him. And I seem to hear Jegudiel's voice echo with faint laughter within this narrow vent in the earth: *Persistence, Ryan. Courage. For you shall need it!*

Then they are gone like a hurricane, my brothers, gone like smoke. Up and out through the manhole cover, which clatters away, leaving a tiny patch of early evening sky framed far above our heads. And I'm suddenly there in Selaphiel's place, on the ladder, a few rungs below where Ryan is, and it's pitch black because I'm just a girl in a black puffer jacket and dark grey jeans who gives out no light. But I can see that Ryan and Selaphiel haven't even reached halfway. There's still a hundred feet, more, to go.

Ryan's voice is strained. 'Tell me it's you, and not some demon that just happened to wander in here smelling like fresh snowfall and moving as silently as a cat.'

He's trying to keep his tone light, but I can hear the exhaustion; that he's about to give way.

'I'm so sorry,' I say quietly. 'About all of this. I warned you. And it's only going to get worse.'

'Just get us out of here,' he says finally. 'You can give me the bad news when we're standing on solid ground with a December gale blowing in our faces.'

'You're sure?'

I hear him swallow. 'It's who you are. And holding you back, not letting you do all that freaky shit you can do, it just puts you at risk. It's time for this ladybug to *man up*.' His voice is suddenly wry in the darkness.

'Well, if you're sure ...' I say softly.

I don't give him any more time to think about it; I collapse into vapour, coil myself around my beloved and haul us up and out through the open manhole. It's over in seconds.

The instant I materialise in my human form beside Ryan, who's breathing hard, like he's just run a marathon, I fall to my knees, my head ringing with the feel of Luc reaching for me across some unfathomable distance.

Underground, the solid rock had sheltered me from his questing consciousness, but out here it's like he's coming at me from all sides, like the wind itself is roaring in his voice: *There's nowhere to hide now, nowhere. When I find you, I will tear you apart for what you have done to me!*

It's as if a breach is opening in the air between Luc and me, as if the shutter of a camera, or a great eye, is turning its gaze upon me, upon Ryan. I know I can't let Luc see us here; am terrified that he might read my thoughts straight out of my head as I think them. Dimly, I feel Ryan's hands on my shoulders, hear him call my name fearfully, and I know he's never been in so much danger.

'*Not unless I find you first!*' I howl in reply, almost blind and deaf with pain.

The force of my fury — born of so much hurt and betrayal; a keen, animal rage — is like the lash of a whip, an open flame, upon Luc's own psyche. I hear him shriek in surprise, in real agony, before that sense of questing is suddenly cut off, and the night no longer seems alive with his malice.

He'll hesitate before he reaches out again, though it has cost me dearly. I roll over, moaning, hugging myself protectively, every part of me raw in the evening air.

Second by second, my senses grow less jammed, begin to return, and I realise that it smells of wet earth out here. It must have rained while we were below. But the air isn't filled with returning birdsong, or the sound of tyres swishing on rain-slicked streets, but with sirens and the reflected glow of flashing lights.

Ryan raises me to my feet, and, without thinking, I pull him to me, needing his warmth, his strength, just to stay upright. I take in my surroundings shakily and see with shock that it's as if we came up out of the ground not in Paris, but back in Milan. All around us is a scene of utter devastation. We're standing on the only section of the street that hasn't collapsed into the earth, taking with it cars, bicycles, trees, street furniture, road signs, the awnings and porticos of buildings. It's not a *Rue* now, but a deep trench.

'My God,' Ryan breathes as he slowly processes the desolation around us. 'What the hell happened up here?'

'*We* happened,' I say quietly.

He turns and stares at me, horrified.

The last of the day's light has leached out of the navy blue sky. My internal clock tells me that it's after four in the afternoon; that we've been gone for hours. There are no faces at the windows of the damaged buildings looming over us, but plenty of emergency personnel on the ground, and a large crowd being kept back at some far remove. I hear someone shout out as they catch sight of us standing in the middle of the road like sightseers. Except that Ryan's covered, head to foot, in white dust, just like those kids were. We might as well have a flashing neon sign over our heads that says we've been down in the catacombs while the world caved in above us.

'*Arrêtez-vous!*' a man roars in the distance.

I don't give him time to point a weapon at us or get any closer; I just grasp Ryan under the arms and leap into the sheltering sky, with Ryan bellowing out his fear.

I take us so high, so fast, that we are soon lost in the underbelly of black cloud that is advancing towards us. Soon, we are specks too small for the human eye to detect. They will have no explanation for us in whatever reports they file of this day.

The direction of the gusting wind is against us. Ryan's stopped yelling, but his eyes are screwed shut and there's a sick look on his face as if this is some crazy carnival ride he can't get off. Once my trajectory starts to even out, he wriggles in my grasp, actually struggling to reach around and get the backpack, half out of his mind with fear.

'We could just c-call Henri,' he stammers through chattering teeth. 'Catch a lift with him.'

It's arctic up here and I hug him closer to me. 'Henri's officially off-duty,' I reply gently. 'And do you really think he'll want to pick up after he sees what's happened to the fourteenth arrondissement? If you can bear it, look down.'

Ryan shakes his head, terrified.

'Street after street, Ryan, collapsed into the earth. If I were Henri, I wouldn't touch us, and I don't blame him. He won't pick up. Please, don't struggle any more. Remember what you told me? *You're not going to fall.* I've got you, I've got you.'

Ryan's breathing erratically and his eyes are still closed, so he doesn't see us leave the chaos around the Île de la Cité and Île St Louis in our wake, doesn't see that we've already left northern Paris far behind us.

To spare him a little, I'm holding back on how fast I can actually go. I feel no fear now as I stretch into the buffeting wind, into the smell of advancing rain. When Ryan is with me, it truly is as if I cannot fall.

The lights are so extraordinarily beautiful, like a net of jewels flung across the darkened land. I feel a surge of inexplicable joy, though I don't think we've ever been so exposed, just two tiny creatures battling a vast and threatening sky.

'I wish you'd look!' I tell him.

He rests his cold cheek against mine, his eyes still closed. 'Just tell me when it's over,' he says, teeth chattering, his whole body one long tremor.

Ten minutes later, no more than that, it is.

'We're here,' I tell him, landing so silently, so lightly, that it takes him a moment to comprehend that solid ground is again beneath our feet. He staggers a little where he stands, opening his eyes with difficulty before raising his head. I see the look of shock on his face as he focuses on the signage on the hangar wall beside us: *StA Global Logistics*. Fear had blocked out the sound of aircraft taxiing down the runway beneath us, blocked out the odour of burning aviation fuel and wet tarmac.

'You're going to walk in the front entrance of that hangar,' I tell him in a low voice, 'and introduce yourself to the ground staff on duty and tell them you need the jet fuelled and ready for take-off as fast as humanly possible, *faster*. We're calling in that favour — get Bianca on the line if you have to, or those mystery telephone wizards. Throw everything you've got at them.'

'But I look like a *terrorist*,' Ryan says, appalled, running a grazed and trembling hand through his dusty buzz cut. 'Those police on the ground — that's what they thought we were. And where am I to say we're going in such a hurry?'

'Tokyo,' I reply. 'By way of the Izu Islands. Specifically, the jet has to make one pass over the uninhabited crag known as Lot's Wife — the Sōfu-iwa.'

Ryan mouths the unfamiliar words, imprinting them on his memory.

'I'll explain more when we get on board,' I add. 'Minimum crew, you know the drill.'

My outline is already beginning to shred at the edges as Ryan squares his shoulders and stumbles around the front of the building.

When the plane reaches cruising altitude — after passing through a belt of heavy rain that gave us a rocky time — Ryan unbuckles his seatbelt and heads for the couch at the back of the plane. 'Scooch over,' he mock-complains when he finds me already there, with a couple of fat pillows under my head and two more set out for him beside me.

There's a pretty, softly spoken crew member at the front of the plane near the cockpit, her hands clenched unhappily in her lap. Apart from welcoming Ryan on board, she's tried to avoid him at all costs. I can feel her towering tension from where I am, and it's rising in me, too. I've had time to think, which is always a dangerous thing.

Ryan's clearly made the most of the passenger lounge inside the hangar during the fifty-seven minutes it took to scramble together a crew and a flight out of Le Bourget: somehow he's managed to shower and get the worst of the dust off his tee-shirt. He smells like soap and the supermarket-brand deodorant Tommy put inside our backpack. He eases himself down beside me, his mobile phone in his hand, and his eyes seem very tired.

'What's at Sōfu-iwa?' he yawns, angling in to face me.

I reach up to trace his freshly shaven jaw, the bruised-looking skin beneath his eyes. He closes them briefly, before placing his hand on mine and pulling our entwined fingers down to rest between us on the couch.

'More like *who*,' I whisper. 'The Eight were supposed to regroup there after Milan. It could be some of Them, or no one. I just need to tell them Jegudiel and Selaphiel are alive; and then maybe that's my cue to stop messing you around and get the hell out of your life. For good.'

Ryan draws breath sharply. 'You're joking, right?'

'I've been thinking,' I say, frowning at the broad wall of his chest, unable to meet his eyes, astonished at my cowardice. 'Every moment I'm here is another chance for Luc to get to me and trigger the kind of "end time" he's been craving since he fell. They all *knew* me, Ryan, those demons that I ... killed. We had ... history. We used to be on the same side. Only at the time I hadn't realised sides were forming.' I raise my eyes to his face. 'They all knew my name. They would have used it, too.'

'So what?' he says sharply. 'So what if they knew your name?'

'I don't just suffer from an inconvenient kind of amnesia,' I say softly. 'Raphael did something to me — he hid my name so deep inside me that I can't bear to hear it without going haywire. Any one of the original hundred that fell with Luc could just speak my name and I'd be his again; it would be that simple. Luc would break free of this realm, the holy war would begin, and the universe would become the kind of contested territory this earth has been, for thousands of years. If I stay, everything gets placed in the balance.'

'I make the mistake of leaving you alone just to take a stupid shower and you come up with *all this*?' Ryan says angrily. 'Haven't you sacrificed enough? Can't the Eight take over for you now? Whatever happened to you and me losing ourselves in the world? When do *you* get to do what you want for a change? Or me?' I hear his bitterness. 'Or maybe you're trying to let me down gently, and I'm not hearing you. All the signals you've been giving out — have I misread those, too?'

'I owe Them my life, Ryan,' I say pleadingly. 'And if I'm not around, the Eight will be able to contain Luc the way he's always been contained — until now. When he didn't know where I was, he was ... constrained. He'll be constrained again, thwarted again, if I'm not here to fuel his ambitions. In the end, I can't take you with me,' I add with a catch in my voice. 'And I can't stay. I can't see any way around it.'

Ryan's eyes are so dark with pain they're almost black.

'But I told my family about you,' he says, pushing a button at the base of his phone so the screen flares into life. I see a cascade of small electronic squares in bright colours with cartoon logos.

'I finally did it. They asked when I was coming home, and I said I couldn't be sure, that it would depend on what you were doing, because I was with you. They wanted to know how "some girl" could be so important that I'd fly all the way to Australia, then turn around and fly to Milan and Paris and Tokyo, then God knows where else, wasting all this time and effort and money when I should be focusing on college. So I had to tell them *why*. Why you're so important to me that I'd drop everything again in a second just to be with you; how we all owe you a debt we'll never be able to repay. At first, they didn't believe me — they said I'd been brainwashed, kidnapped by some dangerous cult — until Lauren explained.

'She's never told them about any of it, you see. She could never bring herself to talk to them in any detail about what happened; not the real way it played out. But she suddenly opened up, and all she wanted to talk about was *you*. And now they want to speak to you. They want to thank you themselves. And I was dumb enough to think it might finally be okay to share your existence with the people I love most in the world.'

He braces himself on one elbow and moves his finger across the screen's smooth surface as if he's painting. Then I see a word appear there: *Lauren*. Hear a dial tone. My eyes widen as Lauren's face is suddenly there. I get a flash of perfect white teeth as she smiles, and I'm astonished at the change in her, how the surface cracks have been so readily papered over. She's still gaunt, still ragged at the edges, but, like me, she's a carefully curated collection of props, put together to make her seem like an ordinary girl again. Under the veneer, though, there's something else entirely.

'Is she there?' she asks Ryan eagerly. 'Can I go get them?'

I get a view of the room Lauren's in. It's morning, I can tell by the background light. And I know that room: it's her bedroom; I recognise the dresser. But it's changed almost out of sight since I stayed in it when I was Carmen. It's not a girly room any more. The stretch of wall I can see has been painted a vibrant purple and doesn't have a single poster on it; and all the photographs and knick-knacks that were on the dresser are gone. It's as bare as the wall.

I look at Ryan, shake my head quickly, mouth: *No. No. Wait.*

But Ryan just shoves the phone into my hand, a dangerous expression on his face.

For a second Lauren just stares at me, puzzled. 'Mercy? Is that you?'

I try to hand the phone back to Ryan and all she gets is a muddled view of the Gulfstream's softly lit interior.

'Ryan?' she says. 'Are you there? What's going on?'

'Tell her,' Ryan says fiercely, refusing to take the phone I'm holding out to him. We wrestle with it for a moment. 'Don't make me look like a crazy on top of everything else. Tell her. No, *show* her.' He shoves the screen back in front of my face. '*Show her*,' he commands.

Lauren and I stare at each other in silence.

'Ryan, can you hear me?' Lauren says finally.

'Yes,' Ryan snaps. 'I can hear you. She's doing this on purpose, Lauren, making me look like a liar. Just unbend, damn you. Just do this for me.'

Lauren studies my electronically mediated features for a long time before her frown evens out. 'Mercy?' she says tentatively. 'It *is* you, isn't it? You have Carmen's hair. It was

242

so wild. It's exactly the same. It's even the same length. I remember looking at you, uh, Carmen in the hospital and wishing I had hair like that. You always want what you haven't got, right?'

She falters to a stop, appalled by her own words.

'You look well,' I say quietly with my stranger's mouth, neither confirming nor denying. 'I'm glad.'

'Thank you,' she whispers. 'This is one of my, um, better days. You just ... left, and I had no one to talk to about any of it after Jennifer went home. No one could possibly understand, you see, if they weren't there ...'

'I'm sorry I didn't get there sooner,' I say.

'At least you got there.' She looks down momentarily, her voice almost inaudible. 'I was ready to die.'

Ryan's still stubbornly refusing to take back his stupid mobile. '*Show her*,' he begs. 'For me? I want her to see *you*, the way I do.'

My eyes snap to his and I see how desperately he wants her to understand and, suddenly, I don't know why I'm fighting him. We're all of us crying out for proof, aren't we? So I hold the screen up before me again and shift. Just long enough for Lauren in the middle of God-knows-where, to see *me* again, the way I truly am. I hear her gasp at my gleaming hair, my gleaming face, everything so different from the girl I was before. I must be shining out from the screen at her like a little sun. Lauren's hands are over her mouth, as if she's going to be sick.

'No trick photography,' I say quietly, 'no special effects. Just me. Doing the freaky shit that I do.'

Ryan slips an arm around me, and gently takes back his phone with his free hand. The plane gives a sudden lurch, riding out a pocket of intense turbulence.

'Keep him safe!' I hear Lauren plead, as if in prayer.

I turn my face away from the screen, let my human guise fall back into place. I can't bring myself to answer her — for I live with that specific fear every moment he's with me.

'I'll call you again when I can,' I hear Ryan murmur. 'And maybe she'll let them see her next time, talk to her. It can't go anywhere beyond us. Love you. Bye.'

It's his turn to put his arm around me from behind, moulding himself to me, his lips against my hair. But I do not bend, I do not soften into sleep; I just lie there facing the seat back, paralysed by love and fear, until I feel sleep overtake his human physiology the way it always does.

CHAPTER 16

Ryan sleeps through a quick refuelling stop somewhere on the Gulf of Aden. We're over the Bay of Bengal when I hear the Frenchwoman walking hesitantly down the central aisle towards us. Instantly, I'm mist. Just a pocket of energy, watching as she stands over him — short, pretty, blonde — wringing her hands a little before tapping him on the shoulder. She straightens immediately and steps back, and he rolls over and looks at her, startled, almost falling off the couch again onto the floor.

'Monsieur Dal-ey?' she says hesitantly, and I sense that weird anxiety coming from her again. It's sky high. Right now, she's just nerves held together by good grooming.

It's not helping that Ryan's looking around wildly for me rather than focusing his attention on the young woman standing before him. His eyes keep moving around the plane and her anxiety hits overdrive. She doesn't want to be here, that's plain.

'The pilots,' she ploughs on gamely, 'they wish me to inform you that we cannot make the requested pass over Sōfu-iwa — it is too far and too dangerous. The closest we

245

can take you is a short pass over Izu-Ōshima,' she stumbles charmingly over the unfamiliar name, 'the first and largest of the Izu Islands, before we land at Narita International.'

It takes Ryan a little while to focus on what she's saying, and she has to repeat her entire message twice before he gets any of it.

'Why?' he replies finally, sitting up and placing both feet on the floor, looking around for his boots. 'Don't we have enough, uh, fuel?'

She shakes her head, already backing away. 'There are current aircraft warnings in place for the entire Nanpō Archipelago.' Again she stumbles over the name. 'Extreme levels of activity, the volcanoes, you understand. It's too dangerous,' she says again nervously, her English beginning to fray. 'I'm sorry, *monsieur*. If you would please to return to your seat?' She turns and hurries away.

Ryan runs his right hand over his scalp. 'Did you get all that?' he says quietly.

I materialise beside him in my usual human get-up, my curly black hair pulled back from my face in a low ponytail. We regard each other warily.

'What we have — you'll never find it again, anywhere. You know that don't you?' he whispers. 'I'll be waiting for you in the arrivals hall. You don't get to leave without saying goodbye.'

In reply, I crawl into his arms. He holds me fiercely and we don't speak.

We're still entwined as the plane flies over the island of Hainan and up the Taiwan Strait before veering northeast, and I imagine — looking through the porthole window — I can see lights in the sea.

'*Monsieur!*' The stewardess calls down the length of the plane from the safety of her seat. 'It passes, Izu-Ōshima.'

Ryan places his hands on either side of my face, lays his forehead against mine, murmurs desperately against my mouth. 'I'll be waiting.'

'I know,' I whisper back against his lips. And we bind ourselves to each other until he can bear no more, gives a gasp against me of real anguish. And I tear myself away, letting my outline shred in his arms as he scrambles to hold onto empty air, almost sobbing.

Then I can no longer feel his sweet breath on my face because I've already left the Gulfstream behind. I'm just a pocket of energy riding the chill and turbulent air above the northwest edge of the vast Pacific Ocean. The jet is a faint gleam in the sky behind me, already turning towards the north having completed its promised pass.

I hadn't imagined it before. There *is* light in the ocean. Fire. Under the water. Like a molten chain that points almost due south, lighting my way towards Sōfu-iwa.

And I wonder who I'll find waiting for me, when I get there.

The air is acrid with gas and steam, as if the earth is breathing out through those underwater wounds, as if it is a dragon beginning to wake beneath me.

It's early morning, not yet dawn, but electric lights gleam on some of the islands that make up the Izu-shotō. I keep flying, keep eating up the miles, until there are no more lights; only treacherous outcroppings of rock, then one dizzying peak after another rising out of the water, inhabited only by birds and sparse vegetation. Until I come to the last isle of all:

a striking pillar of basalt, sheer on all sides, rising out of the water like a knife blade.

No birds occupy that silent island, and the reason soon becomes clear as I descend through the sky, thousands of feet per second, to see a single, seated figure there, shining in the darkness. Pure energy comes off his skin in errant curls that blur and fade in the icy pre-dawn air. He doesn't bother to hide it, because there's no one and nothing to see what he so clearly is. It's Uriel who awaits me upon the peak of that rock, over three hundred feet above sea level. Uriel alone, dressed in his customary robes of such brightness that he is like a shining beacon, a man made of fire.

He lifts his head, sensing something approaching, though I myself give out no light, make no sound, for I am still small, still human-sized, wearing my travelling face.

I feel the same small *frisson* of shock that I always feel when I first see him: for to see him is to see *me*. It's like looking at myself sitting there upon the rock, if I were created male. We're physically identical in almost every way, save that he's a fraction taller, broader through the shoulders, his strong features shading towards the masculine where mine shade towards the feminine. He could be my brother, my twin, and there's never been an explanation for it. We are what we are.

I'm about a thousand feet off landing on the peak when I realise that Uriel is no longer sitting there. All I get is a blur of movement below, the sound of a blazing broadsword igniting in the night, the sensation of giant wings displacing the air, and then I'm suddenly fixed in place by a powerful force-field, frozen mid-descent. He will not let me land, or even approach him.

It's clear he doesn't recognise me at all, for he roars into the space between my eyes: *'Appare!'* *Show yourself!*

I have no time to fight the command. My human disguise shreds instantly, just melts away, and I am completely myself, as I was created.

Uriel moves into view below me, his right hand outstretched, his left grasping his fiery weapon. And he finds himself looking up into his own face, or so it must seem to him, for he gasps aloud, falling back in surprise, and the force-field is suddenly gone.

I land on my feet on an incline so treacherous that only a bird, or an angel, could keep their footing upon it.

'Uri,' I say, shaken, as he lowers his right hand, his sword and wings instantly disintegrating into motes of light.

'You are the very last one I would have expected to come here,' he murmurs, bewildered, looking into my eyes. 'How did you even know to …'

There's suddenly a living flame cupped in his left hand where before there was a weapon. He plays the light across my features, my form, his dark brows knitted together in consternation, seeking a trap, the hand of the Devil in this. Finally satisfied with what he sees, the flame in his palm goes out and he smiles. It transforms his stern countenance utterly.

'You're alive,' he says, and I hear the praise and wonder in his voice.

I'm shocked into immobility when he reaches out and embraces me, murmuring, 'You're safe.'

I close my own arms around him almost awkwardly, seeing the same expression on his face as must be literally mirrored in mine: embarrassed affection, surprise, a softening, perhaps, of entrenched attitudes.

'We used to fight like cat and dog,' he mutters, letting me go.

'Don't believe those days are over, brother,' I reply with a crooked grin. 'But it *is* good to see you, you don't know how much. Jegudiel sent me.' Instantly, Uri's gaze sharpens. 'He told me to tell you that he's taken Selaphiel beyond Luc's reach. Selaphiel will need time to heal, but he lives.'

I see relief flood Uri's countenance.

'What of the others?' I ask, my own anxiety sharpening my voice. 'Gabriel, Raphael, Jeremiel, Barachiel? And what of the great Michael?'

Uriel's smile is instantly wiped clean. 'Of Jeremiel, Barachiel and Michael, I have no word. From Milan, they went in pursuit of Luc and vile Hakael, Luc's paramour Gudrun, a score of fallen *ophanim* and *malakhim* shrieking in their wake. Gabriel and I followed the deceivers Jetrel and Shamshiel to the east, but Gabriel was ahead of me by some leagues, and I saw him taken ...'

My soul seems to go cold at his words. 'Gabriel?'

'Your great friend and protector, yes,' Uri says quietly, 'taken by a score of demons over the mountainous citadel, Machu Picchu — a place that has always reeked to me of blood and untold power. They bore him into the earth there, and, though I scoured the ancient city for two days, I could find no trace of him, though I could still feel his presence very strongly there.' I hear the puzzlement in his voice.

'We have to get him out,' I say, shaken.

Uri shakes his head. 'It falls to *me* to free Gabriel. With Jegudiel and Selaphiel gone, Raphael missing, Barachiel, Michael and Jeremiel unaccounted for, there is no one else. I can no longer afford to wait here for news, or reinforcements, though I will leave a sign here of where I have gone.' His voice becomes very quiet. 'If I must take that place apart, stone by stone, then I will do it.

'And as for you ...' He places his gleaming hands upon my shoulders and looks into my face that is so much like his. 'It is no longer safe for you to remain in this world. You are alone, and we can no longer afford you any kind of protection, for we ourselves are under siege. So you must do the one thing that will secure us all: quit this place, as Selaphiel has done; take yourself out of Luc's reach *forever*. Now. Tonight.'

I go cold as I hear my own thoughts coming back at me from Uriel's mouth. I thought I would have more time; when I should have known that time has been against me from the very start.

I shake my head wildly, hear myself say, as if from a great distance, 'But it's too soon. Not tonight. Let me at least help you locate Gabriel —'

Uriel cuts me off imperiously. 'We are balanced on a knife's edge. You should never have fallen; this "Eden" was never intended for you. Like you, the world beneath our feet is beginning to awaken — Kangra in India has just been levelled by an earthquake greater than the one that destroyed it in 1905; and ruinous tremors have been felt in places as diverse as Ning Xia and Quetta, Erzincan and Aşgabat, Messina, Edinburgh and Sumatra. The world is moving, sister; it is on *fire.*'

He sees me shake my head in denial and his voice roughens. 'You must have seen that the seas around the Izu-shotō are filling with magma. All this must mean that Jeremiel, Barachiel and Michael have somehow failed; they no longer have Luc contained, and his ancient plan of conquest, the war to end all wars, has begun. Hell is coming, sister, and you are our greatest liability, our greatest weakness. Leave now, or doom us all.'

'But I can't just *leave*,' I whisper, seeing flame-haired, emerald-eyed Gabriel, prince among princes, bound by chains of fire far from the light of the sun; seeing Ryan sitting alone in an anonymous airport terminal, surrounded by strangers.

I'll wait, Ryan once said. *I'll wait forever if I have to.*

And he will. It will destroy him if I never come back, if he never knows what happened to me, or how I feel about him.

'You don't understand,' I say, anguished. 'I'm not alone. Not any more. I have ties again, both old *and* new.'

Uriel's voice is uncharacteristically gentle. 'Forget him, as he will forget you, in time. Their lives are but a fleeting moment in ours, and the pain, too, will be fleeting.'

'But I *love* him. And he's waiting for me. I have to say goodbye. At least let me say goodbye. And *I love you*. And *I'm so sorry*.' I begin to shake.

Uriel's fingers tighten in anger upon my shoulders. 'It is your capacity to *love*, that disastrous capacity of yours to *desire*, to *want*, that has brought us all to this pass! You would condemn Gabriel to additional torment for the sake of a mortal man? He is not for you. He is nothing to such as we are.'

'But Ryan is *everything* to me,' I plead, even though I know that it's like pleading with a stone. 'He brought me back to life, and loved me when I was unlovable and untouchable, an outcast. He saw me and knew me, in life after life, even when he'd never seen my true face. Yes, I made the mistake of falling for Luc, and you will never cease to blame me for that single, youthful folly. But what Luc does now, the destruction and terror and evil he brings down on everything and everyone, he does not do those things in my name, but solely in *his*.

'To everyone but Ryan,' I whisper, 'I will always be a marked creature, an exile. He deserves to know that I love him, and that I was forced to let him go. He's been hurt enough, Uriel. Gabriel knows how I feel about him. Gabriel would understand.'

'Gabriel was always too soft-hearted where you were concerned,' Uriel growls, releasing me as if I disgust him. 'And now I must be similarly afflicted, because *this once* I will allow it — I will permit you to exchange your pretty farewells with your pretty human, and then you must go.'

'But Gabriel ...' I plead.

'But Gabriel *nothing*,' Uri snarls. 'I will get him out myself. I will fall upon the demons that hold him like the pestilence that once emptied that sacred city itself of life. But before I do, I will come with you to find this "Ryan", and he and I will both watch you leave. This time, there is no escape.'

I look at Uriel and see all the power and arrogance and inflexibility that so defines our kind. 'You're a bully,' I say bitterly.

His reply is sharp and instant. 'I'm a pragmatist. It is the only choice, and you know I am right.'

I know he is, but it doesn't make it any easier to bear.

I cover my face with my hands and weep then, weep tears of fire. They fall through my fingers onto the stone, each one glimmering for a moment, like a jewel, before dispersing into the chill night air.

'Tears? And for a human?' Uriel murmurs in amazement, making no move to comfort me because this is something I've so clearly brought upon myself. 'What have you *become*?'

'I am what you've made me,' I sob. 'You Eight. Luc, even. Deserving of neither love nor pity. And because I am a creature of my word, I will do my duty. I will do as you command. But if you're coming with me,' and now there's disdain in my voice at the sight of him standing there so regal, so beautiful, the very essence of what it means to be exalted and all-powerful, 'you're going to have to do things my way. For a change.'

CHAPTER 17

It's not hard to find Narita International Airport from the air. Even at four in the morning, the flow of traffic towards it seems steady and endless, and there's a snarl of taxis and hire cars waiting outside the arrivals hall, surrounded by a cloud of exhaust fumes, choking and white.

Inside, the building is blazing with light. As the sliding doors open to emit a rush of hot air, my eyes take in — almost at once — too many things: multiple TV screens filled with reams of flight numbers listed as *Delayed* or *Cancelled*; queues of people at ticket offices and telephone booths; people asleep on almost every available surface, some with luggage, some without. It's a vast and toxic ocean of bodies, of colour, of noise, of smells, of energy. Uriel and I almost reel backwards in a kind of psychic shock.

I'd expected the place to be empty, but it's teeming with people, and I know that Uriel is right. Luc has begun some terrible process that only *I* might be able to contain to this realm, this world. This is just one airport amongst thousands. Only Luc would be capable of setting the very earth upon a course of rebellion that affects so many places, so many people, at once.

I can't see Ryan anywhere.

'Multiply what you see by life *universal*,' Uriel says acidly, 'then tell me you have any other choice but to quit this sphere.'

'Can you see him? Ryan?' I ask despairingly, and Uriel shoots me a look of revulsion as he moves forward into that clamouring sea of people.

He looks awkward in the human form he's assumed; like a smaller version of himself but with a floppy, college-boy haircut, thin steel-framed glasses, and wearing preppy clothes like those we saw on the giant advertising billboards we flew past to get here. It took him more than a few tries to get the look of his skin right, but there's no telltale gleam now on the surface of his neck, face or hands. He's getting more than a few glances because he looks too perfect, almost too neat, clean, handsome, but he definitely passes muster as some uptight, matchy-matchy rich kid on his way home from an overseas holiday. Beside him, I look incredibly dowdy in my usual human get-up of black down jacket, black sweater, grey jeans and boots, hair slung back in a messy ponytail.

'I look ridiculous,' Uri says through gritted teeth. 'Remind me again what he looks like, this Ryan?'

His expression turns to shock as I say distractedly, 'He looks like Luc ... like Luc if he'd been born human, and kind, but with dark hair, dark eyes ...'

My voice trails away as something catches my eye. It's so small, so very faint, just one light among millions, but it's moving in an erratic fashion, winding in and out of the screaming Christmas decorations and glowing airline insignias, moving up the sides of crazily lit-up vending machines and roving across the faces of the sleeping, as if it's searching for something, or someone. But then it vanishes into a bank of flickering TV screens and doesn't reappear. Maybe I imagined it. This place is lit up like an amusement park.

'Let's split up,' I say, indicating the half of the room that I want Uri to take. 'It'll be faster.'

I'm already walking away before Uriel's had a chance to answer me. I want to get to Ryan first, because I don't want Uri to see me with him. There's nothing I can truly call mine in this world except Ryan, and I'm about to let him go. What I have to say to him doesn't require a witness who possesses perfect recall; recall eternal.

I concentrate on all the disparate energies in the room, trying to pick Ryan's. But there's so much noise in here, so much distraction, that I'm having trouble tuning it out. Every braying laugh, snore or angry conversation pulls my focus from place to place.

Uri's well out of sight when that small, coin-sized gleam of light reappears at my feet like a puppy anxious to please. The *malakh* I first met on a street corner in Australia is so weak now, so dissipated, that I no longer feel any fear or uneasiness around it. It's so near death now that if its last act in life is to seek me out, then who am I to deny it?

'If you know where he is,' I plead, 'take me to him?'

The light seems to regard me steadily for a second, before oscillating, as if in response. It leads me without hesitation through a multitude of slumped or sleeping bodies towards a bank of empty luggage carousels, the steel conveyor belts silent and still. Rounding the edge of one, I see the familiar backpack first, then the tall young man leaning against it, playing with his mobile phone.

Ryan looks up and sees me, and the smile that lights his face stops me in my tracks.

'Mercy!' he cries gladly and leaps to his feet.

As he does, the *malakh*, as if startled into flight, darts up the face of the giant advertising poster on the wall and disappears.

Ryan pulls me to him, but then sees my expression. 'What's wrong?' he says instantly, his smile dying, his arms tightening about me like a vice.

I lay my head against his shoulder and the feel of him — his familiar energy and clean, male smell — brings on another fall of tears. They spill onto the battered leather of his jacket, gleaming there momentarily like the embers of a dying fire.

'I love you.' I'm sobbing, hardly coherent. 'I love you, and I'm so sorry.'

There, I've done it, I've finally said the words, and just like that, all the time we ever had together is gone, it's over. We're into overtime now, penalty time. Any moment, Uri will tap me on the shoulder and I will never see Ryan again in this life.

Ryan forces me to look at him, and his hands move to either side of my face. He smears the tears away with the pads of his thumbs as fast as they come.

'Hey,' he says, '*whoa*. I missed you, too. But I didn't mind, it hasn't been that long. I would have been happy to wait longer. I'm just glad you're back.'

He pulls me into him again, breathing me in, kissing my hairline, breathing out all his anxiety, his tension.

'I love you, too,' he murmurs joyously, looking down into my eyes. 'And there's nothing to be sorry about. We got there in the end, right? It wasn't so hard to say.'

'You don't understand,' I wail softly. 'Uriel is here, with me. He says this is it. It all ends now, for you and me. I came to say goodbye. *This is goodbye.*'

'What?' Ryan's dark brows snap together as he scans the arrivals hall feverishly, before returning his gaze to me. 'You're kidding, right?'

I shake my head, and my fiery tears fall and fall as if they will never end. 'Uriel's here to make sure that I do it — that I leave. So I'm finally telling you now: that I love you, and that I'll always miss you, and that I'm sorry.'

Ryan's gone rigid in my arms. I can feel his horror in the way he's suddenly stopped breathing, in the way he's completely speechless.

'Get yourself ... home,' I say haltingly, pulling back from him so I can see his face. 'I'll make Them watch over you, over Lauren, every single day. I'll make sure Luc never has the opportunity to go after you. They have to do that much for me. They have to. You've been through enough.'

I give him a false, tremulous smile and say pleadingly, 'Find a nice girl — you can do way better than me, better even than that Brenda. And have a great, great *life*.' A sob rises again in my throat.

'I'll see you again,' I insist through my tears. '*I'll see you again*. It will seem like today has been ... just a lengthy wait in an anonymous arrivals hall somewhere. But I'll find you, one day, and maybe then we can be together for always.'

Ryan's opening his mouth but no words are coming out, and he tips his head up for a moment, just gazing up at the ceiling. When he finally looks at me, his eyes are red-rimmed and his voice is harsh. 'Mercy, I —'

But then a gloved hand grips his shoulder.

It's such an unexpected thing that we both just stare at it for a moment before taking in the person that's joined to it. It's a man in a dark uniform — dark trousers, dark shoes, dark vest — and a white shirt. He's pale-skinned, clean-shaven, bespectacled, unremarkable. There's a cloth badge picked out in black and gold upon his shirt-sleeve, and a sprinkling of grey through his short, black hair.

He doesn't say anything to us; just gives us a view of his partner standing behind him — younger, similarly turned out — and inclines his head sharply to indicate that he wants us to follow them. Both men are Japanese, of average height and build, and both are sweating heavily in this overheated room. I can see their perspiration gleaming beneath the lights. The energy they give out seems muted, but it's indisputably human.

Still, it seems odd that they don't try to talk to either Ryan or me, or even to each other, though both of them are staring intently at Ryan's face, as if they've seen him somewhere before.

Ryan and I glance at each other edgily, and he picks up his backpack from the floor. The official grasps his shoulder more tightly in his gloved hand and begins to walk so that Ryan is forced to follow, our bag trailing from his fingers.

'Uh, I'm sorry, but you must have me confused with someone else,' he says. 'I'm not boarding a flight or anything. Uh, excuse me, sir? *Sir?*'

The men don't acknowledge me at all, so all I can do is follow behind as they take Ryan through a set of automatic doors that immediately cut us off from the overcrowded waiting area. We're in some kind of processing area now, filled with machines that look like giant, shiny steel portals. It's virtually empty.

A couple of middle-aged Japanese women in uniform are seated near the gleaming portals. They nod deferentially as the officials gesture curtly that they're going to walk Ryan through one of them.

Ryan drops the bag at his feet in resignation. 'You're not going to find anything,' he says under his breath.

One of the women beckons Ryan forward with her gloved hand, and the man pushes him through one of the metal portals with unnecessary force. A small square light on the side turns green. I'm standing just behind the woman's shoulder and am startled to see a ghostly human outline appear on the electronic screen she's positioned in front of. I realise that I'm looking at an image of Ryan, right down to the phone and papers in his pocket, the shape of his body beneath his clothes. The whole set-up is some kind of scanning device, and I lean forward, fascinated, as the woman taps at some keys.

Also fascinated is the official who propelled Ryan into the machine in the first place. He's moved back around the front of the machine and is now leaning in to study the image on the screen over the woman's shoulder.

She points out a couple of places in the image before shrugging and saying, in Japanese, 'Nothing. No threat. Clean.' She beckons to Ryan again, indicating he's done.

Ryan gives the silent official standing beside me a steely, reproachful glare as he moves through the portal. He reaches around the machine to retrieve his pack, and hesitates for a moment before shrugging it back onto his shoulders, as if afraid it will be confiscated. But nobody seems interested in the bag.

I'm watching Ryan walk towards me, when the second official comes up from behind and propels me forcefully into the metal portal. There's a strange noise as I stand there for an instant, before moving straight through it, outraged at being manhandled without warning.

Ryan turns towards me as the Japanese woman taps a few more keys, then looks at the man standing framed in the portal behind me and says apologetically, 'The machine must be malfunctioning, sir.' She turns to the other official, the older man, who's still standing beside her and indicates her screen. 'See, nothing here but clouds.'

Time seems to freeze at her words, before recommencing again.

Ryan shouts, almost in slow motion, 'Mercy! *Behind you.*'

I turn to see the younger customs officer crumpling silently to the floor. Something vaporous and pale, at least eight feet tall, rises up out of his body, towering over me. It's vaguely humanoid but it lacks any distinct features, and the energy it gives off now is less human, more monstrous, setting off a sick, gingery feeling in me. It's swaying a little where it stands, as if testing the air, or getting ready to move.

I can't identify what it is, but I know that it's ancient and capable of possession. And it is cunning: it used its human host's energy to disguise its own strangely part-human energy. This thing is family in some way, but so many times removed that my wariness is in overdrive.

Even before I turn and look at Ryan, I know what I'm going to see: a second creature of vapour rising up out of the motionless body of the other man now slumped at Ryan's feet.

The female customs official gives a terrified whimper.

I startle everyone and everything in the room by raising my hands and clapping them loudly together in front of my face. Instantly, the two creatures of cloud and malice sway in my direction, their eyeless faces searching me out. As they shamble forward, the outline of each shredding and re-forming continuously, I say calmly and quietly in Japanese, 'Madam, move away now. Do you hear me? While I have their attention.'

I clap again, and the spirit-creatures let forth a wordless howl that makes me clutch at my head in pain. I realise that what I'm hearing is that horrific, wordless language I'd first heard in Milan: the common language of the *daemonium*.

The woman is still frozen in her seat, weeping and terrified.

'*Go!*' I growl at her. 'Move!'

She nods tightly before dropping off her chair to the floor and crawling away rapidly, still whimpering. She leaps to her feet some distance away and runs from the room, taking the other woman with her.

Ryan's horrified gaze meets mine through the vaporous outline of the creature standing between us.

'Run, my love,' I say quietly. 'Live a long, full life. You've endured enough.'

I see him hesitate, then take one step backwards as if he would flee. As he moves, the monster between us turns and lifts one of its vaguely arm-like appendages and pierces Ryan through the shoulder with it. He screams in agony as the thing pulls him close, shrieking into his face in cold fury. Then it wrenches its claw free, throws him over its shoulder and bounds away.

For a moment, I'm so shocked, I can't move.

The other creature gazes at me through the scanning portal with its eyeless face, as if taunting me, before turning and leaping after the other.

They sweep furniture, machinery, cordons out of their way with their long, shapeless limbs as they cross the immigration zone, back towards the empty, silent lounges that would usually be full of passengers disembarking from planes. I sprint after them, hurdling fallen chairs and plastic trays, rubbish bins and metal signs, my eyes fixed on Ryan, who's hanging like a rag doll over the shoulder of the demon in front, struggling wildly.

A siren starts to wail somewhere overhead, but I keep running: past cringing maintenance workers, past uniformed men who appear out of nowhere, pulling their weapons, screaming in Japanese that they will shoot. But we leave them all in our wake as we pelt at inhuman speed towards the deserted passenger lounge at the far end of the building. The demons don't hesitate at the sight of the locked double doors near the silent ticket-processing machine — they just wrench them off their hinges and leap out into empty space. I hear Ryan yelling as the monsters fall through the air soundlessly.

I teeter in the doorway for a moment, looking down. There's no ramp there, there's nothing. Just a huge drop to the tarmac.

The creatures land on their feet, look up at me. The one holding Ryan lifts him high off the ground by the back of his leather jacket and gives him a shake. As if to say: *If you want him, come and get him.*

Shots are fired from behind. I feel one pass right through me, without effect. I don't look back, I just leap out through the doorway, landing on my feet before the demons of cloud and venom, my eyes on Ryan. He's shaking from pain and shock, and his lips are tinged with blue.

'It doesn't matter what happens to me,' he hisses. 'Get away from here. I'm bait, they're using me as bait.'

'I know,' I say softly. 'They're not as dumb as they look, these two. They've worked out that my weakness is *you* and always will be.'

As if it understands me perfectly, the empty-handed demon bends and screeches its defiance in my face. The monster that has Ryan in its grip puts its other vaguely claw-like arm straight through Ryan's other shoulder, his good shoulder, and leaves it there. Ryan gives a howl of mortal agony, twisting in anguish at the end of the creature's bladelike arm.

I snarl, 'Let him go! I'll do what you want, go where you want. You have my word. Just let him go.'

I step forward, and as I do the demon holding Ryan tosses him out of the way as if he weighs nothing, as if he *is* nothing. Ryan gives a cry and lies still upon the tarmac.

The two creatures move forward, wreathing me in mist, and take hold of me. Cold moves instantly through me, paralysing me like an anaesthetist's drug. The demons tower over me, drawing me closer, and I seem to see the first blush of morning rising within them, or through them. The stars in the sky seem to go out, one by one, as I feel myself begin to shiver into pieces. They mean to draw me down, down into Hell. I have made my pact with them — my life for Ryan's; a bargain I would make again and again — and there seems no way out.

But there's a flash of something else, something barely glimpsed. A coming together, a coalescence, a rising. Not the sun, but something that seems even brighter. I bow my head, using the last of my energy to wrench myself sideways as

Uriel takes form behind my captors, his giant wings unfurling soundlessly, his broadsword in his hand.

He swings it in one smooth arc and I hear the sizzle of the blade as it connects with the demons' energy. He cuts them both down and they vanish mid-shriek, the wind bearing the last shreds of their dead energy away.

'You are a great magnet for trouble,' Uriel roars over my kneeling figure.

Then he looks up suddenly as he catches rapid movement above and behind me. I turn sluggishly to see men in full riot gear on the ledge above us, weapons drawn. Some stupid order is given, loudly, to *fire*.

But faster than the men can let loose a volley of shots, Uriel has already knotted one of his great fists into Ryan's leather jacket, the other into the stuff of me, and leapt off the surface of the world.

By the time the bullets hit the space where we were standing, turning the air blue with lead and smoke, we've already left Narita International — all of Tokyo — far behind us.

CHAPTER 18

I struggle to pull free of Uriel's mighty grip. As if proving a point, he lets go of me only when he's ready to, hoisting Ryan more securely into his arms. Ryan's still unconscious — head hanging down, limbs slack, backpack still looped over his broad shoulders.

Uriel is silent for a long time as we rise and rise and rise. We're spearing straight into the sky side by side, so far above the surface of the earth that the air is soon choppy and frigid. The blush of a new dawn seems to be following in our wake, as if we are drawing a veil of light across the world, as if we are its sun.

We're so far up now, that I seem to see the world curving beneath us, hear the vast sound of it turning. Like a giant, slowly grinding wheel.

'We're too high,' I say sharply to Uriel.

He flies on in silence, his long, dark hair slipstreaming out behind him. His form is massive in comparison to mine, still winged, still deadly. He's a thing of such singular, gleaming beauty, built along such mythical lines, that I can hardly look away.

'It will kill Ryan, to be this high,' I insist harshly. 'He hasn't moved, he might be dead. We need to take him down. Give him to me.'

Uriel glances at me with an unfathomable expression in his dark eyes, before refocusing upon the horizon, still holding Ryan out of my reach.

'Every moment he's with you puts him at mortal risk,' he says finally. 'Let him sleep until wakefulness is required; it will be less hard on him. He'll do well enough with me.'

I realise then that Uriel is doing this deliberately, keeping Ryan under, keeping him away from me, as if he fears I'll be tempted to do something bold, something stupid, like escape with Ryan; the two of us fugitives forever from all that dwell above and below. And I'm seriously tempted to try, but nowhere on earth would ever be safe again, and no matter how much I love him and ache to be with him, Ryan never signed up for that.

'You still don't trust me,' I say bitterly, almost to myself. 'And why would you?'

Uriel doesn't reply, he just picks up speed, streaking away through the lightening sky. I find myself fighting to keep up, still feeling the effects of the cloud giants' icy, paralysing touch in my system.

'They were *nephilim*,' Uriel calls out suddenly over his shoulder, as if responding to a question I've just asked. 'And you were lucky. Ryan drew them to him first, but you, I think, were unexpected. They were uncertain about you, and it made them slow to act. They are usually fatal to the unwary.'

I draw abreast of him, only because he's letting me.

'Lucky you were there,' I say.

'I had nothing to sacrifice, nothing to lose, unlike you.' His voice is very quiet. 'You've changed so much,' he considers my human disguise wryly, 'both inside and out, that I hardly recognise you.'

'The creature you used to know is separated from the being I am now by an unfordable river. Everything that has happened to me has made me who I am,' I reply.

Without warning, Uriel's luminous wings shred into nothingness, as if we have left some zone of immediate danger.

'We're safe enough, for now,' he says, glancing sideways at me. 'No demon could trouble us for long at this elevation. Though they crave the sun, they have no hope ever of reaching it. If he were not with us,' he looks briefly at Ryan, silent in his arms, 'I would already be in the skies above Huayna Picchu, scouring the great ruins below for any sign of Gabriel. When we reach Cusco, we three must part ways. Ryan will be safer amongst his own kind.'

'At least let us help you find Gabriel,' I plead.

Uriel's gaze is shrewd. 'And buy you both more time together? I think not, sister.'

'I have agreed to nothing; neither has Ryan,' I say fiercely. 'Nothing has been decided.'

Uriel shakes his head. 'But *I* am decided.' His voice is steely, ringing. 'We part at Cusco.'

Without looking at me again, he surges away through the skies, knowing I am forced to follow while he holds my love captive in his arms.

We are silent for leagues, eating up the distance without need of rest — hundreds of miles passing in the blink of an eye. Tiny pinpoints of rock begin to appear in the ocean far below, and I feel Uriel turn us to the south. We fly over a small atoll of islands, scattered like random beads across the ocean. The air beneath us grows grey-dappled, then progressively more impenetrable the further south we move. The skies are thick with a stinking grey haze, a vast plume that is redolent of sulphur, ash and grit.

'Laysan Island, the Gardner Pinnacles, Ni'ihau, Kaua'i, O'ahu,' Uriel says suddenly, taking us down.

We scream through the atmosphere at thousands of feet per second, falling out of the sky like missiles, and I begin to see the red glow of fire deep within the grey. Suddenly I see the cause of the haze: a giant island alive with fire — lava, cinders, ash spewing forth from a multitude of summits and vents and fissures, rocks falling into the sea as if hurled by unruly giants. The name of the place comes to me unbidden: Hawai'i.

'One by one, they come to life,' Uriel calls over his shoulder. 'Every one destructive, a tragedy on its own, but together ...'

He climbs again above the gritty smog and we rapidly leave the long, dirty plume behind, the grey stain stretching away from us to the north and the west.

'Why don't you stop them?' I shout accusingly as I try in vain to chase him down. 'If you're so powerful, so close to *Him*, why let these disasters, these tragedies, even happen? You're the ones with all the answers. *Do something.*'

Uriel flows to a sudden stop, blazing with anger, Ryan still held fast in his arms. I stop, too, suddenly very afraid of what he will do.

'These are the conditions of this world,' he thunders. 'Conditions that Luc now exploits for his own ends. Despite everything that happens here, life continues to flourish;

and that is the continuing miracle — that life *persists*. Do you think that we *rejoice* when any life is lost in unnatural circumstances? Well, do you?'

I shake my head, stunned to see the vehemence and repudiation in his expressive face, the great sorrow brimming in his dark, wide-set eyes.

'You're not the only one among the *elohim* that actually *feels*,' he says bitingly. 'There are simply not enough of us to guard against everything, to save everyone. So some are spared while others perish, and there seems no fairness in anything, no system, no order. But we do what we can, and we can do no more.

'Life in this world is already dark, already messy enough, without the active interference of the Devil and his legions. The vast majority of Luc's *daemonium* will never be as powerful as a single *elohim*, for most did not fall as Luc did, they were created out of the leavings of this world. But what the *daemonium* lack in grace, in speed, in power, they make up for in ferocity and sheer numbers. While our kind can only ever dwindle over time, the *daemonium* can and always will be replenished while Luc lives.

'You have accused us before of being merely "watchers" — but how, in truth, is the life of one man to be balanced against another? Every action has a consequence; and we see each one stretch out before us endlessly even before we act. We fight a battle that has many fronts, and these fronts open and shift and change constantly. Some have "natural" causes, others do not. It is our burden and our rationale, and we accept it.'

His voice is suddenly gentler. 'And that, Mercy, is why you must leave. Life will persist here regardless of what you do. Ryan's people are tenacious — they have weathered so much. But Luc cannot be allowed to export the terror and the evil he deals in beyond this place. It is the time for selflessness, Mercy, for letting go. To rage against the conditions we face — that way lies insanity and paralysis.'

Then he turns and flows away, Ryan held as gently and carefully in his arms as a small child. And I think that this is the closest I have ever come to the mystery that lies at the heart of the Eight, and I am momentarily ashamed to have added to their cares and their sorrows. My love seems so small in comparison to theirs, but it is the very centre of my world now, of who *I* am.

And that is the paradox: I see what I must do, but it would tear me apart to do it.

The sun is high overhead as we cross the equator, and dark clouds gather above us as Uriel begins to take us down. As we cross the seas towards the mainland, he calls, 'The Nazca Plate lies directly beneath us, the Volcán Llaima to the south. See what Luc has wrought in my absence, in mere *days*.'

The coastline we are crossing is obscured by a creeping grey fog. There's nothing but dark above our heads, and a growing darkness before us as Uriel indicates peak after peak to the south spewing forth ash and grit and lava for miles along the coastline.

'Some have been dead for centuries,' he tells me. 'But now Luc brings the Ring of Fire to life on every side; from here to the isles of Japan. It is only the beginning.'

Rain begins to fall as we angle northward along the coast, and develops into squalling winds and a heavy wet-season downpour that obliterates all light. Uriel does his best to shield Ryan from the worst of the storm, which touches neither of us. Lightning cuts through the sky repeatedly, briefly illuminating our approach towards a sprawling river-valley township ringed by immense mountains. The low, white-walled, red-roofed buildings are centred around a great square that gleams a lighter grey in the general greyness and is divided by patches of greenery, electric lampposts, footpaths, flowerbeds, a fountain, green benches. Two towering, Baroque-style stone churches, each in possession of two grand belltowers, face directly onto the square, as do several graceful stone arcades punctuated by archways. There is no one upon the surrounding streets or in the square.

As we approach the square from above at great speed, Uriel says inside my head, *The Plaza de Armas, Square of the Warrior. It is only fitting that this is where we should part. For you have been braver and truer than you know.*

We descend through day that has become night, through howling wind and stinging rain, towards a patch of greenery in the shadow of one of the great churches. We're still about three hundred feet off the ground when Uriel mutters a single word into Ryan's closed eyes: a word of command, of waking. I am above and behind Uriel as we descend, shielded from sight by him, and I alone catch the instant that Ryan's eyes flash open to take in Uriel's stern countenance over his. Uriel's eyes are focused on the distant ground beneath us, and not upon the human he bears.

I see Ryan's emotions chase each other across his face. For he's often gazed upon that simple pencil sketch he keeps of me, I know, meditated upon it, matched it up against reality. Now, I literally see him thinking: *Like Mercy. Not Mercy. Demon.*

All this takes only seconds.

Then Ryan does the bravest, most misguided, stupidest thing I've ever seen him do. He closes his eyes, his lips moving silently in prayer, or farewell, and he dives backwards out of Uriel's arms.

He's falling like a stone through the sky, the rain soaking him instantly, making his heavy, mortal body even heavier, second by second. His eyes are closed and he's as graceful, as accepting, as a diver. There's no messy struggle; the lines of his body are tight and clean, arms outstretched. He makes no sound as he falls, still wearing that stupid backpack across his shoulders. He'd rather be dead, because he thinks that I must be. For he saw me surrender to the demons in Tokyo, and then woke to find himself in the grasp of a being of fire that looked like me but was not me and must therefore be some fiend, some shape-shifter demon.

I am all reaction, no thought, as I pull myself instantly into a tight downward spiral and try to catch him on the way down, catch him before he hits the granite walkways that bisect the Plaza de Armas.

Uriel's so shocked, so unable to credit what Ryan has done, that he's seconds behind me as I catch hold of Ryan by the hands. The force of our coming together threatens to rip his arms from their sockets. His eyes fly open as my fingers tighten convulsively around his. We've formed an imperfect circle, an ellipse, with our joined hands, and we're spinning and spiralling through the air as centrifugal forces, gravity, take us over.

There's no time to do anything but accept the ground rushing up to meet us, and I curve myself protectively around Ryan's body the way I did when we collided with the great glass and steel roof of the Galleria in Milan, using every fibre of my being to cushion the impact of the blow when we hit the ground. Entwined and entangled together, we tumble across the rain-slick grass, skid over the cobbled surface of the Plaza, before coming to rest hard up against the base of a lamppost.

I lie there, shocked into immobility by the fall; a fall that has stirred up echoes in me of that other time. But this time, I am not burnt, blackened or near death. I am whole and very much alive.

It may be seconds, or hours, before I roll Ryan off me onto his back. His eyes are closed, but his life force pulses beneath my fingers and he starts to cough. The sound is harsh and painful. I place a steadying hand upon him as the rain beats down, feel his racing heartbeat below my palm.

I continue to lie there, staring up without blinking into the torrent falling out of the sky, seeming to see every drop, every needle of rain coming down, even up to its source. *Maybe this is all we can ever be*, I think in relief, in anguish. *Only ever one second away from disaster, from ruin.*

And I see that maybe Uriel is right: that if being with me could drive Ryan to do this, then I should go.

Uriel falls out of the sky beside us, landing lightly on his feet. I only vaguely register that he's human-sized again, sporting the floppy, college-boy haircut, thin wire-framed spectacles and preppy designer gear he was wearing in Tokyo.

Ryan opens his eyes, looks up into Uriel's face and some kind of primal recognition flares in them. He sits bolt upright, slamming the back of his head against the lamppost behind him in his haste to put some distance between himself and Uri. Then he realises that I haven't moved at all, that I'm not even faintly concerned, and he looks from Uriel to me, from me to Uriel, in numb disbelief.

'You say Luc and I could be twins,' he says harshly. 'What's the deal with *this* guy?'

He braces himself against the glistening lamppost and uses it to slide upright onto his feet, then checks himself automatically for bruises, for fractures. The rain is seeping into his mouth, streaking down through his spiky, growing-back hair, the stubble on his face. He glares down at me where I'm still lying on the ground, motionless beneath the driving rain.

The tone of his voice and the very sight of him suddenly make me so furious that I'm on my feet before I register it, pummelling his chest with both my fists. Ryan retreats from the force of my blows.

'Why bother?' I scream into his face. 'Why bother asking who he is? Why even check if you're still in one piece when you just tried to commit suicide from three hundred feet? I'll kill you myself if you ever pull a stunt like that again!'

'Mercy,' Uriel says warningly, and my anger dissolves into a tight feeling inside me, like unshed tears. I back away from both of them, crossing my arms tightly against my chest to protect myself from any more hurt.

Uriel walks over to Ryan and they eye each other warily, of a similar height and build, their body language indicating each is unprepared to be cowed by the other.

'I'm Uriel,' he says, putting out one hand awkwardly, in the human way, to be shaken.

'You've never met before,' I interject acidly, 'but he's been inside *your house*, Ryan. He has a habit of just turning up and giving people orders. Like how he wants us to go our separate ways, from here, now, today.'

'In my *house*?' Ryan looks down at Uri's hand almost in horror, as if it might turn into a snake and bite him. He makes no move to take it.

'Penalty time is over, Ryan,' I say, trying to keep my voice light, though I'm gripped by that aching grief. 'Because Uriel says so. I never did tell you, did I, about how much we resemble each other? About how, like you, I'm curiously twinned. Uriel tries to deny it, but our resemblance is proof to me that God exists, and has a sense of humour.'

Uriel glares at me, unamused, and lets his hand fall back down to his side. 'Say what you have to say to each other,' he snaps, 'then get out of the way and let the real work begin.'

Ryan crosses his arms belligerently. 'What happened to the right to *choose*?' he snarls. 'It's not something reserved for you high and mighty *elohim*. I don't choose to leave, and neither does Mercy. Not yet, not now, not when the world is literally going to hell. She can still do *good* down here. She can help you in ways you can't begin to imagine. She can help you get Luc —'

Uriel moves so quickly, bunching one of his fists into the front of Ryan's jacket and hauling him close, that Ryan turns pale with shock. The breath freezes in his throat at something dangerous he sees in Uri's face, only inches from his, but he keeps speaking anyway. 'The only beings that can contain Luc are you Eight and Mercy. She can still play a part. She's already killed some of them, you know, some of Luc's people.'

Uriel's eyes snap to mine, though he doesn't relax his grip on Ryan. 'How many? What order?' he barks.

'Ananel, Remiel, Neqael and Turael,' I say, seeing recognition and then astonishment in his gaze. 'All first order. All once *elohim*, as you well know. Turns out I'm a natural at this killing thing.' My voice dies away.

Uriel's eyes flick back to Ryan's as Ryan adds quietly, 'And I'm still useful. Look at you, look at her, then look at me, and tell me you don't need the kind of help I can give you ....'

Uriel looks down at himself sharply, then across at me, and I think I get it a second before he does. Ryan is soaking wet; he looks like he fell in the Pacific Ocean on his way over. But Uriel and I are both bone dry. There's not a mark on us. Before the rain can even touch our hair, our skin, our fake human gear, it burns off, vanishing completely.

Uriel suddenly releases Ryan's jacket front, and Ryan rocks back on his heels in obvious relief.

That's when I hear the children.

They come out of the stone archway by the church and head for Uriel, chanting, 'Ayar Awqa! Ayar Awqa!'

There are six of them in all, four girls and two boys, wearing colourful coats and knitted jackets and hats, their pretty skirts and patched trousers festooned with hand-embroidered flowers, leaves and animals. They crowd around Uriel, still chanting, and he looks down at them as if he has woken from a dream. He actually smiles; a smile of such radiant beauty that the children seem to sigh and smile back as one.

They lead him back towards the archway, out of the rain, holding onto his hands, onto the hem of his navy sweater with its incongruous preppy logo. He goes with them without a word.

Ryan and I look at each other in confusion. Then he fetches our backpack from where it was torn off during our rough landing and hoists it up by its broken straps. I hook one of my arms through his and we turn and follow the children.

'Why do they keep saying that?' he asks under his breath as

278

we draw beneath the archway where the children are clustered around Uriel, still chanting, 'Ayar Awqa! Ayar Awqa!'

'It's a name,' Uriel says, looking away from the adoring faces of the children for a second. 'In Quechua, the local language. They believe that Ayar Awqa was a winged man who flew down from the sky and transformed into a foundation stone of this place, Qosqo, Cusco.'

The oldest child, a girl of probably no more than seven, picks up a small basket filled with knitted finger puppets from where it was tucked against the archway, out of the rain. She takes Uriel by the hand and indicates he should follow her. The remaining children crowd around us shyly, taking our hands, tugging at the hems of our jackets, calling me 'Sister of Ayar Awqa' and calling Ryan 'Maki Sapa'.

The name makes me laugh out loud, and Ryan says curiously, 'What's so funny?'

I exchange conspiratorial looks with the bright-eyed, dusky-skinned children and try to keep my face straight as I reply, 'Oh, they're calling you Monkey Features — I think your grooming could use a little work.'

Ryan's mouth falls open in surprise, then he screws up his face and lets his arms dangle down. He starts chasing the smaller children up and down the arcade, making monkey noises.

Uriel and I and the older girl look on, smiling. But then she claps her hands together, and we all stride out into the rain.

It beats down as if it will never stop. But the children pull us eagerly by the hands through the deserted streets, pointing out things they think we'd like to see, like special stones and good places to eat. The further we go past rain-soaked squares and quiet *barrios*, past glistening stone churches and the narrow, chaotic workshops of local craftspeople, the poorer and more crowded the neighbourhoods become. Finally, we reach a two-storey shophouse, where the baskets of local wares have been shoved in deep under the dripping awnings to keep their contents dry.

There's no one inside the store, which smells of wool and tobacco and spices, soap and incense, bodies, dust and earth. The children take us up a narrow set of stairs at the back to an apartment with its front door thrown open. Beside me, Ryan's breathing heavily and his face is streaming with sweat. With so many of us here, the tiny place — three, maybe four rooms in all — feels unbelievably crowded.

Ryan suddenly sags over at the waist, dropping the broken backpack on the floor at his feet. He stands there bent over and shivering, wheezing and wet through, his head hanging down, his elbows braced above his knees, oblivious to everything around him. I put a soothing hand on his back, but he doesn't respond, almost gagging for air.

Uriel and I exchange glances. Then, together, we take in the people in the room the same way they're studying us.

There are a couple of elderly women seated on a low, sagging velvet settee beside a radio that's prattling loudly in Spanish. They wear the same colourfully embroidered skirts and short woollen jackets as the little girls do, and have skin like gleaming mahogany and grey hair wound into long, tight plaits. Their seamed fingers fly as they work at intricate pieces of knitting, their black eyes never leaving us.

Two men sit across the room either side of a round, wooden table, small glasses of a cloudy green liquid in front of them, a deck of cards laid out between them. By the similarity of their looks and the degree of grey in the older man's hair, I guess they must be father and son.

I get a glimpse of a woman — maybe the younger man's wife — momentarily framed in the doorway to what must be a kitchen, her eyes wide with surprise, before she moves out of sight, her long, full, red skirt, bordered in gold, twitching out of view.

Nobody speaks, until Uriel says quietly and politely in Quechua, 'We are honoured to be among you.'

Then, suddenly, all the children are talking at once in their high, clear voices.

'They fell from the sky!'

'Upon the Plaza de Armas!'

'Like Ayar Awqa!'

'The woman is his sister!'

'The sister of Ayar Awqa!'

The younger man snorts suddenly and points at Ryan, who is still struggling to get air into his body. 'And this *gringo*? He is like Ayar Awqa, too? The man can barely stand, let alone fly. He has *soroche*, the sickness all the *gringos* get. Look at him.'

The man searches out the oldest child with his eyes and beckons her forward. 'Flor,' he says sternly, 'you were not raised to lie. Nor should you ever bring the *gringos*,' the word is said with disgust, 'into our home. We are not exhibits. How we live is not for them to see.'

'But, Papi,' she says quietly, 'we are not lying.'

She takes his hand, and he gets to his feet reluctantly and allows her to tug him in Uriel's direction.

'Look at the man and the woman, not the *gringo*,' she says. 'Then look at us — at me, Luis and César, Ana, Gabriela, María.'

She takes her hat off and wrings the rain out of it onto the floor.

281

The man — compact, tanned, clean-shaven, his short black hair oiled back neatly — approaches us. He scrutinises Uriel, who stands there calmly in his designer-look clothing without hat, umbrella or baggage. The man looks up sharply into his face, reaches out to touch the skin of his cheek, then quickly withdraws his hand. He does not look at me, but his body language, his thoughts, are no longer unfriendly, only confused.

'It must be some trick,' he mutters, looking back at the older man seated at the table.

'It's no trick,' the older man pipes up. 'If the children say he is Ayar Awqa, and that one is the sister of Ayar Awqa, then who are we to deny it? They are our children, and they are good children. But that one is certainly a *gringo*, and if we do not get him some coca tea, he will be a dead *gringo* before he has even climbed Dead Gringo Pass.' The old man throws back his head and laughs with his toothless mouth.

The young woman sweeps out of the kitchen, looking down shyly as she passes us, and hurries out the open door of the apartment and down the stairs.

When her footsteps have disappeared, the old man shouts in Quechua, 'Welcome! Welcome! Siblings of the Great Owl. Pull up a chair and tell us what it is that you want with us, and we will do everything in our power to help you.'

'A moment,' Uriel tells the old man politely, then he turns to me and says in a fierce whisper, 'As good-hearted as these people undoubtedly are, "pulling up a chair" is the last thing I have time for. I need to reach Machu Picchu *now*. Anything could have become of Gabriel in my absence. Let the mortals nurse Ryan back to health before he heads for home, but you and I cannot remain here drinking their tea. If it's indeed true what Ryan said, that you slew those demons single-handed,' I hear a disbelief in his voice that he's unable to hide, 'then I would welcome your aid in locating Gabriel. We fly in there, we take the place apart and we get out. Then you leave Gabriel and me to find the others.'

Ryan straightens slowly, pale-faced and holding his head. 'Uh, wouldn't they be expecting that?' he wheezes.

'Speak plainly,' Uriel snaps, his dark eyes flashing.

'They'll be expecting you to, um, approach Machu Picchu — shit, in Peru, we're in *Peru*?' He sees Uriel's face and continues huskily: 'They'll be expecting you to go in in full celestial regalia with, uh, swords blazing. It's what you guys do best. But it's too ... obvious, isn't it?'

He turns slowly, wincing, his eyes struggling to focus on the local man standing beside us. 'You trek to Machu Picchu, right?' he says in English, the only language he knows. 'I remember reading about it once. How long does it take, sir?'

The man looks Ryan up and down with his jet black eyes. 'The Camino Inca takes many forms,' he says in heavily accented English. 'The Mollepata is the longest and hardest route. It would not suit everyone,' he adds diplomatically. 'But there is a trek that can take four days, and a trek that can take one. My cousin's son is a guide. He can better answer you.' He turns and says to his father in Quechua, 'Go and fetch Mateo.'

The toothless old man snorts. '*You* go and fetch Mateo, if Mayu has not already brought every one of our friends and relatives back with her. See, she returns now.'

More people spill into the room: handsome, black-eyed women, pretty children in colourful dress, work-worn men and older folk, until we are ringed around by their energy, by

283

their curious faces. Several people touch their hands to Uriel's briefly, almost reverently, and I hear someone exclaim, 'How beautiful he is!'

Uriel smiles and accepts their greetings politely, but in my head his voice is blunt and impatient. *We need to move. Now. We cannot waste another moment in idle talk.*

I disagree, I reply, nodding and bowing in all directions as he is doing. *Ryan is right: the only way to combat Luc is not to behave as he would expect. It would probably never occur to him that the great Uriel would approach on foot. We will infiltrate the site as human trekkers — it will be slower, but may tip the odds in our favour.*

'What are you two up to?' Ryan rasps suspiciously, looking from Uriel to me, intercepting the silent exchanges we make with our eyes.

Abruptly, the room, the building, begins to shake: a long, low tremor that shivers the dust from the ceiling, rattles the light fixtures and the bright ornaments and colourfully painted pottery on the wooden shelves. I almost expect Luc to hit me with all he has; to burst into my head and hold my consciousness hostage while he tears the knowledge of my whereabouts from inside me.

But the shaking suddenly stops, and Ryan staggers, almost falling over. A giggling woman in a brightly striped shawl pushes at him with her hands to steady him.

'Earthquake,' Uriel says, shooting me a worried glance.

I'm so relieved it's just an earthquake that I almost shrug.

The man whose home we're in says quietly, 'For three days it has rained. The guides speak of landslides near Llaqtapata, heavy fog and tremors on the mountain, injuries, cancellations. If you wish to trek, as the *gringo* says, there are permits. We can get them for you, no passports, no waiting, if that is what you want.'

The whole room suddenly seems to be watching Uriel to see how he will respond.

'Don't do that thing with your eyes again,' Ryan finally says, exasperated, looking from Uri to me. 'My advice is that you go in on foot and get the flaming swords out only when you need to. But I'm just the half-dead *gringo*,' his voice is bitter, 'so what would I know?'

Our host pushes a new man forward — younger, moustachioed, fit-looking, dressed in khaki and rubber slides. 'I am Mateo,' he says, studying the three of us keenly. 'My uncle tells me you need a guide and permits?'

'Please,' I urge Uriel quietly. 'Let's do this the way Ryan suggests. He's done as Michael commanded — he's kept me alive in more ways than you would ever understand. None of you has *ever* had someone like Ryan on point guard. None of you would even consider taking direction from anyone remotely like him. To be cast adrift in *this* sea and still find someone to anchor me like he has — you couldn't even begin to calculate odds like those. You'd do a lot worse than to listen to him, Uri. We can reassess the terrain once we're there.'

Uriel regards Ryan silently for a moment before nodding tightly. *One day*, he says grimly in my head. *We do it in one day, or we don't do it at all.*

Then he smiles at the people gathered about him and it's like the sun coming out. The women all around us, young and old, clasp their hands together and sigh.

'Sit, sit,' our host tells us, and a path is immediately cleared for us to the round table in the corner of the room, now groaning with platters of food people have brought from their own homes.

Ryan leans on me a little as he shuffles along like an old guy. 'Can you hear that sound?' he whispers, as I help him into one of the bentwood chairs.

A middle-aged man in a dark shirt and black woollen waistcoat places a warm glass of milky-green liquid with leaves floating in it into Ryan's hand, closing his fingers around it. Ryan's still sweating heavily as he takes a sip and grimaces.

'What sound?' I reply curiously.

The air is alive with sounds, both exterior and interior to all the people here. There's a clock ticking somewhere, voices on the radio, the sound of female laughter coming from the room behind us. People are shoving furniture to one side of the room as an older man tunes a guitar.

Ryan drains the glass and closes his eyes, mumbling sleepily, 'The sound of the clock restarting. We're back in penalty time, you and me.'

He smiles, swaying against me a little in his seat, his eyes still closed. And the happiness that suddenly overtakes me — to be here, beside him still — makes me grasp his left hand in my left and pull his arm across my body. I lean into him, feeling the beat of his heart like bird's wings inside his chest, as Mateo describes how it's possible to get a one-day trekking permit without a passport, and what we're likely to face in the morning.

After we rise from our discussion with Mateo, the children surround us, begging us to try the pumpkin soup and *lomo saltado*, the *buding de chocolate* and a sweet dish made from a kind of stewed purple maize that they fall on excitedly called *mozamora morada*. And we do, we do try. But though it all smells delicious, to Uriel and me the food tastes like ashes. After a while, we discreetly push it away.

Ryan only manages a tiny portion of dinner before he curls up and goes to sleep on the low settee. I beg a blanket from Gabino, our host, to cover him, then hang up his wet jeans to dry. I kneel on the floor beside Ryan's sleeping form and move our belongings from the broken backpack into the replacement Gabino pushed into my hands earlier, made of thick felted wool and crawling with bright Peruvian needlework.

'What's wrong with him? What's the *"gringo* sickness" they were talking about?' I ask Uriel, who's standing there with a strange look on his face.

'We're over eleven thousand feet above sea level,' he murmurs, watching me buckle the bag shut. 'Everything in Ryan's body is working overtime to keep him alive. He's not yet acclimatised to this atmosphere, and, I confess, neither am I. Explain to our hosts that I needed some air? I'll be back before first light.'

As silently as a cat, Uriel leaves the room without drawing anyone's attention — a feat that would be impossible for anyone else in this tightly packed space. It hits me suddenly that this may be the most time Uriel has ever spent in the company of humans. The colour and movement that so delight me must be spinning him out.

A long while later, Mayu, Gabino's shy wife, offers me a place to sleep.

I shake my head. 'I don't need it,' I whisper in Quechua with a smile, 'but I thank you, lady. I'll stay and watch over the *gringo*.'

She inclines her head at me before sweeping away in her beautiful red skirt. When I look up again, Mateo is regarding me with a strange expression in his eyes.

'You need to get some rest,' he says in Quechua, looking around before asking, 'Where is your brother?'

Gabino's father calls out, a little drunkenly, 'Ayar Awqa cannot be caged! He has flown away into the night sky. To speak with the stars!'

'No, really, *señorita*, where is he?' Mateo says worriedly. 'I come back for you in only a few hours. The train leaves Cusco at six, and from Kilometer 104, the trek is short but still difficult for people who are not used to our conditions.'

I look up into Mateo's face with a smile. 'Uriel finds the modern world a little ... claustrophobic. He's not very good with crowds, but he's strong and sure-footed and he can walk forever. He'll be fine, and he'll be back before you are.'

'Then he will feel at home tomorrow.' Mateo looks relieved. 'It is wild, high country where we are going: the country of gods.'

And of demons, I think, shivering despite the light and warmth and music in the room, imagining Gabriel chained by fire, in darkness, in the heart of a dead city.

CHAPTER 19

The apartment is quiet around me — just the creaks and groans of timber settling, breathing out — when Uriel returns. One minute I'm sitting there, gazing into the darkness, peering into those of my memories I can gather together, trying to puzzle out some kind of chain, some kind of workable order — but it's a chain that keeps collapsing, because there are more holes than chain — when he's suddenly just there.

Ryan's still sleeping on the settee, his breathing shallow and hoarse. Uriel kneels beside me, brushes a long curl of dark hair back from my face.

You will never see so many stars as in the skies above Cusco, he says inside my head. *Not unless you are home. Don't you miss it?* he continues. *How could you not yearn to return? Every moment I am away I feel it in my soul, as if I am somehow ... unravelling.*

I don't tell Uriel that he's almost described the way I feel around Ryan. It's like we're bound together now; as if the notion of home that I used to carry around inside me has been transposed, somehow, into *him*. And if we were not together any more, maybe *I* would unravel. It's something I can't bring

289

myself to think about until all this is over — and that day is coming, I can feel it.

Uriel sits down beside me, resting his back against the sagging couch, takes my hand in his. His skin is so warm, seething with his peculiar, living fire.

I'm tired, he says. *Tired of planning and plotting, protecting, fighting, moving. So tired. Am I allowed to say that?* His laughter is ghostly.

I think a little honesty is permissible, I reply wryly. *And you've never been one to hold back.*

Nor you, he says. *How we used to fight.*

I hadn't realised we'd called a truce! I say, before grinning.

He looks at me, really studies me in the darkness. *It's good to have you back. Even this way.*

Don't sound so delighted, I say dryly.

His expression grows embarrassed, even ashamed. *When Raphael first devised a plan to find you and preserve you, I admit to being against it. I thought you were dead the instant you were cast down. All of Luc's intent towards you was there in his face. But Raph kept insisting you were alive, and that Luc would throw everything he had into looking for you because of that vow he made, word of which had already spread to us. Even for creatures as we are, there are no secrets. Someone always hears, always knows.*

To be honest, we didn't know what condition you'd be in if you ever 'woke' again. Of us Eight, I think Gabriel missed you most. He missed your friendship and your singularly opinionated take on every aspect of every thing. Raphael's idea of you is clouded by too much dangerous emotion, but Gabriel just missed you. He said you used to make him laugh — and very few things in life make Gabriel laugh. He will be glad to see you again.

If he's still alive, I think fearfully, and Uriel squeezes my hand before releasing it.

We'll find him alive. His reply is too quick, too certain, as if he's trying to convince himself of the truth of his words.

We sit in the darkness for a while, shoulder to shoulder. And it may not be a feeling with any basis in reality, but I'm somehow connected again, to my people, if only for a moment. I'm part of something far greater than I am, which goes beyond merely existing, merely surviving. I hadn't realised how much I needed to know that. Just sitting in the dark, with Uriel beside me, Ryan breathing at my shoulder, has a healing quality.

But time marches, we two can feel it. We are its keepers, its historians; it beats in us, can never be denied.

We should wake him, I say finally, reluctantly, indicating Ryan.

It is time, Uriel agrees.

He rises silently, holding out his strong hand to me, and I take it.

We're on a tourist train bound for 'Kilometer 104', a station at Chachabamba, about sixty-four miles from Cusco.

Watching Uriel pick a carriage, pick a seat, had reminded me of me: he's sitting with his back to the wall right beside the exit to the next compartment, in an aisle seat that gives him an unimpeded view of the entire carriage, which is empty save for us. I'm between Uri and the window, my back to the wall, too, because old habits die hard. Across from us, Ryan's staring, awe-struck, at the rain slicing down the sheer faces of mountains that drop away into deep ravines, wave after wave of them.

Just before the train left, Ryan had tactfully suggested that maybe Uriel wouldn't want to be seen climbing the Inca Trail in a cashmere sweater, chinos and leather loafers with tassels. A blistering silence had ensued, but Ryan and I had exchanged covert glances when we'd looked up from counting the stash of money in our pack to see Uriel dressed in an anonymous-looking, red and navy hip-length hooded parka with a drawstring waist — like one we'd seen on some other *gringo* at the station — a heavy rollneck sweater, kind of like mine except in navy, and black trousers with cargo pockets, heavy boots, sunglasses, and a black beanie.

Okay? Uriel asks inside my head, when he catches me staring at him, and I give him the thumbs-up.

'Though you could lose the sunglasses,' I say. 'We're inside.'

Ryan's mobile phone rings, drawing Uriel's gaze immediately. Ryan puts his hand inside his leather jacket and pulls it out, surprised.

'Lauren?' he says suddenly.

Across from him, Uri and I are instantly still.

'What is it?' Ryan asks anxiously into the screen. 'What's wrong? I just checked in yesterday, right? From Tokyo.' He looks at me for confirmation.

I nod. It feels like a lifetime ago to me, too.

Lauren's voice comes across loud and clear and frightened, ignoring his questions. 'Ryan, is Mercy there? I need to ask her something. Can you put her on?'

I swing across to the window seat beside Ryan and we put our faces together in front of the screen. 'I'm here, Lauren,' I murmur. 'Shoot.'

'There's a man standing outside our house, right now,' she says, her voice high and panicky, 'and I think I'm the only one who can see him. Whenever I look out the window, he's just ... there. He raises his head when I do it — like he's looking into my eyes.'

I go cold at her words. 'Describe him,' I say.

'I can't, not really.' Her words tumble out in fits and spurts. 'It's, like, when I look at him I can't make out the details because he's, like, *glowing* in this robe thing. Maybe he has dark eyes and dark hair, but I can't be sure. When I look at him, I feel sick. It's like I can't focus. He's there, but he's not there. I can't explain it.'

Uriel says suddenly inside my head: *The colour of the light. Ask.*

I lower my voice, trying to sound as calm and normal as possible. 'It's okay, Lauren, it will be okay. Just tell me what colour the, uh, aura, he's giving out is, if you can.'

Lauren's almost crying. 'It's bright, bright but kind of grey. It doesn't make any sense ... God, I know I'm not making any sense. I can hardly stand to look at him, but when I asked Dad whether he could see anything through my bedroom window he said there was nothing there. But he's there all the time. Not Dad, the watcher. Even when I sleep. When I wake up, he's there. When I look out, he's there.' Her voice has risen rapidly, like a scream.

'How long?' Uri asks sharply.

'Lauren,' Ryan says soothingly, as his sister holds one hand over her mouth and weeps. '*Lauren*. How long has this been going on? How long?'

'Two days, three?' she sobs. 'I'm not sure when I first actually noticed. What do I do? *What do I do?*'

293

Ryan says fiercely, 'You get our parents and get the hell out of there. Take Rich with you, too, if you have to, just get them out of town. Tell them anything.'

Uriel and I exchange worried glances, and he murmurs, 'I'm not sure that's the best idea, Ryan. Away from Paradise, they might be even more vulnerable to —'

'Luc's having the house *watched*,' Ryan explodes. 'We're not like you.' He jabs at the air. 'You can't expect me to tell my family to stay there like, like *targets*!'

I go cold as I remember what Luc said in Milan, inside the limousine, when he'd appeared like a vision to me: *Come to me. Only then will you be safe. Flee the Eight and their legion at whatever cost. But if I should somehow fail, then locate that human boy and return with him to the place where he lives, to Paradise. He, too, will play a part in the final reckoning, when all debts due and owing to me shall be met in full and repaid in blood.*

'Send help!' Ryan says violently, glaring at Uriel. 'You could do that, right? If you wanted to.'

Uriel frowns. 'All the *elohim* and *malakhim* that can be spared to fight Luc are massing somewhere only Michael knows of, awaiting his orders. He is our Viceroy, the one who commands us in the name of our Lord. But now he's missing, and I am *just one* upon this earth; alone except for Mercy, with no word of where the others are. As soon as we locate Gabriel, we'll send what help we can. But we need to free Gabriel first. It's imperative.'

'How is Gabriel more important than the people I love?' Ryan thunders.

He says into the screen, 'Get out of town, Lauren, get

them out of there. If they don't know already, don't tell them why, just make it happen.'

Still weeping, Lauren doesn't reply, she just hangs up.

Ryan throws his phone at the back of his seat, then strides down the length of the carriage to get away from us, his arms folded around his head in anguish.

He doesn't come back, not until the train pulls into the station known as Kilometer 104, and he's forced to get out with us.

Ryan doesn't meet my eyes, and he won't look at Uriel at all, as we pull up our hoods against the downpour and walk the four hundred or so feet to a small guardhouse by a narrow suspension footbridge over the tumbling, swollen Urubamba River. The ground is slick and heavy with mud, but I think I'm the only one who notices how Uriel seems to glide across it without stumbling, how the rain and dirt don't seem to touch him at all.

We line up with all the other trekkers and their local guides and porters — about twenty people at most, some of them clearly having second thoughts about pressing on. Mateo makes his way over to us, his head bent. He's wearing a hooded, heavy-duty khaki parka over dark pants, a pair of battered shoes in place of the rubber slides he'd been wearing the night before, and a large backpack as wide and almost half as tall as he is. We'd requested no porters the night before, and Uriel looks at the large pack enquiringly as Mateo reaches us.

'Food, water, rain ponchos, blankets, first-aid kit,' he explains.

Uriel gestures at him to hand the pack over, offended to see anyone carrying anything on his behalf. Mateo hesitates for a moment, before shrugging it off and passing it to him. Uriel slings the pack over his shoulders, ignoring the waist and chest straps because it weighs nothing to him.

I get the wad of euros Gia gave us out of my pocket and shove them into Mateo's hand. He hasn't yet mentioned any kind of payment.

'This is for you,' I say. 'Thirteen hundred and seventy euros, to cover the three of us. It's everything we've got.'

Mateo shakes his head, tries to push the money back into my hands. 'I can't take it, *señorita*,' he says earnestly. 'It is too much. It is only a few hours of walking — you tell me no porters, no bus, no overnight hotel. I would do it for nothing. It is my pleasure.'

'Please,' Ryan shouts, over the sound of the rain, 'take it. If you can't use it all, share it with Gabino and his family. To thank them for taking care of me, for giving me help exactly when I needed it.'

His voice is bitter and I know he's thinking of his own family.

Mateo nods, finally, and zips the money away in his jacket. He retrieves some paperwork from another pocket, enclosed in a battered plastic sleeve, and blinks at me, at Ryan, through the rain. 'Remember that today you are Estelle Jablonski of Mississauga, Canada, and you are her boyfriend, Clive Butler, also of Mississauga, Canada.'

Ryan looks away without replying.

'And you, *señor*,' Mateo says to Uriel, 'are Gerry McEntee Junior from Johannesburg, South Africa. Okay?'

Uri shrugs, and Mateo hands out the three permits that bear no relation to any of us. The two bored guards at the checkpoint barely lift their eyes to look at them, and then we're on the swaying Chachabamba footbridge, white water roaring below.

Ryan's already in trouble as we begin our ascent up a steep, grassy hillside surrounded by a vast mountain range on all sides, snow lying on distant peaks. From valley to valley, I see dark storm clouds, the occasional flash of lightning. It's only just after nine in the morning, but we're moving through a strange kind of grey half-light and even *I'm* having trouble making out Ryan below us. He's fallen so far back that another tour group coming up behind has almost overtaken him.

I walk back down the slope towards him. When I reach him, it's automatic what I do: I take his arm. He's still so angry that he tries weakly to shrug me off, but I don't let him. His chest is heaving, the almost horizontal rain running down his face in rivulets, like tears.

'I'm so far away,' he grates, as he stumbles along, looking at his feet rather than the astounding, almost prehistoric grasslands around us, and certainly not at me. 'Anything could be happening. I should be there.' Then it slips out before he can take it back. 'I wish I'd never met you.'

'You don't really mean that?' I say, as wounded as if he'd taken a weapon to me. Despite all that has happened, I never wish that. Ryan is synonymous with life for me.

He drops my arm like it's burning him. 'I don't know what I mean. Without you, I wouldn't have Lauren back. With you, I feel helpless, when I used to be known for my strength and speed.' His laughter sounds as harsh as his breathing. 'I'm just some guy you keep around,' he murmurs. 'I don't know why you even bother with me.'

He won't let me defend us, just holds up a hand to silence me.

'Don't go snooping around in my head right now,' he mutters, 'because you won't like what you see there. Go be a superhero, or whatever, with your superhero friends. Just give me some space — I need to think.'

He walks away from me then, deliberately pushing himself to pass Uriel and reach Mateo up ahead, though it looks like it's killing him to do it. And it's such a Ryan thing to do that I want to smile as much as I want to cry.

I rejoin Uriel, who's walking easily. He seems taller, more alive out here, even in his human form, even though the elements are throwing everything they've got in our faces. Wind and water. But not fire. We're bringing the fire.

Ryan falls back again, his face set and miserable, as we continue ascending sharply in driving rain, through the thinning air, thousands of feet up. Mateo warned us the night before that it would take at least three or four hours to reach the first set of ruins along this stretch of the trail, but the punishing pace that Uriel is setting is pushing Mateo, Ryan, even me, to go faster and harder. The other groups we left with are nowhere in sight.

In the middle of a raging downpour, Uriel starts to sing:

Lulley, lullay, lulley, lullay,
The falcon hath borne my mate away.

Suddenly, there's no wind, no rain, just the sound of his voice. I stop dead in my tracks in astonishment — at the aching beauty in his voice, in the words, in the melody, cast in some ancient and peculiar minor key.

All of us have stopped, in a ragged, drawn-out line down the narrow, rocky trail, except Uriel, who keeps walking in long, easy strides, singing in a pure, clear, resonating tenor that seems to come back at us from all the surrounding mountains.

> *He bare him up, he bare him down,*
> *He bare him into an orchard brown,*
> *In that orchard there was a hall,*
> *That was hanged with purple and pall.*
> *And in that hall there was a bed,*
> *It was hanged with gold so red.*
> *And in that bed there lieth a knight,*
> *His woundes bleeding day and night.*
> *By that bedside there kneeleth a maid,*
> *And she weepeth both night and day.*
> *And by that bedside there standeth a stone,*
> *Corpus Christi written thereon.*

Mateo points into the sky, astounded, and a giant, winged shape seems to coalesce out of the darkness above us, out of the rain. I tense instantly, preparing to duck, or to fight if it be demon born — until I see that it's a bird. Not the falcon Uriel sang of, but a giant black condor, its wingspan at least nine feet across. It passes so close overhead, in a single smooth sweep, that I feel a rush of air, hear the sound of its wings passing over, as Uriel finishes with his original refrain:

> *Lulley, lullay, lulley, lullay,*

I join him, feeling almost compelled to do it, singing in an alto counterpoint that is rusty and hesitant, but as weirdly resonant as the thread of Uriel's melody:

The falcon hath borne my mate away.

Our voices echo back at us from the stone before dying away. As the song ends, Uriel just keeps walking, as if we have not just produced the most glorious sound anyone will ever hear on this mountain.

Mateo shouts in wonder, 'I have walked these paths for many, many years and I have never seen a condor pass so close! It's as if he brought it down from the sky.'

Still awe-struck, he hurries to catch Uriel.

I continue uphill, occasionally glancing back at Ryan trailing behind us, head down against the rain. I wish he'd make some attempt to try and catch me; there's so much I want to share with him. *Carmen was a soprano, and I'm not!* I want to tell him, though what use that information would be is anyone's guess. Even when we're not together, I find myself telling him things in my head, or storing up impressions, anecdotes, stories to tell him later, though we might never have a later. It's got to be proof of love, or at least of madness.

I think this is the first bad fight we've ever had; and this edgy, unsettled, unhappy feeling I'm having is the feeling of being shut out.

My feet suddenly hit cut granite: an Inca stairway carved from living stone; and above the sound of the rain there's the sound of something else, something elemental, that's growing in power. Then I round a corner, and see a ruined city of light grey stone clinging to the cliff face, spilling down the side of the mountain in graceful, concave terraces, punctuated by ancient fountains and watercourses. Behind and above it, across a ravine, is a raging, tumbling waterfall — glorious, eternal, uncaring, vastly swollen by the interminable rain.

I turn automatically to share what I'm seeing with Ryan, but, of course, he's not there.

Mateo shouts down to me from the pathway above: 'Wiñay Wayna!'

And I know that the name of the place means 'forever young', but it is young as we are young. It endures, like we do, because we were made to.

I see him turn to Uriel and gesture. I can tell that he's suggesting a break, but Uriel shakes his head. Mateo argues, and points down to Ryan, who is still struggling below me on the stairs, every line of his body telegraphing his sheer exhaustion and misery.

'Ryan? Break?' Mateo calls to him anxiously.

Ryan looks up and shakes his head, proudly, bitterly, before looking back down at his boots. So we don't stop for a break because no one's asking to stop, and Mateo has no choice but to agree.

We pass the mysterious, curving terraces of Wiñay Wayna in the driving, dismal rain, and keep walking, keep moving upwards.

When we finally begin to descend through a cloud forest of twisted tree trunks, ferns, orchids and lush, dark green leafy plants, my internal clock tells me it's just before midday. It's warmer now, and the thick cover overhead shields us from the worst of the rain. Green hummingbirds and butterflies dart amongst the foliage.

Mateo overrules Uriel at last, insisting upon a rest break. He hurries back along the paved Incan roadway to fetch Ryan.

Uriel shrugs off the pack of supplies and studies our surroundings with barely concealed impatience. 'Ryan's holding us up,' he says bluntly. 'Remind me again how he's supposed to be useful?'

'He's committed,' I say tautly. 'He can hardly turn around and go back now. Like I said, *he's with me*, and you don't have to like it, you just have to deal with it.'

Mateo and Ryan stagger into view, and I hurry down the path to meet them, shocked at Ryan's pallor, how badly he's shaking.

'He's hallucinating,' Mateo says worriedly as I take Ryan's other arm over my shoulder, curve an arm around his waist. 'He keeps saying he's seen the Devil and the Devil looks just like him.'

'I wish he *was* hallucinating,' I mutter.

We spread out the rain ponchos Mateo brought along and lie Ryan on them. I hold him until his core temperature rises and his breathing evens out and his anger returns.

He sits up finally. 'I'm *fine*,' he snaps hoarsely, trying to fight his way out of my embrace.

But he's exhausted, and I just lock my arms more tightly around him, refusing to let him go. Suddenly it's a battle of wills, an all-out wrestling match on the grassy embankment, and we're sliding around on mud, getting tangled in the plastic of the rain ponchos, until Uriel drags us off each other, still cursing.

'This is the way you show *love* towards one another?' he says incredulously.

'No,' Ryan rasps, splattered with dirt, his hard expression suddenly dissolving. 'I usually say it with flowers. But flowers are too subtle for someone as pigheaded as she is.' He turns to me and says warily, 'Friends?'

302

'You know I'd always take a round of Greco-Roman wrestling over flowers, so no hard feelings,' I shoot back.

Ryan laughs out loud, and some of that horrible edginess that's been plaguing me all day, like my own personal black cloud, dissipates at the sound.

We smile at each other, and Uriel says disgustedly, 'I don't understand you.'

Mateo approaches hesitantly, handing us each a bottle of water and a plastic plate loaded with food from the pack: slices of fresh bread topped with torn pieces of a soft, white cheese, with a side of some colourful-looking salad involving potato and cucumber, sliced onion, beetroot and mayo. I see him take in Ryan's forlorn appearance, before his eyes slide uncomfortably away from me, from Uri — completely dry and neat as two new pins.

Uriel and I exchange glances of our own.

'The food looks lovely, Mateo,' I say casually, 'but how about you and Ryan take a little more of ours? Uri and I are still working off breakfast.'

Mateo looks down sharply at what's left on my plate, on Uri's, after we've redistributed most of our food to the two of them. But though he's clearly dying to point out that we must have worked up some kind of appetite after hiking for almost three hours straight without stopping, he doesn't. Perhaps out of a natural sense of tact, or to maintain the growing fiction that there's nothing remotely screwy about either Uriel or myself.

When the two men are done eating, Uriel rises immediately and his voice is commanding as he says, 'When we reach Machu Picchu, Mateo, leave us. Take as many of the other guides and porters and tourists with you as you can. Make directly for the car park you talked of last night, the buses to Aguas Calientes. *Do not linger.*' Uriel doesn't actually add: *If you want to live.* But it's in his voice.

Mateo nods, looking troubled as he stows the remains of our meal in the pack. 'There will be hardly anyone on the mountain today. It should be easy, what you ask for.'

'A good day, then, for us to pay a visit,' Uriel replies calmly, hoisting the pack onto his broad shoulders. He turns and looks at Ryan for a moment. 'As for you, do as your "will" dictates. Just keep yourself alive, or there will be no living with this one,' he indicates me brusquely, 'ever again. Got that?'

Then he turns and walks away swiftly, silently.

CHAPTER 20

For a time, our route through the forest is meandering, almost easy. But then the paved roadway transforms back into a steep staircase that's exposed once more to the elements. We find ourselves battling uphill through a curtain of rain upon a slick and infinitely more treacherous surface: Mateo in the lead, followed by Uriel, then Ryan and I, side by side, because to be any other way, we've come to realise, feels wrong.

'I don't even know what day it is today,' Ryan mutters, his hands balled into fists in his pockets in a vain attempt to keep his fingers warm.

'Friday,' I say unerringly.

'Friday in Peru,' he mumbles in disbelief.

I hear him give a gasp as the forest to our right suddenly falls away into thin air and we're staring down a huge cliff face into absolute space. Then we enter more ruins — like standing stones situated upon the crest of a ridge — and Mateo calls out from just beyond them, 'Inti Punku! The Gateway of the Sun!' and we look left through the gate, and down, and we see it at last.

A sprawling complex of ruined stone buildings that lies across the saddle between two mountains, a sheer drop on two sides into deep valleys, a towering mountain peak at its back. The city of Machu Picchu.

As we look down in awe, the rain abruptly stops. The absence of sound is almost disorientating, the silence so intense it feels as if I've momentarily lost my hearing. The heavy pall of cloud that hangs low over the mountain peak framing the city seems suddenly lit up from within, as if the sun is trying desperately to break through.

The cloudy sky is steel grey shot through with silver as we begin our descent down a narrow walkway paved with large flagstones. The zigzagging scar of some modern roadway defaces the steep hillside to our right, a bus — tiny from this distance — travelling back down it. We begin to pass outlying walls and buildings, and it's around 1 pm when we hit the heart of the city. There are stone structures in almost every direction, situated along wide plazas or separated by a multitude of walkways, fountains, ramparts, lookouts, dividing walls, most open to the sky. It's impossible to get a feel for things, or to know what we're even looking at, but I understand what Uriel meant when he said the place reeked of blood and power. The city fell silent centuries ago, but if I listen hard enough, I can almost hear ritual and violence emanating from the stone itself.

The path seems to end at a great three-sided structure, and as Ryan and I reach Uriel and Mateo, I glimpse a few people moving about the complex. I see flashes of colour, feel shifts in energy eddying around me, but nothing I can really put my finger on. Just a pervading sense of menace.

'Where to now?' Ryan wheezes.

Uriel scans the area uneasily. 'Everywhere. We walk every inch of this place until we feel something, see something. He's still here, I know he is. They haven't moved him.'

'That doesn't strike you as weird?' I ask quietly.

He shakes his head. 'I was always supposed to return, Mercy. It was always a trap. In the end, there will be no hiding what we are. All we've done by coming here on foot is to buy ourselves a little more time, some slight advantage. The *"gringo"* was wiser than I gave him credit for.'

Behind Uri's back, Ryan raises his eyebrows and I have to smile.

'Luc's forces will have to work out who we are before they can deal with us,' Uriel murmurs. 'They have to find us first. And while they're looking, we need to locate Gabriel.'

'It's a pretty big place,' Ryan says.

Uri sighs as he considers the elevated structures to the west of us, then below us to the east. 'There's no scientific way to do this. We take as long as it takes to find him.'

His eyes fall on Mateo, still standing there, listening to us talk.

'Go with our thanks, Mateo,' Uriel says quietly but commandingly. 'Find your compatriots, tell them to get their charges back down to the buses. It is no longer safe for you here.'

Mateo nods and starts to walk away, before turning and saying hesitantly, 'The children made me promise to ask what it was that brought "Ayar Awqa" to Machu Picchu. What should I tell them, *señor*?'

Uriel and I exchange glances, before Uriel replies softly, 'Tell the children that he came to seek his brother, upon the mountain.'

Mateo's eyes widen in surprise. 'Lost?' he exclaims. 'Here?'

'If someone were to be held here, against his will,' I say, because it has to be worth a shot, 'where would he be?'

'How could he know?' Uriel says exasperatedly. 'Let us waste no more time, Mercy. What slight advantage we have is slipping away.'

'Held how?' Mateo asks.

'Bound in some way,' I reply. 'Tied up.'

Mateo's face clears immediately. 'But that is easy. It is like a riddle, a puzzle, yes? Like you, like him.' He indicates Uriel. 'I will take you there, follow me.'

The three of us look at each other, scarcely daring to hope.

Mateo descends quickly through street after street of ruins, until we find ourselves loosely ringed around a strangely configured stone that's been roped off to prevent people touching it. It's irregular in shape, with a diameter wider than a man is tall; a broad, stepped area, almost like a bench, cut out of one side; a protuberance of rock — like a blunt finger — pointing up out of it towards the sky. The stone stands above a frightening precipice, framed by cloud.

Uriel says suspiciously, 'What is this?'

'Its name is Intiwatana,' Mateo answers eagerly. 'You understand our language, *señor*, so its meaning will be clear to you.'

'But not to me,' Ryan says apologetically, taking a drink from the bottled water in his pack.

'It means, literally, "sun-tying-place",' Uriel murmurs, walking around the curious stone. 'The instrument to which you tie up, or hitch, the sun.'

'How can you be sure this is the place?' I ask Mateo, feeling nothing more than that general sense of unease.

'This stone has magical properties,' he replies. 'It was built so that on certain days of the year, when the sun stands directly above the stone, it casts no shadow at all. If your brother is like you, then this is the place.'

'I still don't get it,' Ryan says. 'There's nothing here but this rock.'

Mateo points at the ground at my feet, at Uriel's, and I see Ryan's face change as he works out what Mateo's trying to tell us.

Since we left Milan, the sun has barely touched my skin, or has touched it so fleetingly that I never felt its warmth. But here, upon this windswept plateau, its light finally struggles through the cloud. And as its rays move across the face of the stone called Intiwatana, across all of us standing here, I see what Mateo saw before any of us did. There are four people present, but only two cast shadows upon the ground.

Uriel and I glance at each other sharply.

'The Inca believed this stone held the sun in the sky. If he is your brother,' Mateo insists, 'then he, too, is a creature of the sun, bound to this place.'

'Superstition,' Uriel scoffs, saying out loud exactly what I'm thinking. 'How could he be here? I don't feel anything —'

But then, as if in reply, the earth begins to roar, it begins to tremble, and I hear distant screams, the sound of buckling stone, of thousands of roof tiles falling and shattering in the streets. I hear Mateo's cries, Ryan's, as they struggle to remain on their feet in a shifting, rending world.

There's something else, too: like the sound of steel on steel, something fleeting, but so discordant and sharp that it resonates painfully within me, makes me want to claw at my head in agony.

Uriel gasps aloud, similarly afflicted, as the brief sound recurs, then recurs again, and again. Something's coming, something fast. A whole bunch of somethings, erupting from everywhere, but nowhere, all at once.

'Ryan!' I yell through the roar of the physical world being torn apart, through the searing pain in my head. 'Mateo! Lead your people to safety! Find them, get them out.'

Mateo nods, already turning, but Ryan hesitates, crippled by his loyalty to me.

'Every one of them could be your sister, your mother, your father!' I cry. 'Don't just let the bad stuff happen, Ryan. It's penalty time. Every action counts. We have to do what we can with the abilities we've got, don't you see?'

And I see that he gets in an instant what has taken me lifetimes to figure out.

As Ryan and Mateo stumble back up the stairs, a heavy white fog rolls towards the lip of the plateau that Uriel and I occupy. Even as we watch, it begins to ascend *up* the terraces of Machu Picchu, blanketing everything in its path, turning the air an unnatural white that has a tinge of grey, like contagion, at its heart.

Demonsign. Uriel's voice is like a breath of fire in my mind.

Then, without warning, out of that fog sweeps a wraith. It leaps onto the plateau, ghostly braids streaming about its skull-like face, a star-shaped stone axe raised high, mouth stretched in an undying scream. I can see the outline of the man it once was, but the face and form are indistinct, shredding and re-forming like the fog that surrounds us.

Uriel and I are between the wraith and the stone. I see the thing's head questing from side to side as if it's deciding which of us to take first with its ghostly axe.

Uriel puts his arm around me and pulls me close, as if he's Gerry McEntee from Johannesburg, South Africa, and I'm Estelle Jablonski of Mississauga, Canada, and we're lost together in the fog.

Hold your nerve, he roars in my head. *Do not shift.*

The creature throws itself at us, through us — like shards of glass, or a handful of nails — and is gone, subsumed forever by our peculiar energy. *Daemonium* of this kind are no match for us. The ones that wear faces are the ones we fear.

And then an army of wraiths comes boiling over the edge of the plateau, a legion of the violent, mindless dead. Surrounding us, momentarily, like a milling herd of shredded, shredding energy. Those that touch Uriel or me vanish like ether, but hundreds remain. Each one distinct, each one once a man.

Suddenly, as if startled, they flow away, as one, into the trembling streets of the city that once was theirs when they yet lived, mouths stretched wide in silent, ravening screams, taking the unnatural fog with them.

When Uriel releases me from his hold, the roped-off stone lies exposed beneath weak sunlight, and the earth is no longer shaking.

He and I circle the rock warily, studying it, and I tell him of what was done to Nuriel; the forms of punishment that were visited on Jegudiel and Selaphiel.

'If he's in there,' I say, 'he may be compromised. Don't touch him until you're sure he's clean.'

Uriel nods grimly, then leaps lightly over the guard rope onto the upper surface of the stone. He places his right hand upon the granite, effortlessly reaching through and into it, before declaring in ringing tones, '*Libera eum!*'

Nothing. Nothing but storm cloud moving in from the northeast, and the lonely shriek of a hunting bird drifting through the valley below us.

Uriel withdraws his arm from the stone and I watch his forearm, the fingers of his hand re-form in an instant into apparent solidity.

'I'll take the western reaches,' he says finally, 'including the lower terraces. You take this side, and we'll meet back in the middle, near that structure where the path of flagstones ended.'

Uriel — still in his human guise — takes the stairs at a run and is soon lost in the rolling fog above me.

I enter the fog with reluctance; it seems almost impenetrable, even to my eyes. It sucks and eddies around my ankles like a tide, draws its weblike tendrils across my face. Trapezoidal doorways and windows loom up in front of me without warning. All sound seems deadened in the roiling, cloudy atmosphere. I could be the only thing alive on this mountain.

Then the hallucinations start. Snatches of past lives, old demons, stalking me through the streets of the city. I hear Ezra's husband's voice calling her *slut* and *whore*, the dull sound of fist and open palm meeting flesh, a woman's scream. A baby cries, the sound weak and thin, high from hunger and withdrawal, and I know that it's Lucy's baby. I can't escape the crying, try to outrun it. But I lose my footing by a gaping building with walls stained red with earth or old blood, and Susannah's mother roars at me from out of the darkness inside: 'You ruined my life, you little bitch! I wish you'd never been born.' But as I pick myself up clumsily, gripped in the cold fear of memory, I hear her sob, 'Come back, come back! I didn't mean it, oh, how could I? I'm sick, *so sick*.'

Her voice pursues me as I stumble past a row of houses with trapezoidal rooms, scrambling almost on all fours up the staircase beyond them only to hear Lauren say quietly, 'I've been in hell. Am in hell. And now you are, too. You get used to it,' she calls after me. 'Used to it.'

Then I'm lurching uphill, struggling to get away from them all, heading on autopilot towards the place where I'm supposed to meet Uriel, trying to outrun memory. But my own sneering words come back at me in Lela's gentle voice, and stop me in my tracks. 'You'll never get out of here alive, you know,' I hear myself say.

And I hear a dead man reply bitterly, 'I know, and neither will you.'

Then a single gunshot reverberates upon the peak of Machu Picchu, the sound so real and so immediate that when I'm momentarily hit by a hailstorm of sharp sensation — like needles of ice being flung in my face, hurled at my body — I almost fall to the ground, believing I've been shot all over again.

The fog is thick with wraiths. Another one hits the solid force of me and shreds into fragments, then another, and another. I could be standing in a hurricane of broken glass. I twist and flail, trying to shield myself. They're like suicidal insects — the ghosts of this place — drawn to my energy, my warmth, dashing themselves against me in a wave.

The fog parts momentarily and I see that strange, three-sided structure ahead, like a house without a roof, open on one side. There's a winged man standing before it, built along mythical lines, his back to me, wearing raiment so bright I can barely stand to look at it. He has long, dark hair spilling down his back — every strand straight, even and exactly the same — and I'm so filled with panic and shame, fear and relief, that I run towards him screaming, 'Uri, *Deo gratias*. Uri.'

But then he turns, and I see that it isn't Uriel at all. His eyes are a brilliant blue, and there's a blazing scar across his face the size of an archangel's handprint. He is both dazzlingly beautiful and hideously disfigured, and his name springs into my mind unbidden: *Jetrel*.

The instant I recognise him for who he is, I remember Uriel's earlier words of warning: *Hold your nerve. Do not shift*. The advantage we gained from reaching this place on foot, unheralded, is almost gone. One last element of surprise remains to me, and I must hold fast to it.

The fog hides from Jetrel's eyes what happens next: I find a gun in each hand; there because I need them. I raise them with shaking hands, pointing them up into Jetrel's face, where it towers over me. I pray he does not see the single lick of blue flame that plays across the surface of each gun.

'I wouldn't,' he says, and smiles with pointed teeth like the canines of wild animals.

I look behind me to see another shining, winged giant, a feral light in his wide-set grey eyes. With his prominent bones and hairless face and scalp, his vulpine teeth, his heavily muscled bare torso and blazing abdominal scar, he seems even more terrifying and otherworldly than his companion. I

314

know he must be Shamshiel, for Uriel said that Shamshiel and Jetrel were together, but he is so changed I do not recognise him at all.

I train a gun on each of them — one to the south, one to the north along the stone roadway — and they laugh in my face.

Then they look at each other as if I'm not even here.

'There's nothing but condors and humans on this mountain,' Shamshiel spits. 'How much longer must we wait? Our company becomes increasingly restless.' His tone turns mocking. 'And Lord Gabriel grows difficult to control.'

'He's secure?' Jetrel hisses.

'For now. Semyaza and Astaroth, Balam, Yomyael, Beleth and Caym are holding him at the mausoleum. But their powers wane, just as yours do. We are too far from home.' Shamshiel reaches behind himself suddenly and pulls someone forward. 'They found this one stumbling around in the fog. So they gave him to me. Shall I give him to you? Or to her?'

I see that it's Ryan, ashen-faced, staring at me.

I start forward, shocked, and Jetrel's eyes narrow, catching the movement.

'Why? Do they know each other?' he says.

'I saw her face in his mind. He "loves" her. He could not bear to lose her.' Shamshiel chuckles darkly.

Jetrel smiles. 'Then let us see whether those feelings are reciprocated. You, girl,' he snaps, gazing with a sneer at the barrel of the gun that's trained on him. 'Shoot him. Do it, and we will let you live.'

His taunt tells me that they still think me human. They think they have nothing to fear from me and my human weapons.

315

'*Shoot him*,' Jetrel repeats slowly and loudly, as if I possess no more wit than a trained animal. 'Or we will take your puny, mortal handguns and pit you one against the other.' He laughs and turns to Shamshiel. 'They say the female is the more deadly of the species. Let us see if that is the case. This one certainly looks it.'

Shamshiel shoves Ryan towards me until the barrel of the gun that was aimed at him is now pressed against Ryan's forehead.

'*Shoot him*,' Jetrel barks from behind me. 'Do murder.'

I turn my head and look into his brilliant eyes, the shining, disfiguring brand that is burnt across his jaw, his lips, the left side of his face.

'*Fiat voluntas tua*,' I murmur. *Thy will be done.*

Then I pull the trigger of the gun that's still aimed at Jetrel's head.

I see Jetrel's eyes widen at my words, an instant before the bullet — that is no ordinary projectile — hits him between the eyes. The force of his dying bears me to the ground, sends a blast wave of heat and light into the air that is enough to light up the fog from within, like a nuclear cloud.

Let Uriel see, I think fervently. *Let him be warned.*

I open my eyes to find Ryan standing over me, a weird look in his dark eyes.

Bracing myself on my elbows, I say pleadingly, 'I never would have done it, you know. I never would have shot you. It just had to look that way. I'm sorry.'

'And now you'll never get the chance,' Ryan says in a voice that is strangely resonant, like steel on flint, 'because I'm going to kill you first.'

A flaming short sword comes to life in each of his hands, as if they are an extension of his fingers, and I scramble away from him in horror, backwards across the ground. I can't shoot him because it's Ryan. It's indisputably Ryan. I feel his peculiar human energy, the energy I would know anywhere, anytime. But it's mixed up, contaminated, dominated by the energy of another.

Possession.

'Shamshiel!' I scream as I rise to my feet, sickened beyond belief. 'What have you *done?*'

The guns in my hands dissipate instantly into motes of light, replaced by short swords indistinguishable from those in Ryan's hands save for the light of the flames that play across the blades. Mine blaze from hilt to tip with the clean, pale blue of holy fire, but not his. His blaze with a tainted light.

It is too awful to contemplate what Ryan must be going through right now. For it's Shamshiel's laughter coming from Ryan's mouth, the mad light of Shamshiel's eyes in Ryan's own. I shudder as we circle each other, weapons raised. Truly, I am facing a monster.

'Who are you?' Shamshiel growls through Ryan's mouth, crouching lower in a fighting stance, rolling his shoulders, his blades testing the air in intricate patterns that flow and shift into each other. 'One of the *malakhim?* The double-dealer they speak of? If you are she, lay your weapons down, sister, and let me embrace you.'

He licks his lips in a manner so dreadful, so lascivious, so unlike Ryan, that I have to look away for a moment, sickened.

'I'm just a girl,' I say grimly, looking back into his mad eyes, testing the air with my blades in broken figures of eight. The short swords, Shamshiel's weapons of choice, feel unfamiliar and unwieldy in my hands.

'Then have at me, *girl*,' he roars, 'and let me see what you are made of.'

He lunges forward with astonishing, inhuman speed, coming at me so quickly that the tip of the blade in his right hand slices through the front of my jacket, actually nicking the surface of it, of me, before I can leap back. The wound stings like acid burn.

Shamshiel keeps pressing forward in Ryan's body, swinging his blades at me in wide arcs, in hypnotic patterns, like a reaper's scythe. In panic, running on instinct, I throw up block after block. Our blades come together with the *crack* of lightning strikes, and I'm barely able to parry his fluid, two-handed fighting style.

I'm unable to truly attack or land a blow, because although it's Shamshiel I feel in every chop, down stroke and numbing engagement, it's Ryan I'm seeing, Ryan's body that will bleed if I harm it.

How do I do this? I think, panicked. *There's no way to do this without hurting Ryan, or being hurt.*

Uriel! I cry into the ether. But there's no reply. He must be out of range, or fighting his own demons elsewhere on the mountain.

Shamshiel runs at me again, Ryan's teeth bared, sweeping his right blade upwards at my face while he swings his left inwards at my abdomen. I'm trying so hard to avoid the blades that I don't catch him changing the ground rules on me, holding my eyes as he pulls one foot back before sweeping my own from under me. As the back of my head hits the ground with unbelievable force, he throws himself down on me, laughing, teeth exposed and glistening.

I roll sideways frantically, my outline already shredding as I try to get away from him, to re-form elsewhere, out of reach, the way Nuriel showed me was possible in a dirty fight. But Shamshiel catches me by my outflung left wrist, pins it to the stone path with the blade of one of his weapons. The scream that is torn from my lips is awful and echoing, and the earth begins to shake again, as if it feels my pain. It's as if my agony is bringing forth a response in the physical world.

My weapons dissipate in my hands. I cannot hold them.

Shamshiel's blade is anchoring me here, I cannot shift away.

I look at my pinned left wrist and see my scar come to life, see that agonising fire ignite upon the skin, snake upwards from my fingers, cross the back of my hand, take hold of my wrist, my forearm, as if it is alive. As beautiful as it is corrosive.

And I see Ryan's eyes widen as Shamshiel perceives the flames. He thinks me an exile like him, but some turncoat, some traitor to Luc's cause. I see him trying to work out who amongst his fallen brethren carries a scar like mine. It is only seconds that he studies me, his eyes crawling across my skin inch by inch, but it feels like a lifetime.

'Who *are* you?' he rasps finally, crouched beside me. 'Tell me your name.'

I'm shocked when Ryan begins to growl and convulse like a wounded animal, twitching uncontrollably, his facial muscles spasming and contorting, eyes rolling back in their sockets. I know what I am seeing: two sentient beings fighting for control of one body.

'*Tell me*,' Shamshiel screams from Ryan's mouth as Ryan's will and body fight him terribly.

I can feel my options narrowing. Soon there will be none that will not end in the death of one of us; I feel it like a train bearing down upon me at speed.

I beckon the beast inside Ryan towards me, weakly, as if I am mortally wounded. The demon bends until he is looking into my face, and it takes everything in my power not to turn my head away, to retch in horror. For Ryan's human skin seethes with such violence and power that my own soul crawls with disgust.

So fast that Shamshiel does not catch the movement, I plunge my right hand into Ryan's chest, my fingers dissolving instantly like mist.

Ryan roars in a terrible, mortal agony, twists and struggles, but I do not let him pull away. I draw him closer with every ounce of my will, searching desperately for some flaw, some thread that will lead me to where Shamshiel is anchored like a parasite, hooked in so deep that he cannot be shaken out by any means.

But Ryan is no stone angel, just a creature knit of flesh and blood and bone. His body begins to burn, and I know that I am slowly killing him.

'Aaaaaaaah,' he cries in agony, attacked from within and without by fire.

Then something seems to move past my questing will — quick and sinuous, like a serpent escaping — and in the instant that it touches me again, I roar in a voice like sounding brass: '*Ejicie eum!*' Cast him out!

Shamshiel explodes backwards out of Ryan's body, shrieking in rage.

I pull back from Ryan and my right hand rematerialises. I hug it to my chest, weeping tears of fire and contrition as Ryan falls to the ground beside me, clawing at his neck, his torso, trying to put out the flames that are nowhere except inside him.

He badly needs my help, but Shamshiel puts a foot on my left hand before I can reach over with my right to pull his blade out of my pinned wrist.

'*Eloah*,' he growls, 'for that is what you must be, though the strangest I have ever come across. You look and behave like one of *them*, like a creature of clay. But only the *elohim* have the power to cast out demons in this manner, and Lucifer wants you all. You are to be collected like pretty butterflies and brought to him to be dealt with.' He indicates Ryan with disgust. 'But this one *dies*. I tire of the game that cost Jetrel his life; it ends now.'

Ryan gasps and shudders beside me on the ground, curled over in mortal agony, unable to talk, unable to move, his eyes wide with fear and pain.

Shamshiel's remaining sword blazes into life in his hand and I weep harder, tears falling from my eyes like diamonds, as I beg, 'Take me, but spare him. Leave him. Let him live.'

The demon looks into my face from his great height and hisses, 'Die now, die later, it matters not. For soon they all die. From Panama to Mexico, Iceland to Iran, Kamchatka to Sumatra, we will remake the world, its oceans, its climate — for we move at long last. It is only the first step in what is coming, what Lucifer promised us. Soon we will be free of this wilderness, our prison. We shall etch our contempt upon its very bones, upon its face, so that God himself may see what we have written there, then quit it forever.'

Shamshiel wraps his two great hands around the hilt of his short sword and raises it above Ryan's prone and twitching body where it lies beside me. Weeping uncontrollably, I see the great muscles of Shamshiel's shoulders bunch, his face contort, as he readies himself to administer the killing blow, while I watch, unable to move, to do anything.

Then time seems to speed up and slow down all at once.

I see a thin line of blue fire appear like holy writing across the front of Shamshiel's throat, see his eyes fly wide. Hear the howl of indescribable anguish that climbs and climbs into the heavens, only to be lost in a shattering roar of heat and light.

Then Shamshiel is gone; and the fog with him.

As I lie pinned to the ground by the blazing weapon of a dead monster, I see four winged giants standing above me, bathed in a light that comes solely from within.

Then I close my eyes and am lost, for a time.

CHAPTER 21

It's Ryan who pulls Shamshiel's blade from my wrist, Ryan who shakes my shoulders and calls my name and holds me close; Ryan, whole and healed and himself again.

I breathe in the familiar warm, male, human scent of him and cannot help murmuring, '*Jubilate Deo*.'

'Well said,' a familiar voice replies softly, 'well said.'

For a disorientating moment, I open my eyes and look into my own face, my true face, not the false one I'm wearing now. Then I fathom groggily that it is Uriel who smiles down at me, in his customary form, the tail feathers of his great wings trailing upon the stone at his feet, his right hand resting upon the hilt of the great sword that cut Shamshiel down.

My eyes move slowly to the winged Titan standing beside him, also wreathed in glory, and I see that it is silver-eyed, auburn-haired Jeremiel, who says now, in a voice like exaltation, that makes me shiver to hear it, 'Mercy, well met. It has been far too long, sister.'

Beside him stands dark-eyed, dark-haired Barachiel, whose province is lightning. It seems to play within the folds of his shining raiment, the long, sleek feathers of his luminous wings, as he growls at me the way he always used to, 'Here's strife.' But today he's smiling, and I find myself smiling back.

When I look to the last of them, I start to weep again. I can't contain my tears: they spill down my cheeks and down through the fingers that cover my mouth in horror. For his gleaming, sleeveless raiment is rent and despoiled; his wing feathers are broken and torn; the surface of his alabaster skin is marked by signs of terrible torture, by wounds that continually bleed light into the air.

'Gabriel!' I cry, and he bends and takes my hands in his, his flaming hair falling over his pale brow into his pain-clouded emerald eyes. He sweeps it back impatiently, then pulls me close against him.

'Never weep for me, marvellous creature,' he says softly, pulling back and looking into my face for a long while. 'When you and I are together now, there should be only joy. Enough death and pain and evil has marked the time you were lost to us. No more tears, Mercy, I beg you. I am well enough, whole enough.'

But his laughter has a catch in it, as if it hurts him to laugh.

As I smooth my thumbs across the wounds on the backs of Gabriel's great hands, I startle such a strange expression upon Ryan's face. Awe, wonder, jealousy: I see a little of them all there, the greatest being jealousy.

'These are my *brothers*,' I say quietly, with emphasis, with pride, as Gabriel releases me and rises painfully to stand beside Barachiel.

'No more, no less.' Jeremiel addresses Ryan almost reprovingly. 'For if we had not meant you well, you would not now be restored.'

Gabriel makes a stilling gesture in Jeremiel's direction and looks down into Ryan's face. 'We have no words to express our gratitude, our elation, that she is returned to us. You did as Michael asked: you kept her alive in your chaotic, frightening world. Restoring you to health goes no way towards repaying your care of her.'

'What of Michael?' Uriel asks, turning to the others, his wings dissolving into ether. At the same moment, Jeremiel and Barachiel also relax their guard and their wings melt away into the chill air.

'Yes, what news?' Gabriel adds, flexing his own giant wings stiffly for a moment. The torn feathers catch the weak sunlight, seem to hold it, magnify it momentarily, before they also shred apart.

'Luc's forces gather in Panama,' Barachiel replies. 'They have some vague, self-important intention of bringing the Pacific and Atlantic Oceans together. I had it from Semyaza himself before he inconveniently died. If Luc is there, then Michael and Raphael will not be far off. They are too valuable to Luc, he would want them close.'

'Luc did promise Michael an exceptional form of vengeance,' I remind the others quietly, flexing my scored left wrist that still burns with pain from Shamshiel's blade. 'This might be what he intended. Destroying a nation. Creating a new climate, a new world order. He was always ambitious.'

The four turn and refocus their eyes upon Ryan where he kneels beside me on the ground.

'Then it is time to see him home, Mercy,' Uriel says quietly. 'It cannot be further delayed. While we hold Luc's attention, get him home. Get yourself home. There is no other way. I'm sorry.'

I feel my eyes brim again with tears and am appalled at my weakness.

'*Why?*' Ryan says bravely, violently, and I see Barachiel frown. 'Why must she always sacrifice her own happiness for others? Hasn't she done enough? Can't you keep that monstrous bastard away from her for good? You put him here in the first place — take him back, or finish him off. We don't want him, either. You're, like, the most powerful angels in the universe. *Do something.*'

'While Luc lives,' Jeremiel says quietly, 'she remains the catalyst and the key. As powerful as we are, he is nearly untouchable here on earth, able to hide himself indefinitely, like a worm, or a snake, crawling beneath the earth. Once our most perfect son; now our paradigm terrorist. If we could "finish him off", we would have done it years ago. We all,' Jeremiel's eyes move over me before he returns his shimmering, argent gaze to Ryan, 'must play our part, do what we can.'

Barachiel takes up the argument in his rumbling voice. 'With Mercy gone, the threat is not gone, but it is reduced. As is the arena of battle that we must defend. It is the only way.'

I place a stilling hand on Ryan's arm before he can say anything more, and address my brethren harshly through my tears.

'I may not accept it, but I understand, and I will do as you ask. Evil has no community, and I am no longer evil. Though the free will that was supposedly gifted to our kind alone has proved a most bitter thing to swallow. I am free, but not free. Constrained always by what is greater than me, better and more selfless than me. There's no possibility of balance, of compromise, but how I wish there were. How I wish ...'

Even Ryan can feel the force of the longing and desperation blazing out of me.

My four kinsmen regard me sorrowfully for a moment. Then Gabriel draws me to my feet, also helping Ryan to stand, before linking our hands together. Ryan looks down for a moment, unable to speak for sorrow.

'Come,' Barachiel says, his mighty visage grim once more. 'Let us keep company with you along the coast until you must turn for "Paradise" — that most incongruously named place — and we make for Panama, and for Raphael and Michael.'

I glance at Uriel, stricken. 'So soon?'

He says softly, 'You knew this was only temporary, a reprieve. A small measure of time out of time. It is kinder this way, sister. Let him go. Let it all go. You have earned a measure of peace. Some day, you will be together again.'

'How can you be sure?' Ryan says bitterly, still staring at our joined hands, gripping my fingers so tightly that his are white with constricted blood. 'How can you really be sure that we'll ever be together again? What if I want to take *now* over *later*? What if I don't believe?'

'Then you are already lost,' Barachiel murmurs. 'And there *is* no later.'

'Bear him home, Mercy,' Gabriel says quietly. 'Do not delay, do not linger. As soon as Michael and Raphael are secure, we will return for you.'

'How long do we have?' Ryan asks, looking up at Gabriel, his dark eyes shining with unshed tears.

'Not long,' Gabriel murmurs. 'You will know when it is time.' He places a hand on my shoulder. 'His care of you — his love — will be repaid in ways that cannot be measured.'

Then Uriel, who was my watcher when I was Carmen, grasps my hand tightly and lets me into his thoughts, showing me the way. I see the approach up the coast to Ryan's home town of Paradise; see it from above, from the ground; the main street, Ryan's house, even the tree Ryan set fire to. All through Uriel's eyes. It's no longer a mystery to me, where Paradise is.

'You saw it?' Uriel murmurs.

I hang my head, nodding, bright tears spilling down my cheeks onto the stone at my feet. Then, still weeping, I embrace Ryan in my arms — for he is and always will be my burden — and we six leap off the solid surface of the world into the lowering skies above Machu Picchu, and turn west for the coast.

The sun is setting as we pass through the heavy skies over Chiclayo. We travel in silence, each buried in our own thoughts, our own agonies.

Without warning, as we begin to cross over open sea, Gabriel, Uriel, Barachiel and Jeremiel splinter into light; they are already halfway to the Gulf of Panama before we've even registered they've gone.

'Now that it's just the two of us,' Ryan says suddenly, trying hard to smile, 'I have to confess that this is one thing I won't miss, flying.'

I spiral slowly to a stop, and as I do, I shift, so that Ryan is looking at *me*. At my wide-set brown eyes, my long, straight, dark brown hair, my strong-featured face that I've always thought suits Uriel so much more than it suits me. We're alone. It may be the last time I can truly be myself with him. Though I know I should be careful — careful every moment I'm still in this world — I want him to remember me like this, no other way.

Ryan's eyes light up as he takes me in. He runs a finger down my luminous bare arm in the way that always makes my soul shiver. My robes flare and shift of their own accord, as if carried by ghostly winds, curls of energy lifting and curling into the night air.

Ryan cups the side of my face gently as I hold him braced in my arms. 'Welcome back from wherever you've been,' he says.

'I've been here all along,' I murmur. 'And we've had fun, right? Hasn't it been fun? A blast?'

My laughter has a ring of desperation to it as I try to make light of everything that has happened. Already gone forever, already memory.

In reply, Ryan captures my lips with his, his mouth opening over mine, searching and hot and sweet. But he releases me before we hit the invisible barrier that will always separate us.

'We've been hurt enough today,' he whispers raggedly, resting his forehead against mine. 'We don't need to hurt each other, too.'

Suspended together, we gaze down at the darkening sea below.

'Seeing the world with the girl you love,' I say despairingly. 'What more could any guy wish for?'

'A whole lot more,' Ryan says harshly. 'A whole lifetime.'

My voice is very quiet as I reply. 'You say that now, but I've lived enough lifetimes to know that you start off with love and then everything hits you, everything swamps you, and you can't help it, you change — or those around you do — and you have to bear the consequences. I've been beaten, cheated, abused and left for dead, Ryan. Not a great track record. Those are some of the things I will remember from this world. That's what I've learnt about life.'

'But none of that is *me*,' Ryan replies hotly. 'It won't *ever* be, and I won't let anything like that touch you again. I can't promise you that life won't ever be boring, or a grind, or just plain hard, because that's what it's like for us down here, but I will always love you. If you remember anything, remember *that*.'

The words tumble out before I can stop them. 'Luc said the same thing, once.'

Ryan's eyes blaze dangerously. 'Luc is the biggest asshole in the history of assholes. The only thing we have in common is *you*, and he blew it. Which just goes to prove he's an asshole.'

'Why are we even talking about this?' I mutter. 'This is it; this is all we're ever going to get. Of course, we'll have "some day",' I add bitterly, 'but who knows if you'll even remember me by then? You'll have moved on, with your nice life, your nice family. While I will be exactly the same. Frozen in time. Sifting through shattered memories, living through them.'

'You think it'll be any easier for me?' Ryan yells. 'That's *me* you're talking about. You've just described what it's going to be like for me. You blow through my life like a hurricane, and then you leave me?'

We stare at each other, seeing no way out.

'It won't last, this feeling,' I murmur, trying to convince myself it's true. 'It's just a feeling, chemicals. You'll get over me. Soon, it will seem like a dream. To both of us.'

Before Ryan can say anything more, make any more of a case for the impossible, I grip him tightly in my arms and dive down towards the surface of the ocean. And for a moment, that terrible feeling — of falling, falling as if I will never stop — returns.

We soar above the heavy, boiling sea in silence. Me keeping Ryan warm; imprinting every line of his body, every quirk, every expression, into my consciousness, for later.

As we turn back towards land, the Gulf of California streaming away from us to our right, we begin to see lights in the darkness.

Ryan says suddenly, 'What *is* that? Can you see it?'

From the air it looks like a thick slurry of sticks and debris, just sludge. But as I change trajectory, moving lower, I make out shapes in the darkness: tiled surfaces and window frames; the roofs of houses, pancaked so they resemble books laid down flat, their spines facing up. Just floating out to sea.

'My God,' Ryan murmurs, sickened, as we skim low over a bobbing soup of submerged boats, broken-off pylons, oil drums, corrugated iron, sections of road and jetty. 'What happened here?'

Then we smell burning, and see the glow of fire, a mile or so inland, amongst the electric lights of evening. There are unimaginable things in the water. Cars, bobbing like bath toys; the tail of a light aeroplane pointing upwards; the smashed hulls of maxi yachts; overturned freighters and shipping containers just lying in the shallows as if a giant hand reached out of the sea and pulled them over. Or a giant wave. And bodies. So many bodies.

Ryan and I look at each other in horror. 'Lauren,' we both say, as I put on a burst of speed and the lower edge of the wild Coast Ranges are suddenly beneath us.

331

CHAPTER 22

We pass over Port Marie in near darkness. Up the coast road, Paradise gives off the same eerie feel of neglect and abandonment. The small, dusty-looking town is laid out in a strict grid on the edge of a swampy peninsula that just seems to peter out into the ocean. It looks as if only the streetlights are still working.

When we move lower, skimming over the main drag, we see that it's deserted and there are very few lights on in the houses, so neatly and regularly spaced. There are crazy Christmas decorations on the rooftops of some, but none are lit up. Many driveways are empty of cars.

Ryan looks at me enquiringly as I head south, intending to approach his place from another direction.

'Someone's watching the house,' I remind him quietly.

I come in over the back fence, land lightly near the steps by the back door. There's a light on in the kitchen, and one somewhere upstairs, but otherwise the house is in complete darkness.

Ryan mounts the back porch and opens the screen door, but before he can raise his hand to knock, something comes charging out of the darkness at our backs. The Daleys' three Dobermans — all sleek and vicious and bullet-headed — howling and frothing like dark-hearted demons.

'Stay!' Ryan roars, but I move back down the stairs into the garden and say grimly, 'Let them come, let them do their worst.'

I am ready for them, ready to stop them in their tracks; for if they dash themselves against me, as they long to, they will die.

But when they see me, see the luminosity coming off my skin, they begin to whine, circling me at an uneasy distance, before all three lie down in the grass at my feet, as if exhausted.

A faint glimmer begins to coalesce upon the black and tan coats of the panting, shuddering dogs. It pools and lifts, shifting away from them, and now I see the dogs through a veil of light that grows and changes and becomes the outline of a young girl. She's just a sketch, a suggestion, grey and ghostly. But I know her, though I have never known her name. Behind me, I hear Ryan gasp.

'*Malakh*,' I say, 'you have followed me through life after life. What is it that you wish me to know?'

The apparition raises her eyes to me and I see that she would have been very beautiful, once, like a doll. 'Come closer,' she whispers. 'Listen well, for I am dying.'

The dogs whimper. I hear the back door to the Daleys' house open, but I don't turn around, too intent am I on hearing the creature's message. 'Speak,' I urge her, 'for I am listening.'

'Lord Lucifer wishes to parley,' the *malakh* murmurs. 'Raphael for you. At sunrise, at the beach named for that reef shaped like a devil's crown. If you come quietly, he will be just. Even with the Eight. But if you do not ...'

333

For a moment, her outline wavers, and the dogs lift up their heads and howl in terrible anguish, as if she speaks through them.

'If you come armed for battle,' she gasps finally, 'or with deceit, then he will remake the universe as he sees fit.'

I see that she had long, pale, curling hair once, and large eyes, like a greeting-card angel.

'How credulous you are,' I say pityingly. 'At sunrise, no matter what I do, he will destroy us all. It has already begun.'

The *malakh* shakes her head in denial.

Anger explodes in me: that my last hours with Ryan should still brook interference from monsters I'd thought well behind me.

'Double-dealer,' I hiss. 'It was *you* who betrayed my presence in Milan to Luc, wasn't it? You ran messages between Michael and K'el, between those that remained of the Eight, and then you betrayed us all. *Why?* What did he promise you?'

When she raises her own eyes to look at me, I see an answering, ugly fury in them. 'You dare to ask *why?*' Her voice is like a death rattle. 'I owe you no loyalty. I begged you, and you would not help me. He will give me what you *elohim* will not — a living body in which to end my days. I have suffered, how I have *suffered!*'

She shrieks, and the dogs scrabble at the grass and dirt at her heels, in agony.

'Sunrise,' she screeches, raising a pointing finger, 'or *he* dies, *she* dies. Everything you ever loved or touched in this world will be slaughtered, damaged, despoiled.'

I turn to see what the *malakh* gazes on with her empty, shredding orbs. Lauren and Ryan are framed in the doorway — one so tall and dark, the other so slight, so pale, both scarcely daring to move or breathe.

When I turn back to face the *malakh*, she is gone, and the dogs are dead.

It's surreal to be helping Ryan bury his dogs under a moonless sky in a ghost town. Surreal to feel grief for creatures that so feared and hated me. But I do.

When we finally get inside, we watch in numb silence as Lauren deadlocks the back door and draws the chain across. It's so strange to be back inside the Daleys' white-on-white house. The ceilings seem too low, everything too small, as if the house was built for children. But it must be an illusion of my shattered mind, for everything is exactly as it was, and I am no taller than I was as Irina. But that feeling that I might dissolve, might blow apart at any second, seems to have returned. The world feels as if it is pitching beneath me; any moment, I might fall off and never find my way back.

As we trail through the kitchen, through the hallway and up the stairs, everything is exactly as I last saw it; save for Lauren's bedroom, which I hardly recognise. There's colour everywhere, lights, softness, warmth, as if the room is a bright, downy cocoon from which she might one day emerge, whole again.

Lauren sits on the edge of her bed and beckons me to sit, too, her blue eyes wide with wonder. But I'm too wired to do anything but pace, and I catch her eyes following me around the room.

Ryan's leaning against the dresser, almost asleep on his feet. He looks tired and rumpled and sexy, and he will never,

ever be mine. I'm suddenly swamped by so much pain that I stumble and almost fall to the ground.

'What do I *do*?' I wail.

Ryan just reaches out and catches me, pulls me close. And all I let myself hear for a while is his heartbeat, the murmur of blood beneath his skin. The last thing I want to hear at night; and, in the morning, the first. But it's never going to be that way.

There's a loud knock on the half-open door and Ryan and I look up, startled, as a male voice calls out belligerently, 'Lauren? Who's in there? Are you okay?'

The door's shoved open and Richard Coates is standing there. He's wearing blue jeans and nothing else but tatts, and his dark blond hair is still wet from the shower. It's longer than I remember it, falling into his extraordinarily pale, ice-blue eyes. When he sees me, he just freezes; the blood runs right out of his face. It takes him a little while to work out who else is in the room, because I'm all that he can see. I can tell that even though he's never seen me like this before, like a being carved out of titanium, wreathed in light and sorrow, he recognises me. Our minds met once, when I was Carmen and searching his memories for traces of Lauren.

'Hey, Rich,' Ryan says tightly.

I see that he's looking at the way Richard is dressed, then at his sister on the bed, her long, ash blonde hair unbound, her emaciated frame draped in a shapeless blue tracksuit, like something a child would wear, her bird-like legs tucked beneath her.

'Ry,' Richard whispers, his eyes still welded to me leaning against Ryan. 'When did you ... get back?'

'Just now,' Ryan says shortly. 'This is Mercy.'

'I kind of figured,' Richard replies.

He tears his eyes away from me at last, then takes a seat on the other side of the bed from Lauren, his head up proudly, refusing to feel ashamed.

'What are you doing here?' Ryan growls.

Richard and Lauren exchange glances, before she looks down at her new, bright red coverlet. Her thin hair falls forward over one shoulder, hiding her ruined face and haunted eyes.

'Tsunami warning system's been activated,' Richard replies when Lauren doesn't speak. 'The epicentre was nowhere near us, but they evacuated everyone to Little Falls Junction anyway. Lauren was desperate to come back when it didn't look like anything was going to happen. She couldn't handle the crowds. Said people were staring and talking. And they were — it was a circus when word got out she was there. I couldn't let her stay here on her own.'

'Where are Mom and Dad?' Ryan snaps, and Lauren bristles at his tone of voice.

'I did what you said!' she cries, suddenly furious. 'I arranged two tickets to a show in Portland I thought Mom might like to see — dinner, hotel, the works — then I told them everything was fine, that they needed to get away now that I was back, that I badly needed space. And I *did it*. I got them out of town. And now they're stranded on the other side of the highway. Nobody's getting in or out, not tonight.'

'Why didn't you go with them?' Ryan mutters, his face softening.

'I'm not ready to see a show or have dinner, Ryan, *look at me*. Today proved that. I thought I was going to die just from all the eyes. Besides, look outside my window. It wouldn't matter where I went.'

Ryan strides over to the window and pulls one of the cheerfully patterned curtains aside, peers out. 'There's nothing there,' he says with a frown.

Lauren looks at me numbly and I head across to the window, glance out quickly through the side of a curtain. And I see him. Over the side fence, outside the house next door, standing on the footpath, shining in the darkness with a sickly light. He looks up sharply as if he can sense me.

I nod at Ryan and his shoulders slump.

'Semyaza probably sent Barachiel and Jeremiel on a fool's errand,' I say dully. 'Luc's not in Panama, neither is Raphael. They're here, they have to be. It was *me* he always wanted, not Michael. I think he always intended to lead us here — from Europe through Asia to the Americas. Nuriel, Selaphiel, Gabriel were all bait. It's the kind of thing Luc would do. He wanted to wear us down. Let us think we were in control. This is exactly where we were supposed to end up. Without friends, without allies. Completely isolated and alone. He will never stop punishing me. Never.'

'Back up,' Richard interrupts, frowning, trying to understand.

Ryan tells him and Lauren what happened after Carmen: about Lela and Irina and all that followed. 'It feels as if we've been running forever,' he finishes tiredly. 'And now I'm supposed to just stand back and watch as Mercy hands herself over to the Devil on Coronado Beach.'

'You're not alone,' Richard says. 'You've got us.' He indicates himself and Lauren.

'Don't be ridiculous,' Ryan says flatly. 'Lauren isn't going anywhere near that beach.'

'Lauren is in the room,' she says in a steely voice that I recognise, because it's the same tone Ryan uses on me sometimes. 'And maybe she wants to walk right up to the Prince of Darkness and spit in his face. *Leave Lauren to Lauren.*'

She and Ryan glare at each other.

'It's too dangerous —' he begins, but she cuts him off.

'What else could anyone do to me that hasn't already been done?' she screams.

Richard lays a hand on her arm, but she shrugs him off angrily, saying automatically, 'Don't touch me.'

Richard sighs, turns to me. 'I have a bike you could use. You wouldn't have to face him on your own.'

I am obscurely touched. 'I can't risk any one of you,' I tell him. 'And machines and weapons are no use against Luc's people. But I thank you,' I add softly.

'If we choose to go, how could you stop us?' he insists.

'Choose to go?' I parrot incredulously. 'I don't see how *I* have a choice, let alone any of you.'

'Come, come,' a familiar voice says quietly into the air beside me, 'someone like you always has a choice.'

And the room is suddenly filled with light and a power of archangels. Gabriel and Uriel, Jeremiel and Barachiel, Jegudiel and ... Michael. Towering and wingless, beautiful and inhuman.

'Sister,' they all say as one, as Lauren and Richard scramble backwards on the bed, shielding their eyes in awe against the light.

Michael's dark eyes are clouded with pain. He drifts towards me slowly, bleeding from his manifold wounds, engulfs my small hands in his strong ones.

'Tell me,' he says quietly.

And I tell him of all that has occurred since we last met in Milan, and of the bargain that Luc would strike. 'Me for Raphael,' I finish hopelessly, 'and justice and fair treatment for all in the new universal order, if you can believe that.'

'Treachery,' Michael murmurs.

'Of course,' I reply in anguish. 'He is incapable of anything else.'

Michael looks down into Ryan's face where he stands behind me. 'Thank you,' he says simply. 'For keeping your word. And for letting her go, as she must.'

'I can hardly make her stay,' Ryan says bitterly. 'But she doesn't deserve to *die*.'

'And nor will she,' Michael snaps, his steely tone causing Ryan to pale. 'We are not in the habit of sacrificing our own to Lucifer. Look out there.'

Michael points to Lauren's window and Ryan hurries to draw the curtains open. When we peer down into the street, Ryan pulling me close, the watcher has vanished. I beckon Lauren and Richard over, and lean into Ryan.

'Watch, *watch*,' Michael says.

His voice is like a warm zephyr moving through the room as we look out over the darkened rooftops of Paradise. Against the thick covering of billowing black cloud overhead there are pinpoints of light in the sky, scores of them. They drift down towards earth, like the spinning clocks of dandelion flowers somehow illuminated, before coming together in a shimmering mass that vanishes suddenly, faster than sound, than light itself. A sight both extraordinarily beautiful and eerie.

'*Elohim, malakhim, ophanim, seraphim*, others,' Michael's voice is quiet. 'As many as may be spared.'

'It's like Judgment Day,' Richard breathes beside me.

At my shoulder, Lauren is so still she could be made of marble. She watches, a heavy frown pleating her pale brow.

'How could you guys possibly lose with those numbers?' Ryan exclaims. 'Aren't you always going to be more powerful than those mutants Luc uses? Take him down, *finish him.*'

From behind us, Jeremiel murmurs, 'Those angels that came down to earth, there will be no more reinforcements if any of them fall. Unlike Luc, we cannot "create" more.'

I stare at the sky, which is dark and blank once more with cloud. 'Luc will get what he wants,' I say finally, and I feel Ryan freeze beside me. 'Me for Raphael. Like for like. That's what he'll get.'

Ryan spins me around, shakes me. 'What are you saying?' he cries. 'That will trigger the "end time" you're all so afraid of! Why aren't you fighting it?' He looks accusingly at the archangels gathered around us. 'Why are you allowing this to happen?'

'Listen to her,' Uriel urges, his face so like mine.

I know he is the key to this whole damned mess. He is the one to buy us the time we need to save Raphael, then get me back home. A home I can't even imagine now, don't want to return to, because Ryan won't be there.

I place my hands on either side of Ryan's face and force him to look into my eyes. 'What Luc will get is an illusion. When we reach Coronado Beach, "Mercy" will surrender herself to him.'

Ryan shakes his head in angry denial, but I turn from him to look at Michael. 'But the moment Raphael is back safely with us and Luc places his hands upon that Mercy, there must be a shift,' I say with quiet urgency. 'A vast shift so that Luc's forces see *my* face reflected in every direction. So disguised, our people must disperse across the landscape. In the chaos, I will leave.'

'*Merce* ...' Ryan's voice is low and anguished.

'Put Luc back in his hole, Michael,' I say wearily. 'Repair some of the damage he's done. The time for mere watching is past.'

Michael nods grimly.

Ryan releases me as if I'm radioactive. 'I need to take a shower,' he mutters. 'I don't feel clean.' He leaves the room abruptly.

'I'll get the bikes,' Richard says, hooking a sweater and a bunch of keys out of a duffle bag lying in one corner of the room. I hear his footsteps pound down the stairs, the bang of the front door opening and shutting.

I walk across to Uriel, look up into his face. 'It must be you,' I say, and he nods, then smiles.

'Who else?'

He stares down at me for a moment with a quizzical expression, as if I'm a wondrous painting or a poem he must commit to memory.

'*His* little joke,' I remind him, and he shakes his head at me in mock exasperation. Then his outline seems to glow more brightly for a moment, before vaporising.

One by one, Jegudiel, Barachiel, Gabriel and Jeremiel do the same.

But Lauren throws herself in front of Michael before he can disappear, too.

She is shaking with fury as she cries, 'Why didn't you help me? If you can do *this*,' she stabs her fingers at the air where the others were standing only seconds before, 'why didn't one of you save *me*?' Tears spring out of her eyes, run down her cheeks. 'You could have done it. Or put me out of my misery,' she wails.

Michael bends and takes her clenched fists in his great hands, looks into her eyes from which the tears fall and fall.

'What has been done to you will one day be made right. There will be an accounting. Until that day, Lauren Daley, I take your pain, I take your suffering, I will bear your burden. And I am sorry, sorrier than you will ever know, that we were not there when you needed us, that evil was done to you.'

Then he's gone, too, and Lauren is moving like a sleepwalker towards her bed. She pulls the covers over her wasted, pain-racked body and in moments she is asleep.

I turn left unerringly, past Lauren's bathroom, making for Ryan's bedroom. I open the door tentatively and see that he's asleep too, his short, spiky hair standing up all over his head, contrasting with the stark white of his pillowcase. He's bare-chested and smells of clean, male skin and soap. The covers are drawn up to his waist, and I slip beneath them, lie down beside him.

He's so tired that he does not stir, does not waken. All I can do is hold him and let his energy, his life force, wash over me, through me, one last time, like the strains of a familiar love song.

This, I think, *is what I will miss most when I am gone. The closeness, the beating of his heart beneath my ear.*

CHAPTER 23

It's still dark when we leave the Daleys' house, Ryan, Lauren and I. None of us touching each other, keeping our distance. Lauren's dressed in a shapeless navy parka over a pink sweatshirt and baggy jeans, her hair plaited back so tightly that her face looks skull-like. But she seems less jittery today, less defensive. I can tell by the way she's moving.

I'm wearing my 'human' travelling face and the deeply unsexy outfit that I wore across half the world, which Ryan has probably grown to hate. He's still got on his torn and stinking leather jacket, over a fresh long-sleeved tee and jeans, as if it's a talisman that will somehow bring him luck. He hasn't said a word to me since he woke alone in his bed, probably never knowing I'd even been there.

Let him think me callous and uncaring, I tell myself. *It's easier that way.*

Out on the street, beside the nature strip, Richard Coates jumps out of the cab of his rusting, red, two-door truck. In the open tray there are a couple of mud-splattered bikes — one green and white, the other blue and yellow — anchored with black and yellow cables. He starts moving them down onto the road, and Ryan hurries to help him after he's rechained the front gates to his parents' house and pocketed the key, for no good reason except maybe habit.

Wordlessly, Richard hands Ryan the key to the green and white machine, and takes a bunch of helmets out of the cab of the truck. He hands a couple to Ryan before shoving one on his head, then beckoning Lauren over and placing a helmet carefully over her plaited hair. He reaches back into the truck one last time and takes out a long, cylindrical black bag that he clips to the back of the blue and yellow machine. He swings his leg over the saddle, then turns and helps Lauren up behind him. I see her hesitate before she closes her arms around his waist, tightly.

'Ready?' Ryan mutters, handing me a red helmet and putting a black one on over his head. We look at each other from behind the visors like two blank-eyed aliens, before Ryan swings onto his machine and waits for me.

I get on behind him and wrap my arms around his waist and we roar off through the silent streets, down the main drag with its faded front-window displays screaming *Shop here for heavenly savings!* Past the boarded-up front door of the Decades Café where I tried to down a cup of coffee with Spencer Grady and failed miserably because I will always hate the stuff.

We hit the deserted coast road heading away from Paradise down towards Port Marie, drawing closer and closer to Coronado Beach, which I've only ever seen in dreams, in the thoughts of others. As we pass the abandoned military base that's halfway out of town — miles of rusting steel fence ending in a set of chained gates at least twenty feet high — Richard and Lauren pull out from behind us with a roar, putting on such a clean burst of speed that they are soon lost to sight.

We catch up with them at the turn-off for the oil refinery. In the distance, across the salt plains that run right up to the refinery gates, the towering concrete chimney stands still and silent, belching neither flame nor smoke today.

'Coronado Beach!' Ryan yells, turning his helmet towards me briefly, as we take a right at the next crossroads, Richard and Lauren leading the way.

We see the trees first, a long stand of them, like sentinels upon the crest of a steep hill, their dark, twisted, leafless boughs raised to the slowly lightening sky. Then the road goes down over the hill, long grass waving in the stiff breeze on either side, and ends in a small car park. A set of stairs leads down to the beach below.

Neither Richard nor Ryan stops as we hit the car park. There's a rev of engines — like the buzz of multiple chainsaws — and both bikes sweep down the stairs, onto the damp sand of the beach.

Richard does a complicated set of wheelies for the sheer hell of it on the wet sand near the water's edge, before burning to a stop in front of Ryan and me where we've parked high up the beach, near the staircase.

Ahead of us, the water is grey and tempestuous, pierced by jagged rocks that rise up beyond the shallows like claws. As I gaze back, I see the stand of gnarled black trees in the far distance, the undulating line of stark and beautiful cliffs that hug the perimeter of the beach. It seems prehistoric, even primeval, here. A fitting arena of battle.

We all take off our helmets, and Ryan moves towards his sister, who's still laughing and breathless from doing wheelies on the back of Richard's bike.

'Hey,' he says, his expression softening. 'It's good to see

you like this,' he adds uncertainly, half-raising a hand to touch Lauren before thinking better of it and letting it drop.

Lauren tips her small face up to the strong breeze that's blowing off the water, straight tendrils of pale hair whipping around her face, her skin almost translucent.

'It's good to be out,' she says, sounding surprised. She looks at me, then down at the sand. 'I'm feeling better today, kind of ... lighter.'

We four stand there awkwardly, like the first people ever created. Ryan's got his hands in his pockets and he's scuffing the sand at his feet like he doesn't want to know me. The wind picks up, sending the sand stinging against our faces. The sky begins to lighten, just a little, at the horizon.

Suddenly, pain bursts into life behind my eyes, almost bringing me to my knees. And I know that Luc's searching for me, that he's close and gaining, trying to force that strange mental connection we've always shared but which I no longer welcome.

Luc knows me well enough to be sure I would want to be here, personally, to ensure Raphael's freedom. For I did love Raphael, once, and deeply, as one would love a brother. And I owe him a debt that cannot be repaid. I owe him for this life, for gifting me Ryan.

Ryan sees me buckle and catches me easily before I crumple to the ground. He holds me tightly, keeping me on my feet, as the noise that no one else can hear intensifies so that I feel as if I'm made solely of pain.

I want to shriek my agony at the leaden sky as Luc murmurs in my head, his voice dark and low and seductive, *You're mine, still mine, and I will do with you as I will.*

When he feels no flowering of contact with me, no

acceptance, no acknowledgment, everything around us changes in an instant, as if we are players on a stage and someone has changed the script, the set, the backdrop, the lighting, without any warning.

There must be fault lines running below our feet in every direction, for the ground begins to roll beneath us as if it's alive, as if the fearsome tremors are merely a physical manifestation of Luc's anger. We fall to the sand beneath a sky that is as black as pitch. It's like the sky from my dream: when I stood here with Luc in the very centre of a perfect storm and gazed at vast waves breaking over the reef that he called the 'Crowned One'. Heavy rain pours down as if Luc would drown us where we lie.

The sea turns against us, too, the waves reaching four or five feet in height before smashing onto the beach, surging inland. They drag Lauren back towards the sea, sucking her into an angry whirlpool of boiling white water. The storm is so loud that although I see her mouth moving, I can't hear her cries for help.

Ryan, Richard and I crawl down the beach towards her, but the water from above and below tumble-turns us, making us lose any sense of direction. And Lauren is pulled further and further out, towards the rocks.

And then they are among us, my people, as far as the eye can see along the beach. They come clothed in glory, the light of them piercing the darkness, brighter even than the lightning that hits the distant water and illuminates the teeth of the jagged, offshore reef. The storm touches none of them, from lowest *malakhim* to the Archangel Michael himself, our Viceroy, who commands in place of our absent Father. The water burns away before it can even touch them.

348

It is Michael who drifts through the angry swell, bearing Lauren up the beach to where Richard is kneeling.

Then Michael walks back down into the water and all my people follow him. Waves of up to ten feet, then twenty, break over them as they keep moving out towards the reef without faltering.

The four of us who remain cluster together in a tight knot on the beach, like drenched cattle, watching. Everything in me wants to be with my people, wants to shift so that I might wreak my fury upon Luc with my own hands, but I can't move. I have to stick to the plan, pretend I'm human just one last time.

Still the waves beyond the reef keep growing, until they are forty feet, sixty feet, eighty feet in height, their crests as tall as apartment buildings — and then the jagged black teeth of the reef seem to move, too. The reef that gives Coronado Beach its name rears out of the surf, water streaming down its sheared-off, deadly facets. Raphael is bound to its black and twisted crown, by chains of fire that crisscross his body.

Everything stops then, time stands still.

There is no wind, no rain, even the sea is as still as glass, the waves beyond the reef — those eighty-foot, no, hundred-foot waves — frozen there like icebergs.

Luc and his people come, thousands of winged and monstrous faceless or misshapen beings that he and his exiles have created to do their bidding, like murderous dogs. I see three or four score of his original fallen shining here and there amongst the mass. They part around the base of the crowned reef, before rejoining and coming to a standstill before Michael, his forces ranged behind him.

349

A quarter of a mile of sea, no more, separates two halves of a people that were once whole and united.

Michael's forces are far fewer in number, less than three hundred brave souls to meet the most putrid and evil force this earth has ever witnessed. I don't see how we could ever win, could ever hold back such a gruesome host.

Seeing Luc paralyses me. He is as he was in Milan, that sexy, modern Luc that I never knew, as dazzling as the sun, drawing all eyes to him. And even now — even when I know what he did to me, how I was hurled down from Heaven by his own hand — the thought of what he used to be like, what we once shared, hits me like a sucker punch to the head.

Something splinters inside me as I see Gudrun, with her bright yellow hair, sapphire eyes and ruby red mouth, step forward from amongst Luc's people. She places her hand upon Luc's arm, possessively, and, for a moment, I feel jealous and ugly and cast off. It's crazy, I know it is, but I can't help it, seeing Luc again. Almost as if I'm sleepwalking, I wrench myself out of Ryan's arms and move towards the water.

I hear him curse and stumble after me. Lauren and Richard follow, to keep me hidden, to keep me safe, loyal unto the end. Where the waterline is frozen upon the sand, Ryan enfolds me in a vicelike grip and will not let me go any closer.

'Are you *nuts*?' he hisses at me.

I can barely drag my gaze away from Luc to meet Ryan's eyes, and what he sees there makes him shudder.

Luc and Michael glare at each other across the frozen waves: one so pale, beautiful beyond belief; the other dark and fiery in countenance, his black eyes snapping with anger.

'Mercy for Raphael,' Luc snarls, his voice echoing off the cliffs, the iron-hard water, 'or I waste Raphael, I waste this planet, nothing survives. And even when Raphael is back among you, you'd better start running. Because once her soul is back within my grasp, nothing will be safe. It will be open season on the *elohim* and their servants and on the Kingdom of Heaven.' His voice drops to a murmur. 'You should have killed me when you had the chance. For when the new regime arises from the ashes of the old, you will be the first put to death for exiling me all those years ago.'

Michael stands his ground calmly. 'By that same measure, you, too, are guilty. For you sacrificed Mercy, who was innocent of any crime but loving you.'

Luc laughs, and the sound makes me flinch within the tight circle of Ryan's arms. 'Ancient history, *brother*, the old rules no longer hold. Your bargain was false. You agreed to recognise me as standing higher than God if I gave up the one thing that was most precious to me. And I did. *I gave her up.*'

'You tried to murder her,' Michael bellows.

'I gave her up — utterly!' Luc snarls back. 'While you broke your word. Give her to me now,' he roars. 'Or I start with Raphael. Then we will rend all of you limb from limb.'

He scans the small force arrayed behind Michael with narrowed eyes and the searing pain returns as I feel Luc's consciousness searching for me, trying again to single me out, to open that deadly two-way channel that only we share.

I fight to keep myself closed off from him. Ryan feels me tremble within his embrace and whispers so that only I can hear: *Stay strong. I love you. God, how I wish it was enough.*

Luc raises one of his beautiful, long-fingered hands high and the chains of fire that bind Raphael flame up with shocking brightness. Raphael cries out in anguish from where he is bound high upon the rock.

Maybe only I see the small, drifting light that moves into the space between the Archangel Michael and his eternal nemesis. It stills upon the surface of the frozen sea for a moment, drawing power from the two beings on either side of it, then it flares more brightly and takes the form of the young girl I saw in the Daleys' garden, blurry and unstable in outline, but clearer than she was last night.

'Lord,' she says beseechingly, kneeling before Lucifer, head bowed, turning her back upon Michael and those she knowingly betrayed. 'I am dying. Give me what you promised, before it begins and you forget. I found her when no other amongst your people could find her. I shadowed her as you asked — across half the world — and I have suffered, how I have suffered. Give me a warm body, a living body in which to end my days. There are humans upon the beach; give me one of them for my own.'

I feel the others draw tight around me at the creature's words, sense their fear.

Luc looks down upon her bowed head for an instant, then puts a hand beneath her chin, lifts her sweet, lost face to his, so far above.

'You have been faithful, my child,' he says kindly. 'And for your faithful service I give you what you ask — an end to your suffering.'

Faster than the human eye can follow, there's a blazing dagger in his hand and he cuts her throat, the way he cut K'el down, without a flicker of emotion.

There's no heat, no energy, when she dies. Her outline just seems to collapse, like a cloud of dust, and she's gone.

I think I try to scream, but Ryan has felt it building in my body and he's got his hand over my mouth, his arms binding me to him fiercely, before I can make a sound. My keeper, my anchor, my rock. Always.

'Release him to me, Devil,' Michael thunders.

The chains of fire that hold Raphael to the stone dissolve and he falls from a great height onto the surface of the glassy, unmoving sea, lying still for so long that Richard mutters against Ryan's ear, 'Dude, *está muerto.*'

But Raphael finally stirs, pushing himself up from the ground, his long, dark hair straggling across the strong, angular planes of his face. He drags himself slowly to his feet and stumbles through the ranks of Luc's bastard children, who jostle and assault him as he passes. His sable eyes are clouded with agony, light bleeds from the wounds of his torment. I cover my mouth with my hands at the sight of him.

I'm suddenly overwhelmed by snatches, fragments, of memory. Of Raphael laughing; of him and me walking arm in arm upon the surface of some lonely world; of me telling him it would always be hopeless, that I'd never love him the way that I loved Luc. Raphael was patience and kindness, compassion and propriety, but none of it had mattered to me then.

The way Raphael has tried to keep me alive all these years — all of it was motivated by love. Even if the way it all panned out felt like the opposite of love, felt like punishment.

'Luc has hurt everyone I ever cared about,' I say tautly. And I feel the muscles of Ryan's body go rigid at my words.

Across the water, Luc roars, '*Give her to me* then you shall have your "brother".'

He spits the word, throwing his right arm out like a barrier. Raphael cries out from behind him, held in place by some invisible force.

There is a ripple of movement amongst the ranks standing behind Michael, and from the very back of that shining throng comes ... me. In robes of blazing white, my long dark hair hanging down my back, my arms and feet bare.

I see myself drift through the gathered angels towards Michael, see Michael place a hand upon my shoulder to halt me beside him.

'Like for like,' he bellows.

At Michael's words, Luc lowers his right arm, causing Raphael to lurch into motion again.

He stumbles forward towards the false Mercy standing next to Michael, indescribable longing on his face. He falls to his knees, and looks up as if begging for forgiveness.

'It was my fault you were sacrificed,' he says. 'You know I loved you beyond measure. You know that, more than once, I tried to win you from Luc, because I knew his true character — the one he hid from you. I knew how he sought to place himself higher than Michael, higher even than God. In desperation, I begged Michael to force Luc's hand. *Make a bargain with him,* I urged. *Get Luc to declare before us all what it is that he wants and let him believe he will have his way.* But first, Luc had to give you up forever.

'But Luc saw what moved me. If he could not have you, then neither could I. For exiling you when it was not within his province to do so, Luc was himself summarily exiled.'

Luc doomed me for millennia because he was jealous of Raphael. I let out a small whimper and Ryan grips me fiercely. I turn my face into the hard line of his body so that

354

no one will see the tears — hot and bright — spilling down my face.

Raphael looks up at the being he thinks is me. 'Forgive me,' he pleads. 'For I thought I was the truest friend you would ever have. I tried to save you — and in saving you, I damned you for centuries.'

I start to shake again in Ryan's arms as I turn and gaze at Raphael in the distance. Love and loyalty lay at the heart of everything, but how dark and twisted a path grew from them.

Raphael lurches to his feet, moving into the space between Luc and Michael. 'Return to your rightful place at my side,' he begs. '*Be with me.* Let me somehow counterweigh the years, the suffering.'

Luc laughs derisively, the sound like steel on steel, ugly and grating, filling the skies.

I almost tear myself away from Ryan then and run, down towards Raphael's bent and wounded figure. I want so desperately to hold him in my arms again and tell him not to speak of fault or blame; that I understand, and that I'm finally at peace with what was done to me. But I have to maintain the fiction, hold the line.

Uriel, wearing my face, says brusquely in my voice, 'The choice is made, the bargain struck.'

And Raphael, hanging his head in grief, has no choice but to walk past me, to let me go.

But before Uriel can reach Luc and seize him, Gudrun steps forward and grabs him by the hand. The left hand.

Horror rises in me as I realise, even before Luc does, what she is doing.

'Betrayal!' Gudrun shrieks. 'We are betrayed!'

She raises Uriel's left hand high and Luc sees in an instant that it does not burn with an incandescent scar — for it does not burn at all.

Uriel's disguise falls away and he is himself once more. For a moment — like an ache in time, a breath suspended — every soul upon that beach freezes.

Then Luc's blazing weapon is in his hand and he plunges it towards Uriel's chest before any of us can move or cry out. But Uriel is almost Luc's equal in power — for he is counted second in strength only to the great Michael himself — and he throws himself sideways. Luc's blade slices across his forearm, leaving a deep and blazing score, but it does not kill him. Then Uriel vaporises.

'*Where are you?*' Luc screams, scanning the beach wildly, and that terrible pain lashes me anew as he seeks a way in, a weakness, an opening. It feels as if I'm being torn apart from the inside, and then he begins to bellow: '*H—*'

CHAPTER 24

The instant Luc begins to say my name, every angel on Coronado Beach, from lowest to highest, transfigures to resemble *me*. They scatter in every direction, flaming swords igniting in every hand. But in this whirl of white fire and movement, I fall to the ground, convulsing and helpless. For Luc is roaring my name, my true name, again and again.

Ryan curses and scoops me up into his arms.

I hear Richard gasp, 'Move, *chicos*. Move or die,' and get a dim sense of him and Lauren running and stumbling for their lives.

Ryan hauls me towards the motorbike we left parked further up the beach. The air resounds with the crack of blade meeting blade, the sizzle of holy fire meeting its polar opposite. Over and over, I catch glimpses of myself everywhere — my face, my dark eyes, my long, straight hair, my strong-limbed form. It's like a nightmare I can't wake from: seeing myself flee and fall, fight and die, time and again, in a howl of vaporising energy.

I'm sobbing uncontrollably from the horror as Ryan throws me onto the bike, then guns the engine, not bothering with the helmets, shouting at me to *hold on*. I clasp my arms around him from behind, press my tear-streaked face against the back of his battered jacket as we take the stairs at full throttle.

I know I shouldn't look back, but I do, and I'm so overwhelmed by what I see that I almost let go of Ryan, almost fall. Every single angel does battle in my name. Every demon battles *me*. I have been a legend, a pariah, a lost cause, for many, many years, yet many of my brethren make the ultimate sacrifice to protect me.

I can't stop my left hand flaming into life the way Uriel's never could have, and the wound that Luc gave me all those years ago burns so brightly, so fiercely, that Ryan cries out as he catches sight of it wrapped around him, almost losing control of the bike as we crest the hill.

As we speed past the trees, the rain starts again, obliterating the world around us.

At the crossroads, Richard pulls up alongside Ryan and screams, 'Where to now?'

I gesture left, indicating the gates we passed on our way here what feels like a lifetime ago. Richard nods, and roars off up the coastal highway towards the abandoned military installation, Ryan and me following.

At the gates, Richard jumps off his bike and fumbles open the black bag clipped to the back. He digs through the jumble of human weaponry stashed inside it and takes out a pair of boltcutters, slices open the chains that keep the gates closed against trespassers.

It's some kind of abandoned airbase. There's a vast expanse of cracked tarmac beyond a row of identical houses to our left, their front doors riddled with bullet holes. Long grass has overtaken a lot of the land. In the distance, through the pounding rain, I can make out an iron jetty that extends into the water; concrete bunkers built into some of the hills overlooking the sea. There are a couple of large, rusting steel hangars each with a double band of broken windows running around the walls and loudspeakers mounted in groups of three on the roof.

We ride up to the first of them, and Richard dismounts and studies the sliding doors for a moment before simply pushing one of them open. Then we're inside. The sound of the rain upon the steel roof is very loud.

As the others take off their helmets, I say, 'This is the place. For me, time stops here.'

Ryan turns and looks at me, his heart in his eyes.

Lauren takes one look at her brother's face and drags Richard away, to give us space. They clutch each other tightly by the hangar doors as Ryan closes his arms around me fiercely.

I shift, one last time, so that he's looking at *me*. And I whisper, 'I told you once how miraculous you are: that you were somehow able to find me and love me when I had no face of my own, no body. From life to life you've been my rock, my friend, my protector, my constant. You were right when you said I'd never find anyone like you, or what we have, anywhere else. You've been my solace and my greatest joy, and I love you, Ryan Daley, and I thank you. And I will always, always miss you and be thinking of you until "some day" comes.'

He tips his head back in that way I've come to recognise: as if he can somehow rein in strong emotion, hold back his tears.

I lean up and pull his mouth down to mine and kiss him,

as the wind shrieks through the catwalks and steel beams crisscrossing the space above our heads. Then he's kissing my face, my eyes, pulling me into him, weeping into my shining hair, his strong, lean body racked by the strength of his feeling.

'Touching,' a voice drawls, 'but ultimately pointless.'

Ryan and I freeze in horror as we see Luc outlined against the back windows of this empty, dusty space, Gudrun beside him. A dozen of his strongest fallen are ranged around them.

Luc walks forward, his long, luminous robes open to the waist to display his preternatural shining beauty to its best advantage, that scar that burns in the centre of his chest. The sight of him makes me recoil, causes me to stumble backwards.

'Seen from the air, your telltale scar such as we all wear,' he gestures around him at his faithful, 'cannot be disguised.'

Gabriel, Michael and Uriel materialise behind Ryan and me, wings outspread, flaming swords raised before them.

'You're already too late,' Luc roars, surging forward to grasp my left hand, wrenching me out of Ryan's grasp.

At Luc's touch, the flames grow brighter, flare higher, and I cry out in agony.

'She is *mine*,' Luc snarls. '*I* made her what she is. She is my chattel, my possession, my slave once more, and I will do with her *as I will*.'

Ryan starts forward, but Gudrun swiftly bars his way, planting a long, red-painted fingernail in the centre of his chest. 'So pretty,' she purrs.

'But a hindrance,' Luc snaps, releasing me suddenly.

Before I even see him move, he is gripping Ryan by the front of his throat. He plunges his other hand into Ryan's chest as if he would pull Ryan's soul free of his living body and devour it before us all.

'NO!' Lauren and I scream together.

Ryan convulses and falls to the floor at Luc's feet, looks up at me, wide-eyed, struggling to breathe.

Luc lets his hand fall back to his side. 'Your entire life has been for nothing,' he sneers as he looks down at Ryan, twitching and shuddering on the floor. 'Someone as worthless and powerless as you are could never hope to hold onto a being like her. Soon, I will end *her* life,' he indicates me. 'And *hers*, too,' he gestures at Lauren, 'the way it should have ended inside that monster's dungeon.'

He laughs as he sees all the life, the colour, flowing from Ryan's face like the receding tide.

He turns and looks at me. 'The moment we quit this accursed place forever, everything becomes possible for me again. *Everything*. We have been too long apart, my love. Look at me. Take my hand.'

His voice is so full of dark seduction that I almost forget where we are; that we are no longer those two lovers who lay entwined in a bower of flowers, vowing eternal love for each other. He holds his hand out to me as if whole centuries have not come between us, as if he doesn't bear the blood of millions upon it.

I back away from him, my burning left hand held up between us in a gesture of negation, screaming, 'Azraeil! *Azraeil!*'

There is no sound but the harsh rattle of Ryan's breath inside his chest, the sound of him dying. Luc has stopped time to let me hear Ryan die, to watch him die. His life is ebbing away at my feet. I feel it the way I felt it within the Duomo. The light of his dark eyes is failing; he has no strength even to tell me he loves me, and to say goodbye.

I scream again into the echoing space, 'Azraeil! I know you want him, he's one of yours, you've marked him for your own. *Azraeil!*'

'Azraeil is in the business of listening to and helping no one,' Luc taunts.

He gestures at Gudrun, at dead-eyed, auburn-haired Hakael beside her. 'Keep them all back,' he orders. 'Once I take her beyond the boundaries of this vile planet, do as you will with all of them; do your *worst*.'

But then a sudden wreath of fog, a fine silver mist, twines rapidly across the floor. It coils around Luc's ankles, and he leaps back from it, cursing God.

When Azraeil materialises between us, clad in his customary black, there's actual fear on Luc's face, for even Death takes precedence over evil. Death is a power unto itself.

I fall to the ground beside Ryan and cradle his head in my hands, weeping tears of bitter light.

'Give him back to me,' I beg Azraeil brokenly, 'for he goes beyond my power. I have no power to heal a mortal wound dealt by Lucifer himself.'

Azraeil looks at me measuringly with eyes as blue as the daytime sky. 'You hold free will in such regard, sister,' he says quietly. 'If it were to come down to a choice, who would you be for?' He indicates Luc, then Michael, with his eyes. 'Choose correctly and the mortal lives; incorrectly, and he dies. It is a gamble, as all life is. I am in a wagering mood today.'

'Why make me choose, why test me with riddles, when this good man lies dying?' I sob. 'He is my love, and I will never find his like again, not in any life, yet you ask me to choose between two warring houses that shall never agree a peace, not until the other is utterly destroyed?'

'*Choose*,' Azraeil says in a steely, ringing voice. 'And choose wisely because the world turns on your decision; though your choice has always been pre-ordained.'

'Nothing is predetermined, pre-ordained!' I cry brokenly. 'How could that single heinous act of Luc's — of casting me down — mean that Ryan *must* die? The human world and the celestial world will always be spheres that operate independently, that only ever briefly collide from time to time. We are just random acts to them, Azraeil, like the Ebola virus, or a nuclear bomb dropped from the sky on a clear day. Random, unpredictable, rare; so often destructive. They exercise free will as much as we do. Ryan chose *me*,' I sob. 'When he could have chosen safety, normality, *life*.'

'But we are the highest beings in creation,' Azraeil parries. 'Weren't we created to do God's will? Are we not God's will? How could this man even presume to "choose" you?'

'We were *formed*,' I cry. 'We are acts of God in living form, mere instruments of His power, as senseless and directed as every mortal upon this earth. We are the same ...' I weep. 'Underneath it all, we are the same. There is no fate, Azraeil, only coincidence. I have lived as a human for millennia. Nothing is predetermined. It is all chaos, and from it you must wrest your life. You make your own fate. You see the cards that you are dealt, and you play them, as they come, you play them.'

'Choose,' Azraeil says quietly, implacably.

I raise my burning eyes to him.

'Then, before God,' I cry, 'before all here assembled, I reject you all.' I turn to Luc. 'You, Lucifer!' I spit. 'I reject you utterly. And you, Michael! I reject the rigid determinism that you espouse. And even you, Azraeil: I reject Death. I refuse to choose sides. I choose him, I choose Ryan, and a life lived in simplicity and goodness that hurts no one. That is what I choose.'

Azraeil kneels and wrests Ryan from my arms, and I cannot hold onto him, though I claw and weep and plead.

Ryan's breathing is rapid and erratic and his eyes struggle to hold mine as the glorious face of Death smiles down upon him.

Azraeil places his hand upon the spot where Lucifer wounded Ryan. Without looking at me, he says quietly, 'That is your final choice?'

'Yes,' I sob, 'that is what I choose.' Understanding, at last, the gift that he is giving me.

'Then rise, *Mercy*,' Azraeil says, looking up at me from where he holds Ryan on the floor. 'And prepare yourself for the consequences of what you have chosen.'

And I feel such a shock of joy when I understand his meaning. For Death consents to kneel to me here, upon this cold concrete.

I remember how it felt when I tried to heal Karen Neill of her cancer. How it felt when I tried to stop Lela bleeding to death on the floor of the Green Lantern Café. I remember pursuing Ryan's soul through the corridors of his dying body on the roof of the Duomo; of wresting Irina Zhivanevskaya's soul out of the purgatory Luc had left it in.

One last shift. And no one here but Death comprehends the choice that I am making.

Azraeil's blue eyes meet mine. He reaches up and takes my burning left hand before Luc can lurch forward, fingers outstretched; before Gabriel can even finish saying, 'Mercy, *no*!'

364

I let out a shattering scream as Azraeil's will moves through me, like a breath of holy fire.

Light begins to pour off me, out of me, in waves. I have no sense of up or down, no sense of place, of time. I am the world, or the world is in me, and like the world, I can feel plates moving, floes breaking, separation, reconfiguration, transfiguration, an unlinking.

Azraeil releases my hand and I look at my trembling fingers with wonder. My skin is matte, flat. The scar is gone, will never return.

Azraeil lays Ryan's head carefully upon the ground and Ryan blinks up at us, unsure whether this is real or dream or afterlife.

The Archangel of Death rises, looks around challengingly at all who are gathered here. 'My touch can mean death, or life,' he says.

He turns and pins me with his bright gaze. 'I gave him to you because your choice was just, it was considered. You *are* what you wished to be — a creature of clay, subject to the whims, cruelties and mercies,' there's the ghost of a smile on his face, 'of this human life.'

He scans those gathered here again. 'And none of you,' he roars, so loudly that even Luc, even Michael, quail to hear him, 'may touch them. I have marked them for my own. Any of you who reaches out to them in hatred or in anger will bring death upon your own head. They are mine,' he says more quietly, 'and in time I shall collect what is due to me.'

And he vanishes.

Ryan sits up, whole and unmarked, breathing easily, blazing with joy.

'Mercy?' he says uncertainly, scarcely able to believe I'm standing here, in a simple white dress, my feet bare on the cold concrete floor, my long, straight brown hair hanging forward over my shoulders.

I look around and everything seems two-dimensional. I can't read anyone; I get no sense of the life force of anything alive in this room. I see the same faces I saw before Azraeil touched me, but the colours have no depth, the sounds I hear have no extra resonance. I have no ability any longer that is not super-natural. Only natural. Only human.

I am split by joy, but also by grief, for I can no longer read the mysteries inside Ryan's heart. He is as blank and opaque and walled off from me as everyone is.

He rises slowly to his feet and we move towards each other like two people stumbling out of a fog. He catches me and spins me around lightly, as if we are dancing, and laughs.

Michael looks at Luc across the room. 'She is beyond your power now. Find some other means to bring the end of the world upon us all, for you won't find it here.'

Luc is looking not at Michael, but at me, as he hisses his reply. 'Even Death cannot rule over me. Walk carefully in this world, my lost love, for harm comes in many guises, many forms.'

Then, without warning, he and his followers are gone.

I blink, unsure what to feel. I've been threatened and belittled and lied to for so long, survived so much, that Luc's threat barely moves me. Just like that, I'm no longer necessary to him. I'm nothing, expendable, just clay.

'I think I'm ... *free*,' I say to Ryan in dawning wonder. 'Free at last.'

'As free as any human will ever be,' Gabriel says, moving forward.

Ryan releases me as Gabriel places a hand on my shoulder. He looks down into my face from his great height. 'You are sure?'

'It's done, brother,' I murmur. 'There's to be no undoing.'

He nods, a touch of sadness in his bright green gaze.

Uriel moves up behind him, gazes down at me, too. 'You make a pretty human, sister,' he says, and smiles.

'And you a pretty angel,' I tease him.

Michael calls out sternly behind them, 'Come, brothers, the battlefront shifts again. Mercy has earned her rest. We shall see her 'ere long.'

He raises his burning black gaze to me and then they're all gone, vanished into motes of light.

By the doors, I see Lauren and Richard craning their necks up, watching the light stream towards the ceiling before it disperses.

Ryan takes me in his arms. 'Are you scared?' he whispers.

'I'm terrified,' I reply. 'Listen to the way my heart's beating.'

I place his hand above my heart and his face collapses into shock.

'I'll try and keep things, uh, exciting,' he says tentatively. 'I know how much you've ... given up. You can throw it in my face every day, if you want to.'

'Standing still seems pretty exciting right now,' I murmur, wrapping my arms around his neck and kissing him.

We don't come up for air until Richard starts hooting and telling us to 'get a room, already, people'.

'I'm tired,' I say suddenly, realising it's true. 'I could sleep for a year. And I'm ... *hungry*.'

Ryan hears the surprise in my voice.

'Are you ready to start again?' he says, putting an arm around my shoulders and walking me towards the hangar door.

Outside, the rain has stopped, and soft sunlight bathes the cracked tarmac, the motorbikes and the shot-up houses in a soft, wintry glow.

'Yes,' I reply, as the others put on their helmets and climb onto their bike.

I turn and look at Ryan and kiss him again, because I can, and say fervently, 'Yes, I am.'

ACKNOWLEDGMENTS

With loving thanks, as always, to my husband, Michael, and to my children, Oscar, Leni and Yve, who give me so much joy and put up with my award-winning vagueness.

To my brilliant, brilliant A-team who has been with me every step of the way — Lisa Berryman, Rachel Denwood, Lizzie Ryley and Nicola O'Shea. To you all, and to the lovely Mel Maxwell and the very talented Natalie Winter and Kirby Jones, my thanks for helping to bring Mercy home. Thanks also to Tim Miller, Lara Wallace, Melanie Saward and Allan Paltzer for working so tirelessly on my behalf.

To the wonderfully dedicated and insanely hardworking Catherine Onder, Hayley Wagreich, Stephanie Lurie, Ann Dye and Hallie Patterson at Disney-Hyperion, and to the marvellous Iris Prael, Ilse Rothfuss and Marie Kubens at Ravensburger Buchverlag, and to all my international editing and publishing teams, thank you for giving Mercy wings.

I am forever indebted to the indomitable Norma Pilling for reading the initial drafts of *Mercy*, *Exile*, *Muse* and *Fury* and wading through my truly appalling Latin and Italian 'stylings' in order to suggest sensible alternatives. Thanks also for climbing to the rooftop of the Duomo for me when I couldn't be there myself.

A huge *merci* to M. Michel Rateau for fixing the French and providing useful guidance on the usage of French oaths.

With thanks also to Quino Holland for tweaking the Inca Trail material and the Quechua. It's an honour to have you in the family.

To my father, Yean Kai Lim, and mother, Susan Lim, and to Barry and Judy Liu, my thanks for, literally, holding the baby. To my sisters, Ruth and Eugenia, you rock, and always will.

And in loving memory of Ngo So Khim, Lim Koon Yaw, Lau Eng Swan, Koh Boon Chiang, Ko Keng Hoo and Frank Liu. Still, and always, missed.

This is a work of fiction. Most of the locations described in this book are entirely fictional, as are all of the characters and events. Again, certain authorial liberties may have been taken with those buildings and places that do actually exist in the real world, and for those, the author apologises and, once more, begs your leave.

Please note that the inscription on the stone statue of the Archangel Jegudiel was taken directly from a Bernini angel on the Ponte Sant'Angelo in Rome, Italy, and the lyrics for the song sung by the Archangel Uriel during the trek towards Machu Picchu are taken from the sixteenth-century Corpus Christi Carol (author anonymous), but with the original Middle/Early English modernised to assist the twenty-first-century reader.

Mercy 'wakes' on a school bus bound for Paradise, a small town where everyone knows everyone else's business — or thinks they do. But they will never guess the secret Mercy is hiding ...

As an angel exiled from heaven and doomed to return repeatedly to Earth, Mercy is never sure whose life and body she will share each time. And her mind is filled with the desperate pleas of her beloved, Luc, who can only approach her in her dreams.

In Paradise, Mercy meets Ryan, whose sister was kidnapped two years ago and is now presumed dead. When another girl disappears, Mercy and Ryan know they must act before time runs out. But a host of angels are out for Mercy's blood and they won't rest until they find her and punish her — for a crime she doesn't remember committing ...

An electric combination of angels, mystery and romance, *Mercy* is the first book in a major new series.

REBECCA LIM

EXILE

An angel searching for answers, for her destiny.

All Mercy knows is that she is an angel, exiled from heaven for a crime she can't remember committing.

So when she 'wakes' inside the body and life of eighteen-year-old Lela Neill, Mercy has only limited recall of her past life. Her strongest memories are of Ryan, the mortal boy who'd begun to fall for her — and she for him.

Lela's life is divided between caring for her terminally ill mother and her work as a waitress at the Green Lantern, a busy city cafe frequented by suits, cab drivers, strippers, backpackers and the homeless, and Mercy quickly falls into the rhythm of this new life.

But when Mercy's beloved, Luc, reappears in her dreams, she begins to awaken to glimpses of her true nature and her true feelings for Ryan. How can she know that her attempts to contact Ryan will have explosive consequences?

Meanwhile, 'the Eight' — responsible for her banishment — hover near, determined to keep Mercy and Luc apart, forever ...

Mercy's search continues in the second book of this major new series.

In the third MERCY novel, Mercy wakes in a new unknown host, her love for Ryan and Luc burning stronger than ever. But who will she make the ultimate sacrifice for?

Mercy is thrust into the excessive world of fashion when she awakes in the body of a troubled Russian supermodel, Irina: bitchy, hot-tempered and known to be dabbling in things she shouldn't, Irina is on the verge of a very public breakdown. Against the glamorous background of opulent Milan, Mercy continues her increasingly desperate search for Ryan to lead her back to her immortal lover, Luc. But this time Mercy is aware that her memories and powers are growing ever stronger – and she begins to doubt Luc as The Eight reveal more of her mysterious past. Are Luc's desires as selfless as her own or does he want her for a more terrifying purpose?

The grand scale celestial battle for Mercy's soul builds to an incredible stormy crescendo as archangels and demons clash in a cataclysmic showdown that not all will survive …